**Trapped in one of the loneliest places
in the galaxy . . .**

There was no time for planning or even conscious thought. Even before the full ramifications of the situation had sifted completely through my brain I was on my feet, weaving madly through the maze of chairs as I raced for the car's door. I came within an ace of tangling myself in the conductor's legs as I dodged around him; and then I was outside, sprinting across the platform toward the macabre do-si-do still going on.

One of the Juriani half turned, but he had no time for more than a startled gasp before I slammed my shoulder into him, bouncing him in turn off his companions and finally throwing off their rhythm. My hand darted past the Cimma to grab Bayta's wrist, and I turned us back toward the train.

Only to see that it was already in motion.

I tried anyway, nearly dragging Bayta off her feet as I pulled her toward the train. But we were too late. The doors were closed, and there wasn't nearly enough time for Bayta to get a conductor to open one of them. Swearing viciously under my breath, I gave up and slowed to a halt.

The Gang of Fifteen, and whatever it was they were carrying, were gone.

"Memorable characters such as Compton and Batya's wise Bellido ally, Korak Fayr; the growing intimacy between the pair; and loving details of the almost-plausible Quadrail technology lift this SF action thriller."
        —*Publishers Weekly*

BOOKS BY TIMOTHY ZAHN

*Denotes a Tom Doherty Associates Book

The Third Lynx

TIMOTHY ZAHN

A TOM DOHERTY ASSOCIATES BOOK
NEW YORK

This is a work of fiction. All the characters, organizations, and events portrayed in this novel are either products of the author's imagination or are used fictitiously.

THE THIRD LYNX

Copyright © 2007 by Timothy Zahn

All rights reserved.

Edited by James Frenkel

A Tor Book
Published by Tom Doherty Associates, LLC
175 Fifth Avenue
New York, NY 10010

www.tor-forge.com

Tor® is a registered trademark of Tom Doherty Associates, LLC.

ISBN-13: 978-0-7653-5669-7
ISBN-10: 0-7653-5669-4

First Edition: November 2007
First Mass Market Edition: August 2008

Printed in the United States of America

0 9 8 7 6 5 4 3 2 1

For Randy and Cheryl,
creating the music of the shears

The Third Lynx

ONE

From the Stars' End sector of the Filiaelian Assembly to the Darmisfar colony worlds of the Bellidosh Estates-General, the one thing everyone in the galaxy agrees on is that the best thing about traveling between the stars via Quadrail is the food. The Spiders who operate the vast system of trains and Tubes and stations have made a point of seeking out the very best recipes and cuisine from each of the twelve star-spanning civilizations and making them available for their passengers' enjoyment. It's like visiting the Alien Quarter of any of a thousand cities, only you get to travel while you do it.

Even in the second/third-class dining cars the food was delicious, intriguing, and eclectic. Here, in first class, where it was now my privilege to ride, it was all that and more.

And I was ready. More than ready. I'd suffered through a wearying twenty-day round-trip torchcruiser voyage across the Yandro system, living on ship's rations the whole time, followed by the much shorter fourteen-hour Quadrail ride from Yandro to Terra Station, most of which I'd spent sleeping. Now, with a sizzling plate of artistically arranged Shorshic pili tentacles in front of me, I was finally going to get a decent meal.

"Mr. Frank Compton?"

I sighed. And the other thing everyone in the galaxy agrees on is that one of the greatest frustrations of Quadrail travel is some overly jovial fellow passenger interrupting you in the middle of your meal.

Reluctantly, I looked up. The man standing over me was Human, in his fifties, with blue eyes and white-streaked brown hair. As befit his first-class Quadrail passenger status, he was dressed in a quiet but expensive traveling suit that had been tailored within a millimeter of its life. Also as befit the average first-class passenger, he had the steady gaze and solid manner of someone used to having his every word listened to and obeyed.

And his expression was anything but jovial. The man was worried. Seriously worried.

"Yes, I'm Compton," I confirmed. "And you?"

"My name's Smith," he said. His voice carried a slight central EuroUnion accent. "I wonder if I might have a moment of your time."

I glanced across the table at the dark-haired young woman seated there. Bayta had been my sort-of-informal partner for the past several months, ever since I'd gotten myself involved in this strange twilight war between the Spiders and the group mind known as the Modhri. She was looking up at Smith, her face showing her usual wariness of strangers but nothing that might indicate she knew anything more ominous about the man. "Fine, but only a moment," I told Smith. "As you can see, we've just started dinner."

"My apologies for that," Smith said. Pulling over a chair from the unoccupied table beside us, he sat down. "To put it bluntly, I'm on my way into a situation that might require a man of your abilities and experience. I thought I might be able to persuade you to join me."

"What specific abilities and experience are you refer-ring to?" I asked.

He smiled. "Come now, Mr. Compton, let's not be modest. Your record of service in Western Alliance Intel-ligence speaks for itself."

"You might possibly have missed the last page of that record," I suggested. "The page where Westali summarily booted me out."

Smith snorted in a genteel sort of way. "For your very proper attempt to alert the world to the Yandro colonization boondoggle," he said. "Personally, I consider that a point in your favor."

"Nice to see *someone* appreciates it," I said. "Unfortunately, as to your job, I'm afraid I'm otherwise engaged at the moment."

"This would take very little of your time," he assured me. "I'm on my way to Bellis to negotiate the purchase of a small but very valuable item."

I felt my ears prick up. As it happened, Bayta and I were also on our way to Bellis, the capital world of the Bellidosh Estates-General. "What sort of item?"

"A piece of artwork," he said. "I'm afraid I'm not at liberty to say anything more right now. I assure you, though, the transaction will be completely legal."

"I'd certainly hope so," I said. "And my part in this transaction would be . . . ?"

"I merely want someone competent and trustworthy at my side," Smith said.

I nodded toward his fancy suit jacket. "It seems to me a man of your means should be able to hire carloads of extremely competent people."

His lip twitched. "The competency part isn't the trick," he said. "And you come highly recommended."

"Really," I said, intrigued in spite of myself. There were very few people out there these days who would recommend me for any job higher than that of chief sewage handler. "May I ask by whom?"

He considered, then shrugged. "I suppose it's not really a secret. Deputy UN Director Biret Losutu."

I looked again at Bayta, saw my own surprise reflected in her eyes. "Interesting," I said.

"Isn't it?" Smith agreed. "Especially since I would have expected your part in the Yandro affair to have earned you a certain degree of hostility from him. You must be very special for his opinion to have turned around that completely."

He had that right, anyway. My whistle-blowing on the Yandro affair three years ago had made me an enemy in Losutu's eyes. A few months ago, when we'd next met, that status had eroded to the point where I merely qualified as an irritant.

But that was before Losutu himself had been dragged into this quiet war.

The fact that Smith had dropped Losutu's name made this a shade more intriguing. Unfortunately, there was no way of knowing whether or not he was telling the truth about Losutu having recommended me to him.

Even if he was, there was the whole question of whether I was willing to trust either of them. "You and Director Losutu are very kind," I said. "But as I said, I'm otherwise engaged." I picked up my fork, trusting Smith would take the hint.

He didn't. "Mr. Compton, let me put my cards on the table," he said, making no move to get up. "I postponed my trip to Bellis in hopes of linking up with you. In fact, I ended up staying on Terra Station for an extra six hours waiting for you to get back from wherever it was you were."

I eyed him closely, the hairs at the back of my neck doing a gentle tingle. I *had* in fact been almost exactly six hours off my original timetable in returning to Terra Station, a timetable Losutu was very much aware of. That part, at least, checked out.

Problem was, Losutu wasn't the only one who would have known the timing on that mission. "Sorry for the inconvenience," I said.

"Oh, I wasn't blaming you," Smith hastened to assure me. "I was simply pointing out that the delay made the whole thing a bit more awkward. Especially since Losutu wouldn't tell me where you were coming in from, but only when you were expected back. That meant I had to keep an eye on every incoming train."

"You're lucky you found me at all," I said. If, of course, it *had* been luck.

"Yes, indeed." He nodded to Bayta. "I'd just spotted you and your lovely companion and was on my way to talk to you when you got up and headed to the platform for this train. I was barely able to get a reservation in time to make it aboard myself."

"You're obviously a very lucky man," I commented.

"In my experience, luck comes to those who don't rely on it," he said. "The point is that I want your help." He raised his eyebrows slightly. "And as you suggested earlier, money's no object."

There it was: the end point I'd been waiting for. Eventually, if you waited long enough, it always came down to money. "I'm sure it's not," I said. "But as I said, we're busy."

For a moment he studied my face. "May I at least ask you to think it over?" he said. "Feel free to drop by my compartment if you'd like more details." He glanced around. "With more privacy, I can be a bit more open."

"We'll see," I said noncommittally.

"Please do," he said, finally standing up. "Compartment eleven. Drop in anytime."

With another nod at Bayta, he returned his chair to the other table and made his way through the room to the corridor bordering the dining area. Turning left, he disappeared toward the first-class car in front of us and the compartment car beyond that. "His compartment's right across from yours," I commented to Bayta, finally slicing off a piece of pili. "Handy."

"I wonder if that's a coincidence," she said, scooping up a bite of her own meal. "What do you think?"

"About Smith? Or about Smith's offer?"

"Either. Both."

I shrugged. "He personally is probably legit. His little

transaction is more doubtful. Either way, it's kind of irrelevant."

"Why?" she countered. "If it *is* a genuine offer, it might be a good cover for us."

I took another bite, mulling it over. She had a point. The Modhri homeland had been destroyed, but the Modhri himself was unfortunately still very much alive.

It was, without a doubt, the most bizarre enemy anyone had ever faced. The Modhri was technically a single entity, a group mind composed of the telepathically linked polyps that lived in the decorative and highly prized Modhran coral. He'd been created as a last-ditch weapon of the Shonkla-raa, a vicious race of conquerors, during the last stages of a revolt that had wiped them out sixteen hundred years ago.

Unfortunately, the Shonkla-raa's little fifth column weapon hadn't died with them. The Modhri had remained dormant for centuries, until the coral had been rediscovered and the Modhri inadvertently unleashed on the galaxy. Before the Spiders and their secretive Chahwyn masters had finally tumbled to his existence, he'd gotten his claws firmly planted in the power centers of most of the Twelve Empires served by the Quadrail system.

The presence of an aggressive group mind hidden in clumps of coral would have been bad enough. What made the whole thing infinitely worse was that the polyps could also invade and live inside living beings: Humans and Bellidos and Juriani and pretty much everyone else in the galaxy. A polyp hook could move in with just a scratch of the coral and reproduce enough polyps inside their host to create a new Modhri mind segment.

In some ways it was like the terrorist wars of the early century. Only worse, because the newly created walker was completely unaware of the fact that he or she had been co-opted into the Modhri's quiet war of conquest. Most of the time the colony lay quiet, occasionally making subtle mental suggestions that the host would usually obey and afterward find a reason to rationalize away.

But that was under normal circumstances. Under more urgent need, the Modhri mind segment could take complete control of his host, overriding the resident mind and turning the body into a sort of life-sized marionette. The host would have no memory of that period, but would merely end up with a strange blacked-out chunk of his or her day.

Even then, if the Modhri was clever, he could avoid suspicion. A short blackout could be rationalized in any number of ways, especially if the walker was accustomed to drinking intoxicants. Since most of the rich and influential who were the Modhri's targets of choice had learned social drinking at an early age, it was an easy and obvious explanation for the Modhri to push.

If that wasn't bad enough, each walker mind segment could also telepathically link up with the segments of other nearby walkers, or with outposts of the coral itself, creating a larger, smarter, more dangerous mind. A given Modhri mind segment was never static, but continually added pieces and information to itself as new walkers came into telepathic range and losing pieces as old ones moved away off the edge of its consciousness. The result was a fluid, ever-changing opponent that was as hard to pin down as a drop of mercury.

Fortunately, even slippery enemies weren't infallible. One of our few allies in this war, a rogue Belldic commando squad leader named *Korak* Fayr, had taken upon himself the goal of ridding his own worlds of Modhran influence. To that end, he'd spent the last few months moving around the Bellidosh Estates-General, destroying every coral outpost he could get his hands on.

The Modhri had spent those same months trying his damnedest to find Fayr and throw a rope around him. Making Fayr's job all the more difficult was the fact that the high monetary value of the coral meant that even owners and police who *weren't* carrying Modhran colonies under their skins were trying to nail him to the wall.

Fayr was the sort who enjoyed a challenge. Still, I

doubted he would turn down any reasonable offer of assistance, which was why Bayta and I were on our way to Bellis to offer him some.

Which brought me back to Bayta's question. The Modhri was undoubtedly still looking for us, and might have a few walkers hanging around the transfer station where Quadrail passengers bound for the Bellis inner system went through customs. If Mr. Smith's mysterious errand could provide Bayta and me with a legitimate reason to enter Belldic space, it might be worth a few days of our time to accommodate him.

The problem was the other side of coin . . . because if Smith himself was a Modhran walker, then no matter how legitimate he might think his offer, going with him would probably walk us straight into a trap.

Up to now the Modhri hadn't shown himself to be a particularly vengeful sort. But that was before we'd destroyed his homeland. I wasn't eager to find out what his new attitude toward us might be. "Forget it," I told Bayta. "Not worth the risk."

"But—"

"We're not interested," I said firmly, cutting off another bite.

"Maybe *we* aren't," Bayta said, a little crossly. "But someone else is."

I knew better than to abruptly stop what I was doing and spin around. "Where?" I asked, putting the pili into my mouth.

Her eyes flicked over my shoulder, then returned to her own plate. "There are two of them: a man and a woman," she said. "The man's about your age, the woman about the same age as Mr. Smith."

"How's their meal going?"

"I think they're almost finished," she said. "But the man was definitely watching your conversation with Mr. Smith."

And watching was pretty much all he could do at that

distance. The acoustics in Quadrail dining and bar cars were designed to make eavesdropping from more than about a meter away effectively impossible. "Let me know when they get ready to leave," I said.

I got three more bites of pili and had tried the accompanying cornleaf mash when Bayta murmured her warning. I looked down into my lap, pretending to adjust my napkin, and was gazing at the floor as they walked past.

Their shoes were the first items up for consideration. The woman's were very much upper class, while the man's were nice but nothing special. I let my eyes move upward as the two of them continued by, giving each article of clothing the same quick analysis, then checked out the backs of their heads and their hairstyles.

There was no doubt about it. The woman belonged here among the stratospheric wealthy of the galaxy. The man was just as definitely traveling first class on someone else's budget.

And then, as they reached the corridor, the man turned and looked at me.

It was a short, expressionless glance. But it was enough. "Well, well," I murmured as the two of them turned right toward the first-class car behind the dining car.

"You know him?" Bayta asked.

"No, but I know his type," I said. "He's someone's Intelligence agent. Probably Westali or the EuroUnion Security Service—he doesn't look Asian or African enough for any of their groups."

"What's he doing here?"

"The same thing I used to do way too much of," I said. "He's playing escort. The lady's probably some ranking politician who decided her status demanded she get an official government guard dog to hold her hand out here in the big, scary universe."

Bayta pondered that for another two bites. "So why was he watching us?" she asked.

It was the same question I'd been asking myself ever

since Bayta mentioned them. That backward glance all by itself had been way too interested for a man who was supposed to be busy watching his client's back.

There were, in fact, only a limited number of reasons I could think of why he might be that interested in me. Unfortunately, most of those reasons involved the Modhri.

"Maybe he just recognized me from somewhere," I said, picking the least threatening of the possibilities. "I was in that same business, after all."

"I don't know," Bayta said slowly. "He seemed interested in Mr. Smith, too."

"Maybe Mr. Smith's completely legal secret artwork transaction isn't as secret as he thinks," I said. "Either way, our best bet is to keep a low profile the rest of the way to Bellis and hope all of them forget about us."

"It's only twenty-five hours to Bellis," Bayta pointed out.

"Then they'll have to forget real fast."

WE FINISHED OUR meal in silence against the steady clacking of the train's wheels on the tracks beneath us as we traveled along at a steady hundred kilometers an hour. Or a light-year per minute, however one preferred to think about it. When we were finished, we headed back to our double compartment.

We reached the car to find Smith's door was closed. I half expected him to jump out into the corridor as we passed and try his sales pitch on me again, but the door stayed shut. Either he'd gone to bed, or else he'd given up on me. Either suited me fine.

I ushered Bayta into her compartment and then continued on to my own. I hung my jacket on the clothes rack for a quick cleaning, then settled down on the bed with my reader and the complete guidebook to Bellis I'd picked up at Terra Station before Bayta and I had left. As Humans we were going to look out of place enough among all those chipmunk-faced Bellidos. There was no point in looking like tourists, too.

I'd been reading for an hour, and was just thinking about taking a quick shower and getting ready for bed, when a piercing scream from the corridor knifed through the wall.

TWO

I was at the door in two seconds flat, slapping at the release even as a small, sane part of my mind warned that this was not a smart thing to do. There were probably at least a couple of Modhran walkers aboard, and uncorking a pitiful scream was a time-honored way of enticing a victim into a trap.

But the sane part of my mind wasn't winning many arguments these days, and it didn't win this one, either. Reminding myself that the Spiders were very good about keeping weapons off their Quadrails, I stepped out into the corridor.

Standing a couple of paces inside the car's rear vestibule was the lady politician who'd passed us in the dining car earlier. Her mouth was open, her lungs filling for a reprise of her scream, her hands scrabbling at the corridor walls as if trying to find something to hold on to.

Her wide eyes were staring down at Mr. Smith's battered body, sprawled on the corridor floor barely two meters from my door.

"What happened?" I demanded as I dropped to one knee beside Smith. He was still wearing the traveling suit I'd seen him in earlier, now badly rumpled. The front of his jacket was rising and falling feverishly with short, shallow breaths.

"I don't know," the woman managed. "I was—I think he fell—" Abruptly she turned and disappeared back into the vestibule.

I sent a brief hope skyward that she could hold on to her dinner long enough to reach the restroom at the front of the first-class car behind us, then put her out of my mind. Gingerly, I opened Smith's jacket, trying to remember my Westali first-aid training. His shirt, I saw, was peppered with small bloodstains, a ghastly contrast to the diamond fastening studs.

The door to Bayta's compartment slid open, and I glanced up to see her gazing out at us, her eyes wide. "Whistle up a conductor and have him find a doctor," I ordered. "Then get the LifeGuard."

"The conductors have been alerted," she said as she stepped gingerly past me and over Smith's body and hurried toward the bright orange box set into the corridor wall near the front of the car.

"Make it a trauma specialist if they have a choice," I called, hoping at least one of the Spiders was close enough for Bayta's telepathic link with them to work. Carefully, I unfastened the diamond studs and opened Smith's shirt.

One look at the bruise pattern and oozing blood was all I needed. The lady with the excellent lungs might think he'd gotten this way tripping over his own feet, but I knew a professional beating when I saw one.

And then, to my surprise, his eyes fluttered open. "Who—?" he rasped, bits of blood flecking his lips as he spoke.

"It's all right," I soothed, the small sane part of my mind noting the banal stupidity of that comment. Traveling through interstellar space, hours away from a real medical facility, he was probably a goner. "It's Compton. Who did this to you?"

"Know what's . . . really funny?" he asked, his swollen eyes fighting to focus on my face.

I grimaced. Why did so many badly injured people get

stuck on inessentials? "The Marx Brothers," I said. "Who did this to you?"

"He hates you," Smith gasped. "Funny thing is, that was . . . even better than Lo . . . Losutu's rec . . . recommenda . . ."

"Recommendation," I finished for him, wondering which of the collection of people who hated me he was referring to. Not that it mattered. "I'm glad my reputation is so solid. Now who *did* this?"

He shook his head weakly. "Never saw . . ." Abruptly, his right hand jerked upward and clutched at my sleeve. "Lynx," he croaked.

Lynx? "His name's Lynx?" I asked.

His face spasmed with pain. "Nemuti Lynx," he said. "He wanted . . . third Lynx. Daniel—Daniel Mice—" He broke off, his face spasming again.

"Okay," I said. The Nemuti part, at least, I understood. The Nemuti FarReach was one of the Twelve Empires, with territory stretching across a few thousand light-years near the galaxy's central core area. The Lynx I didn't have a clue on. "Did Daniel Mice do this?"

He closed his eyes, and with one final heave his chest went still.

I swore under my breath as his hand dropped limply away from my sleeve. "Bayta!" I snapped as I rolled Smith onto his back and started to check his windpipe for blockages.

And suddenly the Quadrail became a cheap kaleidoscope as I was grabbed by the front of my shirt, hauled to my feet, and thrown violently backward down the corridor.

I slammed to the floor at Bayta's feet, hitting hard enough to see stars. Bayta gave a little gasp as I grabbed a piece of floor and pushed myself upright again. Blinking to clear my vision, I looked back down the corridor.

Trouble was definitely on its way, striding toward me in the form of the biggest Halka I'd ever seen, two meters of short brown fur, back-jointed legs, and muscle.

His flat bulldog face was simmering with righteous anger, his nostrils making little puffing sounds, his short claws extending whitely from their fingertip sheaths. Behind him, the Intelligence man I'd seen in the dining car was hurrying toward Smith's body, the lady politician trailing shakily behind him.

"Easy," I said, taking a step back and holding out my hands toward the approaching Halka. "We're just trying to help."

The Halka kept coming. "What you do to this Human?" he demanded.

"We didn't do anything," I said, taking another step back and hoping I could talk some sense into him before Bayta and I ran out of corridor. "We're trying to get the LifeGuard."

"Then get on with it," the Intelligence man called, his unexpected British accent carrying an extra edge of authority as he knelt beside the body. "Make sure it's set for Human. You—sir—out of his way, please."

The big Halka rumbled something, but obediently stepped to the side of the corridor. Taking the orange box from Bayta, I punched the button marked "Human" and hurried back down the corridor.

The Intelligence man had gotten Smith's head in position by the time I arrived. Up close, I could see that he was in his mid-twenties, a few years younger than my own thirty-two, with light brown hair and the smooth, unweathered skin of someone who preferred the indoor life. His pale blue eyes brushed over me like radar painting a target as I knelt down beside him. "Get the arm cuff on," he ordered as he unlimbered the breather mask and oxygen tank. He took a quick look to make sure the mask had configured to Human facial shape, then fastened it over Smith's face.

I got the cuff in place around Smith's right jacket sleeve. "Ready," I said.

He punched the start button. There was a brief hum that shifted into a soft chugging sound as the respirator kicked in. "You know how to read this?" he asked, peering at the LifeGuard's display.

"Green is good; red is bad," I said. "For anything more complicated, we'll need a Spider."

He grunted. "I think they're all off hunting up a Human doctor," he said. "What's your name?"

"Compton," I said. "Yours?"

"Morse," he said. "What's your relationship with him?"

"Haven't got one," I said.

"Really?" Morse asked, turning his blue eyes on me again. "You were having a rather intense conversation earlier in the dining car."

"He invited himself to our table to offer me a job," I said.

"What kind of job?"

"Unspecified," I said. "Also unaccepted. End of story."

"Did he give you a name?"

"Smith."

Morse grunted. "So what happened here?"

"I heard a scream and found him bleeding in the corridor."

"Did you move him?"

"I rolled him onto his back to clear his windpipe," I said. "Nothing more."

Morse let out a hiss between his teeth and glanced over his shoulder at the vestibule. "Where the *hell's* that doctor?"

"They probably had to go all the way back to third to find one," I said. "Unless you know any working doctors who can afford first-class Quadrail seats."

"Not many, no," he conceded, his eyes shifting pointedly to my neat but hardly expensive suit. "Speaking of affording things, may I ask what *you're* doing up here?"

"Traveling legally and minding my own business," I said.

"Are you paying for your compartment yourself?"

"I have a rich uncle," I said, pointedly running my eyes down his own suit. "What's *your* excuse?"

He eyed me a moment as if wondering if he should challenge my conclusion. "I'm here on business," he said instead.

"You have one hell of a generous boss," I said. "You want to get Smith's wallet, or should I do it?"

Morse gave me a measuring look, then slipped a hand inside the bloodied suit coat, probing one side's pockets and then the other. "Not here," he said. "Hopefully, it's in his compartment and not in someone else's pocket."

The LifeGuard gave a soft beep, and the display lights went solid red. "Damn," I said.

"Keep it going," Morse said, pushing the start button again. "At least until the doctor gets here. What's your business in the Bellidosh Estates-General, Mr. Compton?"

"What's your reason for asking?" I countered. Maybe a little too tartly, but my back was aching where I'd hit the floor and I was getting tired of the interrogation.

"I'm attempting to establish some facts," Morse said. "You *were* found here on the scene, remember."

"Your lady friend was here first," I reminded him.

"The lady couldn't have done this by herself."

"Maybe she had help."

"Maybe I'm looking at it," Morse said, letting his voice go deep and ominous.

The LifeGuard beeped, and again the red lights came on. "You want to try for three out of three?" I asked. "Or shall we let the grim reaper have him?"

Morse's answer was to hit the start button again.

Mentally, I shook my head. I knew the quality of the Spiders' medical equipment, and if the LifeGuard said the victim was dead, he was dead. All Morse was going to accomplish by running the cycle again was to cover his own rear in case of an inquiry. "No, by all means let's run it again," I said. "We don't want to look like we're doing nothing when the doctor gets here."

Morse's eyes narrowed. "I don't think I like your attitude, Mr. Compton."

"Then let me get it out of your face," I offered, standing up and starting back toward my compartment door.

Morse was faster, jumping to his feet and inserting his shoulder between me and the door. "Certainly," he said. "*After* I have a look inside."

He was half a head taller than I was, and probably better muscled. The mood I was rapidly sliding into, I didn't care. "When hell freezes over or the Spiders elect you king," I told him. "Get out of my way."

"I don't think so," Morse said, extending an arm across the doorway to block it. "The victim was definitely beaten in the privacy of a compartment. It's only an assumption that it was done in *his* compartment." He raised his eyebrows. "And we have only *your* word that you hadn't arranged an after-dinner meeting with him."

"All very true," I agreed. "Tell me again why that means I should let you grub around my compartment."

"Because I'm entitled," he said. Pulling out a wallet, he snapped it open to reveal the gold-and-platinum badge and matching ID card of the EuroUnion Security Service. "Special Agent Ackerley Morse, ESS," he said quietly, his voice gone suddenly very formal. "You, Mr. Compton, are under suspicion of murder."

THERE WAS ONLY one Human doctor aboard, and the Spiders did indeed have to haul him all the way up from third class. By the time he arrived, I'd allowed Morse a quick look at my compartment.

Technically, I didn't have to. Inside a Quadrail Tube the only laws or regulations that applied were those of the Spiders. But Morse had clearly latched on to this theory that I'd enticed Smith to his doom, and letting him into my compartment seemed the simplest way of defusing it.

Sure enough, and to his obvious disappointment, he

didn't find any bloodstains or other telltale signs of mayhem.

The doctor fussed over Smith's body a few minutes before pronouncing him dead. One of the conductor Spiders opened compartment eleven, and with his help Morse carried the body inside.

There we *did* find blood. Lots of it.

"Cause of death was massive trauma and internal bleeding," the doctor told Morse as he covered the dead man's bruised face with the bed's blanket. "There may have been an underlying heart problem, as well. No way to tell without a full autopsy."

"I'll see if the Spiders at Bellis Station can give you access to an examination room," Morse said. He'd found Smith's wallet in an evening jacket in the sonic cleaning rack and was sorting through it, a frown creasing his face.

"I'm sorry, but I won't be able to help you with that," the doctor said as he cleaned his hands. "I'm on my way to a conference on Bellis, and I'm already running late."

"I can order you to assist," Morse warned him.

"No, you can't," I said. "He hasn't committed any crime, except possibly to annoy you." I gestured the doctor toward the door. "Thanks for your help. Enjoy your conference."

"Thank you," he said, glowering briefly at Morse as he closed his bag. "I'll leave a report with one of the conductors before we reach Bellis."

He stepped to the doorway. The conductor standing watch from the corridor tapped his seven-legged way to the side to let him pass, then resumed his silent vigil. "Thank you so very much," Morse growled, unloading a standard-issue ESS glare at me with both barrels. "You have any idea how important a timely autopsy is in collecting and preserving evidence?"

"Absolutely," I assured him. "I also know it's no less important than a close examination of the crime scene. You probably aren't going to get *that,* either."

Morse looked around the room as if suddenly remembering where we were. "You're right. I'll need the Spiders to detach the car."

"Good luck," I said. "Unfortunately, this train has a schedule to keep, and that schedule includes a compartment car pulling out with the rest of it. If they've got a spare at Bellis they can throw in on the spur of the moment, you might get lucky. Otherwise, forget it."

Morse threw a hooded glare at the conductor in the doorway. "There should be agreements to cover this sort of thing," he muttered.

"There should be free beer and onion rings at every roadside pub, too," I said. "You don't always get what you want."

"*Look*—"

"Meanwhile, what we *do* have is twenty-two hours until we reach Bellis and a couple of carloads of first-class passengers," I interrupted him. "We should probably start with interviews in the next car back. See if anyone remembers who's been coming in and out of this one."

"*We* should probably start?"

"You'd rather do it all yourself?" I shrugged. "Fine—you're the one with the badge. Have fun."

I started to turn away. As I did so his hand snaked out to catch my arm, a look of sudden recognition on his face. "*Compton*," he said, making the name a curse. "*Frank* Compton? Damn—I *knew* you looked familiar."

"You're one hell of a detective," I said, twisting my arm out of his grip.

"And you're one hell of a bloody bastard," he shot back.

I blinked. Even Losutu hadn't reacted this strongly the first time I'd met him after the Yandro embarrassment. "So I've been told," I said. "What does Yandro mean to you, anyway?"

His forehead furrowed slightly, then cleared. "That's right," he said, still growling. "You were involved with the Yandro thing, too, weren't you?"

"It's been a busy few years," I said, frowning in turn. If he hadn't been talking about Yandro, what *had* he been talking about? Nearly everyone who knew me at all knew me because I'd tried to blow the whistle on the UN's Yandro colonization scam. "But this isn't about me," I added, gesturing to the wallet in his hand. "Did our mystery guest have a real name?"

For a couple of seconds Morse continued to stare at me. Then, almost reluctantly, he dropped his eyes back to the wallet. "According to this, his name was John Smith."

I cocked an eyebrow. At least he'd told the truth about that. "Really?"

"Really," Morse said, his voice odd. "*Or* it was Kevin Abrams, *or* Emile Dorfmann, *or* Homer LaGrange."

"Come again?"

"Four IDs; four credit tabs," Morse said. He held up a handful of cash sticks. "And just over a million dollars in cash."

"Interesting," I said. "Sounds like he was expecting to be on the buying end of the business transaction he mentioned." I pointed toward the wallet. "May I?"

He hesitated, then handed it over. I sorted quickly through the contents. "At least we know he wasn't murdered for his cash or credit tags," I said, handing it back.

"Unless there used to be more than just four of the latter," Morse countered. "Maybe someone was hoping to pick up a new identity."

I shook my head. "The indentation pattern in the leather doesn't show anything missing."

He took another look at the wallet. "Yes, of course."

"They're excellent forgeries, though," I said.

"That they are." He gave me a speculative look. "Rather the sort of documents a former Westali investigator might know how to get hold of."

"You'd better make up your mind as to which slot you want me in," I warned. "You can't tag me as his killer *and* as his loyal private watchdog, too."

"Of course I can," he said. "The case files are full of watchdogs who changed sides when the price was right."

"Right. Whatever you say." I turned and headed toward the Spider still standing in the doorway. "I still suggest you talk to the rest of the first-class passengers before we hit Bellis," I added over my shoulder.

"Don't worry," Morse assured me, "I will."

Motioning the Spider aside, I walked past into the corridor and returned to my compartment.

The divider between my room and Bayta's was still closed as I locked the door behind me. But as I took off my shirt the curve couch collapsed into the wall, and the wall itself retracted into the side of the half bath to reveal Bayta standing facing me, her hands making nervous little twitching movements.

"You get all that?" I asked as I hung the shirt in the sonic cleaner. I might have picked up a few traces of Smith's blood while we were working on him, and I wanted them gone before it occurred to Morse to confiscate my whole wardrobe as evidence.

"I was listening in through the conductor," Bayta said, her voice tight. "What are we going to do?"

"For starters, we're not going to worry about Morse," I said. Crossing into her compartment, I took her arm and eased her gently back toward the bed. "What do the Spiders think of all this?"

"They're concerned," Bayta said, still looking troubled as she let me sit her down on the edge of the bed. "They're really not sure what to do."

"I thought the Spiders had a procedure for everything."

She hunched her shoulders slightly. "The procedure in the case of a major crime is to turn the likely suspect over to his own people."

I grimaced. "Ah."

"Oh, don't worry, they aren't going to hand you over to Mr. Morse," she promised. "Even if they wanted to, I certainly wouldn't let them."

"Thanks," I said. That wasn't just plucky assistant talk, I knew. Bayta had been raised by the Chahwyn, and was herself a strange sort of amalgamation of Human and Chahwyn minds and bodies. As such, she could pretty well order the Spiders around if and when she needed to.

But doing so in any obvious way would draw unwelcome attention, and attention was something we very much wanted to avoid right now. Far better if I could arrange things so that blatant manipulation of the system wouldn't be necessary.

"But they can't just take a whole car out of service, either," she went on. "Keeping the trains on schedule is their first priority."

"I know," I said. "Any chance of substituting another car at Bellis, like I suggested to Morse?"

"Maybe, if they have a spare available," she said. "They can send a message ahead when we stop at Helvanti."

"Good." Though even if they had a substitute available, they'd have less than forty-five minutes to swap out the cars and transfer all the passengers and their stuff. Even for Spiders, that would be pushing it. "Looks like we may have to do without a full crime-scene analysis for once," I said. "Maybe that's a good enough reason all by itself to kill him here instead of somewhere else."

"Do you think we should mention that to Mr. Morse?"

"I'm sure it'll eventually occur to him," I said. "Meanwhile, we have more immediate problems to deal with. Starting with the fact that our plan of sneaking quietly into the Bellis system is now pretty well shot."

Her throat tightened. "Oh," she said.

"Well might you say 'oh,' " I agreed. "We've got three stops between here and Bellis. That's three chances for someone to sniff out the story and load it into a data cylinder bound for the nearest Intragala News office. By the time we make Bellis, the sensational story of Mr. Smith's murder will be on its way to every corner of the galaxy."

"And Mr. Morse will make sure your name is in there somewhere," she murmured.

"Definitely," I said sourly. "Which means that if the Modhri isn't already aware that we're on this train, he will be well before we reach Bellis."

"Which means we can't go looking for *Korak* Fayr."

"Not unless we want to do it with a parade of Modhran walkers behind us," I agreed.

Bayta turned her head to gaze toward the compartment door. "Do you think that was why he killed Mr. Smith? To alert the rest of the mind?"

"Who says the Modhri was even involved?" I countered. "There *is* other crime still going on out there in the galaxy."

"I suppose." She shivered. "It seems like such a horrible way to kill someone."

"It's also very inefficient," I said. "That's why the only time you bother with it is for revenge or for information."

"Information about what?"

I shrugged. "All I know is what Smith said before he died. He said someone wanted the Nemuti Lynx. Or maybe the third Lynx—he used both terms. He also mentioned someone named Daniel Mice."

"Do you know this person?"

"Never heard of him," I said. "But I'm starting to think I should correct that omission. Next station where we have time, I want you to get the stationmaster busy sifting through the master records. If there's a Daniel Mice riding the Quadrail right now, I want to know it."

"All right," she said. "What about us?"

I grimaced. "As far as Fayr is concerned, the best thing we can do is turn around and go somewhere else."

"You have someplace in mind?"

"Not really."

For a moment we sat together in silence. Then Bayta got up and walked to the display window, gazing out at the faintly lit Tube surface rushing past. "Could Mr. Morse himself be involved?" she asked.

"There were no obvious blood spatters on his clothing," I told her. "And his hands didn't show any bruising or other marks."

"Yet he seems very anxious to put the blame on you."

"Unfortunately, I'm a very logical suspect," I said. "I was on the scene, and I have the training to know how to do this."

"But you have no motive."

"He's probably working on that as we speak," I said. "What's he doing right now, by the way?"

"He's in the first first-class coach car," she said, frowning in concentration. "He's asking one of the Halkas if he saw anyone going into or coming out of our car in the past three hours."

"Can you get that conductor to stay with him?"

"He was already planning to do that."

Which meant Bayta would be able to listen in on Morse's investigation via her handy little telepathic link. "Good," I said. "Be sure to take notes."

"I will." Bayta hesitated. "Frank . . . what did Morse mean when he said you were involved with the Yandro incident, *too*?"

"Obviously, he must have originally recognized my name from somewhere else."

"Obviously," she said patiently. "I was asking where that someplace was."

"I have no idea," I said. "Whatever it was, though, he wasn't remembering it fondly."

Her throat tightened. "He's not going to let you go on this, is he?'

"I'm sure he'll give it his best shot," I said. "But it's over twenty hours to Bellis. We'll think of something."

THREE

Twenty hours later, I still hadn't thought of anything. Morse, unfortunately, had.

He was waiting on the platform with a pair of well-dressed Bellidos as Bayta and I disembarked from our car. The Bellidos were looking very solemn, their dark eyes staring hard at me out of their striped chipmunk faces.

The typical Bellido was shorter than the typical Human, which meant they were looking up at me. But that particular stare had an amazingly effective leveling effect.

Standing a few paces behind them was the lady politician who'd discovered Smith's body, still looking a little shaken. "There he is," Morse said to the Bellidos, pointing at me. "That's Mr. Frank Compton."

"Can I help you?" I asked, giving the Bellidos a quick once-over as Bayta and I walked up to the group. Along with their expensive clothing, each of the two aliens was wearing a double shoulder holster on each arm, making a total of eight small-caliber handguns between them.

Not real guns, of course. The Spiders banned weapons of any sort aboard their trains, and had a highly sophisticated layered sensor array in every Tube station to enforce that edict. The Bellidos' real guns were safely secured in lockboxes beneath the cars, which the drudge Spiders were busy packing aboard one of the outgoing cargo shuttles for shipment to the transfer station floating in space a hundred kilometers away.

But guns were an indication of Belldic social rank, and the soft plastic substitute guns currently riding the Bellidos' holsters were no less valid a mark of their status than were the real things.

Four guns apiece implied that status was pretty high. Whatever Morse had up his sleeve, I was pretty sure I wasn't going to like it.

I was right. "Mr. Compton is under suspicion of felony murder," Morse informed the aliens. "I'm going to go and speak to the stationmaster about having him officially handed into my custody for return to the Terran Confederation. But in case I can't persuade him, I wanted to lodge a formal warning with the Bellidosh Estates-General as to who and what this man is."

"Who he is and what he *might* be," I corrected stiffly. "Mr. Morse has absolutely no evidence against me."

"Mr. Compton had both opportunity and ability," Morse countered. "Belldic law, if I'm not mistaken, allows extradition or temporary confinement under such indicators while an investigation is launched."

"It does," one of the Bellidos confirmed, eyeing me thoughtfully.

I eyed him right back with all the innocence I could dredge up at such short notice, and sent a few mental daggers in Morse's direction. I'd already decided we weren't going to Bellis, but there had still been the option of getting off somewhere else in the Estates-General and backtracking again after the uproar over Smith's murder had died down.

Now, that option was also down the plumbing. The minute I stepped onto a shuttle and headed for any Belldic transfer station I would be out of Spider jurisdiction. If Morse could persuade the Bellidos to arrest me and extradite me over to him, he could bypass the Spiders completely.

A little obfuscation was clearly called for. "What Mr. Morse fails to mention is that everyone with a compartment on this train had the same level of opportunity that I had," I pointed out.

"A moot point, since everyone else is continuing on," Morse said before either of the Bellidos could respond. "All we can do here is to send a warning on ahead to the various Belldic stations down the line." He looked expectantly at me, and I could tell he was dying for me to also bring up the passengers in the other two first-class coaches as possible suspects.

Fat chance. I already knew from Bayta and her eavesdropping conductor that no one in either car remembered seeing anybody leave the compartment car during the hour before Smith's body had been discovered.

Obviously, they'd simply forgotten. People did that a lot, and every cop knew it. But just the same there was no point in offering Morse the opportunity to add that bit of weight to the case against me. "Still, we do know of at least one person who entered the compartment car prior to the discovery of the crime," I said instead.

"Who?" one of the Bellidos asked.

I pointed to the lady politician still hovering behind them. "Her."

The woman's eyes widened. "What did you say?" she demanded. Unlike her screaming voice, her demanding voice was solidly in upper-crust territory.

"Just stating facts, ma'am," I said mildly.

"Lady Dorchester had nothing to do with the crime," Morse put in hurriedly. "I can personally vouch for her."

"So what?" I scoffed. "Bayta here can personally vouch for me, too. That proves nothing."

The mental daggers I'd been sending Morse earlier reversed direction. "This is nothing but an attempt to muddy the waters," he ground out. "I've shown you my credentials. If Mr. Compton has any of his own—"

"Excuse me, but Mr. Compton and I have business to

attend to," Bayta spoke up unexpectedly. "You three go ahead and continue your discussion."

"Don't be ridiculous," Morse growled. "Until this is settled you can't go anywhere unattended."

"What's to settle?" I countered. I had no idea where Bayta was going with this, but I was willing to play along. "As long as we're still in the Tube none of you has any right to hinder our movements."

"That may change momentarily," Morse warned darkly.

"When it does, be sure and let me know," I said. "Until then, we have lives to lead. Honored sirs; Lady Dorchester," I added, nodding in turn to the Bellidos and the woman. Taking Bayta's arm, I turned us in the general direction of the stationmaster's building and started walking.

I half expected Morse to try to stop us, but he didn't. I gave us five or six steps worth of distance, then leaned my head toward Bayta. "What's up?" I asked quietly.

Her answer was to pull subtly on my arm, changing our course a few degrees to the left. "Those hatchways," she murmured, nodding toward a set of shuttle hatchways fifty meters ahead.

I craned my neck to look over a line of goose-feathered Pirks that were hurrying past across our path. Two of the hatchways had the glowing rims that proclaimed the presence of docked shuttles. A crowd of travelers had gathered in the area, waiting their turn to embark for the transfer station and the torchliners that would take them to their ultimate destinations here in the Estates-General's capital system. As I watched, one of the two glowing hatchways opened and began disgorging a line of passengers, upperclass Bellidos with lots of plastic guns riding beneath their arms. "What about them?" I asked Bayta.

"I just saw another shuttle from that same group only let out five passengers," she said. "All of them upper class."

"So they had a short load," I said. "So what?"

"But then only five outgoing passengers got on," she said. "Belldic shuttles are supposed to carry sixty passengers."

I frowned. She was right about the number. And given that it cost as much to run a half-empty shuttle as it did a full one, nobody deliberately ran short loads without a good reason. "Let's take a closer look," I suggested.

Sure enough, before we'd gotten twenty paces the flow of incoming Bellidos from the shuttle stopped. Five of them, just as Bayta had said. The outgoing passengers started filing down the stairway; again, only five made it in before the hatchway light went out, indicating the shuttle was full.

"Interesting," I said, shifting my attention to our five new arrivals. A dozen paces from the shuttle hatchways they joined up with another group of five, possibly the ones from the shuttle Bayta had first noticed. The first five were standing casually enough, looking at first glance like any other collection of travelers regrouping before heading for their trains.

But they weren't talking among themselves or looking at their tickets or admiring the brilliantly flashing Coreline that ran through the center of the Tube above our heads. Instead, they stood silently, their attention focused outward toward the rest of the crowd milling about the station.

Even more interestingly, their carry-on luggage, instead of hugging their owners' sides like well-behaved self-rolling luggage should, was gathered together in the middle of their circle like the women and children in an old dit rec western.

The other lighted hatchway opened, and a third group of upper-class Bellidos started filing up into the Tube. "Wait here," I told Bayta. Turning off the leash button inside my lapel to keep my luggage from following, I headed toward the hatchway, weaving in and out of the other travelers as quickly and unobtrusively as I could.

Only five Bellidos got out of this shuttle, too. By the time I reached the waiting crowd the first five outgoing passengers had disappeared down the stairway and the hatchway's rim lights had gone out. Picking up my pace, I hurried forward, and as the hatchway started to iris shut I jumped through the opening.

The stairway had already retracted, and I dropped two meters straight down onto the folded metal. I hit with a rattling clang, nearly twisting my ankle on the uneven surface as I threw a hand against the side wall to steady myself. Recovering my balance, I lifted my eyes from my footing.

To find myself staring down the muzzles of a dozen guns.

Not the fake ones Bellidos were allowed to carry into the Tube, either. These were the real thing: large caliber, undoubtedly loaded, and gripped in very steady hands. Hands whose owners were furthermore encased in Belldic military uniforms.

"Who?" one of the soldiers demanded.

Somewhere deep in my chest, I found where I'd mislaid my voice. "Sorry," I croaked, carefully opening both hands to demonstrate their emptiness. "Wrong shuttle."

There was a soft clanking from above me as the hatch opened again. "Go," the Bellido ordered, twitching the muzzle of his gun upward in case my ears had stopped working the same time my voice had.

I got a grip on the edges of the hatch, my eyes flicking once to the five wide-eyed nonmilitary Belldic passengers in the front row, and pulled myself up and out. The shuttle hatch irised closed, followed by the station's own hatch, both of them nearly catching my legs before I could get them out of the way.

"What in the *world* was that for?" Bayta demanded, hurrying toward me with my carrybags in her hands and her own rolling at her heels. "If Morse had seen you trying to get away—"

"I wasn't trying to get away," I assured her as she set down my bags with perhaps a little more force than necessary. "Besides which, the shuttle was already full."

"With only five passengers?"

"That's right." Turning my leash control back on, I let my bags roll into position behind me, then gave a casual glance at the—now—fifteen Bellidos who'd emerged from the three special shuttles. The original ten were still gazing outward, looking for all the world like a group of combat soldiers settled into a defensive ring around their clustered luggage.

The five new arrivals, in contrast, were looking straight at me.

"Come on," I said, taking Bayta's arm again and picking a random direction away from them.

The Bellidos didn't make any move to follow. I waited anyway until we'd built up some distance before speaking again. "Two reasons why the shuttles were already full," I said quietly. "Reason one: they were military layout, with only twenty seats each. Reason two: the other fifteen seats were occupied by armed Bellidos."

Bayta's eyes went wide. "They're not supposed to bring weapons this close to a station," she insisted.

"They must have gotten special permission," I said. "It *did* seem to be an official military operation. And they didn't try to—"

"I don't care *how* official it was," Bayta said. She actually looked angry, an emotion I didn't see in her very often. "No weapons are allowed in the trains or Tubes. They know that."

"And they didn't try to bring the weapons into the Tube," I finished patiently. "Come on. If the Spiders could keep their temper over this, you should be able to, too."

Her lips compressed into a thin line. Then, slowly, the tension lines eased. "It was still a waste of effort," she said. "Once the shuttle has left the transfer station, what good are armed soldiers going to do anyone?"

"Not a scrap," I agreed. "But *someone* aboard must have been feeling nervous about whatever he was up to. Apparently he wanted to get to the Quadrail with at least the illusion of safety."

Bayta started to look over her shoulder, seemed to think better of it. "The Modhri shouldn't care all that much if one of his walkers is kidnapped or killed," she said, her voice almost too quiet to hear. "Why protect them that way?"

"We don't *know* the Modhri's involved in this, any more than we know he was involved with Smith's murder," I reminded her. Still, I'd pretty much come to that same conclusion. "But if he is, you're right, he shouldn't care. So kidnapping and murder are out. That just leaves theft."

"Something valuable in their luggage?" Bayta asked, clearly still working it through. "Is that why it's all bunched together that way?"

"Could be," I agreed. "The question is, what?"

"The Lynx Mr. Smith mentioned?" she suggested. "In fact . . . could he have been on his way here to meet with these people?"

"Could be," I said again. The girl was definitely starting to click with this detective stuff. "Alternatively, maybe he had information on their movements that they didn't want getting out. Speaking of which, how about asking the Spiders where they're all going?"

We'd made it another fifty meters before she got her answer. "Laarmiten," she said. "It's on the Claremiado Loop, one of the five regional capitals of the Nemuti Far-Reach."

An unpleasant tingle went up my back. The Nemuti FarReach. The place Smith's last-gasp Lynx had come from. This was definitely starting to push the edges of coincidence. "When does their Quadrail leave?" I asked.

She glanced at one of the holodisplay clocks hovering in various spots around the station. "Thirty minutes, from Platform Ten. It's an express."

"Get us a compartment on it."

She shook her head. "I can't," she said. "All the compartments are booked."

I scowled at the nearest Spider as he strode purposefully across the station on his seven slender legs, his central metallic globe reflecting the colors of the Coreline's light show. As recently as a few months ago, the Spiders had made a point of keeping a double compartment open for us on all trains in our vicinity.

Still, to be fair, we *had* been heading the opposite direction. "Can you pull rank or something?" I asked.

"There's nothing left," Bayta said with the impatient tone of someone who's already answered the question. "They were all booked three weeks ago."

I frowned. "By our fifteen nervous Bellidos?"

"They—" She broke off. "Actually, yes, they were," she continued, her impatience fading away. "There's one Juri who's continuing on from Misfar, but the rest are all new Belldic passengers."

And all of them heading to a Nemuti world. "What about ordinary first-class seats?" I asked. "Can you get us a couple of them?"

"You mean . . . just *seats*?" she echoed warily. "With walkers aboard?"

"Does that really make a difference?" I countered. "You know as well as I do that if they really want us a compartment door isn't going to hold them for long."

She swallowed. "I suppose not," she said in a low voice.

"Don't worry, the Modhri's not going to throw away any of his walkers just for a little revenge," I soothed. "With his homeland wrecked, he can't afford to waste any of his resources without a damn good reason, and that includes his walkers. As long as we don't bother him, I don't think he'll bother us."

"You assume."

"Okay, yes, I assume," I conceded. "But either way, this is too intriguing to pass up."

She nodded, still looking unhappy at the prospect of sharing a Quadrail car with an unknown number of Modhran walkers. "All right. We have seats."

"Good girl." I glanced at my watch. "As long as the Spiders are tracking down our mysterious Daniel Mice anyway, they might also see what they can find about this Nemuti Lynx. It'll be fairly obscure—I already searched my encyclopedia and came up dry."

"Mine didn't have anything, either," Bayta confirmed. "I doubt anyone here will know. Can they put the information in a data chip and deliver it to us somewhere down the line?"

"That should work," I said. "But make sure they put a high-priority stamp on it. This is no time to be flying blind."

"They'll get it to us as quickly as they can," she assured me.

I looked back across the station at the train we'd just left, where a pair of drudges were crowding close beside the door of the first-class compartment car. Morse was there, too, standing off to the side, Lady Dorchester near him. Even at this distance I could see they both looked stiff and unhappy.

And as we all watched, the Spiders maneuvered a covered stretcher out through the door and onto the platform.

No weapons were allowed aboard the Spiders' nice, clean, safe Quadrail. So someone had simply beaten a middle-aged man to death.

Whoever was playing this game, they were playing it for keeps.

FOUR

Of the twelve civilizations served by the Quadrail system—people-groups which the Spiders liked to refer to as empires—seven had been riding the rails since the beginning. The rest of us had dribbled into the club over the centuries since then, with Humans being the most recent to join, three decades ago.

Our people-group, of course, consisted of Earth and four pathetic little colony systems, while at the other end of the spectrum the Shorshians had literally thousands of worlds to call their own. Nevertheless, to the Spiders we both qualified as galactic empires.

A lot of Humans tended to strut a little over that alleged equality. I had no idea what the Shorshians thought of the whole thing. Probably they just accepted it as one of the Spiders' peculiarities and ignored us as best they could.

The Spiders had a lot of peculiarities, and a lot of secrets. I knew more about them than most people, and even I didn't have anything close to a complete picture. All I really knew was that the Spiders were being directed from behind the scenes by the Chahwyn, a below-the-radar alien race who had survived the galaxy's rebellion against the Shonkla-raa.

I also knew that, strictly speaking, the Quadrail was a fraud.

A benevolent fraud, perhaps, but a fraud nonetheless. The trains, the thousands of light-years of four-railed track, the whole damn Tube system—none of it had anything to do with the light-year-per-minute speeds the galaxy was privileged to enjoy.

The effect was due solely to the Coreline that ran down the center of each Tube. Lurking inside the light-show window dressing the Spiders had set up was some kind of exotic quantum thread. An object moving parallel to the Thread at close range picked up terrific speed, with that speed increasing the closer to the Thread the object got.

That was how the message cylinders that carried the galaxy's information managed to travel so much faster than the trains themselves. Once out of the station and away from prying eyes, an outgoing train would kick its cylinder up into the loose mesh that surrounded the Coreline, where it zipped along until kicked back down to another train coming into the next station along the way.

A cynically minded person might assume the Spiders maintained the fraud in order to rake in the money the rest of us had to pay for interstellar transport. But there was more to it than that. A lot more. With the Tube severely limiting access to the Thread's vicinity, the Spiders could maintain tight control over everything that traveled between the stars. Specifically, they could restrict war-class weapons, limiting such transfers to legitimate governments, and then only in order to beef up the defenses at those governments' own colony worlds.

Which meant that anyone who wanted to make trouble on someone else's turf would end up going against warships with the military equivalent of popguns. With the Tube in place, and the Spiders controlling the Tube, interstellar war was impossible.

With the Tube gone, all bets would be off. Anyone would be able to build warships and troop transports and self-guiding weapons and send them zipping along the Thread to the next empire down the line.

And they would. I knew enough about alien psychology, and more than enough about the Human version, to know that if interstellar travel was open and unrestricted we would soon have the sort of massive power struggles that had plagued Earth for most of its history. The Thread had enabled the Shonkla-raa to enslave most of the galaxy, and the Spiders and Chahwyn were determined not to let it happen again.

They'd been doing a pretty good job of it, too, until the Modhri showed up.

The first-class car Bayta and I found ourselves in was identical to all the others I'd seen during the months I'd been working with the Spiders. The seats were large and comfortable, with automatic cushion adjustments that could accommodate the full range of passenger rear ends. Each seat had its own reading light, drink holder, and music system, plus an eyeshade and sonic neutralizer for when the occupant grew tired of the genteel party atmosphere that usually pervaded first class and wanted to get some sleep. The chairs here were also mobile, and could be moved around to create conversation or game circles, swiveled for a view of whatever was playing on each of the car's display windows, or just moved off into a corner for reading or quiet contemplation.

The passenger roster was also pretty typical of what I'd seen before, consisting of the rarefied upper crust of a variety of the galaxy's species. In second and third class, travelers tended to segregate themselves by species. Not so in first. Juriani and Halkas, Bellidos and Pirks, Humans and Cimmaheem—we were all just one big happy family.

Of course, for the passengers the Modhri had co-opted, the family metaphor was literally true.

But if the Modhri mind segment I assumed was riding our train recognized Bayta and me, he apparently decided to play it cool. There were no obvious stares or scowls from any of the passengers, and certainly no attempts to make any trouble. In fact, aside from a few curious looks at our nonrarefied-upper-crust clothing, the rest of the car's occupants pretty much ignored us.

As for the fifteen Bellidos who'd arrived at Bellis Station under armed escort, they seemed to be keeping to their compartments one car forward.

Still, there was one amenity even a first-class compartment lacked, and that was personal food service. As the hours crept by, in ones and twos, the reclusive Bellidos began passing through our car on their way to the first-class dining car just behind us. Lounging in my seat, my legs propped up comfortably and my reader nestled in the crook of my elbow just for show, I took careful mental notes.

The first stop on our way back toward Human space was the Greesovra system, one of the Belldic regional capitals, seven hours out from Bellis. A few of our car's passengers, mostly Bellidos, got off there, to be replaced by a slightly more varied group of new arrivals. With a Spider conductor standing the usual watch at each of the train's doors, Bayta was able to confirm that all the passengers in the first-class compartments stayed put.

I'd hoped those seven hours would be long enough for the Spiders to do the Nemuti Lynx and Daniel Mice research I'd asked for. But the train pulled out of Greesovra Station without word being passed to Bayta that any such data chips were waiting to be picked up.

Three hours later we reached Dyar, the train's final stop in the Bellidosh Estates-General. Again, there was some shuffling of passengers, though not as much as we'd seen at Greesovra. Again, not a peep from the Spiders about my data requests.

But I'd made some progress of my own with our mysterious Gang of Fifteen, as I'd privately dubbed them. The stripe patterns of Belldic faces were fairly easy for Human eyes to distinguish between, and over the past ten hours most of the Bellidos had made at least one trip back to the dining car.

All of them, that is, except two.

"The conductor says they're in compartments two and three," Bayta said as we had some dinner of our own in one of the dining car's back corners.

"Is that where the two carryout meals we saw ended up?" I asked.

"There weren't any Spiders in the car at the time, so I don't know for sure," Bayta said. "But it's a safe assumption."

I cut off another bite of steak and popped it into my mouth. It was a very good steak, though I couldn't for the life of me identify which animal it had come from. Travel might be broadening for the mind, but it could be very confusing for the taste buds. "Did those two have any special luggage?"

"There were four standard rolling carrybags between them," Bayta said. "One of them was also carrying a shoulder bag."

With something inside he hadn't wanted to risk letting get even a meter away from him? "Is there any way the Spiders can get them out of there?"

"You mean *force* them to leave their compartments?" Bayta asked, looking shocked that I would even make such a suggestion. "No, of course not."

"I'm not asking the Spiders to declare open war on them," I said patiently. "I just want them out for a few minutes so I can see what they're carrying."

"No," Bayta said firmly. "There's nothing they can do." Her cheek muscles tightened. "Not *will* do. *Can* do."

I grimaced. But she was probably right. The Spiders had been genetically engineered to be passive, just like their Chahwyn masters, which was why the whole group of them were forced to rely on less civilized beings like Fayr and me to handle the rough stuff for them.

Still, it was that same lack of aggression that had kept them from simply taking over the galaxy and everything in it after the Shonkla-raa were destroyed. It was, I supposed, a fair enough trade-off.

But it did mean Bayta and I were pretty much on our own. "New question, then," I said. "Is there any way *we* can get them out of there? Maybe create some sort of disturbance, like a fake fire or something?"

I'd thought she'd hit her top scandalization level with my last suggestion. I'd been wrong. "Are you *serious*?" she demanded, her eyes going even wider. "There's never been a fire of any size on a Quadrail train. Ever."

"I'm aware of the Spiders' enviable safety record," I said. "But this is war, remember?"

"*If* they're walkers," she countered. "We don't know that for sure. They might just be nervous businessmen or couriers."

I glared across the bar at a petite serving Spider making his way between the tables. Catch-22. Unless and until I could prove the Gang of Fifteen were an immediate threat to us or the Spiders or the Quadrail, Bayta wouldn't support any drastic action against them. And without drastic action I probably couldn't get her that proof.

I would just have to do something clever.

Taking another bite of steak, I pulled out my reader and called up our schedule. From Dyar to the Human colony of Helvanti was seven hours, four of which had already passed. That left me three hours to talk Bayta into the scheme starting to take shape in the back of my mind.

The mood she was in, I suspected it would take every minute of those three hours to pull it off.

HELVANTI HAD BEEN the first of Earth's colonies, the original colonist survey teams having headed into the system nearly twenty-five years ago and the official Quadrail station being commissioned and built four years after that.

Unlike humanity's other three colonies, though, Helvanti was actually thriving, its people doing a brisk business in rare metals, exotic woods, even more exotic spices, and possibly the finest chocolate in the galaxy. Still, it was definitely a minor stop, and we were only scheduled to be in the station for fifteen minutes.

It had taken me an hour to talk Bayta into my plan. Now she had fifteen minutes to do likewise to the stationmaster.

As far as I could tell, as I looked back and forth through the display window beside me, she was the only one of us getting off here, with only a single young Human couple coming aboard back at the third-class end of the train. That was about the traffic volume I would expect for Helvanti. I watched Bayta disappear inside the stationmaster's office, then checked my watch and started my mental countdown.

The minutes ticked by, the platform outside settling into the character of a dit rec western ghost town. With four minutes yet to go the conductors got back on the train, though the doors themselves remained open. I kept one eye on my watch, the other on the stationmaster's office door, and started trying to figure out what I would do if Bayta didn't make it back in time.

With two minutes left on the clock I finally saw her emerge from the office and head toward the Quadrail at a dead run.

I exhaled a silent sigh of relief. Helvanti Station wasn't very big, and even at a casual walk she should make it with half a minute to spare.

I'd relaxed too soon. Bayta had reached the halfway point when a pair of well-dressed Juriani and a massive pear-shaped Cimma suddenly entered my line of sight, heading across the platform from one of the cars farther back. Chatting animatedly among themselves, apparently oblivious to their surroundings, they moved directly into Bayta's path.

She tried to swerve, but it was too late. Even as I watched the four of them came to a confused face-to-face halt and launched into one of those in-unison side-stepping farces that looks hilarious in a well-done stage comedy.

Only in this case there was nothing even remotely humorous about it. Their last-minute appearance tagged the three of them as Modhri walkers, with the clear intent of making sure Bayta didn't make it back onto the train.

Trapping her in one of the loneliest places in the galaxy.

There was no time for planning or even conscious thought. Even before the full ramifications of the situation had sifted completely through my brain I was on my feet, weaving madly through the maze of chairs as I raced for the car's door. I came within an ace of tangling myself in the conductor's legs as I dodged around him; and then I was outside, sprinting across the platform toward the macabre do-si-do still going on.

One of the Juriani half turned, but he had no time for more than a startled gasp before I slammed my shoulder into him, bouncing him in turn off his companions and finally throwing off their rhythm. My hand darted past the Cimma to grab Bayta's wrist, and I turned us back toward the train.

Only to see that it was already in motion.

I tried anyway, nearly dragging Bayta off her feet as I pulled her toward the train. But we were too late. The doors were closed, and there wasn't nearly enough time for Bayta to get a conductor to open one of them. Swearing viciously under my breath, I gave up and slowed to a halt.

The Gang of Fifteen, and whatever it was they were carrying, were gone.

FIVE

The sounds of the Quadrail faded away, and as they did so I became aware that I wasn't the only one swearing. "What do you do, Human?" the Juri I'd slammed into demanded, glaring at me as he clutched his shoulder with one clawed hand.

"What do *you* do?" I countered. "You kept my friend from reboarding her train."

He bristled, clicking his hawk beak with indignation, his three-toed feet tapping the floor. Probably as annoyed by my lack of proper verbal etiquette as he was by the physical injury itself, I guessed. The Juriani were sticklers for such things, and normally I did my best to accommodate them.

At the moment, though, I couldn't have cared less. "It was completely unintentional, I assure you," he insisted stiffly. "We had suddenly realized that here was the source of all that fine Helvanti chocolate and decided to avail ourselves of the opportunity to purchase some."

The worst part was that probably really *was* all that he and his companions had intended. Or at least, all they thought they'd intended. None of them would be aware in the slightest that there was a small mass of alien flesh tucked away beneath their brains whispering these suggestions to them.

"It's all right, Frank," Bayta spoke up. "Master Juri, we apologize for our actions. To all of you," she added to the others.

She looked expectantly at me. "I also apologize," I said, forcing as much civility into the words as I could manage. "My actions were discourteous and inexcusable, and I crave your understanding and your forgiveness."

The Juri drew himself up to his full height, his polished scales glistening in the Coreline's flickering light. Now that the proper words had been said, he was willing to let bygones be bygones. "You are forgiven," he said, clicking his beak three times to show that he meant it. "And do not be alarmed at the departure of the train. There will be others." With that, he gestured to his friends and they headed together for the station's single shop/restaurant.

I glared after him, fighting back my frustration and sense of defeat. How did you fight someone who didn't even know he was your enemy?

"You all right?" Bayta asked as she watched them go.

"Oh, I'm fine," I said sourly. "You?"

She nodded. "I wasn't hurt."

I looked down the tracks to see our Quadrail ride up the angled end of the station and through the atmosphere barrier into the narrower main Tube. "I don't suppose there's any way to send a warning message ahead."

"How?" Bayta countered.

She was right, of course. Spiders were telepathic between themselves, but only over short distances. Message cylinders traveled a thousand times faster than the Quadrails themselves, but to send one you had to have a train available in the first place. "Any chance we can get another train before that one reaches Terra Station?"

"The next one for this station isn't due for another twelve hours."

And the Bellidos would be at Terra in eight. Plenty of time for them to switch trains or pass their package on to some other group of walkers the Modhri could have waiting at the station. "No express trains we could stop?" I asked, trying one last time.

"There are only two other expresses during that time, and it's too late to get a message to either of them." She hesitated. "Even if the Spiders were willing to stop them."

I nodded. For years I'd admired the absolute precision with which the Quadrail system operated. But now that I knew how the message cylinder trick was done, I realized there was more to it than just professional pride. If the trains weren't in the right places at the right times, those cylinders would be falling from the inner mesh like pigeon droppings over Manhattan. "So we've lost them," I said, making it official.

"I'm sorry."

I focused on her face. Bayta spent so much of her time being in complete emotional control of herself that it was always something of a shock when that control slipped, even for a minute. "Hey, relax," I soothed. "It wasn't your fault. Anyway, we know where they're going. Sooner or later, we'll catch up with them." I raised my eyebrows. "Trust me."

She gave me one of those wryly patient looks she'd honed to a fine art during our months of traveling together. But at least the self-reproach was fading. "If you say so."

"I say so," I said. "Incidentally, just out of curiosity, how did it go with the stationmaster?"

"Oh, fine," she said, making a face. "Right now there's a drone Spider hanging onto the side of one of the baggage cars. Actually, he's probably moved to the top of the car by now."

All ready to work his way forward and try to peek through the window into the compartment where our reclusive Bellidos had locked themselves. A glimpse of what they had in that shoulder bag, relayed telepathically to Bayta, might have given us a clue as to what was going on.

Only now the whole thing was moot, because Bayta wasn't there to guide the operation and receive the image. Spiders were terrific at their assigned jobs, but I was starting to realize that trying to nudge them outside their personal fields of expertise was like trying to teach a cat to sing. Chances were fairly good, in fact, that the drone would still be on the baggage car roof when the train pulled into Terra Station eight hours from now. "I hope he at least enjoys the ride," I said.

"Enjoyment for a Spider comes from doing his job," Bayta said, glancing casually around us. "The stationmaster also had two data chips," she said, pulling them out of her pocket. "One for each of us."

I took the proffered chip, giving the platform a quick check of my own. The trio of walkers had vanished into the shop/restaurant, and aside from a half-dozen drudge Spiders working on one of the tracks down the line we were completely alone. "Let's go sit over there," I suggested, pointing to a pair of benches facing an interactive kiosk offering visitors the Helvanti colony's brief but no doubt exciting history.

We both had our readers out and the chips plugged in by the time we sat down. "Mine has the Nemuti Lynx data you asked for," Bayta reported, peering closely at it.

"That's nice," I said absently, my brain fully absorbed with my own chip. What the *hell*?

I was on my third reading when Bayta nudged me with her reader. "Here," she said.

"What?" I asked, forcing my mind away from the sudden flurry of thought and speculation that had descended on me.

"Here," she repeated. "You'll want to read this."

I put my reader down on the bench and took hers. Scrolling back to the top of the report—and there wasn't all that far I had to scroll—I began to read.

The Nemuti Lynx turned out to be one of a set of nine small abstract sculptures that had been unearthed at an archaeological dig in the Ten Mesas region of the Nemuti colony world of Veerstu two hundred years ago. The set included three sculptures that were called Lynxes, three that had been dubbed Hawks, and three more with the name Vipers.

"They gave them *Human* animal names?" I asked, frowning at Bayta.

She pointed at the reader. "Keep reading."

The sculptures had originally been given Nemuti names, I discovered in the next paragraph, but fifteen years ago a scholar with way too much time on his hands had done some heavy-duty etymological studies and translated the names into what he decided were the most accurate and/or poetic equivalents in a dozen other languages, including English. Over the years the nine sculptures had ended up dispersed around the galaxy, four to various art museums and five to private collectors.

The next page was devoted to pictures of the sculptures, including a scale that showed them to range between twenty and forty centimeters long. All nine were made of some gleaming white stone, they were very definitely abstract, and to me they didn't look anything like lynxes, hawks, or vipers. The so-called Hawk was twenty centimeters from top to bottom and shaped something like a comma, with a rounded top flowing in a wide curve into a somewhat wider base. The Viper was larger, about forty centimeters long, and looked like a frozen tongue of fire, curving upward twice from its base to a slightly rounded point. The Lynx was about thirty centimeters long and mainly tubular, like a short piece of bamboo rising out of a wider base. To me it looked a lot more like a viper than the Viper itself did. All nine sculptures were covered with texturing, but whether it was abstract decoration, miniature bas-relief carvings, or simple erosion I couldn't tell.

There was also a map of the Ten Mesas area where they'd been found, plus a short bio of the Nemut who'd led the team that dug them up. I skimmed the latter without finding anything of interest and scrolled down to page three.

Page three was a police report.

I glanced at Bayta, noting the set of her jaw, and returned to my reading.

The nine sculptures weren't considered all that valuable, certainly not compared to the Mona Lisa or the Cincarian Stand. But that hadn't stopped collectors from trying to acquire a complete set of Lynx, Hawk, and Viper. Collectors being what they were, of course, none of them wanted to part with even their single sculpture, and over the years there had apparently been a lot of Go Fish-style jockeying back and forth among the various owners. The four relevant museums had been approached as well, but most of them were run by equally fanatic collectors, and it had appeared that the status quo would be maintained for a long time to come.

Only someone had apparently gotten tired of waiting and decided on a more direct approach. In the past twelve months all four of the museums had been burglarized and their Nemuti sculptures stolen. *Just* their Nemuti sculptures, as far as I could tell from the reports, which should have sent up red flags or at least yellow ones for anyone who had been paying attention.

Apparently, no one had. Skimming farther down the report, I discovered that four of the privately held sculptures had also been stolen, despite the heavy security their owners had built around their collections. In the most recent of the robberies, the owner had apparently surprised the intruders and been killed.

Eight of the sculptures had vanished. One was still at large.

The third Lynx.

"This," I said, looking up at Bayta again, "is starting to sound like an old dit rec drama."

"Only those are fiction," she reminded me soberly. "This is real."

"Dead bodies do have a way of emphasizing that," I conceded, skimming the dates and locations again and wishing the Spiders had included the full police reports instead of just a summary. Even so, though, there were some intriguing hints to be gleaned. "Did you notice where the last private-collector robbery took place?" I asked Bayta. "The one where the owner was murdered?"

She craned her neck toward the reader. "Somewhere on Bellis, wasn't it?"

"Very good," I said. "For extra credit, *when* did it happen?"

"Just over three weeks ago."

"Right," I said. "Which, if the number you gave me earlier was correct, was the same time all those first-class compartments on our dearly departed train suddenly got booked."

I saw her throat tighten. "By Bellidos traveling to a world of the Nemuti FarReach."

"*And* who left Bellis Station the same time someone with the last Lynx on his mind was due to arrive," I said. "Coincidence is coincidence, but this is starting to push the envelope."

I picked up my own reader and handed it to her. "Or we could push it even farther."

I watched her eyes flick back and forth again as she started to read. They faltered, then started again, moving more slowly.

It was a short message, which meant she must have read it through at least twice before she finally looked back at me. "This can't really be from *Korak* Fayr," she insisted. "Can it?"

I shrugged. "The last reports of coral vandalism would suggest his commandos are still operating on Bellis," I said. "But there's no reason Fayr has to be there in person. For that matter, we're only assuming it was his group who pulled these latest attacks. The way the various Belldic Intelligence services operate, it's entirely possible that someone else has put the pieces together and started running his own private anti-Modhri crusade."

Bayta looked again at the message. " 'To Frank Compton: meet me at the Fraklog-Oryo Hotel, Magaraa City, Ghonsilya, Tra'hok Unity.' Isn't Magaraa City where one of the Nemuti sculptures was stolen?"

"Very good," I said approvingly. "One of the Vipers, to be exact."

"And the Bellis theft was of one of the Hawks," she said slowly. "And Mr. Smith talked about one of the Lynxes."

"A complete set, in other words," I said. "The final set, actually, if we assume the other two sets were appropriated by the same people."

"Don't you mean the same *person*?"

I glanced at the store where the three walkers had disappeared. "Either that, or we've got a large and organized gang working," I agreed soberly. "The Magaraa museum theft took place about two months ago, with the Bellis one only five weeks later. That's not nearly enough time for the same team to travel from Nemuti territory to Bellis, case the joint, and prep and pull off a second robbery."

"So the Modhri has them all now?"

"Well, he hasn't got the third Lynx, anyway," I said. "At least, I don't think so."

"Then why was Mr. Smith killed?" Bayta asked.

"Not to get the Lynx," I repeated. "Though come to think of it, that might have been the original plan: lure Smith and the Lynx to Bellis so that the walkers could grab it on their way out of the system."

"If so, they cut it a little fine, didn't they?" she commented. "Mr. Smith was coming in less than an hour before they were scheduled to leave."

"Right, but remember he was delayed six hours waiting for me to get back to Terra Station," I reminded her.

"That would have given them plenty of time to negotiate and finalize any transactions." I grimaced. "And possibly to consign Smith's body to deep space."

"What do you suppose went wrong?" Bayta asked.

"That one's easy," I said. "Smith apparently double-crossed them and didn't bring the Lynx."

"Are you sure?"

"I'm positive," I said. "It would have been a three-minute job to search a Quadrail compartment for something that size. If Smith had had it with him, they would have found it, and there would have been no need to beat him to death."

"Unless they wanted to cover their trail."

"A quick snap of the neck would have done that," I said. "No, they don't have the Lynx. But I'd say they really, *really* want it."

"Enough to lure us into a trap?" she asked, lifting my reader for emphasis.

"Possibly," I said. "But if so, that message isn't it. It was sent long before we stumbled into the middle of this Lynx thing."

"But not before the Magaraa museum robbery," she pointed out. "It could be a trick by the Modhri to make sure we were out of the way when they went after the Hawk and Mr. Smith's Lynx."

"No," I said. "Note the P.S. just below Fayr's name."

Bayta looked back at the reader. " 'Bring with you that strange but interesting gift of Human humor.' "

"That's a reference to something he said to me just before our first raid on the Modhri homeland," I said. "You weren't there at the time."

"He finds Human humor strange?"

"I think half the galaxy finds Human humor strange," I said dryly. "The other half doesn't believe it at all. The point is that it's nothing a random stranger would have known to include. Even the Modhri shouldn't know about it."

"Unless Fayr is now himself a walker."

In which case, Fayr would be unaware that his idea to invite me to Ghonsilya was not, in fact, his idea. "That's a possibility," I admitted. "But I think Fayr's sharp enough to suspect if that had happened to him. If he did, I also think he'd try his damnedest not to allow the Modhri to finish its entrenching."

"Suicide?"

I felt my throat tighten. Fayr *did* typically drag a small arsenal around with him. "Regardless, the Spiders should at least be able to settle the question of whether or not he's actually in the Ghonsilya system," I said instead. "See if the stationmaster can start a trace. Speaking of which, was there anything on Daniel Mice?"

"There was nothing on my data chip, so I assume not," she said. "They might still be searching."

"Or maybe Mice also has a walletful of fake IDs to choose from," I said. "Actually, now that I think about it, Fayr's almost certainly traveling under an alias, too. Means we're probably not going to be able to track either of them."

"We can still try," Bayta said. "Remember that *Korak* Fayr was traveling under false names before we met him. The Spiders might be able to link him with one of those."

"It's worth a try, I suppose," I said. "Go ahead and get them on it."

Her eyes glazed over a moment, then came back to focus. "The stationmaster will put the request aboard the next cylinder."

Which was, unfortunately, still almost twelve hours away. But there was nothing we could do about that except cultivate our patience. "Thanks," I said. "You hungry?"

Bayta glanced at the shop. "Not just yet. What's our plan, then? To try to find this third Lynx?"

"How?" I countered. "We don't even know Smith's real name, let alone whether he was the one with the Lynx, or what he might have done with it if he *did* have it."

"And the Bellidos are gone," Bayta murmured.

"Long gone," I confirmed. "Our best option now is probably to head to Ghonsilya and hook up with Fayr. Maybe he's got some leads he'd like to share with his fellow playmates."

"I suppose you're right," Bayta said with a sigh. "I just hate . . . you know."

"Letting the Modhri get the better of you?"

"It's not like that," she insisted. "This isn't personal."

"I know," I said, pretending to believe her. "It isn't for me, either."

For a few seconds she sat quietly, her eyes staring down the Tube. Then, stirring, she handed me back my reader. "You might want to destroy Fayr's message," she said. "Just in case."

"Actually, I had something a little more devious in mind," I told her, keying for an edit.

"What do you mean?"

"You'll see." I finished my edit and held the reader out for her perusal.

" 'Meet me at the Supreme Falls viewing area on *Laarmiten*'?" she read, sounding a little taken aback.

"As long as the Gang of Fifteen are heading there anyway," I said. "The Modhri's reaction might be interesting if he finagles a peek at this."

"An expert will be able to tell the message has been modified," Bayta warned.

"Not with this reader he won't," I said. "This is that special high-tech job I got from Larry Hardin, back when I was working for him. Chock-full of interesting goodies. Did you also notice the new P.S.?"

She frowned. " 'Remember that victory belongs to the daring.' "

"There's no point in letting a private joke go public, either," I said. I pulled out the chip and put it in my side pocket, then returned the reader to its usual place inside my jacket. "So. Are we planning to just sit here until the train arrives?"

"Unless you want to take a shuttle across to the transfer station," she suggested. "There might be more to do there."

I looked at the shop. "I think I'd rather keep an eye on our walkers."

"I agree," she said, shutting off her reader and putting it away.

And then, to my mild surprise, she slid across the dozen centimeters that separated us and snuggled up against my side. "I'm going to take a nap," she said, her voice a little muffled as she rested her head on my shoulder. "Wake me when it's my turn to keep watch."

She exhaled a deep sigh; and with that, she was asleep.

Bayta's approach to the universe had a natural reserve to it, which acted as a psychological barrier to keep people at arm's length. Part of that was undoubtedly her wariness about the Modhri and his little bag of telepathic tricks, the rest of it her own natural personality. But she and I had been through a lot together, and over the months she'd gradually accepted me into her inner circle.

Apparently, I'd made it deeper into that circle than I'd realized.

It felt a little awkward, and more than a little embarrassing. My own personality was every bit as closed as hers was, though that probably wasn't so much natural tendency as it was having had all my alleged friends turn their backs on me during the Yandro controversy. I'd gotten used to my own company since then, and wasn't entirely sure I wanted to start with the whole friendship thing again.

I gazed down at the top of her head, tracing locks of her dark hair with my eyes. Still, Bayta was my partner in our little corner of this war, and it was part of my job to humor her.

Shifting position, I put my arm around her shoulders and turned my head just enough to keep the shop/restaurant in view. Now that they'd succeeded in getting us off the train and away from the Gang of Fifteen, I wasn't expecting the three walkers to give us any more trouble.

But I'd been wrong before.

SIX

Eleven and a half hours later, precisely on time, the next Quadrail arrived at Helvanti. Together with our three walkers, each of them now lugging a large bag of chocolate, we went aboard.

The usual lack of communication with a moving train meant that Bayta hadn't been able to arrange our accommodations ahead of time, and once again it turned out that all the compartments were booked. Still, with the trip only eight and a half hours long, a compartment hardly seemed worth the trouble anyway.

After having been on guard duty most of the previous twelve hours, I spent the majority of the trip dozing in my seat. I doubted that Bayta, with her nervousness about being in an open car surrounded by walkers, even closed her eyes.

The trip passed without incident, and we were soon weaving our way through the relatively large and bustling crowd at Terra Station toward the stationmaster's office. First on our list was to figure out the fastest route to Ghonsilya for our rendezvous with Fayr, while a close second would be to see if the Spiders had retrieved our luggage from the train we'd been bounced from. Third on the list would be checking on Fayr's and Daniel Mice's passenger histories.

We were studying one of the floating schedule holodisplays when I heard a familiar voice behind me. "Well, well. Look what the budgie left in the bottom of his cage."

I turned around. ESS Special Agent Morse was striding toward me, his expression hovering between angry and sour. "I could say the same thing about you," I countered. "I thought you were on lapdog duty this week."

His face drifted a few percentage points further onto the angry side. "We're more terriers than lapdogs, actually," he corrected. "Bred to drive burrowing animals into the open, where they can be properly hunted down and killed."

"And I take it I'm the rat du jour?"

"I'd like nothing better," he said. "Unfortunately, I have other more pressing matters to deal with. I merely stopped here to pick up my messages and arrange the transfer of Mr. Kün—Mr. Smith's body."

I felt my ears prick up. "So you've identified our victim?"

"Good day, Mr. Compton." Turning on his heel in an almost military-precise about-face, he stalked away, his bags trailing behind him.

And as he headed through the streaming travelers, three well-dressed Halkas casually turned in unison and set off after him.

Bayta touched my arm. "It looks like we want the express to—"

"Hold on," I told her, watching the procession. The Halkas were still following Morse, but with an air of leisure and unconcern that even professional Intelligence agents had trouble counterfeiting when they were on the hunt.

Only in this case, it wasn't an act. The Halkas genuinely didn't realize they were following anyone.

Walkers.

Beside me, Bayta inhaled sharply as she spotted the procession. "Frank—"

"I see them," I growled, handing her my leash control. "Wait here."

I headed into the flow of passengers, trying to look as casual as the three Halkas. There was a lot about Morse I didn't like, but that didn't mean I was going to just stand off to the side and let the Modhri have a free poke at him. Especially since there was at least half a chance that it was Morse's contact with the late Mr. Smith that had drawn the Modhri's attention to him in the first place.

The Modhri had bounced Bayta and me out of the Lynx investigation once. Maybe this was our chance to get back in.

A dozen meters ahead of Morse were a pair of Juriani with long hard-sided golf cases rolling along behind them. They paused, and one of them reached down and picked up his case. He tucked it under his arm and they continued on their way, their path now shifted subtly onto an intercept course with Morse's.

The pursuing Halkas, meanwhile, were steadily closing the gap. At current speeds, I estimated, the three of them and the two golfers would converge together on Morse in about ten seconds. Keeping an eye peeled for anyone else the Modhri might decide to throw into the mix, I picked up my pace.

Abruptly, one of the two Juriani who'd blocked Bayta at the Helvanti Station loomed in front of me. "Ah—my Human friend from last night," he said cheerfully, raising his arms wide in welcome.

I ducked beneath one of the outstretched arms and kept going. So the Modhri had spotted me, too. I thought about shouting Morse a warning, decided it would just distract him—

"Mr. Morse!" one of the Halkas behind Morse shouted. Morse half turned, slowing but not stopping.

And in that split second of inattention, the Modhri struck.

It was, from a professional standpoint, beautifully

done. The two Juriani cut directly in front of Morse with no more than half a meter to spare, and the golf case still trailing behind them rolled into position just in time for Morse to trip over it. As he thrust out his hands to break his fall, the other Juri spun a hundred eighty degrees around, ostensibly to see what was going on, and slammed the end of his case solidly against the side of Morse's head.

Morse went down like a lassoed calf, rolling half over as he sprawled across the rolling case and slammed the back of his head solidly on the Tube floor.

The three trailing Halkas were there in an instant, dropping to their knees around him like solicitous Good Samaritan bystanders at an accident scene. Their positioning, probably not coincidentally, managed to block my view of Morse and anything they were doing with him. "Someone get a Spider!" the Halka whose shout had distracted Morse at the fatal moment called to the station in general. "We must find a Human doctor."

Cue for Compton. "I'm a doctor," I said, striding up. I dropped to one knee at Morse's side, deftly elbowing the nearest Halka out of my way.

And as I did so, out of the corner of my eye I saw his hand dip briefly inside his own inner vest and come out empty. The left side of Morse's jacket was open, I noted, as if someone had pushed the flap aside. "No—don't go," I said, grabbing the Halka's wrist as he started to get up. Pulling him firmly back down to his knees, I put his hand on Morse's left wrist. "Hold him right here," I instructed.

"But—" the Halka started to protest.

"And put your other hand up there on his right shoulder," I interrupted, putting some authority into my voice as I started to take off my own jacket.

Clearly wondering what this had to do with medical treatment, but just as clearly unwilling to argue from his ignorance of Human physiology, the Halka leaned forward and stretched out his hand. As he did so, he started to lose his balance—

"Careful," I warned, turning at the waist and putting a supporting hand on his chest. My jacket, which I hadn't yet pulled off that arm, dangled down across Morse's legs. "First shift your knee over there to his other side."

The Halka complied, and from his new position was able to get his hand to Morse's shoulder without trouble. I kept my hand protectively against his chest until it was clear he was stable again, then let go and finished taking off my jacket. I bunched it together and laid it beside me, making sure that the slim, flat case I'd removed from inside the Halka's vest was safely hidden inside it.

I had taken Morse's pulse—which seemed steady enough—and was making a show of checking for pupil dilation when a pair of drudge Spiders finally arrived on the scene.

"There you are," I said, grabbing my jacket and standing up. "He needs to be taken immediately to the medical center. Carefully, now."

I supported Morse's head myself, pillowing it on my wadded-up jacket as the drudges got three legs each under him and lifted him up. Feeling the stares of the Juriani and Halkas on my back the whole way, I snagged Morse's luggage and followed the Spiders through the crowd of onlookers.

Terra Station was a pretty unsophisticated stop, certainly when compared to the elaborate facilities and ornamentation of the other eleven empires' homeworld stations. But despite its backwater appearance, it included a pretty decent medical center. One of the doctors examined Morse, diagnosed a mild concussion, assured us that he would recover, and fitted him with a bandage and a QuixHeal injection. A few minutes later he was in a Fibibib-designed monitor bed in an otherwise unoccupied ward, sleeping soundly, and Bayta and I were seated in a couple of chairs across the room near the door where we could keep an eye on him.

Only then, with some time and privacy on our hands, did I dig out the flat case I'd stolen back from the Halka.

"Where did you get that?" Bayta asked as I pulled it from my jacket pocket.

"From the walker who'd just taken it from Morse," I told her.

From the feel as I'd picked the Halka's pocket I'd guessed it was a data chip case, and I was right. About fifteen centimeters long, two wide, and one deep, it could hold up to thirty data chips in protected, padded niches.

"Is that why the Modhri attacked him?" Bayta asked.

"Either that or he just felt like giving his walkers some exercise," I said, turning the case over in my hands and studying in particular its lock and hinge sides.

Bayta watched me in silence for a few more seconds. "Well?" she prompted.

"Patience," I said, pulling out my reader and inserting the data chip that turned it into a powerful sensor. "Data chip cases are sometimes booby-trapped to fry the chips if the wrong person opens it."

For once, my paranoia was unwarranted. The case wasn't rigged. "Let's see what the well-equipped ESS Special Agent is reading these days," I said, and popped it open.

Inside were a dozen data chips. None of them, I guessed, was light summer entertainment. "Let's assume he's the organized type," I suggested, pulling out the last one in the line. It was the same type of chip I'd gotten at Helvanti, the sort the Spiders used for cross-Quadrail messages and information packets lasered to the Tube from the collection center in the local transfer station. Wondering who was sending Morse fan mail, I inserted it into my reader.

The display filled with lines of apparently random characters. What the well-equipped ESS Special Agent was reading these days was heavily encrypted. "Can you decode it?" Bayta asked.

"That may not be necessary." Handing the reader to Bayta, I got up and went across to the rack where Morse's outer clothing had been hung. His reader was in the standard inside jacket pocket. "People running the same routine day after day sometimes get careless," I told Bayta as I rejoined her. "Specifically, they sometimes neglect to scramble-clear the decryption program after they've read something." I turned on the reader and inserted Morse's chip.

He hadn't been as careless as he might have been. But he'd been careless enough. The display still came up gibberish, but there was now a helpful tab at the bottom of the screen asking if I wanted the message translated into another language. I keyed it, and a moment later we had clear, readable text.

"Good thing the Modhri didn't get the reader, too," Bayta commented.

"That was probably next on his list," I told her. Scrolling down past the standard classified-document warning and a five-color ESS logo, I got to the meat of the document.

Some meat.

TO: Ackerley Morse, Terra Station
FROM: ESS Central, Geneva
RE: Urgent information request
Confirm your report re death of Rafael Künstler on Terra-Bellis Quadrail #339721. Current data attached.
Current assignment re Lady Dorchester suspended. Locate and detain Daniel Stafford immediately as person of extreme interest. Current data attached.

"DO YOU KNOW these people?" Bayta asked as she read over my shoulder.

"I know one of them," I said. "At least by reputation. Rafael Künstler is—*was,* rather—one of Earth's upper-crust multibillionaires. Maybe he'd made it all the way to trillionaire; I'm not sure. He was something of a recluse, which is probably why I didn't recognize him."

"He was one of Earth's rich and powerful?" Bayta asked pointedly.

I grimaced. Up to now the Modhri had mostly left humanity alone, for which we were all very grateful. But every other time he'd made a play for power across the galaxy, his attack pattern was to target a people's leadership: political, military, economic, and social. The typical Human trillionaire would fit nicely into at least two of those categories. "Hard to imagine the Modhri letting one of his walkers get beaten to death," I said. "All that shared pain through the whole mind segment, remember."

"Maybe that's what he wants us to think," Bayta said. "And don't forget, Mr. Künstler did say *he hates you.* Who could he have meant besides the Modhri?"

"Could be any number of people, actually," I said. "Besides, referring to the Modhri that way would imply Künstler knew something about him. Walkers usually never figure that out."

"Maybe he was smarter than most." Bayta paused. "Or maybe he had friends who could figure it out for him."

I scratched my cheek thoughtfully. As far as I knew, there were only two Humans besides Bayta and me who were even aware of the Modhri's existence: Bruce McMicking, chief troubleshooter for multitrillionaire industrialist Larry Hardin, who I'd once worked briefly for; and Deputy UN Director Losutu, who had supposedly put Künstler on my trail to begin with.

Both men had been sworn to secrecy, but I wasn't naive enough to think their solemn oaths would hold traction forever. Calling up the reader's search page, I punched in McMicking's and Losutu's names.

McMicking's came up dry. Losutu's didn't. There, tucked away at the bottom of the document, was what looked almost like an almost-forgotten afterthought:

ADDENDUM
FROM: Deputy Director Biret Losutu, UN Directorate, Geneva.
Bona fides of former Westali agent Frank Compton confirmed beyond question. He can be taken into your fullest confidence.

"UNCOMMONLY KIND OF Director Losutu," I commented, angling the reader to show Bayta the note. "Though in my experience ringing endorsements like that usually come with fairly nasty situations attached." I scrolled back to the top of the document. "Let's see how nasty this one is."

The first data file was a summary of the life and times of the late Mr. Künstler.

Like many of Earth's wealthiest people, he'd gotten a head start by arranging to have himself born to parents who were themselves already stratospherically rich. Unlike many in that position, though, he hadn't rested on their laurels or frittered his inheritance away with riotous living. Instead, he'd taken the money and run with it, building an economic empire that had dwarfed even that of his parents. According to the best estimates, he had indeed made it to trillionaire status before his untimely death.

The wealth and power hadn't come without a few speed bumps along the way, of course. In his early twenties he'd been lured briefly into the stereotypical rich kid's skating-on-the-edge life mode, which had been quickly and inevitably followed by half a dozen paternity suits. He'd taken the quick route back to peace and quiet, paying off the claimants without wasting time contesting the charges, and having learned from his mistakes retired to his estate in the Bavarian Alps to focus on business. From that point on, he'd largely limited his Human contacts to his staff, his business associates, and his older and more trustworthy friends.

And with a frenetic social life no longer a viable hobby, he'd turned his thoughts and bankroll to art collecting.

He'd gotten pretty good at it, too. Somewhere along the line he'd built a warehouse-sized gallery on his estate, constructing a labyrinth of passageways inside it with nooks and display cases and panels along every wall and around every turn. The report included a few quotes from art critics and connoisseurs who'd toured the place, all of whom praised the experience as unique and exciting.

Two of the critics had expressed hope that the collection might someday be opened to the public. A counterquote from Künstler made it clear that would happen when hell froze over.

The rest of the file was taken up with a summary of Künstler's various business ventures, plus lists of colleagues, family members—all the way out to fourth cousins—and friends. That last list was definitely the shortest of the three.

Bayta spotted that, too. "He didn't have many friends, did he?" she murmured.

"Who do the superrich have to hang out with except the rest of the superrich?" I pointed out. "Hardly the gene pool *I'd* want to have to choose my friends from."

"And that opinion is based on what?" Bayta asked dryly. "*One* man?"

"I'm sure Larry Hardin is good to his dog and has a wonderful singing voice," I said, thinking back to our last meeting, when I'd stuck him for a trillion dollars, and our subsequent less-than-amicable parting. "Doesn't mean I'm in any hurry to renew our acquaintanceship."

"He *did* help us out, you know."

"Unknowingly, and only after I blackmailed him into it," I reminded her, scrolling past the list of Künstler's business addresses and contact information to the second data file on the chip.

It was yet another police report.

"They have a report already?" Bayta asked, frowning.

"This isn't about his murder," I said, my eyes automatically finding the line marked Crime Description. "Looks like there was an attempted burglary of his art gallery a few weeks ago."

An extremely strange burglary, too, I saw with growing interest as I read through the report. The perps had been an unlikely gang of six midlevel bureaucrats from the UN's Geneva HQ, who nevertheless had handled themselves with a professionalism that had apparently impressed even the police officer who'd written up the report. He'd gone into considerable detail, in fact, on their technique in penetrating the grounds and the art gallery, including their disarming of the alarm system.

Incredibly, though, especially after all that care, they were still wandering the twisting pathways and staircases an hour later, the shoulder bags they'd brought with them still empty. At that point they'd been surprised by Künstler himself, who had apparently come in to commune with the Old Masters. He'd sounded the alarm, and in the resulting very one-sided fracas all six burglars had been killed.

But not before one of them had found the strength to ask Künstler where the Nemuti Lynx was.

"Well, if we still had any doubts the Modhri was involved, this pretty well clinches it," I told Bayta as I handed her the reader.

"Which part?" she asked, frowning at the text.

"The part where one of the perps wastes his dying breath asking where the Lynx is." I pointed to the place.

I saw Bayta's throat tighten. "The walkers weren't all inside the grounds," she said. "There was at least one still outside."

"Exactly," I agreed. "Hoping Künstler would tell him where he'd stashed the Lynx."

"Unless the inside man had an open radio channel to someone?" Bayta suggested.

I shook my head. "Standard procedure in a case like this is to immediately jam all communications except the private rolling-link system the security people themselves are using. No, the only messages getting out right then would have been across a Modhri mind segment."

"I just hope Künstler didn't tell him."

"He didn't," I assured her grimly. "His lethal interrogation aboard the Quadrail proves that much."

Bayta shivered. "What in the galaxy does he *want* with these things?"

I shrugged. "Between our attack on his homeland and the pressure Fayr's been putting on his Belldic outposts, he has to be finding himself a bit on the ropes these days. Every good soldier knows that the first rule of retreat is to have someplace to retreat to. Could be he's made a deal with one of these ultrarich collectors to trade the complete Nemuti collection for a chunk of cold-water territory he can call his own."

Bayta stiffened. I didn't blame her. The thought of the Modhri going underground, regrouping, and relaunching his campaign against the galaxy on his own terms and with his own timing was very much at the top of my Things We Don't Want To Happen list. "How do we stop him?" she asked.

"We start by ignoring the big, scary view and focusing on the immediate job at hand," I told her. "Künstler's murder shows the Modhri's still after this third Lynx. We have to make sure we get to it first." I took back the reader and scrolled to the next file. "And we start by finding out what they've got on this person of extreme interest."

The third file on the chip, as expected, was a brief biography of one Daniel Josef Stafford.

He was twenty-six years old, the son of one of Künstler's top business managers. Born into the Künstler inner circle, he'd spent a lot of time on the estate when he was growing up, hobnobbing with the rich and powerful among his father's friends. The usual pattern in these cases, I knew, was for the kid to be groomed for goldencog status, then inserted into some cushy midlevel corporate job as soon as he graduated from college.

That might still be the plan, but as yet the big event hadn't happened. Stafford had taken to the collegiate lifestyle with a vengeance, so much so that he'd apparently decided to make a full-time career of it. In the past eight years he'd bounced his major around like a fumbled football, switching from business to economics to art appreciation to psychology. If the attached course schedule was up-to-date, he was currently splitting his class time between the odd duo of alien sociology and techniques of advertising.

His free time was equally well packed. During his teen years he'd become adept with both skis and lugeboard, and every chance he got he was off Earth and onto the Quadrail to match his skills against some of the galaxy's most challenging slopes.

Despite his unfocused ambitions, relations with his parents seemed to have remained good. He still dropped in on them at the Künstler estate a couple of times a year, where he also made a point of touring Künstler's art gallery to see what the boss had added since his last visit. Showing off his art appreciation classes, no doubt.

His last visit had been the weekend of the abortive burglary. He hadn't been seen or heard from since that night. Nor had his ID been logged through at any air, sea, or land entry portal, nor had he used any of his credit tags anywhere in the Terran Confederation. As far as ESS could tell, Daniel Stafford had simply dropped off the edge of the universe.

"Do you think he was killed?" Bayta asked.

"I doubt it," I told her. "His body wasn't found on the

scene, and I can't see the Modhri dragging him all the way across the grounds just to kill him somewhere out of sight."

"Unless the Modhri thought Mr. Stafford had the Lynx," Bayta suggested.

"Which is a pretty good bet anyway," I agreed. "Stafford on the estate; Stafford and the Lynx no longer on the estate. Hence, person of extreme interest."

"I don't know," Bayta said doubtfully. "It sounds like the Lynx had been sitting around there for years. Why wait until now to steal it?"

"The simplest and most obvious answer is that the Modhri got to Stafford with an offer too good to pass up," I said. "That's probably ESS's current reasoning, too. Except the Modhri part, of course."

"But you don't believe that?"

I shrugged. "Cops like simple answers," I said. "And to be honest, most crimes do end up shaking out that way. But this case has a few too many unanswered questions."

"Such as?"

"Such as why Künstler was on the Bellis Quadrail," I said. "Was he chasing Stafford, or was he on some mission of his own? He was certainly doing *something* underhanded—there's no other reason for him to be running alone and under a false ID. And whatever he was up to, if the Modhri already had the Lynx or knew it was on the way, why beat him to death?"

"Maybe Mr. Stafford is planning to sell the Lynx to someone else," Bayta suggested. "Maybe the Modhri realized that and needs to find him before the Lynx disappears into another private collection."

"That's sort of where I'm leaning on the whole thing," I agreed.

"You think Mr. Stafford is the Daniel Mice Mr. Künstler spoke about?"

"I'd say it would be straining the bounds of probability to have a second Daniel running around this case," I told her. "But since we can't find Daniel Mice and ESS can't find Daniel Stafford, it would seem he's got at least one other name in his collection."

"So we're basically stuck."

"At least as far as his name goes." I raised my eyebrows as a sudden thought struck me. "Unless we don't *need* his name. Could the Spiders locate him if we provide them with a photo?"

Bayta pursed her lips. "Probably not," she said regretfully. "Conductors can learn to distinguish Human faces—they can recognize the two of us, for instance. But they aren't going to be able to pick a random Human face out of a crowd."

I grimaced. But I really should have expected that answer. "In that case, we're back to old-fashioned detective work," I said, scrolling to the next page. "Let's see if ESS was kind enough to provide us with a search platform."

They had. The next two pages of the file listed Stafford's relatives, closest friends, classmates, and fellow lugeboard junkies. It was, I noted cynically, a considerably longer list than Künstler's own. Apparently there were social advantages to being only *slightly* obscenely rich.

The three pages after that included Stafford's favorite hot spots, on Earth and elsewhere, a list of every place he'd visited during his wanderings, plus every travel, work, and play habit anyone had been able to statistically dredge up from his life's history. "I can't believe how fast they pulled all this together," Bayta commented when we finally reached the end.

"They've *had* five weeks since he and the Lynx disappeared," I reminded her. "This wasn't something they came up with after Morse messaged them that Künstler had been murdered."

Bayta's eyes went slightly unfocused. "Two drudges have arrived outside with the luggage we left aboard the last Quadrail," she reported.

"Good," I said. "Go let them in—I'll be with you in a minute. Just leave the bags in the waiting room, though, until I've had a chance to look them over."

She nodded and left. Turning off Morse's reader, I returned the data chip to the case and took both of them back to his jacket. I slid the reader into its tailored pocket, and returned the case to its own slot.

I had turned toward the door when Morse's voice croaked at me from the bed. "That does it, Compton," he said. "You're under arrest."

SEVEN

I turned back and looked at Morse. His face was still pale, but there was nothing uncertain about the disbelieving anger in his eyes. "Welcome back to the living," I said pleasantly.

"Did you hear me?" he rasped. "You're under arrest."

"I heard you," I confirmed. "Unfortunately, you still have the same jurisdictional problem you had at Bellis."

"Not at all," he countered. His voice was sounding stronger now. "This medical facility is Human-owned and Human-run. That makes it Human territory."

"An interesting interpretation," I agreed. "However, unless you know of an arraignment court on the premises, you still have to take me through Spider territory to get me to a shuttle."

"The Spiders can—" He broke off, twisting his wrist around and looking at his watch. "Bloody hell," he snarled, fumbling for the call button beside him on the rail. He squeezed it and then swung his legs over the side of the bed, pushing himself up into a sitting position. He spotted his shoes beside the bed and leaned over to grab them.

And toppled straight to the floor.

I was ready for it, and managed to grab one of his arms in time to keep his head from bouncing off the tile. "What happened?" the doctor said sharply from the doorway.

"Nothing," Morse's slightly muffled voice came before I could answer. "I'm all right."

"He tried to pass out," I told the doctor. "Almost made it, too."

"Help me get him back on the bed," the doctor said.

Together, he and I helped Morse back into a prone position on the bed. Morse fought us the whole way. "Let me alone," he insisted. "I have to leave."

"You'll leave the minute you're ready," the doctor countered firmly. "Not before."

"Then give me something to speed up the process," Morse demanded. "I'm already an hour behind the train I'm supposed to be on."

"And, what, you're going to chase after it on a dit rec western handcar?" I asked.

Morse tried his dagger-glaring technique, but with his eyes still woozy it wasn't very effective. "Mr. Compton is right," the doctor said. "There'll be other trains."

"Doctor, I need whatever you can do," Morse said, pitching his voice low and earnest and reasonable. "I can finish recovering once I'm on the train. I'm a EuroUnion government agent, and I *have* to get out of here."

The doctor looked at me. "He is, and he probably does," I confirmed.

The doctor grimaced, but nodded. "Wait here." Turning, he left the room.

"Don't think this is helping," Morse warned me. "Even if you manage to slide on Künstler's murder, I can still get you for theft of official ESS property and data. The penalty for that is eight to ten in the Minsk Four facility."

"That's good to know," I said. "I'll be sure to mention that to the next pickpockets I run into."

An uncertain frown edged across his forehead. "What are you talking about?"

"I'm talking about three Halkas out in the station, one

of whom called your name, thus enabling two of his buddies to trip you up and knock you cold, thus enabling them to steal *this*." I snagged his jacket and pulled out the data chip case. "Luckily for you, I got there in time to steal it back. No, no—don't thank me. That sunny smile of gratitude is all the thanks I need."

That one got the daggers up and running again. "Compton, if you think—"

"Hey, relax," I interrupted what would probably have been an impressive threat. "Believe it or not, we really *are* on the same side. Besides, Deputy UN Director Losutu has given me a clean bill of health."

"That might mean something if I actually cared about Losutu's opinions," Morse growled. "As it happens, I don't."

I shook my head and dropped the case onto the bed beside him. "You know, Morse, it's exactly this kind of simmering rage that starts popping capillaries when you hit fifty. Are you just mad that you lost your bird dog?"

"My what?"

"The late Mr. Künstler," I said. "You were following him in hopes that he'd lead you to Daniel Stafford and the Nemuti Lynx."

"I was escorting Lady Dorchester," he corrected stiffly.

"Whom you dropped like an election-year tax hike the second Künstler was murdered," I countered. "Since when does art theft fall under ESS's jurisdiction, anyway?"

For a dozen heartbeats he stared at me in silence. I was starting to wonder if he'd fallen asleep with his eyes open when he stirred and picked up the data chip case I'd dropped beside him. "My reader, please?" he asked.

I pulled it out and handed it to him. "It's the last file on the lower right-hand chip," I said helpfully.

In silence he inserted the chip, keyed on the decryption program, and scrolled down to Losutu's vote of confidence.

He was still studying it when the doctor returned with a hypo. "This is a mild stimulant," he told Morse as he gave him the injection. "It'll keep you going for an hour or two, but once it wears off you'll find yourself exactly where you are right now. Maybe even a little worse."

"That's fine," Morse said. "Like I said, I can sleep all I need to on the train."

"And here's a packet of QuixHeals," the doctor added, handing him a package. "Give the shot a few minutes to take effect, and you should be able to get to your train all right."

"Thank you," Morse said. "You wouldn't happen to have a schedule handy, would you?"

"I can do better than that," I offered. "Doc, did you see a young lady out in the waiting room?"

"The one looking through her carrybags?" the doctor asked. "Yes, she's still here."

I grimaced. I'd told Bayta *I'd* check for Modhran surprises. "Ask her to come in here, will you?"

"Wait a second," Morse growled. "It says *your* bona fides are in place, not anyone else's."

"Just ask her to come in," I repeated to the doctor.

He gave me the kind of look of strained patience I seemed to get a lot from people and left the room. "Losutu knows all about Bayta," I told Morse. "If you'd mentioned her in your report, he certainly would have included her in his note."

"Of course," Morse said. "By the way, in case you're interested, I've got ESS running a full check on you even as we speak."

"They're welcome to waste their time," I said, with just a twinge of concern. There was nothing blatantly illegal anyone could point to, but over the years I'd had my share of incidents that might easily be misinterpreted. "Meanwhile, if I were you, I'd try very hard to stay on Bayta's good side. If you need to make up time on a Quadrail, Bayta's the one who can make it happen."

He snorted. "What is she, a travel agent?"

"Way better than that," I assured him. "But if we're going to help you, you need to tell us what exactly is going on."

For another moment he studied my face. He still looked weak, but the color was starting to come back to his skin. Whatever the doctor had given him, it was working. "All right," he said at last, laying the reader aside. "What do you know about three sets of Nemuti sculptures called Hawk, Viper, and Lynx?"

"Never heard of them before yesterday," I told him truthfully. "Not until Künstler's dying words, actually."

His eyes widened. "Künstler *talked* to you? What did he say?"

"You first," I said. "Tell me about these sculptures."

His lips compressed. "There are nine of them," he said. "Smallish things, the size of your forearm or perhaps a bit smaller. They're very old, apparently from some vanished civilization that predates the Nemuti colonization of Veerstu. Even so, the art community doesn't put a lot of value on them." He tapped the reader. "I presume you read all this?"

"Enough to get the gist," I said, glancing over my shoulder as the door opened and Bayta slipped into the room. "I know about the attempted robbery and Daniel Stafford's mysterious disappearance. We both do," I added, nodding toward Bayta.

Morse turned a brief glare on Bayta. "What you *don't* know is that all nine of the sculptures have disappeared over the past year, stolen from various collectors or museums," he continued. "The last of them, one of the Hawks, was stolen from a Belldic collector just over three weeks ago."

"I thought the report said that the attempt on Künstler's Lynx failed," I reminded him.

"No, *that* group didn't get it," Morse said with a touch of impatience. "But it *is* gone. Odds are Stafford stole it, either at the time of the botched burglary, or else earlier, with the other attempt merely exposing its absence." He raised his eyebrows. "Curiously enough, in the five weeks since then Künstler never filed a missing-item report with his insurance agency. That tells me he knew where it was and thought he could get it back."

"From Stafford."

"Or whoever Stafford has sold it to," Morse said. "Unfortunately, there isn't enough actual evidence to issue a detention order."

"He *is* apparently traveling under a false ID, though," I said.

"Which we'll be happy to charge him with once we catch him at it," Morse agreed. "But we have to find him first. At any rate, when Künstler suddenly made plans to travel to Bellis right after the theft of the Hawk there we thought he might know something. Since Lady Dorchester already had plans to visit friends on Bellis, ESS put me aboard as her escort to keep an eye on him."

"Only Künstler never made it that far," I murmured. "Do we know if he had any communications from the Estates-General before he headed off there?"

"He received communications every day from all over the galaxy," Morse said patiently. "Barring a complete tap-and-strain, there's no way for us to tell if any of them mentioned the Lynx. Now, what did Künstler say before he died?"

"One more question," I said. "If you don't know where Stafford is, where exactly are you heading in such a hurry?"

"Stafford has friends," Morse said. "Eight of them are currently on their way to a ski resort in the Halkavisti Empire."

I looked at Bayta, noting the sudden tightening of her face. Our last visit to a Halkan ski resort had nearly gotten both of us killed. "Which one?" I asked.

"Carvlis Fang Mountain," he said. "It's on Ian-apof, one of the systems bordering the Tra'hok Unity."

Nowhere near Sistarrko, then. I started breathing again. "And you think they'll lead you to Stafford?"

"I don't know, but at the moment, they're all we have." Morse's lips compressed. "Unfortunately, they were on the express train that left an hour ago."

"Any of these friends particularly close to Stafford?" I asked.

"Penny Auslander," Morse said. "Twenty-three years old, daughter of the financier Charles Auslander of Zurich. She was Stafford's girlfriend all last school year, and there's no indication the relationship has cooled any."

"Really," I said. Penny's name had been the first one on ESS's list of Stafford's friends, but there hadn't been anything about them being snuggly. "How do you know?"

Morse smiled tightly, patting the side pocket on his slacks. "Not *all* the data chips end up in the data chip case," he said. "There was a set of follow-up information that came on its own chip."

"I'd like to see that."

"I'm sure you would," he countered. "Not going to happen."

I shrugged. We'd see about that. "Fine. What class are you traveling?"

"I have a six-week first-class pass," Morse said, his smile fading into a frown. "Why?"

"We need to know what kind of seats to get," I said. "Get your shoes and jacket and meet us in the lobby."

"Just a moment," he growled as he sat up. This time, he didn't fall over. "You haven't told me what Künstler said to you before he died."

"It wasn't much, actually," I said. "I told him who I was, he said he trusted me, then he told me about the Lynx—"

"Wait, wait, wait," Morse interrupted. "He said he *trusted* you?"

"Or words to that effect," I said. "He mentioned the Lynx, then he mentioned Daniel, then he died."

"Just Daniel?" Morse asked. "Not Daniel Stafford?"

Künstler's fading voice echoed again in my ears. *Daniel—Daniel Mice.* "No, just Daniel," I told Morse. "Now finish getting dressed while I get us some seats."

"You just get seats for wherever you're going," Morse said as he started putting on his shoes. "I can get my own."

"Fine," I said. Nudging Bayta, I moved us out into the corridor.

"Are we just getting two seats, then?" she asked as we headed toward the lobby.

"We're getting three," I told her. "We need to find Stafford and the Lynx before the Modhri does, and Morse has some of the pieces to that puzzle. I want to stay with him as long as we can."

"He may not like that."

"He's welcome to wait for another train," I said shortly. "First things first. I presume our friend Ms. Auslander will need to change trains at some point on her way to Ian-apof?"

"At least twice," Bayta said, frowning in concentration. "The first change will be at either Homshil or Jurskala."

"Have the stationmaster pull her itinerary and find out which it is," I said. "Then have him send a message ahead to the stationmaster there to keep her from getting on her next train."

Bayta blinked. "How is he going to do that?"

"Have the Spiders tell her there's some problem with her transfer," I said. "Or that her ticket record's been lost, or her ID's not reading right and they'll need to message back to Terra for confirmation."

She gave me the same look she'd used earlier when I'd suggested smoking the Gang of Fifteen out of their compartment with a fake fire. "I suppose they can do that," she said reluctantly.

"Don't worry, it won't go on anyone's personal record," I soothed her. "We just need to hold this girl in one place long enough to catch up with her."

"And then what?" Bayta asked. "What if she doesn't know where Mr. Stafford is?"

"Let's play this one move at a time, okay?" I said, a smoothly evasive way of saying I didn't have the foggiest idea. "Once you've got that in the works, see how fast you can get us moving after her."

Bayta's eyes defocused. "There's a local leaving in forty minutes, or an express leaving in two hours. Both of them stop at both Homshil and Jurskala."

"Let's try for the express," I told her. "Three first-class seats."

"You don't want a double compartment for us?"

"Homshil's less than a day away by express," I reminded her. "Hardly seems worth tying up two compartments for."

"I'd rather we had compartments."

I shrugged. "Fine. Whatever you want."

"Thank you." She paused. "By the way, Mr. Künstler didn't exactly say he trusted you," she said. "He said 'he hates you.' "

"Which is something we should probably avoid mentioning to Morse," I warned. "In case you hadn't noticed, he's the only one around who makes no bones about the fact that he hates me."

Bayta glanced over her shoulder. "You have any idea why?"

"I wish I did," I said. "Maybe I was part of some Westali operation that stepped on ESS toes."

But deep down, I knew that wasn't it. Morse's antagonism was way more personal than just misplaced professional rivalry.

Maybe there was a way to find out. "Can you get the Spiders to encode a message and send it to Earth?" I asked Bayta.

"If it's simple enough," Bayta said. "They'd prefer you to go to the message center and do it yourself."

"I'd rather not be seen at the message center right now," I told her. "Too many people might notice and wonder who I'm writing notes to. I just want a simple message sent to Losutu: 'Verify Ackerley Morse's bona fides—reply via Spiders.' Sign my name and send it."

"I suppose they can do that," Bayta said, a little doubtfully.

There was the sound of footsteps behind us, and I turned to see Morse hurrying down the corridor. "No need to rush," I called. "We've got your seat."

His expression darkened. "I told you not to do that," he growled. "You're not coming with me."

"No, *you're* coming with *us*," I clarified for him. "At least, if you want to catch up with Penny Auslander before she gets to Ian-apof."

His eyes narrowed. "What's that supposed to mean?"

"We're getting her pulled off the train at either Homshil or Jurskala," I told him. "Our train—"

"*You're* getting her pulled off?"

"Our train leaves in two hours," I went on, ignoring the question. "That gives us all time to get something to eat and compare notes a little."

For another few seconds Morse continued to eye me. Then, his lip twitched. "You've already seen most of my notes," he said. "And I don't especially care about yours. You really booked me a seat?"

"The ticket can be picked up at the stationmaster's office," Bayta said.

"You're not on this case," Morse warned. "This is official Euro-Union business, and you aren't involved in any way, shape, or form. Make *very* sure you understand that."

"We're just on the way to meet up with a friend," I said, stifling a sigh. There was something about Morse's attitude that was just plain tiring. "We just happen to be traveling on the same train as you, that's all."

He raised his eyebrows. "Imagine that," he said in mock surprise. "Frank Compton actually has a friend."

With that, he brushed past me and strode through the lobby to the exit. A moment later, he was gone.

I turned back to find Bayta gazing at me, a look of compassion on her face. "What?" I demanded. I didn't need friends, I certainly didn't need Morse, and the last thing I wanted right now was sympathy.

Fortunately for her, she got the message. "Nothing," she said, her expression going back to its usual neutral.

"Good," I growled. "The stationmaster get that message encoded?"

"It'll go out on the next scheduled laser transmission to Earth."

"Good," I said again. "I'm hungry. Let's get something to eat." I started us toward the door, putting my hand in my side pocket as I walked.

And stopped. "Well, well," I said.

"What?" Bayta asked.

"Clever," I said, feeling my stomach tighten. No wonder I'd gotten away so easily with picking that Halka's pocket.

"What's clever?" Bayta asked.

"The Modhri," I said, pulling my hand out of my pocket. "I'd been wondering where I got my newly improved pickpocket skills. Now I know. Turns out the Modhri didn't actually care about Morse's ultrasecret ESS reading material after all.

"The data chip with Fayr's message." I opened up my empty hand. "It's gone."

EIGHT

Morse was waiting at the platform when we arrived there an hour and a half later. Our Quadrail was visible in the distance, the red glow of the laserlike beams flashing between the train's front bumper and the Coreline and turning the Coreline's already impressive light show into something frighteningly manic. The lasers winked out, the train angled down the Tube's sloping side into the wider section that was the station, and a few minutes later it rolled to a brake-squealing halt beside us.

Our double compartment was, as usual, in the first car behind the engine. Morse's seat was three cars back, just behind the first-class dining car.

Bayta and I stayed close to home during the trip, emerging from our compartments only for meals, to stretch our legs, and occasionally to check on Morse. As far as I could tell, he too seemed to be keeping mostly to himself in the midst of all that noisy first-class camaraderie.

I made a couple of attempts to wheedle the other data chip out of him, the one that had been hidden in his pocket. But it was a waste of effort. Now that he was finally on the Quadrail and had Bayta's assurance that we could link him up with Penny and her friends, he wasn't making even an effort to be civil to me anymore.

I spent the rest of my limited time outside my compartment eyeing the other first-class passengers and wondering which of them might be walkers. That was even more of a waste of effort. As long as the Modhri colony inside a person stayed dormant, there was no way, barring serious micro-level surgery, to know it was in there.

Twenty-one hours after leaving Terra, precisely on time, we pulled into Homshil Station.

Most Quadrail stations carried between ten and forty sets of tracks, spaced more or less evenly around the inside of the Tube. Homshil was different. Though its main purpose was to provide service to the Jurian colony world of Homshiltristia, it also happened to be one of the fifty or sixty node points in the Quadrail system where the Spiders had brought several different lines together. One of the most important was a set of cross-galaxy tracks that headed out of our spiral arm entirely and traversed a wide swath of relatively empty space before skirting the edge of the galactic core and Fibibib space and heading across to the Pirkarli, Shorshian, and Filiaelian territories in the other spiral arm. For anyone traveling to those empires, shifting lines at Homshil could cut two or more weeks off their transit time.

As a result, Homshil carried a lot of traffic, and the Spiders had built accordingly. The station was half again bigger than the usual Quadrail station's diameter, with no fewer than sixty sets of tracks running along the floor. Between the platforms were dozens of restaurants, shops, waiting areas, and three full-service hotels for travelers who wanted to take a break before continuing their journeys. The stationmaster's office had been expanded into a four-building complex that included the office itself, separate booking and message centers, and a small computer library where newcomers to this spiral arm could grab up-to-date information on the worlds and cultures they would be visiting.

Between and around the various buildings, the Juriani

who were responsible for maintaining the service structures had set up planters and air-vine hedges, providing decoration, agreeable aromas for those species who went in for that sort of thing, and a modicum of badly needed pedestrian traffic control.

Across from the main passenger areas, looking upside down as you gazed up past the Coreline, the station's cargo facilities were equally crowded, except that instead of restaurants and shops the space was filled with cranes and sidings and transfer pallets. Through it all bustled dozens of drudge Spiders, looking like seven-legged ants crawling on a distant ceiling as they shifted crates back and forth between freight cars and cargo hatchways. At both ends of the five-kilometer-long station, away from the passenger and cargo unloading areas in the middle, were the maintenance and assembly areas.

Once again, we found Morse already on the platform when we disembarked from our car. The man was nothing if not quick on his feet. "You told me she'd be here," he said. "Where?"

"Over there," Bayta said, pointing to a long, low waiting room with classic Jurian architectural curlicues at the roof line.

Morse grunted. "Would have been safer to put her in the stationmaster's office."

"It might also have clued her in that there was something serious going on," I countered. "Her and anyone else who might have been paying attention."

The waiting room was comfortably full. Most of the passengers sitting around reading or chatting or playing cards were aliens, but there was a fair scattering of Humans as well. Despite the crowd, Penny Auslander was easy to spot. She was seated in a far corner of the room, the only person in that entire block of seats, flanked by a pair of watchful conductor Spiders.

We made our way through the aisles, dodging Juriani balancing frothing cups of pale yellow ale and Pirks carrying containers of some of the horrible things they liked to eat. Penny lifted her glare from the floor in front of her as we approached and transferred it to us. "About time," she said stiffly. "What took you so long?"

"My apologies for the delay, Ms. Auslander," Morse said, inclining his head in polite old-world manner.

"Apologies are cold comfort to the lost and vacant hour," she countered.

I winced to myself. Light-stick aphorisms, especially deep pithy light-stick aphorisms, always left me cold.

"I understand your distress," Morse said, still politely. Apparently he had a higher tolerance to brainless philosophy than I did. "But I think I can clear this up." He pulled out his badge wallet and flipped it open. "My name is Morse; EuroUnion Security Service."

Penny's glare slipped a little. "You're not with the Terran consulate?"

"No, ma'am," Morse said, tucking the wallet away.

Penny's eyes flicked to me, then Bayta, and finally back to Morse. "What's going on?" she asked.

"We're looking for your friend Daniel Stafford," Morse said. "We need to ask him a few questions."

He launched into a standard police-style explanation, a spiel tailored to evoke sympathy and cooperation without giving away any actual information. Listening with half an ear, I touched Bayta's arm and took a casual step backward. "Check with those conductors," I murmured to her. "Has she been alone this whole time?"

"They don't know," she murmured back. "They only came on duty fifteen minutes ago, replacing the others who'd been watching her. She was definitely alone then."

"Then find the ones who were here earlier and ask *them*," I said. "Her eyes shifted just a fraction to her left when Morse mentioned her friend Daniel."

Bayta shook her head. "I can't. They just left on one of the trains."

I swallowed a curse, looking around the waiting room. The Spiders *really* needed some training in proper police procedure. "Get everyone in the station looking for another Human," I ordered, pulling up my mental picture of Daniel Stafford. "Dark hair, mid-twenties, slender build—"

"Most Spiders don't know how to estimate Human ages," she interrupted.

"Then just go with dark hair and slender build," I said impatiently as I looked around the waiting room. All the Humans I could see were either older, bigger, or female. "At this point, I'll take any Human who's even close."

Morse was still trying to sell Penny on the idea that she could trust him. Penny still wasn't buying. I looked around the waiting room again, wondering if I ought to give up on the Spiders and start a search of my own.

"Got it," Bayta announced suddenly. "There's a dark-haired Human male at the TrinTrinTril restaurant carry-away counter. He's dressed in red and blue."

I'd noticed the TrinTrinTril on our way in. It was the direction Penny's eyes had flicked a minute ago. "Tell the Spiders I'm on my way," I told Bayta.

"Do you want me to come with you?"

"I'd rather you keep an eye on Morse and Ms. Auslander," I said. Confirming that neither of the other two was paying attention to me at the moment, I slipped away and headed through the milling passengers toward the door closest to the TrinTrinTril. I made sure to watch the other doors as I did so, just in case my quarry decided to come in through one of those instead.

No dark-haired Human males had appeared by the time I reached the far side of the room. I stepped outside, nearly getting run down by a Fibibib and a Nemut who were on their way in, and craned my neck to look over at the TrinTrinTril.

There he was, exactly as advertised: a youngish dark-haired kid in his early or mid twenties, wearing a red and blue ski outfit and holding a carry tray containing a pair of cups and a small closed box. He was talking earnestly with a well-dressed, smooth-skinned Shorshian, whose protruding dolphin snout was partially obscuring the kid's face.

Or rather, the kid was *listening* earnestly—the Shorshian seemed to be doing all the talking. Dodging around a pair of older Humans with double-knotted bankers' scarves, I headed over. I saw the boy's eyes flick past the Shorshian's head and lock on to me.

And to my astonishment, he dropped the carry tray and took off like all of hell was after him.

"Wait!" I shouted. "We just want to talk!"

The assurance was a waste of breath. If anything, the kid just ran faster.

And now that his back was to me, I could see for the first time the long backpack slung securely over his shoulders.

A long backpack just about the size of the Nemuti Lynx. Cursing feelingly, I took off after him.

In theory, running from the law inside a Quadrail station was an exercise in futility. There was literally nowhere to go where you couldn't eventually be tracked down. In practice, though, it was clear that the kid was intent on giving it a really good try.

He couldn't have picked a better station for it, either. With its maze of buildings and decorative shrubbery, Homshil was definitely a runner's paradise. Wishing now that I'd invited Bayta to join this party, I concentrated on keeping him in sight without bowling over any innocent bystanders in the process.

It was as I rounded one of the shops and nearly shinned myself on someone's luggage that I suddenly realized that the boy and I weren't the only ones on the move. On the fringes of my vision I could see two Halkas and three Juriani moving swiftly through the crowd in the same direction I was. None of them, as far as I could see, had any luggage with them.

No one simply abandoned their luggage in a Quadrail station. Not without a damn good reason.

Apparently, the Modhri wanted Daniel Stafford, too.

For the moment, though, the walkers weren't making any effort to close with the kid, apparently content to merely parallel the chase. Meanwhile, I had other troubles to deal with. My near miss with the luggage had cost me a couple of seconds, and as I came around another corner I saw that my quarry had gained some distance on me. He was nearing the end of the public areas, where he would have only three options: to keep going into the Spider maintenance section, head cross-country toward the cargo platforms, or double back and try to get past me.

"Where is he?"

I half turned to see Morse come up beside me. "Where's Ms. Auslander?" I countered.

"The Spiders have her," he said. "Bayta said Stafford was running."

"There," I said, nodding toward the distant figure. "Don't know . . . where he's . . . going."

"Wonder where he's—damn; there he goes," Morse said.

The kid had apparently decided on Option B and was angling toward the edge of the passenger platforms and the cargo areas beyond. Morse and I reached the edge of the hedge we were paralleling and turned to match his new direction. "Can you sic the Spiders on him?" Morse asked.

"They don't need . . . me to . . . tell them," I said, silently cursing Morse the lung capacity that let him run and talk at the same time. ESS apparently made its agents do laps every morning.

"Well, they'd better get to it," Morse warned. "Lot of places over there where he can go to ground."

"Only temp . . . orarily," I said. Our Juriani and Halkan friends, I noted uneasily, had changed course as well. "We've also . . . got outriders."

Morse glanced to both sides. "Damned amateurs," he rumbled. "Looks like he's making for that warehouse."

He was right. The kid had shifted direction again and was heading for one of the big maintenance buildings. "It's a . . . maintenance . . . building," I corrected.

"Whatever," Morse said impatiently. "Come *on,* old man. Run."

But it was too late. Even as Morse started to pull ahead of me, the kid ahead reached the closest of the maintenance building's doors, pulled it open, and vanished inside.

"I'm going in," Morse shouted over his shoulder. "You circle around in case he comes out the other side." Without waiting for a reply, he put on a burst of speed and left me in the dust.

I scowled as I veered to my right, heading for the nearest edge of the building. How I was supposed to cover all four sides of a warehouse-sized building by myself he hadn't said.

But there was nothing to do but try. The outriders were still paralleling me, I saw, apparently no more interested in following Morse into the maintenance building than they had been in converging on the kid out in the open air.

Only now, where there had been five outriders, there were only four.

One of the Halkas had disappeared.

I turned my eyes forward again, scanning the area. He might have simply run out of air and dropped out of the race. But I would hate to bet on that. I'd already seen how the Modhri presence inside a walker could push its host beyond normal limits of stamina and strength.

I was nearly to the corner of the building when the kid flashed into view, emerging from one of the side doors and running toward the next building over, a much smaller repair shop. He crossed the open space in a mad dash and disappeared inside.

I swore under my breath and changed direction. My walker escort had turned the same time I had, and unless I put on a pretty respectable burst of speed the two Halkas on that side were going to get to the door before I did.

But I'd run close to a kilometer already, and I didn't

have the reserves left for a last-minute sprint. The two Halkas reached the door a good thirty meters ahead of me and disappeared inside. Ignoring the small sane part of my mind that warned me this was a stupid thing to do, I charged in after them.

For once, the sane part was right. I'd barely made it in out of the Coreline's pulsating glow when they attacked.

Fortunately, Modhri walkers or not, they were as worn-out from the run as I was. Their lunge was slow and disorganized, and I was able to dodge out of the way with only a single glancing blow off my shoulder. I took the nearest one down with a leg sweep, tried unsuccessfully to do the same to the other, and danced back out of his way, taking a moment to look around.

As our young fugitive had picked a good station to run in, he'd similarly picked a terrific place to go to ground. The repair shop was reasonably large, but over half of the open space in the center was currently occupied by a freight car with a disassembled rear wheel assembly. Between the car itself, the various equipment cabinets lining the walls, and the catwalks and crane tracks crisscrossing the space above us, we had the makings here of world-class hide-and-seek.

And with the Halka I'd tripped now back on his feet, I was again on the short end of two-to-one odds. "Stafford!" I shouted as the two Halkas advanced toward me. "Get out of here—fast—and get back to the stationmaster's office."

Nothing. Behind the Halkas the door we'd come in through opened again and the two Juriani who'd been on my other flank appeared, panting heavily but clearly game to join in the fun. Four-to-one odds, now. "Stafford, you're in danger," I shouted again. "Get out of here." Again, the only response was my own echo off the high ceiling.

And I was running out of time. Westali combat training was all well and good, but four to one was still four to one. I backed up, looking vainly around for some sign of my quarry, wondering too where that missing Halkan walker had gotten to. There was a soft tapping sound behind me, and I spun around, whipping my hands around into defensive position.

But it was only a drone Spider. The smooth globe and slender legs hardly lent themselves to expressions or body language, but just the same I would swear this particular Spider looked startled. "Don't just stand there," I growled at him. "Give me a hand."

The Spider's response was to take a couple of rapid steps toward the Quadrail car to get out of my way. Radically nonaggressive beings, I reminded myself, as constitutionally unable to fight as the Chahwyn who had created them. I continued to back up, keeping ahead of the advancing walkers, hoping to find a spot narrow enough that they would have to come at me one at a time.

But I was nearly halfway through and hadn't found anything yet. I would have to try circling around the front of the Quadrail car when I got there and see if there was anything on the other side of the building.

And then, as I passed one of the tool cabinets, it gave a soft click.

The sound of a lock unlocking.

The drone still cowering over by the car couldn't simply wade in and help me fight the four walkers. But he'd done the next best thing.

He'd offered me a chance at a weapon.

I took a sideways step to the tool cabinet and swung open the door, grabbing the first long tool—a wrench—that caught my eye. Jumping back, slamming the door closed again, I once again faced my attackers.

The Modhri mind segment that included these four walkers must have known in that moment that he'd lost this group. But after having taken full control of them for this long he probably would have had to kill them anyway. The Modhri preferred to operate in the shadows, and four upstanding citizens of the galaxy who had inexplicably blacked out for this length of time might wonder about it a little too hard and a little too loudly.

So with absolutely nothing to lose, he sent them charging to the attack.

Four bodies under the control of the same mind made for an awesome fighting machine. But these four weren't fighters, and as such had no training or reflexes or combat experience the Modhri could draw on.

And it showed. I moved against one side of the circle as they closed in, taking out one of the Halkas with a blow to his knee before the others could get close enough to double-team me. I danced back again, ducked under a flailing Jurian arm, and jabbed the owner in one of his upper thigh nerve points. He went down even more spectacularly than the Halka had, and then there were two.

Normal attackers might have paused at this point for a little reevaluation. These two just waded in, the Halka going high, the Juri going low. The latter got a wrench across the side of his beak for his trouble, and he was down for the count.

But the numbers had been just a shade too tight. His partner got in outside my arm, and I found myself being crowded sideways with arm and wrench pressed too tightly against my chest to do anything. I managed to shift the wrench to my left hand, but was shoved against a bank of waist-high diagnostic machines before I could get off more than a fairly weak blow across his upper arm.

He grunted with pain and grabbed at my wrist. I evaded that attempt, but his second try succeeded, and multiple jolts of pain lanced through my left forearm as his claws punched through my jacket and sank into my skin. His other hand slashed at my eyes; more by luck than skill I caught his wrist in my right hand.

For a second I stared into that flat, bulldoglike face, the sagging jowls and empty eyes an eerie reminder that what I was fighting wasn't the respectable, civilized being that had once called this body home. Then, clenching my teeth against the pain from the dug-in claws, I twisted my left wrist to the side, bringing the end of the wrench down onto the hand still stretched toward my eyes.

There was the faint sound of snapping bones, and suddenly my left arm was free as the Halka howled and clutched at his broken hand. I lifted the wrench high, aiming for the muscle ridge where his neck and shoulder joined.

The blow never landed. Abruptly, the Halka dropped straight down like he'd fallen through a trapdoor as his legs were swept out from under him. As his head dropped out of my line of sight I saw Morse standing behind him, a thunderous look on his face. He jabbed a single blow into the back of the Halka's neck, and the fight was over.

The physical fight, anyway. "What in *bloody* hell do you think you're doing?" Morse snarled at me.

"Protecting my life," I told him, massaging my arm where the claws had perforated it.

"From *these?*" Morse countered, gesturing at the unconscious bodies around us. "What were they going to do, foreclose your house? Force you to buy some insurance?"

"Maybe protecting Daniel Stafford's life, too," I said. "He came in here right before I did."

Morse looked around. "Stafford?" he called. "Stafford, this is Agent Ackerley Morse of the EuroUnion Security Service. We need to talk to you."

"It's all right," I called. "You're safe now."

There was no answer. "Maybe he went out the other end," Morse suggested.

I shook my head. "I would have heard the sound of the door."

Morse hissed softly between his teeth. "Right," he said, his voice quiet and deadly. "Let's go find him."

Five minutes later, we found him lying behind a diagnostic cabinet that had been pulled a meter away from the wall. He was dead, of course, his neck broken.

Only it wasn't Daniel Stafford. In fact, aside from the hair color, age, and body type, he wasn't even close.

"Check the bag," Morse murmured over my shoulder. "See if they got the Lynx."

The backpack was still slung over the boy's shoulder. Carefully, I reached over and unzipped it.

No one had gotten the Lynx, because the Lynx had never been there. Snugged up inside the padded case was a beautifully decorated, high-priced lugeboard.

Morse and I stared at the board, and at the body, for what seemed a long time. Then, Morse got an unpleasantly firm grip on my shoulder. "Come on," he said. "We need to talk."

NINE

"I'm trying to give you the benefit of the doubt," Morse said as we faced each other in the privacy of one of the stationmaster's storage rooms. "I really am. But you're not making it easy."

"You saw the boy running," I said. "You also saw me in the repair shop fighting off those four attackers—"

"You mean those four respectable industrialists and bankers, none of whom had any reason to bother you?" he interrupted. "Those four upstanding citizens who are all dead?"

Even in death, I reflected, Modhran walkers were a pain in the neck. "*You* took out the last one," I pointed out.

"*After* you'd already had a crack at him."

"You're welcome to ask for an autopsy," I said. "The point is there wasn't nearly enough time for me to have gotten all the way around the building, killed the kid, and then gotten back to where you found me."

"No one said you had to have done everything yourself," Morse said. "There were several Spiders in the vicinity, and you and your friend Bayta seem to have an amazingly cozy relationship with them."

"You ever hear of a Spider attacking anyone?" I countered. On that one, at least, I was on very safe ground. "Or even getting agitated?"

Morse's lips puckered. "The point is, seemingly at every stop, the reason for your presence here becomes ever murkier."

"I have Deputy Director Losutu's endorsement," I reminded him.

"Which I already told you doesn't impress me," he retorted. "What's your game, Compton?"

"There's no game," I told him. "A man who died at my feet a few days ago seemed concerned about his missing sculpture. I'd like to help recover it, for his sake. I was trying to do that when this fiasco happened. End of story."

Morse snorted. "Hardly," he growled. "What about the Juriani and Halkas you just killed?"

"You find medical proof that anything I did killed them, and I'll be happy to discuss it further," I said. "Until then, this conversation is a waste of time. What we need to do is talk to Ms. Auslander and find out what she knew about the boy who was killed."

"Correction: *I* need to talk to Ms. Auslander," he said. "*You* need to stay put until I figure out what to do with you."

I thought about reminding him once again that he had no authority inside a Tube station, especially one surrounded by Jurian space. But it didn't seem worth the breath. "Just make it fast," I said. "Wherever Stafford is, he's getting a light-year farther away every minute we sit here."

"Thank you for the reminder," Morse said acidly. "You can be in charge of keeping track of those light-years." With that witty exit line, he strode out, closing the door behind him.

I made a couple of circuits of the storeroom, just to keep my complaining leg muscles from seizing up completely. I was starting my third circle when the door opened again and Bayta slipped inside. "Any word from the governor?" I asked her.

"What?" she asked, frowning.

"Skip it," I said, making a mental note to add some prison stories to the list of dit rec dramas I intended to show her someday. "What's Morse doing?"

"He's interviewing Ms. Auslander," Bayta said. "She's very upset."

"Sudden death does that to people," I said. "So she *did* know the kid?"

Bayta nodded. "Pyotr Gerashchenko, one of the group going to Ian-apof for that ski trip. He stayed behind with Ms. Auslander when her ticket was canceled."

Which the Spiders had done under my orders. Which meant that ultimately I was the one responsible for getting the kid killed.

I shook away the thought. It was the Modhri who'd killed him, not me. "So why did he run?"

"I don't know." Bayta paused, cocking her head as if listening to something faint. "She's telling Mr. Morse . . . Mr. Gerashchenko was accustomed to using certain illegal drugs. She thinks he must have thought he was going to be arrested."

"I wonder how he came to that conclusion," I said sourly, thinking back to the Shorshian who'd been talking earnestly to Gerashchenko just before he spotted me and took off.

"She doesn't know," Bayta said.

"I do," I said. "The Modhri engineered the whole thing, from spooking the kid into running, to helping us herd him someplace nice and private, to sending someone in to kill him."

"The fifth walker?"

"Or someone else who slipped over there ahead of us and waited for Gerashchenko to show up," I said. "Interesting that the lack of a fifth walker body implies the Modhri didn't want to waste that particular one."

"But why kill Mr. Gerashchenko at all?"

"That *is* the question, isn't it?" I agreed, looking at my watch. Morse had had five minutes alone with Penny. That was plenty. "Let's go find out."

We left the room, walking past the two server Spiders Morse had apparently shanghaied into guarding me. Bayta led the way down a corridor to one of the private conference rooms adjoining the stationmaster's office. Again we brushed past a couple of Spiders and went inside.

Penny was seated in one of the chairs, her head bowed, her eyes on the floor in front of her. Morse was half sitting, half leaning against the table beside her, a standard posture for giving the interrogator intimidating height over the subject. Both of them looked up as Bayta and I entered, Penny with a look of defiance-flavored trepidation, Morse with completely unadulterated annoyance. "What the bloody hell are *you* doing here?" he demanded. "I told you to stay—"

"Ms. Auslander, my name is Frank Compton," I introduced myself, ignoring Morse. "One question: what was it your friend Pyotr wanted you to do?"

The sheer unexpectedness of the question brought Morse's budding tirade to a halt. "What?" he asked.

"Ms. Auslander?" I prompted. "You and Pyotr were discussing something before we arrived. What was it?"

She was staring at me like something that had just crawled out of a fishbowl and quoted Nietzsche. "He wanted me to go home with him," she said. "I mean, not *with* him—just go back to Earth and forget the ski trip and whatever the problem was with my ticket."

Morse heaved himself off the desk and took a step toward me. "Compton, if you're not out of here in five seconds—"

"And you discussed this in the waiting room?" I asked Penny. "In full earshot of anyone who happened to pass by?"

Penny's expression was starting to slide into sudden horror. "My God," she breathed. "Are you saying—? Oh, no. God, *no*."

I looked at Morse, silently inviting him to renew his rant. But he just stood there, a grim look on his face.

"I'm afraid so," I confirmed, looking back at Penny. "Someone wants to find your friend Mr. Stafford, and he's counting on you to help him do that. The last thing he wants is for you to turn around and go back home."

"And he killed Pyotr for *that*?"

"Your boyfriend is very important to him," I said.

The girl took a deep, shuddering breath. "Not boyfriend," she corrected quietly. "Fiancé."

I looked at Morse, noting his complete lack of reaction. Apparently, that was one of the tidbits on his private data chip. "All the more reason we need to get to him first," I told Penny. "Will you help us?"

She dropped her gaze to the floor again. Clearly, the fact that her fiancé's pursuer was willing to play rough had all sorts of potentially unpleasant ramifications for her safety as well as Stafford's. If their engagement had been made in some boardroom instead of heaven she would probably be seriously rethinking the whole thing right now. "What do you want me to do?" she asked at last.

"You can start by telling us exactly what you've heard from Mr. Stafford in the past two weeks," Morse said.

Penny shrugged, a nervous hunching of her shoulders. The haughty young woman in the waiting room who'd demanded to know what had taken us so long had vanished, replaced by someone a little vulnerable, a little scared, and way more human. I definitely liked this version better. "He sent me a message about a week and a half ago telling me he'd found a great new resort on the north side of Carvlis Fang and that I should get a group together to come join him."

"Don't you all have classes?" I asked. "I thought you were students."

Penny shook her head. "We all graduated last semester."

"Except for Mr. Stafford, of course," Morse murmured.

"He's not what you all think," Penny snapped, some of her earlier fire flaring out again. Her lips quirked, her eyes dropping away from Morse's. "Anyway, he's doing an independent study on alien sociology this semester. He can travel as much as he wants."

Or at least, as much as he wanted up to the limit of his parents' bank account and patience. "So you collected the gang and headed out," I said. "I presume you were supposed to call him once you got to Ian-apof?"

Penny nodded. "Only this griggle with my ticket came up and I couldn't transfer trains." She gave me an accusing look. "Only I gather it *wasn't* just a griggle, was it?"

"Meanwhile, Mr. Gerashchenko volunteered to stay behind and keep you company," I said, ignoring the question. "And then tried to get you to go back to Earth."

"Could he have been hoping to steal you away from Mr. Stafford?" Morse suggested.

"No," Penny said, the fire gone again with the fresh reminder of Gerashchenko's violent death. "I don't know. Maybe. If he was, it wouldn't have worked." She blinked a couple of fresh tears from her eyes. "It takes more than a few hours alone with someone, you know."

I felt my breath catch in my throat. *A few hours . . .* "I suppose that depends on the person," I said, keeping my voice casual. "Excuse me a minute."

I touched Bayta's arm and backed out of the room. She followed, a puzzled look on her face. "Is that all you needed?" she asked.

"No, but the rest can wait," I said. "Right now, we need a train. A fast one."

"The next express to Ian-apof—"

"Faster than an express," I cut her off. "I need something that can gain five or six hours over the distance between here and Jurskala. We need to catch Penny's original Quadrail, the express Morse was heading for back on Terra Station when he got clobbered."

"What for?"

I looked at the door we'd just come through. Morse might already be on his way to find out the reason for my sudden retreat. "Because the Hawk the Modhri stole from Bellis is on that train."

Bayta's eyes had just enough time to widen in shock; and then, right on cue, the door opened and Morse strode through, a suspicious glint in his eyes. "Our company suddenly not good enough for you?" he demanded.

"Bayta and I need to get moving," I told him. "Good luck with your investigation. I trust you can take care of Ms. Auslander?"

"I thought you wanted in on this," Morse said.

"I thought you didn't want me."

"I don't," he said. "But as far as I'm concerned, you're still under suspicion of murder. Of six murders, now, actually. I don't intend to let you out of my sight for the foreseeable future."

It was basically the response I'd expected. It was also the one I'd wanted. If the Modhri wanted Penny in on the hunt for Stafford, I didn't want her out of *my* sight, either. "I don't have time to argue the point," I said, trying for the right combination of chagrin and resignation. "Bayta thinks she can get us a train that'll get us to Jurskala ahead of Penny's friends."

"That's impossible," he said, frowning. "They're on an express."

"Bayta thinks she can get something faster."

He gave Bayta a long, speculative look. "All right, I'll play," he said. "Just make sure it has enough seats for the four of us. You think Ms. Auslander's friends can help us find Stafford?"

"Multiple heads are usually better than one."

"Maybe." He grunted. "I'm not looking forward to telling them about Gerashchenko's death."

"I'm sure your natural tact will carry the day," I assured him. "Why don't you get Ms. Auslander's luggage together and we'll meet you outside."

"Just make sure you're still there when we arrive," he warned, and disappeared back into the room.

I started to head the opposite direction, but was brought up short by Bayta's grip on my arm. "Frank, the Hawk can't be on that Quadrail," she insisted. "The

Spiders checked the records, and those Bellidos are still on their original train."

"The Bellidos are; the Hawk isn't," I said. "They transferred it to another walker team at Terra."

"But that doesn't make sense," she protested. "I thought the Modhri trapped us on Helvanti Station so that that group could get ahead of us."

"Right, but they can't outrun a message cylinder," I said. "If the walkers hadn't switched at Terra, we could have easily gotten word to someone ahead of them before the next major station and arranged an ambush. What sidelining us incommunicado at Helvanti did was make it impossible for us to keep track of where the Hawk was."

"But why would he put it on Ms. Auslander's train?"

"I doubt he even knew Ms. Auslander was aboard," I said. "I think he just wanted an express that would get the Hawk to Nemuti space in a timely manner, but not on an obvious straight-line path. The Jurskala–to–Ian-apof line fits that description perfectly."

"So do six to ten others."

"But none of them was the train Morse was heading for when he was clobbered."

That one stopped her. "What?" she asked, frowning.

"Think about it," I said. "If all the Modhri wanted was to get hold of Morse's data chips—or, rather, to get hold of *my* data chip—a simple trip plus maybe a light blow to the head would have done the trick. But instead, he hauled off and really walloped the guy. Why take that kind of risk unless he was desperate to keep Morse—and us—off that particular train?"

"Maybe his goal was to keep us from connecting with Ms. Auslander."

I shook my head. "He had three hours to figure out a countermove while she was sitting here complaining to Gerashchenko in the waiting room," I reminded her. "He certainly would have figured out we were the ones who'd snafued her schedule, and that we were on our way. But he didn't do anything, except make sure Gerashchenko couldn't talk her into going home. In fact, my guess is that he's pleased we're joining forces."

"He'll be watching us, of course."

"As long as that's all he does, I don't mind."

She gave me a slightly strained look. "I'll see what the Spiders can do."

"And tell them to hurry," I said. "The Modhri mind segment here will be sending a message ahead. It would be nice to be in position before the segment on the Quadrail gets the message and dumps the Hawk somewhere else."

I HAD ENVISIONED some kind of sleek, private train out of a dit rec western or EuroUnion drama, perhaps not as luxurious as a Halkan Peerage car but at least to the level of the standard Quadrail compartment car.

The outside, at least, was a serious disappointment.

"You *are* joking," Morse said as a pair of conductor Spiders escorted us across the last of the passenger tracks toward the short train that had been readied for us. "Looks like a cattle car."

"It's called a tender," Bayta told him, a little stiffly. "It's the only thing the Spiders could put together on short notice."

"Looks like a pushmi-pullyu," Penny commented, sounding as doubtful as Morse did.

"What's that?" Bayta asked.

"A legendary animal from an old dit rec musical," Penny explained. "It had a head at both ends."

I gave the girl points—that was indeed exactly what our new transport looked like. It consisted of three windowless Quadrail cars with a small engine at each end facing opposite directions. "What are these things used for?" I asked Bayta.

"They carry drones, drudges, and repair equipment," she said. "There's an engine on either end so they can go wherever they need to without first having to go to a station or siding to turn around."

"I hope you reminded the Spiders that we need air to breathe," Morse said. "Not to mention food and water and rest facilities. Even a regular Quadrail takes over three days to get to Jurskala—this one's not likely to be any faster."

"It's probably faster than it looks," I offered. In fact, I knew it was. The loop gantries on the two end cars extended at least two meters higher than the standard Quadrail. Since a train's speed was determined by how close the closest bit of matter was to the Coreline's quantum thread, this thing could probably do close to double the usual light-year-per-minute if it wanted to.

Assuming that the wheels and structural integrity could handle such speeds, of course. Still, even a modest percentage gain should give us what we needed.

The Spiders ushered us to the center of the three cars, where my original trust in our hosts was fully vindicated. Inside, the car was set up like a double first-class passenger compartment, though without the extendable dividing wall between the sections or the mirror-imaged curve couches that were normally built into that wall.

There were a few other alterations, as well. Instead of the usual overbed luggage racks there was another permanently fixed bunk, giving us upper and lower berths on both ends of the car. There was also only a single half-bath cubicle instead of the usual pair that a double compartment would have, with the space that had been thus freed up given over to a food prep/storage area.

"Interesting," Morse said, setting down his carrybags and making a quick circuit of the car. "Looks like some kind of prototype."

"It's not decorated as nicely as the standard compartment," Penny seconded. "No privacy, either."

"Obviously, you've never ridden third class," I said.

"We'll give you all the privacy we can, Ms. Auslander," Morse said. "It's only for a couple of days."

"I was thinking about Bayta," Penny said, lifting her eyebrows at Bayta. "She seems more uptight about things than I am."

Bayta's face darkened a little. "I can handle it, thank you," she said coolly.

For another few seconds the two women eyed each other. Then Penny shrugged and headed toward the rear of the car. "Fine," she said. "Dibs on the lower bed."

TEN

The trip to Jurskala took just under two and a half days, and was every bit as awkward as it had looked going in.

The lack of privacy turned out to be not as big a problem as I'd feared. The problem of showers, more specifically the dis- and rerobing before and afterward, was solved by dousing the lights during the process. The food was decent enough, too, though for the life of me I couldn't figure out where it was from. My eventual best guess was that it was cuisine from the other end of the galaxy, Shorshian or Filiaelian delicacies that I'd never run across before.

The problem wasn't with the accommodations. The problem was Morse and Penny.

Somewhere midway through the first day Penny apparently got over the initial shock of Gerashchenko's death and started wondering what exactly had happened to him. Unfortunately, Morse got to her with his version of the story before I could get to her with mine.

It created an instant bias that no amount of subsequent explanation or damage control was able to alleviate. The sleeping arrangements, which had started out with Penny and Bayta at one end and Morse and me at the other, changed abruptly after the first night as Penny silently but firmly moved to Morse's end of the car.

After that, the whole thing took on a distinct Us Versus Them flavor. Morse and Penny would sit together on the lower bunk on their side of the car, facing each other from opposite ends and having quiet, earnest conversations. Every time I tried to penetrate the invisible wall they'd built around them all talk abruptly ceased and two pairs of studiously neutral eyes followed my every move until I retreated back to my half of the car.

They didn't think any better of Bayta, either because of her association with me or her mysterious influence with the Spiders.

Bayta spent most of the trip sleeping. I whiled away the hours lounging on my bunk and gazing at the earnest conversations going on at the far end, wondering what useful secrets they might be trading back and forth.

Still, I had some hard thinking to do. A little peace and quiet was just fine.

Besides, it wasn't as if Bayta and I didn't have a few secrets of our own.

I'D TOLD BAYTA I wanted to reach Jurskala at least half an hour before the train carrying the Hawk. She and the Spider driving the tender did me one better, getting us into the station nearly an hour ahead of Penny's friends.

"We have seats in the first of the first-class cars," Bayta informed me as we worked our way through the mostly Jurian crowd toward our platform. Now that the tension of Penny's presence was gone, she was back to her usual cool, competent self. "That's all I could get."

"Any chance of switching later to a compartment?" I asked.

"Two of the members of Ms. Auslander's group have compartments which they'll be leaving at Ian-apof," Bayta said. "They're not connected, though. The stationmaster's still pulling the records for the other compartments. He'll let me know if he spots a double becoming available."

"You okay with open seats?"

"I'll manage," she said. "Ian-apof is only two days' journey away."

It was a little more than that, actually, but I wasn't about to quibble. "Fine," I said. "What about Morse and Penny?"

"Mr. Morse didn't want me making their arrangements," Bayta said, a slight flush coming into her cheeks. "I told the stationmaster to reserve seats in our car for them in case it fills up before they reach the ticket counter."

I nodded and looked around, automatically picking out the best dressed of the travelers milling around us. So far there was no indication that the local Modhri mind segment was aware of our presence. "Have the Spiders keep an eye on them," I instructed her. "Watch especially for any attempt to split them away from us."

"Are you sure we really need them?"

I took another, closer look at her. "She really got to you, didn't she?" I asked.

"I don't trust her," Bayta said flatly.

"Because she doesn't like us?"

"Because she trusts Mr. Morse too much."

"She's EuroUnion," I reminded her. "Morse is EuroUnion Security Service. Of course she's going to take his word over mine."

"You *do* realize we still don't know anything about him, don't you?"

I did, and it was starting to worry me. It had been over three days since the Spiders had sent my message to Losutu. There could have been a reply as early as Homshil; there certainly should have been something waiting here at Jurskala.

But so far not a peep. Either Losutu was ignoring me—always a possibility—or he was too involved in his UN duties to bother with something this low profile.

Or else there wasn't any data to be had on an ESS agent named Ackerley Morse.

"We do know that he wants Stafford and the Lynx, too," I reminded Bayta. "For now, that makes him an ally." I raised my eyebrows. "Ms. Auslander is one, too, whether she likes it or not."

Ms. Auslander didn't, of course. The suspicious look she sent Bayta and me as she and Morse settled into their first-class seats showed that abundantly. But she wasn't annoyed enough to walk off the train.

Her friends—four girls and two guys—greeted her with the surprise and delight of someone meeting a long-lost cousin. Their enthusiasm faded considerably with the news of Gerashchenko's death. The train was barely moving before they all disappeared together into one of the two compartments, no doubt to hear all the details. Before we hit the thirty light-year mark, I suspected, there would be six more people aboard whispering together as they gave me dirty looks.

It was just as well, I reflected, that government service had given me such thick skin.

Meanwhile, I had more urgent matters to attend to. Settling our seats into one of the car's corners, Bayta and I once again began to monitor the comings and goings from the compartment car ahead.

The walkers, as I'd surmised, had changed, with none of the original Gang of Fifteen aboard. But the Modhri's basic strategy seemed to have remained the same. Once again, we were able to account for nearly everyone in there as they made their individual and group sorties to the dining car for food and drink. Once again, we observed meals being brought up from the rear.

But where the Gang of Fifteen had had two of their number on permanent guard duty, this batch of escorts seemed to have only one.

"Not really surprising," I told Bayta as we compared notes in the bar. "On the first leg of the trip, the one from Bellis, the Modhri had time to plan everything out and make sure he got connecting compartments. This time, with the scramble to send the Hawk in a new direction, he had to take pot luck."

"I'm not sure how that's going to help us," Bayta said doubtfully. "As long as there's still a walker in there we're not going to get in."

"It's going to help because there are now *two* ways into the compartment instead of one," I said. "The connecting wall locks from both sides, right?"

She was starting to get that suspicious look again. "Yes," she said cautiously.

"All handled electronically?"

"Yes."

"And if there was a brief power outage, what would the default setting be?"

Her look changed from suspicious to aghast. "No," she said firmly. "Not a chance."

"Why not?" I asked. "Don't walkers sleep?"

"The *walkers* sleep," she said. "I'm not so sure about the polyp colonies inside them."

"We'll just have to chance it," I said.

"Frank, you can't—" She broke off, her eyes abruptly glazing over.

"Bayta?" I asked, resisting the impulse to wave my hand in front of her face like they always do in old dit rec dramas. Instead, I gave the bar a quick sweep, then shifted my attention to the corridor. There was nothing out of the ordinary that I could see.

Abruptly Bayta's eyes came back. "Come on," she said, standing up and heading for the corridor.

But instead of turning forward toward our seats, she headed aft. "Where are we going?" I asked.

"Just come."

She led the way through the other first-class car, through the second-class section, and into third. We kept going, passing the Humans and aliens reading or talking or dozing in their seats, and into the first baggage car.

"We're starting to run out of train," I warned Bayta as

she led us through the meandering passageway that led between the stacks of safety-webbed crates. "What are we looking for, anyway?"

"We're not looking for anything," she said over her shoulder as we went through the door and vestibule and entered the second baggage car.

And now we really *had* run out of train. "What now?" I asked as she finally came to a halt a few steps inside the car.

"We wait," she said. Sitting down, she rested her back against the nearest crate and closed her eyes.

Thirty seconds later, while I was still looking around for some clue as to what we were doing here, there was a gentle lurch and my inner ear told me we were gradually but definitely slowing down. "Have we just been disconnected from the train?" I asked carefully.

Before Bayta could answer there was a second lurch, a stronger one this time, and the gradual deceleration switched back to an equally gradual acceleration. "Uh-oh," I muttered.

Bayta nodded, her eyes still closed, tension lines tightening her cheeks. "The Chahwyn want to talk to you."

THE FIRST TIME I'd had this particular detached-car trick pulled on me I'd been gassed and unconscious for most of the trip. Now, fully awake and alert, I decided being unconscious had definitely been the better way to go. Standing around a Quadrail baggage car, watching the stacks of crates swaying inside their webbing as we went around slight curves, was breathtakingly boring.

Which meant nearly a hundred percent of my available brain power could concentrate on the unpleasant question of what the Chahwyn had up their sleeves for me this time.

Fortunately, they'd timed things so that the trip didn't take very long. We'd been trundling along for no more than twenty minutes when I again sensed that we were starting to slow down. Five minutes after that, with the usual creak of brakes, we came to a halt. "We're here, dear," I said to Bayta as she got back to her feet. "You want to get the luggage while I see about a rental?"

"This isn't a joke, Frank," she warned as we moved to the door near the front of the car. "Behave yourself."

The door irised open as we reached it, and as we stepped out onto the platform I found that we were in one of the Spiders' secret sidings: smaller than a standard station, with only four sets of tracks and lots of drab, functional-looking support buildings. Bayta walked us past the engine that had pushed us here, leading the way to one of the smaller buildings.

Inside, seated at the far end of the typical three-chair triangle setup and flanked by a pair of Spiders, was a Chahwyn.

"Hello, there," I greeted him. "Nice to see some of you getting out a little."

"Sit down, Mr. Compton," the alien said in a grave but melodious voice. He extended a hand, the forefinger visibly lengthening as he pointed to one of the chairs.

Silently, I stepped to the indicated seat as Bayta took the third. The Chahwyn were a humanoid species with pale skin, mostly hairless except for tufts of catlike whiskers extending out from ridges above their eyes. Their limbs and fingers were long and thin, their facial features flat and bland.

Or at least they were normally flat and bland. Their whole physique was so malleable that the only other Chahwyn I'd ever met had been able to pass himself off as Human, at least for a short time. Like that first Chahwyn, this one was wearing soft shoes and an elaborately draped togalike robe.

The two Spiders standing stiffly beside him were also tantalizingly familiar. They were of a type I'd seen on my first visit to a Quadrail siding, about the size of a stationmaster but without the usual stationmaster markings. I still didn't know what class they were.

The Chahwyn waited until Bayta and I were seated. "We had not wanted to have this meeting, Mr. Compton," he said. "But the Elders have concluded we have no choice."

One of the Spiders stirred and tapped its way toward me, and I saw now that it was walking on only six of its seven legs. As it reached me the seventh leg unfolded from beneath the shiny sphere and I saw that it was holding a folded piece of paper. "What's this?" I asked as the leg extended itself toward me.

"The substance of a message between two of Earth's leading Humans of wealth," the Chahwyn said. "Read."

I took the paper and unfolded it; and as I read I felt my eyebrows crawling higher up my forehead with each line. "What is it?" Bayta asked.

"Apparently our good friend Larry Hardin is still sore about that trillion dollars we squeezed out of him a few months ago," I said, leaning over and handing her the paper. "He's sent out a lovely little chain letter warning all his trillionaire buddies to steer clear of me."

"I trust you see the problem," the Chahwyn said. "Mr. Hardin's friends will tell their friends, and their friends will tell their friends, and so on."

"And what, the next thing you know people will be pointing to me in crowds and asking for my autograph?" I asked.

"There's more," the Chahwyn said. "I understand another Human has died violently in your presence aboard one of our Quadrails."

"That wasn't my fault," I said stiffly. Having people turn up dead around me was definitely getting to be a bad habit.

"Regardless, the result is that it raises your visibility," the Chahwyn said. "Your usefulness in this war is dependent upon your ability to remain anonymous."

"Anonymous to whom?" I countered. "The Modhri's known about me for the better part of a year now. We've managed to muddle through."

"Anonymous to those who might notice or detain you for purposes of their own," the Chahwyn said. "The purposes of Mr. Morse, for example."

"I can handle Morse," I insisted. "And if it's anonymity you're worried about, just fix me up with a few false IDs. Names might stick for a while, but faces fade."

"I'm sorry, but the decision is made," the Chahwyn said. "We will regret losing your services."

I looked at Bayta. Her face was set in a tight mask. "What exactly are you saying?" I asked.

"In the idiom of your people"—the Chahwyn's eyes flicked to Bayta, as if probing her mind for the correct phraseology—"you have been fired."

ELEVEN

For a long moment I just stared at him, unpleasant memories swirling into view. Two years ago Western Alliance Intelligence had fired me for rocking the boat on the Yandro affair. Six months ago, Larry Hardin had done likewise, though for very different reasons.

This one made three firings in a row. Another bad habit I needed to work on. "Bad idea," I said, putting on my diplomat's face. "This war is a long way from being over."

"We know that better even than you do," the Chahwyn said, a little stiffly. "As I say, we'll regret losing your services."

"You may do more than just regret it," I warned. "Not to be insulting, but I don't think you and the Spiders can handle the Modhri without me."

"There are others with your capabilities," the Chahwyn said. "A suitable new partner for Bayta will be found."

I looked at Bayta, my throat tightening. Somehow, my brain hadn't yet made it to the obvious conclusion that if I was finished with the Spiders and Chahwyn, I was finished with Bayta, too.

She'd obviously gotten there ahead of me. Her eyes were locked solidly on a patch of floor midway between her and the Chahwyn, carefully avoiding mine. "You bring in someone cold and you could end up regretting it," I warned.

"*You* were brought in cold," the Chahwyn reminded me.

"And you damn near ended up regretting it," I said bluntly. "You can't count on being lucky twice in a row."

"Bayta will know whether or not he can be trusted," he said. "You will be returned to—"

He broke off, his head turning sharply toward Bayta. Her eyes, I noted, had now risen to his.

And as they stared at each other in rigid silence, I had the eerie feeling that a battle was taking place.

I gave it about half a minute before I decided I'd been left at the kiddy table long enough. "Excuse me," I spoke up. "I hate to break in on a private conversation, but I think I can demonstrate that you need *me*, and not just some random leftover Intelligence hack."

With an effort, the Chahwyn pulled his gaze away from Bayta. "There is nothing more you can say," he said, an edge of annoyance audible beneath the music of his voice. Probably as close to actual violence as a Chahwyn could get. "We'll regret losing—"

"Yes, you said that already," I growled. "A word of advice: take a good look at the nine-pack of Lynx, Hawk, and Viper sculptures that were dug up on the Nemuti planet Veerstu a couple hundred years ago."

"The Spiders have already concluded such a study," the Chahwyn said. "It has been delivered to you."

"Yes, I read it," I said. "Now I'm telling *you* to do one."

The eye-ridge tufts twitched. "What exactly do you expect us to find?"

"I don't know," I said patiently. "That's why I want you to do the study."

"You must at least have a theory."

I'd already spun Unpleasant Theory Number One for Bayta, the idea that the Modhri might be planning to barter the Nemuti collection for a new homeland.

Time to trot out Unpleasant Theory Number Two. "I'm simply wondering if there might be something in the sculptures—some rare mineral or enzyme or something— that would allow Modhran coral to grow in something besides arctic-temperature water."

I heard Bayta's breath catch. I couldn't blame her. If the Modhri could create a homeland without that restriction, the oceans of the galaxy would literally be open to him. He could go to ground, and we wouldn't find him again in a thousand years of trying.

"We will search the records," the Chahwyn said. His voice was still melodic, but I had the feeling that some of the air had gone out of his tires, too.

"I suggest you do it fast," I said. "So . . . ?"

I held my breath. But no soap. "You will be returned to your Quadrail and your service will come to an end," he said. "As already stated."

I grimaced. Apparently he wasn't authorized to reverse Elder decisions just because I'd just done them a major service. Again.

The Chahwyn looked at Bayta, and I wondered if we were about to get a rematch of their earlier staring contest. But he then shifted his eyes back to me. "You have one week to return to Terra Station," he continued. "There you will surrender your travel document to the stationmaster."

My handy little diamond-dust-edged first-class unlimited-use Quadrail pass. I'd been hoping he would forget about that. "One week's not much time," I said, stalling.

"It's more than enough," he countered. "One week." With that he stood and walked back to the rear of the room. A door opened, and he disappeared.

"I'm sorry," Bayta murmured.

"Don't be," I assured her grimly. "It's not over yet."

We headed back to the baggage car in silence. *One week,* the time limit whispered through my mind. One week left of freedom among the Quadrail's interstellar travelers and the lurking and conspiring Modhri mind segments. One short week.

It might just be enough.

FIVE MINUTES LATER we were on the move. "What did you mean that we need you and not someone else?" Bayta asked.

"Does it matter?" I countered. "They've made up their minds."

Bayta's eyes were steady on me. "I don't want another partner, Frank," she said quietly.

Unbidden, unwanted, a lump rose into my throat. Bayta had made it clear that she considered me her friend, though I still wasn't ready to make such a commitment myself. "You've got at least one more week to be stuck with me," I assured her. "What do you think of this latest dollop of irony?"

"Which irony is that?"

"Hardin's little hate-mail campaign," I said. "Or had you forgotten Künstler's dying words?"

Bayta's eyes widened. "Is *that* what he meant by 'he hates you'?"

"What else?" I said. "Given the circles a man like Künstler traveled in, I should have thought of Hardin right from the start."

"They must not have gotten along very well," Bayta murmured.

"Hardin's an ambitious multi-trillionaire, Künstler's a rabid collector, and neither type likes losing," I said. "Your basic cookbook recipe for making enemies. Maybe I wasn't so far off with that crack about getting stopped on the street for autographs."

"I'm sure Mr. Hardin has friends, too," Bayta said diplomatically.

"And we'll do our very best to avoid them," I said.

"Anyway, the point is that Hardin's round-robin diatribe is at least partially responsible for getting us onto the trail of the Lynx in the first place. That's the kind of intangible asset the Chahwyn aren't taking into account."

Bayta shrugged. Clearly, she didn't see much benefit in having a trillionaire for an enemy, either. "What are we going to do?"

"I still have a week of free Quadrail travel," I reminded her. "That should be more than enough to get us to Ghonsilya and find Fayr. The next move will depend on what he has to tell us."

"What about Mr. Stafford and the Lynx?"

I ran the question a couple of turns around my brain. Should I tell her, or not?

Not, I decided. "If we're lucky, we'll be able to pick him up along the way," I said instead. "The line out of Ian-apof should take us to Ghonsilya with only one or two train changes."

"I suppose we can do that," Bayta said, and I could see in her face that she was wondering what I would do if I was on Ghonsilya when the time limit on my pass ran out. Quadrail traffic, even back in third class, didn't come cheap.

I didn't blame her for her unspoken concerns. I was wondering about it, too. "In the meantime," I went on, "we'll see about taking a crack at the Hawk the walkers are sitting on."

Bayta gave me that patented strained look of hers again. But she was apparently too drained by the encounter with the Chahwyn to argue the point. "We'll see," she said instead. Lowering herself to the floor, she put her back against a stack of crates and closed her eyes.

I sat down, too, and did likewise.

Because there was another reason the Chahwyn might want to reconsider firing me. A very important one.

But I wasn't ready to let Bayta in on that secret, either. Not yet.

Especially since I might be wrong.

AN HOUR LATER we reconnected with our train. As far as I could tell as we worked our way forward, no one had missed us.

The server Spiders had, of course, long since cleared away our half-empty glasses from the table where we'd left them. I ordered us two more drinks, lemonade for Bayta, iced tea for me. "Where were we?" I asked as we settled into our chairs. "Right—I was asking about the separation wall's default settings."

"And you were talking insanity," she said. "The Modhri would never have put the Hawk on board unless he had enough walkers here to protect it. If we try to steal it, we might trigger the same thing that happened on our trip back from the Sistarrko system."

"I doubt it," I said. "Remember, there he had a source of Modhri coral to work with. I doubt he has anything like that here. Besides, who said anything about stealing the Hawk?"

She was still frowning at me when the server tapped up and delivered our drinks. "You want to break into the compartment and *not* steal it?" she asked at last.

"Of course not," I said, putting some dignity into my voice. "Stealing's against the law. So if there's a power glitch do the wall locks stay on or go off?"

For a moment she continued to stare at me. Then, her eyes flattened as she consulted with the experts. "They'd go off," she said. "But the wall would still stay closed."

"Not a problem, provided the Modhri inside doesn't notice the power glitch," I assured her. "*And* provided we're already on the other side of the wall."

"Which would mean breaking into the other half of that compartment."

"Possibly," I said. "Let's find out first which compartment the Hawk's in, and who has the other half."

Neither bit of information proved difficult to collect. As with every Quadrail, conductor Spiders were continuously roaming the aisles, and a few minutes of silent interrogation and cross-checking on Bayta's part did the trick.

"The Jurian in compartment seven is the one who hasn't been outside since we left Jurskala," Bayta said. "The connecting compartment is occupied by another Jurian, a diplomatic consul."

"We can work with that," I said. "I don't suppose we're lucky enough for one of Penny's friends to have the compartment across the corridor from him."

"No," she said. "But Giovan Toya, one of the group, is two down from it. Will that help?"

"Not really," I said. "But that's okay. We'll just have to do it on the fly."

"How?" she asked.

"Just leave it to me," I said, patting her hand. "Order me another iced tea, will you? I need to go find Morse."

MORSE WAS NOT amused. Not even close.

"You have *got* to be joking," he growled when I'd finished outlining my plan. "You're talking about breaking and entering. That's a felony. *Two* felonies."

"One: there won't be any breaking involved," I corrected. "You're going to get him to leave; I'm going to get inside before the door closes. So no breaking. Two: the Quadrail is under Spider jurisdiction. Human and Jurian laws don't apply."

Morse snorted. "Somehow, I don't think the consul will see it that way."

"And three," I added, "this may be the key to nailing down this whole Nemuti sculpture mystery. Possibly including the key to Rafael Künstler's murder."

His lip twitched at that one. No doubt he still thought

I was involved with Künstler's death. "It's still lunatic," he insisted. "Why would a ranking Jurian diplomat get himself involved in theft and murder?"

"Why does anyone get involved in that sort of mess?" I countered, looking quickly for a reason that didn't require me to mention the Modhri. "Greed, blackmail, bad judgment, even just being in the wrong place at the wrong time. Pick one."

"Wrong place and time certainly seems to be *my* problem these days," Morse muttered.

"A quick look inside his compartment, and I'm done," I promised.

"And that's *all* you're doing?" he asked, gazing hard at me. "Fair is fair, Compton. I'm sticking my neck out here, far enough to look backward down the Chunnel. I need the whole story."

"You have it," I assured him, stifling a twinge of conscience. He didn't have the whole story, of course. He barely had the first page. But I couldn't give him all of it. Not yet. "I get in, I look for the Hawk, and I get out."

"And you promise that this is it?" Morse persisted. "That if the Hawk's not there you aren't going to want to work your way through all the rest of the compartments?"

"Scout's honor," I said. "If the consul hasn't got it, the entire theory department's back to square one."

For a moment he continued to measure me with his eyes. Then, he shook his head. "Losutu had better be right about you," he said. "All right. Tell me what you want me to do."

WE WAITED UNTIL late in the Quadrail's night schedule, hoping to increase the chances that the Hawk's courier would be sleeping. Whether the Modhri colony inside him would also be asleep, unfortunately, was anyone's guess.

Morse didn't know about that part, of course. My

rationale to him was that the late hour would catch the Jurian consul in the other compartment in a half-awake state where he might be more easily manipulated.

It was a few minutes after one o'clock when Morse carefully positioned himself in front of the consul's door and touched the chime button.

A minute went by. Nothing. Morse glanced over at Bayta and me as we leaned against the corridor wall five meters farther forward, pretending to be engaged in a heartfelt conversation. I nodded toward the door, and Morse keyed the chime again. Another half minute went by, and then the door slid open and a Jurian face leaned out, eyes blinking groggily above his beak. "What is this you do, Human?" he demanded.

"My name's Morse," Morse said, holding up his ID wallet. "Terran Confederation EuroUnion Security Service. We have a situation two cars back that requires the assistance of a Resolver."

"I am not a Resolver," the Juri said. But I could hear the growing interest in his voice. All Jurian diplomats had at least a modicum of Resolver training, and a lot of them had ambitions in that direction. Getting called in to fix a social problem aboard a Quadrail would be a nice step toward that goal.

"I was misinformed," Morse said, playing it with a perfect mix of respect and regret. "My apologies."

"Not so hastily, Mr. Morse," the Juri said, lifting a hand to block Morse's departure. "Perhaps I can still assist."

"I wouldn't want to disturb you," Morse said.

"It would be my honor to assist," the Juri said. "Permit me a moment to garb myself."

He stepped back into the room and the door slid shut. Morse looked back at me, his eyebrows raised questioningly. I nodded encouragement as I straightened up from the section of wall I'd been leaning against and prepared for action. I'd spent an hour practicing this maneuver in one of Penny's friends' compartments, but it was still going to take perfect timing to pull it off.

Morse nodded back and gave one last look at my rolled-up belt peeking from between his feet, looking for all the world like a large black snail or nautilus shell. Most people, I knew, seldom looked down unless there was some actual reason to do so. I hoped the Juri was like most people.

The door slid open again and the Juri stepped out into the corridor, nattily attired now in full diplomatic regalia. He must *really* want that promotion to Resolver. "Take me to this conflict," he ordered Morse.

"This way," Morse said, gesturing toward the rear door. As he did, I left Bayta and started walking casually toward them.

The Juri glanced incuriously at me as he stepped past Morse and headed aft. Morse fell into step beside and slightly behind him as the compartment door started to slide closed.

And as I reached the spot where Morse had been standing, I gave the coiled belt a gentle sideways nudge with my foot, sending it unrolling across the corridor and dropping its tip neatly across the path of the sliding door.

Quadrail compartment doors had built-in safeties that were supposed to make sure they didn't close on someone in the process of passing through. But those sensors were clustered midway along the panel. Way down at the bottom, there was nothing but the backup pressure sensors designed to stop the door's movement before it exerted any significant pressure on a Jurian back claw, Shorshian tail, or Human toe.

The key was that, unlike the main safeties, the pressure sensors would merely stop the door and wait there for further instructions.

The Juri fell for it, of course. There was practically no way he couldn't have. He'd heard his door closing, he *hadn't* heard the soft whoosh of it reopening, and the only person who'd been nearby as it closed—me—hadn't even broken stride as I walked along behind the two of them at the corner of his sight.

I made sure to keep walking with them all the way to the end of the car. There I courteously allowed them to go into the vestibule first.

As soon as they'd vanished behind the door, I did a one-eighty and hurried back to the compartment. I had maybe ten minutes now while Morse searched in vain for the alleged travelers whose alleged confrontation had sent him looking for diplomatic smoothing in the first place.

Bayta was waiting, her throat muscles working nervously. "See?" I said. "No worries." I reached into the narrow gap between door and jamb, and as my fingers triggered the safeties, the door gave its little whoosh and slid open again. I ushered Bayta inside, scooping up my belt from the floor as I followed.

The Juri's compartment had the almost pathological neatness I'd come to expect from ambitious rank-climbing members of the galaxy's various diplomatic corps. His personal items were precisely positioned, with the clothing hanging in the cleaning rack actually laid out in descending spectrum order of basic color. If the Hawk had been in here, I reflected, I would probably have found it filed alphabetically in his luggage.

"Douse the lights," I murmured to Bayta as I stepped to the back of the compartment and the wall switch that controlled the collapsing divider wall.

The room went dark. A moment later, I sensed the movement of air that meant she'd joined me. "You ready?" I asked.

"As ready as I'm going to be," she said. "Wait—the window."

"Right." Reaching over to the control, I opaqued the window, cutting off the last bit of faint reflected glow from the Coreline overhead. Moving back to the wall, I pressed my ear against it.

Nothing. Still, given the Spiders' soundproofing and the clickity-clack of the wheels below me, the courier would have to have a live-spec music party going in there for me to hear anything. "Okay," I murmured to Bayta. "Glitch number one: now."

With the room's lights out, there was no obvious indication that we'd just suffered a quarter-second power flicker. "Ready glitch number two," I said, and pressed the wall release.

Against my hand, I felt the wall begin to retract.

It didn't open very far, making it only about half a meter before Bayta's mental order to the Spiders again shut down power to the double compartment. But that was all I needed. Squeezing Bayta's arm reassuringly, I slipped through the gap.

The courier had also opaqued his window, with the result that the compartment was as black as a politician's financial records. Fortunately, our trip in the tender had given me a fair amount of experience in moving around a blacked-out Quadrail compartment. Hoping the courier wasn't the sort to leave his laundry piled in the middle of the floor, I made my way toward the bed.

I could hear the sound of slow breathing now. If the Modhri colony was awake and aware of my presence, he was being very quiet about it. I reached the bed and located the rack above it. There were three good-sized pieces of luggage up there, none of them the easily carried hand bag I was expecting.

Had the Modhri mind segment decided that the shoulder bag idea was too obvious and stashed the Hawk in with the courier's regular stuff? I hoped not. Opening and digging through someone's luggage in pitch-darkness wasn't something I really wanted to try.

But there was one other possibility. Using the sound of the Juri's breathing to orient myself, I eased my fingertips toward the spot where his chest ought to be.

There it was: a leather carrying bag, about the size of the late Mr. Gerashchenko's lugeboard case, gripped in the Juri's arms like a child's beloved stuffed animal.

I smiled tightly in the darkness. With the sleeper's arms wrapped around it, the bag would be nearly impossible to steal or open. Even if the Modhran colony was sleeping or otherwise unaware of his surroundings, a disturbance on that scale would surely startle both him and the walker himself awake.

But as I'd told Morse, I wasn't here to steal anything.

My reader was already tricked out into its sensor mode. Pulling it out, I started moving it slowly and deliberately down the side of the bag, a centimeter or so above the leather.

"Compton," the Juri murmured.

I froze. The sleeper hadn't stirred, and the word had come out with a definite slurring to it. Was the Juri talking in his sleep? Setting my teeth, I got the scanner moving again.

"Compton," the mumbled word came again. "Give me the Lynx."

I felt the hairs on the back of my neck begin to tingle. This wasn't anyone's sleep-talk. The Modhri was talking to me. "I don't have it," I murmured.

"Find it," the Modhri said. "Give it to me. Then you may retire in safety and wealth."

"Thanks for the offer," I said, forcing myself to continue moving the scanner in the same slow and steady motion. Maybe in the darkness the Modhri didn't realize what I was doing. But whether he did or not, it was for damn sure that I wasn't going to get a second crack at this. "I'll think about it."

"Bring me the Lynx," he repeated. The Juri gave a little sigh and readjusted his shoulders before settling down again.

Conversation over, apparently. I finished the scan and shut down the reader. Then, just out of curiosity, I reached to the top end of the bag and got a grip on it.

The sleeping Juri stiffened, his arms tightening reflexively around his prize. But he didn't wake up; and I, for my part, wasn't interested in pushing the Modhri any farther than I already had. Letting go of the bag, I backed carefully across the compartment. As I slipped through the opening, I felt Bayta reach around behind me and touch the control, and the wall slid shut again.

"I heard voices," she whispered tensely in my ear. "Was that you?"

"Later," I said, taking her hand and leading her back to the door.

We were sitting in our chairs watching the dit rec comedy playing on the nearest display window when Morse and a disappointed-looking Juri consul headed through on their way back to the compartment car.

TWELVE

We waited another half hour, just to make sure everything had settled down. Then, once again retreating to the bar, we examined the sensor record.

And found nothing.

"What the bloody hell is this?" Morse demanded, frowning at the reader screen. "This your idea of a joke?"

"Hardly," I said. I hadn't wanted him along, but he'd insisted, and after his help I couldn't really refuse him. "Or if it is, it's being played on the universe at large. We're talking one very interesting object here."

"No, we're talking one very harmless carrybag," Morse retorted, dropping the reader back on the table. "Unless you're going to tell me these Nemuti sculptures can morph into brocade dressing robes?"

I spread my hands helplessly. "What can I say? All the signs pointed to the Hawk being in there."

Morse snorted. "And here I always thought it was the Yandro fiasco that got you kicked out of Westali."

"Meaning?" I asked, feeling a stirring of anger.

"You're the big clever Yank detective—you figure it out." Abruptly he stood up. "If you'll excuse me, we're due into Ian-apof in an hour and I have to make sure Ms. Auslander's packed and ready to go." He strode out of the bar and headed forward.

I watched him go, then turned to Bayta. "Well?" I invited.

"Well what?" she said. Her eyes were troubled, but there was none of the contempt or disappointment in her face that Morse had just spilled out onto the table. "The sensor must have failed."

I shook my head. "I've already run a self-test. The sensor was working perfectly."

"Then where is the Hawk?"

"It's in the Juri's bag, right where we expected it to be," I told her. "Before I left the compartment I got a grip on the bag, just to see what the Modhri's reaction would be, and I could feel something hard and solid in there. Something that felt very much like the slightly bulbous tip of the Hawk that we saw in the pictures."

Bayta craned her neck to look at the reader's display again. "I don't see that at all."

"Neither did the sensor," I said grimly. "Apparently, the Hawk and its brother sculptures are sensor transparent."

She looked up at me, her eyes widening. "They're *what*? How can that be possible?"

"I have no idea," I said. "Actually, no, let me back up a little. The Hawk's not simply invisible—if it was, there'd be a hole in the middle of the sensor image. It's more like a sensor chameleon, something that takes on and mimics the characteristics of its surroundings."

"But then how can we see it and take pictures of it?" she protested. "Visible light is just another part of the electromagnetic spectrum, like infrared and radar."

"How can we see through ordinary glass while it still blocks ultraviolet and some infrared?" I countered. "Like I said, I have no idea how it's done. Especially since sitting alone all by itself the Hawk must look like *something* on a sensor scan. Otherwise, they sure wouldn't have been relegated to the status of third-rate folk art."

Bayta lowered her eyes to the display again, and I could see in her expression that she was starting to work through the serious implications of this whole thing.

Because Unpleasant Theory Number One had just been kicked out of the lineup. Whatever the Modhri wanted with these sculptures, it wasn't a simple trade of exotic but ordinary artwork for a new homeland site. The Nemuti sculptures were either a weird material à la Unpleasant Theory Number Two, or something even worse.

And with their self-generating cloak of sort-of invisibility, even the Spiders' massive and wide-ranging Tube station sensor system might not have a hope in hell of spotting them.

Bayta was obviously thinking the same thing. "The Spiders can't detect them," she murmured. "The Modhri can take them anywhere he wants."

"That's the bad news," I agreed. "The good news is that he apparently still needs the third Lynx to make his plan work."

"How do you know?"

"Because he offered to let me retire in peace if I got it for him."

Bayta's eyes were steady on me. Possibly she was remembering that the Chahwyn were basically forcing me into retirement anyway. "What did you tell him?"

"That I'd think about it," I said. "It seemed the safest thing to say."

"But he'll be watching you."

"Me and everyone else," I agreed. "Especially Morse and Penny and the rest of Penny's friends."

Bayta grimaced. "Who are going to lead him right to Mr. Stafford."

I looked around the bar. None of the other patrons was within hearing distance of us. "Hardly," I said, lowering my voice anyway. "Stafford's not on Ian-apof."

Bayta frowned. "But he told them to meet him there."

"Your classic red herring," I told her. "You haul out something big and fat and obvious and slap it down on the table in the hope that the bad guys will be so busy staring at it that they won't notice you sneaking off somewhere else."

"You're saying he's using them?" Bayta asked, apparently still not believing it. "He's using his *friends*?"

"Why so surprised?" I asked. "This is a guy who spent his summer vacations hanging around Rafael Künstler, trillionaire and rabid art collector. Using your friends, acquaintances, and enemies is standard procedure with that crowd."

"So you've said," Bayta murmured. "It still doesn't . . . never mind. But if he's not on Ian-apof, where is he?"

"That's the wonderful irony of it," I said. "He's—"

I broke off. Across the bar, Penny Auslander had appeared in the corridor. For a moment she stood there, her eyes sweeping the room. Then she spotted us and started across. "Play it cool," I murmured.

Penny reached the table and sat down. "I need to talk to you," she said, her voice low and urgent.

"Please; sit down," I said, gesturing to the chair she was already planted in.

A waste of good sarcasm. "It's Agent Morse," she said. "I'm starting to wonder if I can trust him."

"I thought we were the ones you didn't trust," I said.

She lowered her eyes a little. "I didn't," she admitted. "But I've been thinking about . . . what happened to Pyotr. Even Agent Morse admits you were somewhere else at the time."

"Yes, I believe we tried telling you that."

"I know," she said tartly, some of the old Penny peeking through. The girl had fire, that was for sure. "I'm trying to say I'm sorry."

"Apology accepted," I said. "Thank you for—"

"And I want you to come down to the ski resort with us."

I shook my head. "I'm sorry, but we have urgent business elsewhere."

"But we need you," Penny said. "Daniel needs you. I'm—" Her throat tightened. "Mr. Morse says he's in danger."

I thought about Künstler, beaten to death amid the quiet luxury of a Quadrail compartment. "That's possible," I conceded. "But Mr. Morse himself seems capable enough of dealing with any trouble."

"You're not listening," Penny said impatiently. "I don't *trust* him."

I looked at Bayta, and it wasn't hard to read her thoughts. I only had a few days left on my Quadrail pass. If I spent those days riding a torchliner from the Ianapof Station inward to the inner system, I would likely end up stranded there. I would certainly never make it to Ghonsilya and our hoped-for rendezvous with Fayr. "I'm sorry," I said again. "For whatever comfort it might be, I don't think anyone's actually out to hurt Mr. Stafford."

For a long moment Penny stared at me, her expression bringing the full weight of her family's wealth and position to bear. I returned her gaze without flinching, and with a twitch of her lip she turned the glare back down to low power. "I see," she said stiffly. "Thank you for your time." Standing up, she strode out of the bar and disappeared again down the corridor.

"Some people are never satisfied," I commented, taking a sip of my iced tea. "I wonder what kind of man she *does* like? Rich kids with rich daddies, I suppose."

"I don't know," Bayta said thoughtfully. "How sure are we that Mr. Morse isn't a walker?"

I shrugged. "Statistically, the odds are against it," I said. "We know the Modhri hasn't made much of an incursion into Human space."

"Or he hadn't as of a few months ago," Bayta countered. "Even then, though, he had some walkers at the UN and other places."

She had a point, unfortunately. With Earth law banning the import of corals and corallike substances, the Modhri hadn't been able to bring in the outposts that he'd used as base camps for his infiltration of most of the other societies throughout the galaxy. Still, we knew he'd managed to create a certain presence for himself, mostly among the behind-the-scenes personnel in Earth's various power centers.

And an ESS agent like Morse probably got out into the galaxy enough for the Modhri to have possibly snared him somewhere along the way.

"It's certainly possible," I told Bayta. "But he seems awfully antagonistic toward me for someone with a Modhran mind segment whispering behavioral cues in his ear."

"Unless the Modhri's keeping quiet and trying not to influence him."

"Sure, but why?" I countered. "You catch more flies with honey than vinegar, to dust off an old saying. Even if Morse had a good reason to hate me, it would pay the Modhri to try to suppress that and make him a more enthusiastic ally."

"Maybe he thought you'd be suspicious of a total stranger who wanted to assist us."

"Maybe," I agreed. "On the other hand, we're fellow toilers in the Intelligence service trenches. That should automatically raise me above the standard random citizen in his eyes."

"Except that he doesn't like you."

"Which the Modhri should be able to suppress, as I said." I shook my head. "Bottom line is that we're probably not going to know for sure whether Morse is a walker unless the Modhri makes a mistake."

Bayta shivered. "Or takes him over."

"Right," I said, suppressing a shiver of my own. "But at least he can't do that without our knowing about it. There are definite vocal and facial changes I know how to spot." I took another sip of my tea. "Meantime, we just pretend Morse is as untrustworthy as everyone else and play our cards as close to our chests as possible. *And* try to get to Stafford before the Modhri does."

"Yes," Bayta murmured. "You may have been right about the Modhri not wanting to hurt Mr. Stafford. But at the same time, he won't hesitate to do so if he thinks it necessary."

I grimaced. "I know."

"But you say you know where he is?"

"Pretty much." I took a last swallow of tea and stood up. "Come on. The least we can do is see Penny and her friends off."

THE IAN-APOF STATION was fairly small, reflecting the modest size and ambitions of the planetary system itself. As far as I could tell from my encyclopedia, the planet's skiing, lugeboarding, and rock climbing facilities were about all they had that might appeal to the interstellar tourist.

Still, those facilities were apparently pretty impressive, and the station's designers had worked hard to make sure that no one who passed through their Quadrail station forgot it. Each of the dozen restaurants, waiting rooms, shops, and sleeping-room facilities had been painted and textured to look like craggy cliff sides, snow-covered forests, or majestic glaciers. With trains stopping less frequently than at larger stations, the Halkas here had even put in a public dit rec facility, whose tall sides had been sloped upward into a Matterhorn-like peak. Looking at it all, I could practically feel frostbite working its way into my feet.

We said our good-byes to Morse and Penny and her friends at the platform. Penny was rather subdued, probably still annoyed that I hadn't properly fallen all over myself obeying her request to escort her to the inner system. Morse, for his part, seemed to have gotten over the—to him—perceived fiasco of my midnight reconnoiter and had gone back to his normal attitude of simmering dislike.

I was glad to be rid of the pair of them.

Bayta and I watched the group make their way toward the exit hatchway waiting area—apparently Ian-apof transfer station shuttles ran on an on-demand basis—and then headed for the main Quadrail waiting room. "How soon until the next train to Ghonsilya?" I asked Bayta as we walked.

"About two hours," she said.

Way too long, I decided, to just sit around a waiting room counting the cracks in the fake rock formations. "In that case, let's get something to drink," I said, changing course toward a restaurant decorated to look like a very intimidating rock chimney. I'd never done any rock climbing myself, but I'd heard enough stories to know it wasn't a hobby I would be taking up anytime soon.

"By the way, there was a data chip waiting for you with the stationmaster," she said as we walked. "I went and got it while you were telling Ms. Auslander—again—that we weren't going with them."

I winced a little at the frost in her tone. She very definitely didn't like Penny. "And?"

"It was from Deputy Director Losutu," she said. "Agent Morse is indeed who he claims to be."

"He's sure?"

"He sent us Agent Morse's complete ESS personnel file," Bayta said, handing me a data chip. "From what I glanced at, it looked fine. But you'll be able to tell better than I can."

So much for the possibility that the Modhri had tried to throw in a ringer. Still, that had never been more than an outside chance anyway. With modern technologies making a person's identity easy to check, a charade like that wouldn't hold up long enough to be very useful. "I'll look it over later," I said.

The restaurant's outside wilderness decor unfortunately carried over to the interior, with the added bonus of a whistling-wind soundtrack running in the background. The floor was painted to give the illusion that your table was halfway up the side of a cliff that even a mountain goat would avoid. Idly, I wondered how many acrophobes they got who took one look and ran out screaming.

Our iced tea, lemonade, and onion rings had just arrived when the door opened, and I looked up to see Morse hurrying toward us. "Where is she?" he demanded.

"Where is who?" I asked, frowning.

"Don't play the fool," he snapped. "She's been trying for the past hour to get me to order you to come to Ianapof with us."

"Like you could actually do that," I said, looking past him out the window. There were maybe twenty or thirty other waiting passengers milling around out there. None of them was Penny Auslander. "When did you see her last?"

"She went to the washroom about fifteen minutes ago," Morse said, turning to follow my line of sight. "When she didn't come out, I sent one of the other girls in to check on her. She must have sneaked out the other door."

I looked at Bayta. Sneaked out, or was helped out. "Where are the rest of them?" I asked, pulling out a cash stick and plugging it into the table's jack to pay for the drinks and onion rings that it looked like we weren't going to be enjoying.

"At the shuttle waiting room," Morse said. "I told them to stay together and not move until I got back."

"Were they good with that?" I asked as the three of us headed for the door.

Morse made a noise in the back of his throat. "Who knows? I don't exactly have authority to order *them* to do anything, either. Are you telling me Ms. Auslander *didn't* come looking for you?"

"If she did, she didn't find me," I told him, pausing outside the restaurant to take stock of the situation. "Okay. She didn't get on a shuttle, because you would have seen her."

"Correct," Morse said. "Besides which, none have docked since we arrived."

"Ditto for any trains," I said. "Ergo, she's still somewhere in the station."

"Brilliant, Holmes," Morse growled. "Problem: there are fourteen buildings, not counting the Spiders' private ones, and only three of us to search them all. If she cares to, she can play hide the button all day." He looked at Bayta. "Unless you can persuade your Spider friends to join in the hunt."

Bayta looked along the curved Tube floor to a pair of cargo trains with Spiders swarming busily around them. "They're all already occupied," she told him. "We'll have to do it on our own."

Morse grunted. "Lovely. Any suggestions as to where we begin?"

"We begin by splitting up," I said. "Like you said, there's a lot of ground to cover."

"I thought you'd probably say that." Morse pointed toward one end of the station and a triad of gift shops clustered around a restaurant. "I'll start with that end."

"We'll take the other," I said. "I suggest you start at the far side and work your way back toward the middle."

"Thank you; I *do* know something about the technique," Morse said acidly. Giving the area around us one final visual sweep, he strode off toward his target buildings.

I took Bayta's arm and headed us off in the other direction. "You think she's in danger?" Bayta asked quietly.

"I don't know why she would be," I said. "The Modhri must have realized by now that she doesn't know where Stafford is."

"Maybe Mr. Künstler told them he didn't know where the Lynx was, either."

I grimaced. At which point the walkers had beaten him to death just to make sure. "Point," I conceded. "The Modhri doesn't seem to be the trusting sort." Directly ahead of us, a wiry Pirk with an expensive plumed headdress came to a halt in front of one of the schedule holodisplays, his hands idly preening his feathers as he gazed up at the listings.

It was the sort of thing Quadrail travelers did all the time. Problem was, this particular traveler had been looking at an identical display when Morse and Bayta and I had first emerged from the restaurant not two minutes ago. Either he had the galaxy's worst short-term memory, or he wasn't here to look at schedules. "But we can sort out the details once we find her," I continued, keeping my voice casual. "Why don't you start with those two cafés over there"—I pointed to the buildings nearest the working Spiders—"and I'll hit the dit rec and sleeping-room buildings." I indicated the two window-less structures directly past the Pirk. "If she's not there, we'll expand the search to the service buildings."

"You think we should split up?" Bayta asked, her tone making it clear that she herself didn't think much of the idea.

"We'll be all right," I soothed, patting her shoulder and then giving her a gentle push. "Go on, get going. Meet me here when you're done."

She studied my face a moment. But whatever her doubts or suspicions, they weren't strong enough to override her basic tendency toward obedience. Turning, she headed toward the two cafés.

I let her get a few steps away, then continued toward the Pirk. He was still studying the display, standing in fact directly between me and the dit rec building. As I veered a little to go around him, he swiveled and tufted his ear feathers in the traditional gesture of greeting. [Ah—a Human,] he said in scratch-voiced Karli. [May your day be rich with joy and profit.]

"May your day be likewise," I said, touching my hand to the top of my ear in the proper response by those of us whose biomechanical design had somehow neglected the need for full-range ear movement. "You are well?"

[Well and most content,] he replied. [I have just finished savoring the pleasure of one of your classic Human dit rec dramas. Its name—what was its name again?]

"I'm afraid I can't help you on that," I said politely.

This Pirk seemed even more aromatic than usual for his species, and I had to force myself not to widen the circle I was already making around him.

[*Ten Angry Men,*] he said suddenly, his ear feathers making little circles. [That was the title. *Ten Angry Men.*]

"An excellent drama," I agreed. The other standard response to Pirkarli aroma, aside from creating more distance, was to talk a lot, permitting more air to bypass the nose on its way in and out of the lungs. "But I believe you'll find the title is actually *Twelve Angry Men.*"

[Ah, yes, indeed,] he said. [That was the number. Thank you. We shall have to remember that.] His ears flattened slightly. [Rather, *I* shall have to remember. You have no such need, as you already know.]

"You're welcome," I said, nodding as I finished my half circle and thankfully started widening the distance between us. "A fine furtherance of the day to you."

[And to you, Human.] Briskly, he strode away.

Mentally, I shook my head. A dit rec drama, and the number twelve. If they ever handed out prizes for unsubtlety, the Modhri would take the top three places.

From the outside, as I'd already noted, the dit rec building looked like a miniature Matterhorn. Inside, I discovered, its designers had gone even more overboard. The central corridor, instead of carving a clean, straight line through the middle of the building, twisted like the meandering path of a drunken sailor trying to find the door. Its walls were craggy and angled, the light overhead dim and diffuse, the overall effect that of a narrow northside mountain crevice straight out of some Icelandic saga.

Even more impressive, it came complete with a set of Icelandic trolls.

There were three of them, all Halkas, grouped loosely together in the corridor like watchful statues a few meters past the door marked *12*. The biggest of them was an unexpectedly familiar face: the Halka on the Bellisbound Quadrail who'd pulled me away from Künstler's dying body and tossed me down the Quadrail corridor.

One of the other two was the fifth walker from Jurskala, the one who'd conveniently disappeared during our mad chase after Pyotr Gerashchenko. Apparently, the Modhri was consolidating his best forces here. Probably not a good sign. Watching the Halkas out of the corner of my eye, I opened the door and went inside.

Public viewing facilities like this normally included a variety of room sizes, ranging from those suitable for single viewers to larger ones that could accommodate groups of ten to fifteen. Room Twelve was in the middle of that range, with five large seats arranged in a semicircle around the dit rec display. At first I thought the room was deserted, but as I walked around one end of the semicircle I saw there was a single middle-aged Human lying along the farthest of the seats, his head pillowed on one armrest and his knees angled somewhat awkwardly over the other. There was a silk scarf across his face, as if there to shield his eyes from the dim light, covering everything down to his upper lip. His mouth was slightly open, his breathing the slow and methodical rhythm of a man in deep sleep. Playing to itself on the display was a classic Harold Lloyd dit rec silent comedy.

"Nice choice," I commented quietly as I continued around the end of the seats and came to a halt facing the sleeping man. "A silent dit rec means no annoying soundtrack to interfere with your friend's nap."

"Thank you," the man said.

Though not really the man, of course. The stiffness of his shoulders, the subtle tightness of voice and jaw and throat muscles, were all I needed to know that I was once again speaking directly to the Modhri.

"You're welcome," I said. "You're both missing a good dit rec, though."

"He needed the sleep," the Modhri said. "And I find Human humor tedious." He stretched his arms once, the gesture somehow making him look even less Human than he already did. Unhooking his legs from the chair arm, he swiveled himself back up into a sitting position.

The scarf covering his face started to slip off, but he got a hand up in time and readjusted it back into place. "Please; sit down."

"That's okay—I've been sitting all day," I said, staying where I was. Sitting in any of the remaining chairs would mean putting my back to the door, which I wasn't interested in doing. "What did you want to talk about?"

"The third Lynx, formerly owned by the Human Künstler," he said. "I want it."

"So I've heard," I said. "What I *don't* understand is what kind of appeal an old Nemuti sculpture can possibly have for a galaxy-spanning supermind like you."

"They intrigue me." He paused, as if searching for the right phrase. "Perhaps they will go well together on my mantel."

"I thought you said you didn't like Human humor."

"I said it was tedious," he corrected. "I didn't say it wasn't a useful tool. What would it take to persuade you to deliver the Lynx to me?"

"Number one: I've seen how trustworthy your promises are," I said. "Number two: you couldn't afford me even if I *did* trust you. And number three: I haven't got the Lynx."

"But you know where it is," he said. "That puts you ahead of the fools who seek the Human Stafford on Ianapof."

"You don't think he's there?"

"*You* don't think he's there," the Modhri countered. "Else you would be preparing to travel to the inner system with them."

"Who says?" I countered. "Maybe I just don't fancy an eight-day torchliner trip in the company of people who don't like me. Maybe I'm planning on taking a later torchliner, or renting myself a private torchyacht."

"Or maybe you already know where the Human Stafford is." He cocked his head. "Tell me, do you find the Human Auslander an attractive female?"

"I hadn't really noticed," I said, trying to keep the sudden tension out of my voice. There was only one direction he could be going with this particular change of topic.

"Really," the Modhri said interestedly. "I would have said she is. Certainly judging by my host's reaction to her. She is also somewhat younger than you, I believe. Like most species, I've found Humans to be especially protective toward their young."

"That only applies to children," I told him. Probably a waste of effort, but I had to try. "Ms. Auslander is an adult. Who, I might add, can't tell you anything about Stafford that you don't already know."

"Yet her presence might be useful in bringing him into the open."

"Stafford's on the run," I reminded him. "He's going to be suspicious of anyone who shows up with unknown friends in tow. Even Ms. Auslander."

"So she is truly of no use to me?" The Modhri shrugged. "Pity. Then I suppose I might as well kill her."

"Hardly seems worth the effort," I said, keeping my voice even. If anything happened to Penny, there was no way in hell that Morse wouldn't find a way to pin it on me. "Besides, vengeance is for the weak and small-minded. That hardly applies to you."

"You flatter me," he said. "Still, you're right: I kill only when necessary. But perhaps in this case it *is* necessary. Why do you think I have my host's face covered this way?"

I shrugged. The answer was pretty obvious, with some ominous implications. "I assumed it was because you *really* don't like Human dit rec comedies," I improvised.

"Come now, Compton," he chided. "You surely know better than that. I still have use of this Eye, and don't wish his identity to be compromised by your sight."

"Ah," I said, as if I hadn't already figured that out. "He's one of your spies in the UN, I suppose?"

He gave me what was probably intended to be a sly smile. "Please. No one gives away information for free. But I *will* trade you his identity for the Lynx."

I snorted. "And then suicide him before we can get anything of value from him? No thanks."

"Yet therein lies my dilemma," he said. "It may be that the Human Auslander saw this Eye's face. In that case, killing her would not be vengeance but a necessary act of self-preservation."

"*Did* she see his face?"

"It may be," he repeated.

I puffed out a breath of air, the small sane part of my mind appreciating the neat little box the Modhri had put me in. If Penny had indeed seen the hidden face, the Modhri genuinely would be justified in killing her, at least from his point of view.

Of course, she was still on the station, which meant that Bayta and the Spiders still had a chance of finding her before the Modhri could do anything drastic. But even if they could, the Modhri had the advantage in position and recon setup, and it was a long way back to Earth. If he really wanted Penny dead there was probably no way any of us could stop him.

Which meant her life was now squarely in my hands, which was clearly where the Modhri wanted it. "I already told you I don't have the Lynx," I said.

"I believe you," he said. "But you *do* know where the Human Stafford is. I would be willing to trade the female's life for that information."

"First bring Ms. Auslander here," I said. "When I see she's all right, I'll tell you."

For a moment the faceless face studied me through the filmy silk. "And then?"

"Then we say good-bye, Ms. Auslander goes skiing with her friends, and you and I race to see which of us can get to Stafford first."

He smiled again. It was even more grotesque this time. "With the Spiders who control the Quadrail as your allies? I think not."

Briefly, I wondered what his reaction would be if he

knew the Spiders had already fired me. Probably best not to bring that up. "You want me to stay here, then?"

"We will go find the Human Stafford together," he said. "You *and* the female, with my Arms accompanying you. She will be useful as leverage."

"Against whom?" I asked. "I already told you she can't help pry Stafford out of hiding."

"Not leverage against him," he said. "Leverage against you."

Behind him, the door opened and Penny appeared, stumbling in as if some unseen person had given her a shove. "Mr. Compton!" she said as she recovered her balance. "What's going on? They said I couldn't leave—"

"It's all right," I interrupted her soothingly. "Just a misunderstanding."

Her eyes narrowed slightly, flicked to my companion, then back to me. "Look, I don't know what he's been trying to sell you—"

"But it's all cleared up now," I said. "You ready to go find your fiancé?"

"—but this was no—" She broke off as her brain caught up to her ears. "What?"

"We think we know where Daniel is," I said, watching the Modhri out of the corner of my eye. "He's somewhere in Magaraa City on the Tra'hok Unity planet of Ghonsilya."

Penny's mouth dropped open a centimeter. "*Ghonsilya?*" she echoed. "What in the galaxy is he doing *there*?"

"We'll ask him when we get there," I said, taking a step around the chairs toward her. "Let's go get your things and say good-bye to your friends."

"I think Ms. Auslander deserves to know first why we're going to Ghonsilya," the Modhri said.

Or in other words, he wasn't going to let me lead him across the galaxy on a wild goose chase without something solid to back it up. "If you insist," I said, wishing briefly that Bayta was here. I always liked her to be around when I was being clever. "Everyone's been assuming that Daniel stole Mr. Künstler's Lynx. He didn't. Mr. Künstler gave it to him."

"He *gave* it to him?" Penny asked. "When?"

"Sometime before the attempted burglary." I raised my eyebrows toward the Modhri. "Probably shortly after Mr. Künstler was approached by agents trying to buy it."

The Modhri's lip twitched, just enough to confirm my guess was right. Of course he would have tried the straightforward approach before attempting anything as risky as a burglary.

"Daniel never mentioned that," Penny protested.

"Mr. Künstler probably told him not to tell anyone, including you," I said. "The fact that the other two Nemuti Lynxes had already been stolen from their owners would have made him extra cagey with his. The point is that Daniel didn't leave Earth running *from* anything. He left running *toward* something."

"The Viper," the Modhri said suddenly.

I nodded. "Exactly."

"What Viper?" Penny asked. "You're not making sense."

"On the contrary, he makes perfect sense," the Modhri said, as if unknown pieces were suddenly dropping into place. "Mr. Künstler was killed on his way to Bellis, where the last Hawk had been stolen. He was hoping to contact the thieves and buy the sculpture from them."

I felt my stomach tighten. I'd already guessed that was the reason Künstler had been on his way to Bellis. But the certainty in the Modhri's voice strongly implied that it hadn't been entirely Künstler's idea. "Or else he was lured with a promise to trade the Hawk for his Lynx," I said. "The people who killed him clearly expected him to have the Lynx with him."

If I could have seen the Modhri's face I would have been ninety percent sure I'd nailed it exactly. As it was, I could only make it to about seventy percent. But it was enough. The Modhri had indeed enticed Künstler onto that Quadrail and to his death. "Unfortunately for them, the Lynx was already on its way in the opposite direction," I continued. "Daniel was heading toward the art museum where one of the Vipers had also been stolen, probably also hoping to wheedle the sculpture out of the thieves."

"Or also planning to falsely offer a trade," the Modhri said darkly.

Penny was staring at me with horrified eyes. "Are you saying Mr. Künstler was killed over a stupid piece of *art*?"

I shrugged. "Collectors can get pretty fanatical."

"No," Penny said, her voice firm. Fire, *and* a sharp, intelligent mind. "There has to be more to it than that."

"You can ask Mr. Stafford when you find him," the Modhri said. "You'd best see now to your preparations— the Quadrail for Ghonsilya will be arriving in the station in a little over an hour. Good luck with your search, Ms. Auslander." He turned his covered eyes to me. "And to you as well, Mr. Compton."

The three Halkas were nowhere to be seen as Penny and I made our way through the twisting corridor and out again into the reassuring light of the Coreline. "We'll find Bayta and have her get us reservations," I told Penny as we headed toward the shuttle waiting area.

"That was weird," Penny murmured, walking very close to me. "That man—he won't be going with us, will he?"

"I'm sure he won't," I said. It was clearly the answer she wanted, even if it wasn't entirely true. "But I imagine he'll have friends aboard keeping an eye on us."

"Keeping an eye out for Daniel and this stupid sculpture, you mean," Penny said harshly. Her fright was fading away, leaving a growing anger in its place. "But it won't work. Daniel's too smart for them."

"It'll be all right," I assured her. "Trust me."

"I will," she murmured. "I do."

I looked sideways at her. She didn't return my glance, but there was something in her profile I hadn't seen before. A softness, and some actual genuine trust.

The Modhri had been right: she *was* an attractive woman. She was also rich, still single, and not all *that* much younger than I was.

Resolutely, I turned my eyes and mind away. I was here to protect her, Daniel, and the Lynx. Nothing more.

And I would. Because what the Modhri didn't know was that Fayr wasn't waiting for me on Laarmiten, as he'd read in the message chip he'd stolen at Terra Station. Fayr was on Ghonsilya, in the same Magaraa City neighborhood where we were all heading.

I hoped he'd brought all his guns with him. Knowing Fayr, I rather expected he had.

THIRTEEN

Penny's friends didn't understand the abrupt change of plan, of course. Given Penny's vague and rather incoherent explanation, I probably wouldn't have understood it either. One of the boys offered to accompany us, but it was a token offer and he was easily talked out of it.

Morse, in contrast, was grimly serious in his insistence that he go along. I'd expected nothing else, and didn't even bother to argue with him. I had no illusions that he would ever stick his neck out for me, but I was pretty sure I could count on him to protect Penny when the shooting started. That made him worth putting up with.

Besides, when push came to shove against unknown assailants, he might even take my side instead of leaving me to sink or swim on my own. Stranger things had happened.

Paradoxically, for the moment at least, we were probably as safe as we were ever going to be. Certainly as safe as I'd been since I stumbled into this war. We had something the Modhri wanted, and until he got it he was going to take exceptionally good care of us.

Just the same, Bayta made sure to get us our usual double compartment for the trip to Ghonsilya. Lockable doors are a good thing to have. I had her upgrade to a compartment for Penny, too, for the same reason. Bayta wondered a little about that, but I pointed out the girl was our only solid connection to Stafford and that we therefore needed to make sure she was as safe as possible. Her daddy could certainly afford the extra cost.

I did let Morse take only the standard first-class seat his pass permitted. I figured he could take care of himself, and I knew the kind of conniption the ESS accountants would throw over any unauthorized expenditures. There was nothing to be gained in getting him into any more trouble than he was probably already in over all this.

Besides, he might very well have to spring the extra cash for that locked door on the way out of Ghonsilya.

It was a five-day trip from Ian-apof to Ghonsilya, and it went off as smoothly as any I'd ever taken. At Ghonsilya Station we collected our luggage and took the shuttle to the transfer station, where we breezed through customs and reserved tiny staterooms aboard the next torchliner headed for the inner system. Ghonsilya's current positioning vis-à-vis the Tube translated to another six days of travel, and we all settled in to enjoy the ride as best we could.

It wasn't nearly as easy as it sounded.

Morse, while cordial enough, was still nursing the secret resentment against me that he still refused to talk about. Penny was brooding with an equally potent nervousness about the situation she'd been unexpectedly drop-kicked into. Bayta was even quieter than usual, probably worried about the two of them in addition to her usual worrying about the two of us.

And as the forced idleness of torchliner travel built up toward boredom, I found my thoughts turning increasingly toward Penny.

It was absurd on the face of it. I knew that. Her family's wealth created a social chasm between us that I could never hope to cross, she was already engaged to someone else, and despite her twenty-three years she was clearly a babe in the woods when it came to stuff like this. My focus needed to be on the Lynx: finding it, getting it away from the Modhri, and then *keeping* it away from the Modhri long enough to find out what he wanted with it. Anything that fell outside those parameters came under the heading of potentially lethal distractions.

It was a litany I repeated to myself at least once a day. Usually more than once. But the harder I tried to push my feelings into the background, the more they stubbornly popped out somewhere else. Somewhere along the line, I knew, this growing obsession was going to get me into trouble.

The last evening before we reached Ghonsilya, it did.

I HAD TAKEN to eating dinner quickly and then escaping from the general press of other passengers to the aft observation lounge. That particular lounge, with its view marred somewhat by the blazing nuclear fire of the drive, was usually fairly empty, which was just the way I wanted it.

Not that the solitude was helping my mental wrestling. If anything, being alone with my thoughts actually made things worse. But at least I didn't have to put up with any mindless prattle from Tra'ho'seej excited about returning home. The ultrasonic overtones in their voices always made my teeth hurt.

I'd been sitting there for maybe half an hour when Penny showed up. "There you are," she said, working her way between the chairs and over to my two-person couch. "I wondered where you've been disappearing to. That's very rude, you know."

I glanced over at the lounge's only other occupants, a pair of lanky Fibibibi cuddled close together at the far side of the room. Their full attention was on the coruscating fire of the drive, which their ultraviolet-sensitive eyes made more spectacular than Human vision could appreciate. "Sorry," I apologized to Penny. "I have a lot on my mind."

"I can imagine," she said gravely as she sat down beside me. Way too close beside me. "*Real* men of action are also men of thought."

"I wasn't just thinking," I told her. Aptly and succinctly put, I noted to myself. "I've also been keeping an eye on the rest of the passengers."

It was half a lie, but only half. I had indeed done a little looking and speculating. But at this point it was mostly just academic. The walkers would identify themselves soon enough, as soon as we sorted ourselves out among the various transports at the Ghonsilya spaceport.

Penny, of course, didn't know anything about that. All she knew was that she was in danger from dark and mysterious forces, and that she was counting on me to protect her from them. "Mr. Morse is worried about them, too," she said. "He told me I should stay in my stateroom the whole trip except for meals."

I had to smile at the thought of Morse trying to keep someone with Penny's spirit caged up that way. "I take it you didn't think much of that advice?"

"You've got to be kidding," she said, her nose wrinkling. "There's nothing to do in there except read and sleep. At least the Spiders put computers in *their* compartments."

"I wouldn't be so quick to dismiss Mr. Morse's advice," I cautioned her. "He *is* a professional security agent."

"I know." Her nose wrinkled again. There was something rather endearing about the way she did that. "It's just that he's *so* British."

"And you're, what, German?"

"Austrian, actually," she said. "But I mostly grew up in Paris."

"Ah," I said, nodding. The Brits and French had had a running feud going for at least the past six hundred years. Sometimes it had been almost friendly, other times decidedly not. "Say no more."

Her forehead creased, and for a moment I thought she was going to take issue with my comment. But then her skin smoothed out again. "Anyway, I've got you here to protect me, right?"

"I'll certainly do my best," I said, gazing at her face, feeling all those unwanted emotions stirring inside me. It was bad enough when I was just watching her from across a room. To have her staring trustingly at me with those big brown eyes barely half a meter away was pushing things way past the line. "But in this case I have to agree with Mr. Morse," I managed. "Now that you've finished dinner, maybe you should go back to your stateroom for a while."

Her face fell a little. "Well . . . all right. But only because it's you who's asking me." Her expression brightened again. "Will you walk me there?"

"I—" It had been a long time since I'd stumbled over my own tongue. This wasn't just a stumble, but a full-blown barrel-roll reverse in the pike position. It took me a solid three seconds just to bring my voice back on line. "I can do that," I managed. "Sure."

"Because I feel a lot safer when you're with me," she breathed.

She shifted position; and suddenly that half meter of open space between us was gone. "You're not like any man I've ever met, Frank," she whispered, her breath making little hot puffs against my lips. "Thank you for caring about me." Her lips moved closer, brushing gently against mine.

I should have pulled back. Failing that, I should at least have frozen in place.

Instead, I moved in for the kill.

I don't know how long we sat there like that, our lips locked in a solid, passionate kiss. No more than a few seconds, probably. My blood was pounding in my ears, my whole body starting to tremble with adrenaline and desire and guilt.

But for those few seconds, the rest of the universe had ceased to exist. There was no Daniel Stafford, no mysterious Nemuti sculptures, no Modhri, no Bayta, no—

"What in *bloody* hell are you doing?"

And very definitely no ESS Agent Morse.

I tried to pull back, only to find that somewhere along the line Penny's right arm had gotten itself crooked around the back of my neck. I reached up and gently but firmly forced it away as I looked sideways past the sheen of her hair toward the door.

Morse was standing just inside the lounge, his eyes wide, his expression still trying to decide whether it wanted to be astonished, appalled, or just plain furious. Penny's face, in contrast, was flushed, slightly defiant, and completely unapologetic.

"Evening, Morse," I greeted him as I finished easing Penny away from me and rested my hands on her shoulders to make sure she stayed there. I was feeling rather defiantly appalled myself, but since both of those were taken I decided to go with unconcerned casual instead. "You must have skipped the dessert cart."

The contest taking place across Morse's face was instantly over, with furious as the clear winner. Quietly, genteelly furious, perhaps, but furious nonetheless. "That's more than I can say about you," he retorted, his voice gone stiff with a thousand years of proper British decorum. "May I see you a moment?" His eyes flicked to Penny. "*Alone?*"

"Certainly," I said, shifting my eyes to Penny's. They were big and brown and still unrepentant. "If you'll excuse us, Penny?"

She nodded silently and got up, weaving her way back through the chairs to the door. She passed Morse without a glance going in either direction and disappeared. "What can I do for you?" I asked, gesturing Morse forward.

He took his own sweet time in ungluing himself from the deck, and wasn't any faster in working his way over to me. By the time he pulled one of the other chairs around to face me and sat down, he seemed to have cooled down a bit. "We'll pass over for the moment the utter inappropriateness of your behavior," he began in a growl. "For the moment."

I nodded, returning the favor by passing over for the moment the fact that he had no authority over me and that I wasn't subject to any bureaucratic rules of behavior anyway. "Fair enough."

"What we cannot pass over any longer is what exactly is going on here," he went on, glancing at the Fibibibi and lowering his voice. "We make planetfall tomorrow, and you obviously know more about this situation than you're letting on."

"Not so much as you think," I said. "There's a group of people who want Künstler's Lynx—"

"What people?" he cut me off. "That's the real question, isn't it? Who are they, and who are they affiliated with? Are they a criminal gang, an insurgent group, a government—what?"

"As near as I can tell, they have ties and links to all three categories," I said, angling the truth only a little. "I know they've infiltrated several galactic governments, some of them at the highest levels."

His face hardened. "Including Earth's?"

"They've got a few people scattered around the UN and probably elsewhere," I acknowledged, frowning. Clearly, some unknown puzzle pieces had just fallen into place behind those pale blue eyes. "Fortunately for us, they've mostly been concentrating on other governments."

"I see," he murmured, darkly thoughtful. "That would explain a great deal. I suppose our four Halkan friends will be continuing with us the whole way?"

I'd only tagged the three Halkas who'd been on Ianapof as the Modhri's local walker contingent. Apparently, there was one more I'd missed. "Until we decide to lose them, yes," I told him.

Morse's forehead wrinkled a little at that, but he let it go without comment. "Well, then, if you have nothing else for me, I'll be off." He stood up. "I trust you'll be spending the night in your own stateroom?"

My first impulse was to tell him it was none of his

business. He could hardly dislike me more than he already did.

But I was counting on him to protect Penny if and when the shooting started. I couldn't afford for his disgust with me to bleed over onto her. "Absolutely," I assured him.

"I would hope so," he said. "Good evening, Mr. Compton." He gave me a stiffly polite nod of the head and moved off.

I watched as he made his way back to the door, quiet alarm bells going off in the back of my head. I had long experience in reading faces, and I was pretty sure that some significant threshold had just been crossed in Morse's mind. Problem was, I had no idea what that threshold was.

But I was very sure I wasn't going to like it.

I THOUGHT ABOUT dropping in on Penny before retiring to my own stateroom, just to make sure she'd gotten there safely. But I decided against it. She might invite me in, and then I would have to say no, and then there'd be more confrontation of the sort I'd just gone through with Morse.

So I headed instead back to my own stateroom. I was finished with confrontation for the night.

Unfortunately, confrontation wasn't finished with me.

I'd been in the stateroom no more than ten minutes when there was a tap on the door. Wondering whether it was Penny or Morse or one of the Modhran walkers, I opened it.

It was none of the above. It was Bayta.

"We need to talk," she said without preamble as she strode into the room.

"Come in," I murmured, closing the door behind her. "What exactly do we need to talk about?"

She turned to face me, a determined look on her face. "Ms. Auslander," she said.

My stomach rumbled with a stirring of anger. "That was quick," I growled. "What did Morse do, come straight to your stateroom?"

Her forehead creased. "I haven't seen Mr. Morse since dinner," she said. "Is there something he's supposed to tell me?"

"No, not really," I said, cursing my carelessness. The first rule of subterfuge was to never, *ever,* offer information that hasn't been asked for. Especially information you didn't want anyone knowing. "What specifically about Ms. Auslander did you want to talk about?"

"I want to talk about the way you've been behaving toward her," Bayta said, still frowning.

"I'm just trying to be civil," I said. "Just because *you* don't like her—"

"You're trying to be *civil*?" she interrupted.

"Civil, friendly—whatever," I tried again. If Morse hadn't blabbed, could she somehow have heard about the kiss from one of the Fibibibi who'd been in the lounge? "We need to earn her trust if we're going to get to Stafford and the Lynx."

"Frank, what *are* you talking about?" Bayta repeated. Her puzzlement, I noted uneasily, had edged into irritation. "I'm talking about the way you've been ignoring her practically since we got on the torchliner."

I swallowed. Uh-oh. "Oh," I said.

"Is that what you call being friendly?" Her eyes narrowed slightly. "Or is there something I don't know about?"

"Nothing that's any of your business," I said. Even to my own ears it sounded lame.

Apparently, it sounded exactly the same to her. "Really," she said, her tone dipping below the frost line. "Shall I go ask Mr. Morse what he thinks of that?"

Silently, I cursed myself, Morse, Bayta, and the universe at large. But there was no way out. Letting Morse frame the details of Pyotr Gerashchenko's murder had turned Penny against us for days. I didn't dare let him frame the details of this one, too. "Okay, fine," I bit out. "I kissed her, okay? Is that a crime?"

I'd expected Bayta to stare at me in disbelief, or explode in anger, or at the very least launch into a lecture on proper decorum. Instead, she twitched backward, her breath catching in her throat, her expression that of someone who's just been slapped hard across the face.

Slapped across the face by a friend.

It was so unexpected that it took me a couple of seconds to find my brain and then my voice. But by then, it was too late. Bayta was already on the move, brushing past me and making for the door. "Bayta!" I called, spinning around.

Again, I was too late. Bayta was out of the stateroom, the door sliding shut behind her.

My first impulse was to run after her, to try to explain that it wasn't as bad as it sounded. But she hadn't looked like someone who was ready to listen to explanations.

Besides, maybe from her point of view it *was* as bad as it sounded.

I spent the rest of the evening alone in my stateroom. Between Penny, Morse, and Bayta, suddenly the Modhri was starting to look like the least of my problems. I hoped that by the time we made planetfall tomorrow morning everyone would have calmed down.

But I wasn't really expecting it.

FOURTEEN

We touched down at the main Ghonsilya spaceport outside Portline a little after six in the morning, torchliner time, which had been gradually adjusted during the past few days to match that of the local spaceport. We'd already gone through one set of customs formalities at the transfer station outside the Tube, but the local groundsiders wanted a crack at us, too, and we spent two hours running through their particular collection of bureaucratic hoops. Finally, we were released to make our individual ways to the other end of the terminal where we could catch one of the various planes, trains, or suborbital transports that would take us to our final destinations across the planet.

Morse's count had been correct: there were indeed four Halkas who joined us aboard the Magaraa City transport. I wondered briefly if the Modhri realized how they would stand out of a crowd of the thinner, more delicately featured Tra'ho'seej, then put the question out of my mind. That was the Modhri's problem, not mine.

Morse wasn't speaking to me much, basically limiting his conversation to necessary information exchanges. All of those were short and formal. Bayta wasn't speaking to me at all. Penny, in contrast, was almost chatty, though most of her conversation was of the casual cocktail-party variety. Usually I had little patience with that sort of thing, but I recognized it here as a cover-up for her nervousness about what might await us.

She also was showing a new penchant for hanging on to my arm as we walked. It would probably have made Bayta even quieter if she hadn't been at absolute zero already.

Off we all went for a fun-filled excursion together.

The suborbital transport took three hours to get across the Ghonsilya landscape, which when added to the local time zone change put us on the ground again just after local sunset. At my suggestion we parked our luggage in the depot storage lockers, with the idea that we'd pick it up later after we'd figured out what our long-term plans were going to be. We took the subway to the neighborhood of the art museum that had been burgled, and a few minutes later disembarked into the gathering dusk.

By our own internal biological clocks, of course, it was only lunchtime. Travel could be very wearing on the stomach.

"What's your plan?" Morse asked quietly as he, Penny, Bayta, and I walked along a street lined with small shops and quaint-looking houses, our four silent walkers running a wide screen formation around us a few meters away.

"I thought we'd try something outrageously clever and give the nearby hotels a call," I said, pulling out my comm and keying for a local directory.

Morse snorted under his breath. "And here I thought you'd be looking for a trail of bread crumbs."

Penny half turned toward him, her eyes glowering. But whatever crushing retort she'd been preparing to offer on my behalf, she never got to it. As I lifted the comm the biggest of the four Halkas, whom I'd privately dubbed Gargantua, moved in from his place in the screen formation and plucked it from my grip. "No," he growled.

I was actually perfectly willing to let him have the

comm. Stafford hadn't been traveling aboard the Quadrail under either his own name or the Daniel Mice moniker Künstler had gasped at me, and I doubted he would go back to one of them here. That made a hotel survey pretty much useless.

Of course, Modhri already knew the Stafford name was a bust, since he would certainly have done a survey of his own the minute our walker escort got close enough to the planet for their Modhri colonies to meld with the locals and sound the alert. My suggestion had been pure red herring, designed to make Morse and the walkers think I knew something that they didn't.

Which, technically speaking, I did. But that wasn't the point. The point was to keep the Modhri thinking in the wrong direction, and if taking my comm away made him feel safer, he was welcome to it.

Unfortunately, Morse didn't know any of that. He apparently thought I was about to reveal Stafford's traveling identity, and figured it was therefore the right time to try to lose our escort. Slipping his hand inside his jacket, he turned toward Gargantua.

It was a complete waste of effort. The Modhri had easily anticipated the move. Two of the other Halkas moved in even before he completed his turn, and in typically perfect coordination one of them threw his arms around Morse's shoulders to trap his hand inside his jacket while the other reached inside and twisted the gun out of his hand.

Penny gave a little gasp as she jerked back from the sudden fracas. The fourth Halka was ready, catching her shoulders to discourage any thought of flight and relieving her of her own comm. She started to give him a withering over-the-shoulder look, but midway through her eyes seemed to catch on something behind my back. "Frank?" she breathed.

I turned. Somewhere along the line, the four Modhran walkers who'd accompanied us from the Ghonsilya spaceport had picked up reinforcements. Twenty reinforcements, to be precise, all of them Tra'ho'seej. They were arranged in a loose but very deliberate guard ring around us about thirty meters away.

They didn't look like guards, of course. They were grouped in casual-looking twos and threes at corners or loitering silently as individuals in the various shop doorways around us. Most of them were dressed in the expensively embroidered clothing and multiple earrings of upper-class citizens, while the rest had the severe half-shaved heads and contrasting flowing topcuts of oathlings who'd taken the vow of government service.

Apparently, the Modhri had turned out most of his local mind segment in honor of our visit.

"Frank?" Penny repeated, more urgently this time.

"It's all right," I soothed, studying the newcomers. They were making no move to approach, but were merely continuing with their conversations or private meditations. The Modhri would have maneuvered them here through his usual technique of quiet and reasonable suggestions, but was apparently holding off on the more drastic and riskier step of taking direct control of their bodies.

Playing it low-key . . . and it was going to cost him. Whispering subtle instructions in their ears had gotten the Tra'ho'seej here just fine, but it was highly unlikely that the hosts' rationalizations could have been made to stretch to the extent of bringing weapons along on their innocent evening group stroll. Twenty walkers were bad enough, but twenty armed walkers would have been a hell of a lot worse.

Of course, Gargantua and his buddies *did* have at least one gun now—Morse's—plus whatever hardware they might have brought with them from the Quadrail lockboxes. Morse and I would just have to deal with that as best we could.

Assuming it was still *Morse and I* and not just *I*. Judging from the look he was giving me as the Halkas continued frisking him I wouldn't have bet large sums of money on it. "Lovely move, Compton," he growled acidly. "Lovely *non*-move, rather."

"Sorry," I apologized. "But I try not to start fights when I'm on the short end of ten-to-one odds. Little rule I have."

His glare slipped a little, his eyes flicking away from me. From the sudden change in his expression, it was clear he hadn't yet noticed our new outrider collection. "Bloody hell," he muttered.

"At the very least," I agreed. "I suggest we not make any sudden moves."

The Halkas finished their search without coming up with anything else and took a step back. "You through?" I asked, addressing Gargantua for convenience.

"For the moment," he said, eyeing me closely. "There will be no more trouble?" His eyes flicked significantly to Penny.

I followed the look. The Halka who'd taken Penny's comm had shifted his grip pointedly from her shoulder to the back of her neck. A squeeze, followed by a good solid twist, and she would die the way her friend Pyotr had. "Understood," I told Gargantua, a shiver running up my back. "Come on. We start at the art museum."

For the first time since I'd walked into the dit rec viewing room at Ian-apof the Modhri seemed genuinely startled. "Why?" Gargantua asked.

"Who's the detective here, you or me?" I countered. "You want the Lynx, or don't you?"

His eyes burned into me, but he nodded. "Lead the way," he said, gesturing me forward.

We set off again, Penny walking close beside me on my right, Bayta a bit farther away on my left, Morse bringing up the rear, the Halkas flanking, and the oblivious Tra'ho walkers wandering along more or less in formation. Half a kilometer directly ahead, I knew from the city maps I'd studied on the flight, our street dead-ended at the grounds of the art museum where the Viper had been stolen. Much closer than that, only a couple of blocks ahead, in fact, I could see the marquee of the Fraklog-Oryo Hotel.

Where Fayr's message had said he would be waiting for us.

I could feel Bayta's tension as we moved closer. She was onto the plan now, and preparing herself for action.

Or rather, she was onto half of it. I had the feeling she wasn't going to like the other half.

We were twenty meters from the hotel entrance when I stopped. "Look, there's no reason we all have to go there," I told Gargantua. "Why don't we leave the others here and you and I can go alone?"

Gargantua eyed me suspiciously. "Is the Human Stafford there?" he asked.

"Possibly," I lied. "If he is, all the more reason for us not to spook him by bringing a crowd. Besides, together we may be able to do the trade right there and then."

"What trade do you mean?"

"The obvious one," I said. "If he has the Lynx with him, you'll let Penny, Bayta, and Morse leave and join us. Once I see they're alone and unharmed, you can have the Lynx, and all of us will walk away. All of us plus Mr. Stafford, of course."

Gargantua flicked a measuring glance at Morse. "I accept," he said.

I had expected nothing less. Suspicious or not, he had more than enough eyes in place to risk lengthening my leash a little. "Then let's get on with it," I said.

"You can't leave us here," Penny said, her voice tight. "What if they—?"

"They won't hurt you," I assured her, taking her hand and giving it a squeeze. Morse and Bayta, I noticed peripherally, didn't miss a bit of the byplay. "Just hang in there. I'll be right back."

Gargantua and I started off again, leaving the others standing in the middle of the walkway like abandoned orphans. We walked in silence until we were at the level of the hotel entrance. "Oh, there was just one other thing," I said, stopping suddenly.

Automatically, Gargantua stopped and turned to face me. "What?" he asked.

Smiling sweetly, I buried my fist in his abdomen.

The sheer surprise of it froze him in place. I took advantage of the moment to hit three more of the most painful and incapacitating Halkan nerve centers I could reach, dropping him into a quivering heap on the walkway.

For a moment the shared pain rippling from Gargantua into and through the Modhri mind segment sent the rest of the walkers quivering. But it didn't hold them for long. A glance behind me showed that two of the other Halkas were on the move, charging toward me at full speed. Behind them, ten of the twenty Tra'ho'seej were closing their circle to bolster the fourth remaining Halka guard as the Modhri dropped his earlier subtlety and took direct control of their bodies. The rest of the Tra'ho'seej were spreading out, clearly planning to cut off my escape no matter which direction I decided to run.

And in that same quick glance I saw the fourth Halka draw a gun and press the muzzle into the side of Penny's neck.

Another shiver went through me to see her in danger that way, as it was clearly intended to. But I had no choice. Without Fayr we were all dead, and I had to alert him to the fact we were here. Jumping over Gargantua's twitching body, I sprinted to the hotel door and ducked inside.

The lobby was tastefully dark and quiet, its walls and end tables adorned with a wide variety of small paintings, sculptures, and other art works. A handful of Tra'ho'seej were seated in the various overstuffed chairs and couches, apparently in deep contemplation of the culture arrayed around them. All of them looked up with varying degrees of shock or outrage as I sprinted through their midst to the check-in desk and its self-service computer terminals.

I was still punching keys when Gargantua's two Halkan buddies caught up with me.

I'd fought against walkers enough times to have a fair idea of the sort of tactics the Modhri favored. This mind segment was no exception. The first Halka came at me with arms spread wide, ready to take the brunt of my attack and then immobilize me with a bear hug, leaving his partner free to mete out whatever punishment the Modhri decided I'd earned.

Naturally, I had no intention of playing it that way. Waiting until the last fraction of a second, I dodged to my right toward one of the unoccupied couches. The second Halka had anticipated the move, angling past the first in an attempt to cut me off. I reached the couch ahead of him, and as he jabbed a fist at me I ducked down and rolled over the couch back, landing on the cushions and continuing my roll off the couch and onto the floor.

The Halkas were already onto the change of plan. The first continued with his forward motion, probably aiming to circle around the far side of the couch, while the second braked and reversed to go around the near side. Two more seconds, and they would have me neatly corralled.

Or so they thought. Rolling back up to my feet, I killed my own momentum; and as they came charging around the ends I dived again for the couch, jumping on the cushions and leaping over the back.

At this point most normal opponents would probably have cursed or spat or otherwise shown some annoyance. Not the Modhri. He fought in silence, his Halkan walkers merely reversing direction in response to my move. I took a long step toward one end of the couch, and as the nearest Halka again reached for me I scooped up the delicate metalwork sculpture from the end table and threw it into his face.

I was still dodging and sparring when the police finally arrived.

THE HOTEL MANAGER was livid.

[Payment from the criminal,] he kept repeating over and over in Seejlis as the cops cuffed my hands behind me, the normally fluid Tra'ho language sounding a lot less melodious than usual. [Payment in art and in money.]

The cops made the sort of soothing noises cops everywhere in the galaxy make to outraged victims and marched me out into the street.

Where I found myself smack dab in the middle of a jurisdictional dispute.

It was a beaut, too, as near as I could decipher from the rapid-fire argument going on. On the one side was the chief cop on the scene, who had me dead to rights and clearly wasn't interested in handing me off to anyone else. On the other side were two of the government oathlings I'd just run out on, whose Modhran controller was equally adamant that I not be locked up where I couldn't help him find Stafford and the Lynx.

Of course, the oathlings had no idea of why they were fighting so hard to keep me out of jail, and it was weirdly amusing to watch the mental and verbal gymnastics they were throwing themselves into to make their point. Still, words and arguments were their profession, and I gave them five to three odds of winning.

I hoped they would, too, for the cops' sake. From the look on Gargantua's face as he gazed at me from one of the knots of gawkers it seemed likely that if the cops took me away their friends guarding the jailhouse might not survive the night.

Casually, I sent a gaze around the area. From the size of the muttering crowd out there it looked like my little fracas had roused pretty much everyone within a two-block radius. Certainly it should have roused anyone in the Fraklog-Oryo Hotel.

But there was no one in the streets except Tra'ho'seej, no one peering out the windows except more Tra'ho'seej, and no one on the rooftops at all.

Which meant I'd ruined a few perfectly good art objects, not to mention risking my neck, for nothing. Fayr was apparently out for the evening.

If he'd ever been here in the first place.

A light rain began while the argument continued, and everyone in sight proceeded to either pull out a fold-up hood from their coat collars or produce a compact hooded plastic poncho from some pocket. Apparently, sudden rains were a part of the local climate, part of the guidebook I must have missed.

The Halkan walkers didn't seem to notice. They stood there motionlessly, water running down their heads and dripping off their snouts, their eyes focused on me. Morse took off his jacket and offered it to Penny, who draped it hoodlike over her head for protection, while Morse himself held a forearm pressed to his forehead to at least keep the water out of his eyes. Bayta, for her part, seemed as oblivious of the precipitation as the Halkas, her eyes haunted as she gazed at the crowd surrounding us.

As for me, with my hands cuffed behind my back, I had no other option but to simply get wet.

It took a good fifteen minutes, plus at least three comm calls from each side of the argument, but eventually the cops gave up. My cuffs were removed, the hotel manager was soothed some more, and with baleful looks that were evenly distributed between me and the oathlings the cops piled back into their cars and took off.

That was apparently the signal the bystanders had been waiting for as well. A few of them shook the rain from their hoods or ponchos and trooped into the hotel with the manager, presumably to commiserate with him over a drink and survey the crime scene for themselves. The rest melted back away to their homes and gardens and cafés.

A minute later we were standing alone under the dripping sky. Penny, Bayta, Morse, me, and the Modhri's other twenty walkers.

"A waste of time and energy," Gargantua said. He was no longer glaring, but merely studying me expressionlessly. In some ways, his calm was more unnerving than the glare had been. "Did you really think you could escape me?"

Briefly I wondered what his reaction would be if I told him I'd merely been trying to make enough noise to attract the attention of a homicidal chipmunk-faced commando. But I was still hoping we might run into Fayr somewhere else along the way. "I wasn't trying to escape," I said instead, wiping some of the rainwater off my face. "I was curious to see how far you'd go with your walkers."

"And did you learn anything?"

I looked at the rich and powerful Tra'ho'seej still loitering around the area. Their expressions and eyes were back to normal, the brief episode of full Modhri control long since over.

But their attitude had definitely changed for the darker. No longer did they imagine—no longer could they persuade themselves—that they'd all simply stepped out for an evening stroll with friends and acquaintances. They were watching the four of us intently, apparently convinced that potentially dangerous aliens shouldn't be allowed to run free and wild without someone in authority guarding them. "I still wonder how you get away with these personality blackouts," I said, looking back at Gargantua. "You'd think *someone* would eventually catch on."

For a moment he gazed at me in silence. "I saw an old book on Human stage magic once," he said at last. "One of the illusions it described involved a large wheeled war device for hurling round shot at an enemy. I don't know the proper term."

"A cannon?" I suggested.

"Yes, that was it," the Modhri said. "In this case, it was to be loaded with a Human, who would then supposedly disappear as it was fired. After the Human entered the barrel, the cannon was swiveled completely around on the stage so that the audience could see that there were no tricks involved."

"And the trick was . . . ?"

"The trick was that as the cannon finished its rotation, a set of false spokes slid into the openings between the lower spokes of the wheel facing away from the audience," the Modhri said. "They were so engineered that they appeared to be the spokes of the front wheel, which had just happened to block the observer's view of the rear of the stage."

I nodded as I understood. "And every observer simply thought *he* was the one in the bad seat," I said, "not realizing that everyone else was seeing the same blockage and was thinking the same thing."

"Exactly," the Modhri said. "With the audience's sight thus completely blocked, the Human was free to slip invisibly through a hidden door in the base of the cannon and lower himself behind the rear wheel to a concealed trapdoor in the floor without being observed." Gargantua's doglike snout curled slightly. "I trust you see the similarities."

I did, of course. As long as each Tra'ho in the group thought he was the only one having strange memory lapses, he wasn't going to think much about it, especially with the Modhri continually whispering soothing theories and rationalizations in his ears. If all of them ever got together and compared notes, they might begin to wonder.

But that would never happen. The Modhri would make sure of that. "We have much better magic tricks now," I said.

"Illusion is still only illusion," he said. "But I grow weary of this stalling. Take me to the Lynx."

"Fine," I said, gesturing down the street. "Like I said, we start at the art museum."

I took a step in that direction. Gargantua didn't budge. "You think me a fool?" he demanded, some of his earlier anger peeking out again.

"Don't worry, this time we can all go together," I said. Looking over his shoulder, I caught Penny's eye and beckoned.

She started to move forward, came up short as the Halka guarding her tightened his grip on her arm. "No," Gargantua said flatly. "You and two of my Arms."

"I need Ms. Auslander," I insisted. "Stafford won't show himself unless she's there."

"The other Human female is similar enough," Gargantua countered. "She will go with you."

I looked at Bayta. Her face was as expressionless as Gargantua's had been a minute ago, but her body language was tied in tension knots. She also didn't look a thing like Penny. "She's not nearly similar enough," I said. "Not to other Humans."

Two of the Halkas took Bayta's arms and walked her over to us. "If she does not go, then she will die," Gargantua said.

Bayta was staring unblinkingly at me. "In that case, I guess she goes," I said.

"And no others," Gargantua said.

"No others," I conceded, trying to avoid Penny's sudden look of stunned panic. Clearly, she'd expected me to fight harder for her freedom.

And I wanted to. Desperately. But there was nothing I could do against odds like these. I would have to cooperate and hope the Modhri made a slip somewhere along the line.

"But first," Gargantua continued, "you will give me the name."

Bayta's face went suddenly very still. "What name?" I asked carefully.

"The name you were searching for in that hotel," Gargantua said. "The name the Human Daniel Stafford is traveling under." His snout curled back to reveal his teeth. "The name the Human Künstler gave you before he died."

I flicked a glance at Bayta, my back muscles twinging in memory. Apparently, Gargantua hadn't reached the scene in time to hear Künstler's actual last words. But he'd been in time to see the dying man's lips moving. "He didn't give me any name," I said.

From behind me came a sudden gasp. I spun around, my stomach tensing, to see one of the Halkas gripping the nerve center on Penny's forearm. Her face was contorted in surprise and pain. "I can hurt her much worse than that," Gargantua reminded me.

I took a deep breath. Penny was watching me closely. So was Bayta. "Daniel Mice," I said. "Now stop hurting her."

A flash of surprise and disbelief flashed across Bayta's face as Gargantua took a sideways step and gazed at my profile. "Speak the name again," he ordered.

"Daniel Mice," I repeated.

For a moment he was silent. Then, to my relief, the Halka released Penny's arm. "Yes," he said at last. "Those were indeed the lip movements. Daniel Mice," he repeated, his voice gone thoughtful. "But Mice is a form of Earth vermin."

"It also refers to a famous cartoon figure you may have seen in dit rec animations," I said. "Apparently Stafford has a sense of humor."

Out of the corner of my eye I saw several of the Tra'ho'seej pull out their comms. The Modhri would have certainly already done a planetwide search for the name Daniel Stafford. Now, he was about to do the same for Daniel Mice, plus all the variants he could come up with.

One of the oathlings who hadn't hauled out his comm broke away from the rest of the group and came toward us, pulling off his poncho as he did so. [For the female,] he said, handing the poncho to Gargantua. He gave Bayta a courteous little bow, as befit a culture that held females of all species in high regard. Then, with a brief glower in my direction, he returned to his place in the informal picket line.

"Put it on," Gargantua said, handing the poncho to Bayta. "It will help disguise you."

So the Modhri had conceded my point that Bayta and Penny didn't look alike. Interesting. "You might as well," I confirmed to Bayta. "That's the kind of sky that could rain on us all night."

I looked around again as she began to work her way into the garment. Gargantua didn't wait for her to finish, but headed silently back to where the fourth Halka was guarding Penny and Morse. Either the Modhri wanted to keep him back in reserve, or else he'd decided that Gargantua's presence at Penny's side would be more of an incentive for me to behave myself.

Or maybe I'd hurt him badly enough that the Modhri wanted to let him recover a little before throwing him into battle again. I rather hoped that was the case.

I looked around us. Now that the non-Modhran spectators had dispersed, the streets were nearly deserted. Two streets away, I could see a couple of Tra'ho'seej walking arm in arm, young lovers perhaps out for a romantic stroll in the evening rain. Occasional vehicles appeared briefly as they crossed the various intersections in the distance, though none came our direction. Half a block ahead, at the mouth of an alleyway on the far side of the Fraklog-Oryo Hotel, a lone figure in a rain poncho and badly worn clothing had broken into a public trash receptacle and pulled out several of the compressed blocks. Two of the blocks had already been prodded apart into little piles of assorted garbage at the edge of the sidewalk, and he was laboriously poking at a third with a crooked stick, searching for food or buried treasure or God only knew what.

And at the edge of the nearest pile to us, squarely in the middle of the sidewalk, was possibly the last thing I would have expected to see on an alien world: a bright yellow banana peel.

Bring with you that strange but interesting gift of Human humor, Fayr had said in his message. The whole galaxy seemed to be either intrigued or outraged by what we Humans considered funny. And without a doubt one of the strangest and most outrageous forms of Human comedy was classic vaudeville slapstick.

Including the venerable tradition of slipping on a banana peel.

I took another, harder look at the scavenger's back. It could be, I decided. It could very well be.

And suddenly our odds were looking a whole lot better.

Bayta finished settling the poncho into place. "I suggest you hang back a little," I told the two Halkas as I stepped to Bayta's side. "Stafford isn't likely to come out if he sees a crowd."

Neither of them replied, but in unison they took a step closer to us. It was about the response I'd expected. "Fine—have it your way," I said. Taking Bayta's arm, which was oddly stiff and unyielding, I started us toward the museum.

We were about ten paces from the hooded scavenger when he gave a startled little yelp, his hands bobbling something in front of him as if he'd suddenly come into possession of a bird that was trying desperately to get away. A second later the unknown object shot out of his grasp, arcing high over our heads.

And as every other eye in the area automatically swung to track its flight, I grabbed the back of Bayta's head and buried her face against my shoulder. Pressing my own face against the side of her head, I squeezed my eyes shut.

The blast was surprisingly quiet, not much louder than a kid popping a paper bag. But the intensity of the flash more than made up for it. Even through closed lids and with my face turned mostly away it was bright enough to make me wince. God alone knew what it was doing to all those unshielded Tra'ho and Halkan eyes.

Though perhaps the strangled gasps from our two watchdogs were a clue. Getting a grip around Bayta's shoulder so I wouldn't lose her, I veered sharply to my right, hoping to get us out of grabbing range before the Modhri recovered from the shock and got his Halkas hunting us by sound and touch.

We'd made it barely three steps when a pair of louder cracks, the sound of large-caliber killrounds, rendered the point moot.

And then a strong hand grabbed my arm at the elbow, urgently pulling me along. Cautiously, hoping he didn't have a second sunburst grenade already on line, I opened my eyes to slits.

It was Fayr, all right. The stripe pattern on his chipmunk face had been radically altered, and there were the first signs of age-graying on his cheek fur. But his eyes were bright and steady as he peered over his shoulder from beneath his hood, and there was no mistaking the professional steadiness with which he held the large handgun pointed warily past my side. Turning my head, I looked at the crowd of walkers behind me.

It was as if Fayr had lobbed a concussion grenade squarely into their midst instead of just setting off a sunburst half a block away. All of the Tra'ho'seej had dropped to the ground and were writhing on their backs in agony. Writhing in perfect unison, actually, with each to and fro and squirm duplicated by all of them. It made the whole thing look like some strange dry-land version of synchronized swimming.

Gargantua and the other Halka weren't in much better shape. They weren't exactly writhing, but they had dropped to their knees and were swaying back and forth, their faces buried in their massive hands. Penny was half collapsed on Morse's shoulder, her body shaking with silent sobs, her face likewise buried in her hands. Morse himself had his back to us, and I couldn't tell what shape he was in.

But it didn't really matter whether he could see or not. With the whole cadre of walkers incapacitated, this was our chance to get them free. "Wait a second," I muttered toward Fayr, leaning against his guiding hand to try to stop us. "We've got friends back there."

We didn't even slow down. Fayr was stronger than his diminutive size suggested. "Leave them," he muttered back. "Too dangerous."

"They aren't walkers," I insisted.

"Are you certain?" Fayr countered.

I grimaced. But he was right. In this shadowy war, you could never tell for sure who the enemy was. "Not a hundred percent," I conceded.

"Then leave them," he repeated. "The Modhri won't hurt them without cause. Besides, there is no time."

He was right on that one, too. The sunburst had lit up the sky over the entire neighborhood, and already I could hear the sounds of sirens as the police headed back to see what the hell had happened now.

Their reaction when they found out the government oathlings had managed to lose their Human prisoner ten minutes after I'd been left in their custody would probably be highly entertaining. But it wasn't a conversation I wanted to hear with my hands cuffed behind me. "You have someplace to go?" I asked Fayr.

"No fears." He gestured with his gun toward the next side street. "There." As he drew back his hand, he slid the gun back into concealment inside his poncho.

I took one last look at the two dead Halkas lying crumpled behind us on the sidewalk. *We have much better magic tricks now,* I'd told the Modhri earlier. Such as making a pair of walkers disappear forever. "Hey, presto," I murmured.

FIFTEEN

The sirens were still approaching when Fayr turned off the sidewalk onto a garden path leading to the back door of a modest house on a block full of similar residences. He opened the door and slipped inside, leading us through darkened hallways to a windowless room in the center of the house. "I had this place prepared in my mind in case the Modhri should locate me at the hotel," he explained as he turned on a small flashlight and set it in the corner to shine against the ceiling. "The family is on vacation and not expected to return for five more days."

I looked around. The place was decked out like a cross between a conversation room and a traditional Japanese garden. There were a couple of couches and a recliner chair in the center, accessible via curved flagstone paths winding their ways from each of the two doors. One of the couches had a shimmery gray cloth, window curtain–sized, draped casually over one end. The rest of the room's floor space was filled with potted plants of various types and sizes, with concealed fixtures in their bases that probably provided a muted, understated light. "Interesting place," I commented.

"It's a contemplation room," Fayr said, crossing to the other door. He opened it, peered briefly out, then closed it again. "The design is Filiaelian in origin, though the

Tra'ho'seej have adapted it to their own cultural personalities."

"They must spend hours just keeping the plants watered," I commented, looking around.

"I believe that's one part of the contemplation aspect," Fayr said, returning to the recliner and sitting down. "That, plus the maintenance and the observation of the plants in general. Are either of you hungry?"

"I never pass up a chance to eat," I told him. I reached for Bayta's arm, but this time she was having none of it. Evading my grasp, she took a step away from me.

Fine. Whatever. "What have you got?" I asked Fayr as I headed alone along the flagstones toward the center, leaving Bayta to follow on her own.

"The pack is under there," he said, pointing to the couch without the gray drape. "Take whatever you wish."

"Thanks." I sat down at one end of the couch and pulled a thin shoulder bag from beneath it. "Bayta?" I offered.

"No, thank you," she said, coming up behind me and seating herself at the other end. "We're grateful for the rescue, *Korak* Fayr."

"No fears," he said grimly as he inclined his head to her. "I'm always looking for ways to strike against the Modhri."

"I'm glad we have such an ally," she said. "But I wonder if we should perhaps move a little farther from the hotel."

"We aren't going anywhere until the police finish poking around out there," I pointed out. "Especially not with a double homicide to keep them busy."

"Yes; the killings," she said, her eyes still on Fayr, a little color rising into her cheeks. "I wonder if that was wise."

I glanced at Fayr, noting the hard set to his chipmunk face. That, and the large shoulder-holstered guns beneath his arms. "I'm sure *Korak* Fayr did what he felt necessary," I said diplomatically.

Bayta didn't take the hint. "They were just walkers," she continued. "They aren't responsible for their actions when—"

"They weren't walkers," Fayr interrupted her. "Not anymore. The preliminaries have ended, Bayta. The war has begun in earnest." He nodded in the direction of the hotel. "Those Halkas were soldiers."

"Only under the Modhri's influence," Bayta persisted.

"What do you mean, soldiers?" I asked. There'd been something extra ominous in Fayr's voice just then.

"The Modhri has changed tactics," Fayr said, shifting his attention from Bayta to me. "He knows he can no longer rely on untrained walkers to suddenly act when necessary. He has therefore begun to build a cadre of dedicated fighters under his continual control."

I felt a shiver run up my back. "Zombies," I murmured.

"What are zombies?" Fayr asked.

"Something from Earth legend," I told him. "Corpses magically reanimated and under the control of the voodoo priest who brought them back."

Fayr nodded. "That is exactly what these soldiers are. The beings those Halkan bodies once contained are long gone."

"Are those consciousnesses actually dead, then?" Bayta asked. Clearly, she still wasn't ready to concede this one. "Or are they merely suppressed, the way any walker's personality is when the Modhri takes control?"

"Does it matter?" Fayr asked.

"Of course it matters," Bayta shot back. "In the first case all you did was end the Modhri's use of innocent beings he'd already killed. In the second, *you're* the one who killed those innocent beings."

"What about what we did on the Quadrail train after Sistarrko?" I asked.

Her eyes flicked reluctantly to me, a bit of color again showing briefly in her cheeks. "We had no choice," she insisted.

"Neither did *Korak* Fayr," I said.

"The situations aren't the same," she said. "If we hadn't killed those walkers, we ourselves would have died." She looked back at Fayr. "Here, we could simply have run away."

"Leaving them alive and free to create more havoc about the galaxy?" Fayr countered. He seemed more puzzled than angry at her criticism. "A poisonous groun-lyve is also not responsible for its actions as a predatory creature. Yet when a gardener finds one among his seedlings, he kills it without second thought."

For a few seconds the room was filled with a taut silence as he and Bayta stared across the room at each other. Then, abruptly, Bayta got up from the couch and strode to the door we'd come in through. "Bayta, I don't think that's—" I called softly.

She pulled open the door and stomped out, closing it behind her. "—a good idea," I finished, getting reluctantly to my feet. "I'll go get her."

"She'll be careful," Fayr said, his eyes hard on me. "While she's gone, perhaps you'll tell me what the difficulty is."

"We're on the trail of a sculpture that the Modhri wants for some reason," I said. "He's also taken hostages—"

"Not your mission," he interrupted. "Tell me what the difficulty is between you and Bayta."

I grimaced. I hadn't thought Bayta's snit was that obvious.

But then, Fayr *was* a trained observer. "She thinks I've been unprofessional with a client," I told him. "Actually, the lady's not really a client. She's a—well, we just sort of fell in with her along the way."

"This is the female Human I saw with the Modhran walkers?"

"Right," I said. "As I said, she's being held hostage. The other Human you saw is—"

"*Have* you been unprofessional with the female?"

"What kind of a question is that?" I growled.

"A quite reasonable one," he said calmly.

"And it's your business how?"

"Do you and Bayta intend to walk out of here right now and not contact me again?" he asked pointedly. "No? Then a problem between allies is very much my business."

I sighed. It *had* been a stupid thing for me to say. "I know," I said. "I'm sorry."

He inclined his head, wrinkling his chipmunk nose a little in acceptance of my apology. "Then tell me. Have you been acting unprofessionally?"

"I was just being friendly to her," I said. "For some reason, Bayta's blowing the whole thing way out of proportion."

The second part, I told myself firmly, was certainly true. The first part was just as certainly open to legitimate debate, no matter what Bayta might think.

"You must talk to her," Fayr said. "You must listen to her complaints and straighten out the coldness between you."

"Right," I growled. "In case you hadn't noticed, we're a little busy right now, what with the Modhri and everything."

"You will make the time," Fayr said, the weight of command in his tone. "Lack of trust and care between allies carries a risk more deadly even than the enemy."

"I don't know about that," I muttered. But he was right, and we both knew it. "Fine. Next opportunity I get, I'll talk to her. Meanwhile, why exactly did you call us here?"

"You mentioned a sculpture a moment ago," he said. "I presume, then, that you have heard of the nine Nemuti sculptures called Vipers, Lynxes, and Hawks?"

I nodded. "As a matter of fact, I happened to be with the owner of one of the Lynxes when he died."

"Of natural causes?"

"Hardly," I said grimly. "He was beaten to death. In a Quadrail first-class compartment, no less."

"Interesting," Fayr said. "The price for these sculptures continues to rise."

"Tell me about it," I said. "How come *you* know about them?"

"I was approached by a Bellido collector who had one of the Hawks in his possession," Fayr said. "He offered a great deal of money if we would obtain the Viper for him from the art museum here in Magaraa City."

I felt my eyebrows climbing my forehead. "You were going to *steal* it?"

"You disapprove?" Fayr asked stiffly.

"Not really any of my business," I hastened to assure him. "Even for commandos operating alone, a war is expensive."

"Especially for commandos operating alone," Fayr said, sounding somewhat mollified. Probably wasn't crazy about hiring himself out as a thief, either. "At any rate, I came here to examine the museum and its contents in order to prepare a plan, only to discover the Viper had already been stolen."

"Apparently by the Modhri," I said.

"Apparently by the Modhri," he agreed. He cocked his head. "But perhaps only *apparently* stolen."

"Meaning?"

"The scene of the event has not been changed," he said. "When the additional police presence in the vicinity of the hotel has been lifted, we'll go there and you can see for yourself."

"What, now?" I asked, glancing at my watch. It was only a little past seven, local time. "They don't stay open evenings?"

"Normally, yes," Fayr said. "Tonight they've closed early."

"Handy," I murmured. "On the other hand, I *did* tell the Modhri I wanted to go there."

"Yes, I heard some of that discussion," Fayr said. "Did you genuinely mean it?"

"Not all *that* genuinely," I said. "It was really only a

cover story, first so I could get a ways ahead of the crowd, and second to give us a reason to move into range of your bag of tricks once I'd spotted you. But the Modhri might not realize that."

For a moment Fayr pondered in silence. "I think he will," he said at last. "The Modhri has had a great deal of experience with your tactical methods. He'll surely conclude that the museum request was the feint that it indeed was."

"He might still plant a couple of walkers in the area," I warned. "He has plenty to spare."

"In actual fact, he doesn't," Fayr said with a sort of grim satisfaction. "Not at the moment. Tra'ho balance is strongly tied to their eyes and vision. For the next three or four days, until the effects of the sunburst grenade fade away, the Modhri's local walkers will be largely confined to their beds."

"That's handy," I said. "Of course, that still leaves the rest of the walkers he's got on Ghonsilya."

"If there *are* more," Fayr said. "There may not be. Ghonsilya is a small and fairly unimportant world, with few people of great wealth and power. It's entirely possible that he drew in his entire walker contingent for this occasion."

I scratched thoughtfully at my cheek. That certainly jibed with the low status accorded to Ghonsilya by my encyclopedia's planetary info listing. There was a local government, of course, but I'd already noted how many of the walkers were government oathlings.

It also jibed with the Modhri's known urgency regarding the Lynx. He'd had several hours to collect his troops, and there was no particular reason for him to have kept any of them in reserve. Especially since being stingy that way might enable me to slip away from him. "If you're right, it would just leave Gargantua and his remaining Halkan buddy in relative working order," I said.

"And they won't be of much use to him for at least the

rest of the night, either," Fayr considered. "Of course, when it comes time for us to leave the system, it will be a far different story. He'll have time to alert walkers from other worlds and bring them to the Quadrail station long before you can return there by torchliner."

"One problem at a time," I said. "What's so interesting at the art museum?"

"You'll understand when you see it," he said. "In the meantime, who are Daniel Stafford and Daniel Mice?"

"Daniel Stafford is a person of extreme interest," I said. "Both to the Modhri and to Earth's EuroUnion Security Service."

"How so?"

"I told you I met the late owner of one of the Lynx sculptures, a Mr. Rafael Künstler. The general consensus is that Daniel Stafford is probably the one actually in possession of the Lynx at the moment."

The color in Fayr's facial stripes seemed to deepen. "And Daniel Mice?"

"Mr. Künstler's dying words," I told him. "The Modhri believes that's the alias Stafford is running under at the moment."

"You don't think it is?"

"I know it isn't," I assured him.

"*Do* you know the correct name?"

"Very likely," I said. "I'm not entirely sure, but I think so."

Fayr pondered a moment. "Perhaps we won't need a name," he said. "You know what this Human looks like?"

I nodded. "Unfortunately, so does the Modhri."

"The Modhri is not particularly good at distinguishing between Human faces," Fayr said thoughtfully. "At any rate, for the moment at least we have the initiative. We must do our best to reach the Lynx before he does."

"For whatever that'll gain us," I said. "Best guess at the moment is that he's already picked up all the other sculptures."

"No," Fayr murmured. "Not *all* of them."

I was about to ask what he meant by that when the draped fabric on the other couch gave a soft ping. "Someone approaches," Fayr said, his voice suddenly clipped and professional as he bounced to his feet. "Quickly—under the cloakcloth," he continued, pointing to the drape with one hand as he drew one of his guns with the other. "I'll get Bayta."

He was only a couple of steps along the path when the door opened and Bayta slipped hurriedly back into the room. "There's a police car coming this way," she announced tightly.

"Under the cloakcloth," Fayr ordered her, reversing direction back to the couch. Taking the edge of the cloth from me, he pulled it over and up. Bayta sat down beside me and he sat down on her other side, draping the cloth over all three of us.

And a taut silence descended on the room. "What is this?" Bayta whispered, gingerly touching the inside of the cloth.

"Cloakcloth," Fayr told her, his voice low, his eyes on a row of small red lights built into his edge of the cloth. "It absorbs our infrared signatures and shifts them so that detectors will read us as Tra'ho'seej."

"Clever," I murmured. Of course, these particular Tra'ho'seej were supposed to be out of town. I hoped this wasn't one of those areas where citizens had to register their travels with the local police database. "What about your own sensors?" I asked, nodding toward his row of lights.

"Passive detectors only," he assured me. "Slender wires pressed into the ground in various places around this neighborhood. Virtually undetectable."

The uncomfortable silence resumed. I looked sideways at Bayta's profile, at her tight cheek muscles and her eyes focused on the piece of cloakcloth directly in front of her.

Make the time, Fayr had all but ordered me. And he'd

been right. Conflict between allies was potentially disastrous. "Bayta—"

"He wouldn't have hurt her," she interrupted me, her voice as stiff as her expression. "He wouldn't risk losing the advantage she gives him. You should have just kept quiet."

I sighed. So now we had two problems to deal with. "You're mad at me for caving in so easily?" I asked, deciding to deal with the simpler one first.

"The oathlings have already begun the search," she said. "The effects of *Korak* Fayr's sunburst grenade won't interrupt that. By now probably hundreds of non-walker oathlings will have joined the effort."

"Good for them," I said. "The more of Ghonsilya's official attention is tied up looking for a mythical Human named Daniel Mice, the less they'll have left to focus on us."

Her eyes flicked reluctantly sideways toward me. "Are you saying Mr. Stafford's *not* on Ghonsilya?"

"Oh, he's here, all right," I assured her. "Or at least, he was—it's possible he's flown the coop. But he's not traveling under the name Mice."

"A modification of the word, then?" Fayr suggested.

I shook my head. "I don't think Künstler was trying to give me Stafford's traveling name," I said. "I think he was going for something else."

"What?" Bayta asked.

"Think about it," I said. If the Chahwyn were going to kick me out, Bayta needed to work on her detective and deduction skills. "Stafford's supposedly been spinning his wheels through umpteen years of college, taking every class in the catalog, refusing to graduate, and meanwhile spending buckets of money along the way. What sort of parents put up with that?"

"Rich ones," Bayta said. She still sounded cross, but I could hear a growing interest in her voice. "Agent Morse's report said his father was one of Mr. Künstler's business managers."

"Who undoubtedly has better things to do with his money than support a lazy professional student," I said. "But the report also said Stafford continues to have a good relationship with his parents, with no indication they've ever given him any graduate-or-else ultimatums."

"Someone else is funding his education," Fayr said suddenly.

"Exactly," I said. "And once we have *that,* we can look at his course work with a new eye. Bayta, do you remember the list of the majors Stafford's gone through?"

"Agent Morse's report listed business, economics, electronics, medical technology, history, psychology, art appreciation, alien sociology, and advertising," Bayta said, frowning in concentration.

"What do all those taken together add up to?" I prompted. "Considering especially that Künstler's business empire includes medical equipment and a wide range of electronics products and services."

"That Mr. Stafford is being prepared to be a manager of an interstellar business?"

"Bingo," I confirmed. "Only he isn't being prepped to be *a* manager. He's being prepped to be *the* manager."

Bayta swiveled around to look at me. "Are you saying . . . ?"

"I am indeed," I said, nodding. "The whole Stafford name and family identity have been a scam right from square one. Probably a deal Künstler worked out with his manager before Daniel was born."

"Mr. Künstler wasn't saying *Daniel Mice,*" Bayta said, her voice tight. "He was trying to say *Daniel, my son.*"

"You've got it," I said. "Daniel Stafford is, in reality, Daniel Künstler."

THERE WAS A long moment of silence as Bayta and Fayr did their individual siftings through the potential implications of that revelation. "We must make certain the Modhri never learns that truth," Fayr said at last.

"Absolutely," I agreed. Whenever the Modhri decided to make a full-bore move against humanity, the young heir to a trillion-dollar estate would be high on his list of potential targets. "A more immediate concern at the moment is that it will eventually occur to him that all he has to do is get the cops to haul in every Human on Ghonsilya for a visual check against Morse's picture. There can't be *that* many of us here."

"You might be surprised," Fayr said thoughtfully. "According to the official numbers, there are over eight thousand Humans on this planet."

"Eight *thousand*?" I asked. I'd been ready to guess no more than a few hundred.

"That is correct," Fayr said. "There are also twelve hundred Bellidos, if you were wondering."

"What in the world are they all doing here?" I asked. "The Humans, I mean?"

"Most are skilled workers," Fayr said. "Humans have a manual dexterity beyond that of Tra'ho'seej, especially for detail work. There are also many artists." He cocked his head to the side, one of those gestures the Bellidos had picked up from us. "Many of that group are right here in Magaraa City."

I thought about the hotel lobby where the Modhri and I had had our brief fight. The place had been literally strewn with cheap art. "Working for the local trade, I take it?"

"Indeed," Fayr confirmed. "In Ancient Seejlis, *Magaraa* means *Labor of Artisans,* and the residents take that title quite seriously. They cherish all levels and forms of artwork, from inexpensive wall mountings and table settings to masterpieces designated specifically for contemplation rooms."

And Stafford had come here to buy a piece of alien sculpture. "I don't suppose there's a particular restaurant or tavern where these artistic types hang out?"

Fayr smiled. "We think along the same path," he said. "In fact, I can do even better than that. Come; I'll show you."

He lifted the edge of the cloakcloth and climbed out from under it. The lights on the display strip had gone out, I noted, apparently indicating that the police patrol had moved on. "You think it's safe to travel?" I asked as Bayta and I also climbed out.

"I believe so," he said, refolding the cloakcloth onto the edge of the couch, ready for its next use. "I've spent some time studying Tra'ho police procedure. Once they've swept an area, they seldom return to it. Not unless a serious crime has been committed."

"You don't call a double killing a serious crime?"

"Not in this case." Fayr rumbled deep in his throat. "The victims weren't Tra'ho'seej."

I grimaced. Sometimes I forgot how much specism there was lurking beneath the surface civility of the Twelve Empires. "And neither were the killers."

"Exactly," he said. "Disputes between aliens are hardly a matter of importance unless they also threaten the local citizens."

"What about the sunburst?" Bayta asked. "It specifically targeted the oathlings."

"All of whom will do everything in their power to downplay the effects and the investigation," Fayr said. "The last thing the Modhri wants is for the Lynx to fall into official hands not directly under his control."

He stepped over to the other couch and pulled another of the ubiquitous hooded rain ponchos from beneath it. "Still, we don't wish to make it too easy for them," he said. Handing it to me, he bent down again and busied himself with something else beneath the couch.

The poncho was a shade on the small side, and I had to work a little to get it over my head. By the time I finished settling it into place and could see again, I discovered that Fayr had pulled out a new gun.

Not one of his usual shoulder-holstered handguns this time, but a Rontra 772 submachine gun, a large military snub-nosed multiple repeater with double-clip magazine, midline cooling chamber, integrated underslung grenade launcher, and a sensor-click sighting capability that could pinpoint a target at two thousand meters. The thing looked about the size of the cannon Gargantua had been talking about earlier, and could probably make nearly as much of a mess of anyone who happened to be standing in its way. "Still not wanting to make it too easy for them?" I asked.

"Exactly," Fayr said. Hiking up his poncho, he slung the Rontra's strap over his right shoulder, letting the weapon hang down alongside the holster there. He hesitated a moment, then drew the handgun from that holster and handed it to me. "Lest it be in my way," he added.

"Thanks," I said, checking the safety. "Killrounds?"

His nose twitched a bit. "Clip two has snoozers."

I found the selector and switched it over. Fayr may have worked out the difference between Modhran walkers and soldiers, but I wasn't nearly so ready to make that kind of delicate distinction.

Besides, I didn't need anything else for Bayta to be mad at me about.

I stuck the gun into my belt. Fayr and I both resettled our ponchos—his was barely long enough to conceal the Rontra's muzzle—and then I turned to Bayta.

She was watching us with a mixture of disbelief, distaste, and disapproval. It was the same look I remembered my mother giving me when I used to play soldier with my friends when I was six. "Would you like one, too?" I offered.

"Whenever you're ready," she said, not even bothering to answer the question.

"We're ready," Fayr said. "Follow me."

SIXTEEN

The rain had increased in intensity while we'd been inside, but the lack of wind kept it from blowing beneath our hoods into our faces or otherwise being particularly unpleasant. The neighborhood immediately around us seemed to have reacted to the precipitation by closing down for the night, most of the houses showing cheery lights through their curtained windows as their inhabitants settled in for the evening. There were still a few pedestrians in sight, but none was closer than half a block away. There were also a fair number of cars out and about, but the drivers all seemed intent on taking care of their business and getting back home.

We walked without speaking, surrounded by the sizzle of the rain on the sidewalk and the hissing of tires on wet pavement as cars went by. The homes and other buildings around us gradually changed from our original middle-class neighborhood to a slightly lower-middle-class area, then reversed itself and started up the social scale again. By the time we reached the museum grounds, the houses had become full-bore estates, with the sculpted facades and manicured lawns and fenced perimeters to prove it.

The art museum itself left them all in the dust.

It was as if the designers couldn't make up their minds

whether they wanted a museum, a mansion, or a Greek temple, so they'd compromised and made it a combination of all three. The place was as imposing as the Rock of Gibraltar, had the solid look of a structure built to last into the next millennium, and was big enough to lose a small army inside. Apparently, the people of Magaraa City took their reputation as art lovers very seriously.

And it was currently lit up like Times Square on VI Day. "I thought you said they'd closed early tonight," I said in a low voice as we walked toward it.

"They did," Fayr confirmed. "The staff must be preparing for the auction."

"Auction?"

"An art auction tomorrow evening," he explained. "The objects for sale will be on display during the day for potential buyers to examine."

"This sort of thing happen often?" I asked.

"Not to my knowledge," Fayr said. "The fifty percent commission the museum will be charging for each sale will be put toward repairing the damage caused by the intrusion. Come—there's a side door we can use."

The side door turned out to be a service entrance built to accommodate forklift-sized vehicles and their cargoes. It was locked, but apparently not all that seriously, and in less than thirty seconds Fayr had it open wide enough for us to get through. "Stay here," he murmured, and slipped inside. Nudging Bayta back into what limited shadows there were near the door, I drew my gun, keeping it ready but hidden beneath the edge of my poncho.

Two minutes later Fayr was back. "Come, but quietly," he said.

Beyond the door was a wide service corridor with the utilitarian look of service corridors everywhere. Fayr led us through a maze of several more, each getting progressively narrower as other corridors branched off the main one to other parts of the museum.

Finally, we reached one that dead-ended at a normal-sized door. Fayr eased it open, looked inside, then gestured us in.

Up to now all we'd seen of the museum's interior were the staff and worker sections. With this room we'd finally made it into the public display areas, and I saw that the same people who'd designed the exterior had extended their schizophrenic triple architectural theme inward. The gallery we were in was quite large, with curved marble walls and a cupola-type ceiling with moldings and frescoes and whatnots thrown in everywhere by the shovelful. The carpeted softfloor had an embedded pattern of tiny starlights that could probably be programmed to give a viewer a customized tour, while strategically placed benches allowed the serious art connoisseur to linger in his or her contemplation.

It was truly a place of elegance and beauty. Or at least it had been. Now, squarely in the center of all that splendor, the gallery had become a blackened, ruined mess.

"The damage I spoke of," Fayr said. "Tell me what you make of it."

I walked across the floor, eyeing the destruction as I ran through my mental list of things that go bump in the night. It had been caused by an explosion—that much was obvious. But the radius of the blast and the progressive damage pattern didn't match anything I was familiar with. "What did the police report say?" I asked.

"That there had been an explosion," Fayr said. "Specific cause unknown."

"Any witnesses or security records?"

"The security cameras had been shut down," Fayr said. "Suspicion has fallen on one or both of the two guards on duty that night, neither of whom has been seen since then."

"*Neither* of them?"

"No," he said. "But traces of their nucleic matter was recovered at the site, along with that of an unidentified Jurian."

I rubbed my jaw as I measured distances with my

eyes. The explosion had caused nearly complete destruction within a three-meter-radius sphere, even chewing up the floor, the subflooring, and the concrete foundation. But outside that radius, the damage dropped off dramatically to the point where the floor, display easels, and pillars ten meters away weren't even scorched. "The first part seems straightforward enough, anyway," I said. "The Modhri turned one of the guards into a walker and used him to shut off the cameras and open the door for the Jurian thief."

"But then what of the explosion?" Fayr asked. "Did the second guard surprise them and a grenade accidentally go off?"

"Does seem awfully sloppy on somebody's part," I agreed. "Besides, all short-range grenades I know of leave a lot more body residue behind. Do we know where the Viper was displayed?"

Fayr pointed across the room. "It was in a case against that wall with several other Nemuti artifacts."

"So the thieves were heading for our service door," I concluded, a funny feeling starting to grow in the pit of my stomach. "But before they could reach it, the second guard came in and confronted them. Shortly thereafter, the whole group got themselves vaporized."

There was a long, heavy silence. Bayta broke it first, with the conclusion all three of us had obviously reached. "The Viper exploded," she said, her voice tight. "*That's* what the Nemuti sculptures are. They're bombs."

"And the Modhri already has seven of them," I added, the funny feeling in my stomach changing to a knot as the full implications of that began to trickle in.

"Apparently so," Fayr said. "Still, unless the Modhri can create a more powerful version, I don't see how this gains him very much."

"That's because you don't know the whole story," I told him. "I had the opportunity to do a scan of one of the Hawks on the trip here. It turns out the things are sensor chameleons. Put one of them in a bag, maybe even just wrap a towel around it, and it takes on the characteristics of that object as far as sensors are concerned. It might work with liquids, too. I never got a chance to test that."

Fayr's facial stripes had gone dark. "Are you saying," he said slowly, "that they can be taken aboard a Quadrail train without detection?"

"You got it," I said grimly. "Aboard a Quadrail, through a transfer station, probably even onto a warship. The Modhri doesn't have to learn how to enhance the effect, Fayr. If he can figure out even just how to duplicate it, this war is about to take a very nasty turn."

"He's going to use them against the Spiders," Bayta murmured, a shiver running through her. "He can't infiltrate them or take them over, so he's going to kill them."

"Actually, he's not," I assured her. "Because we're going to stop him."

She turned hot eyes to me. "Will that be before or after we rescue Ms. Auslander from him?"

"Why not do both together?" I said tartly. "I *am* capable of thinking about more than one thing at the same time, you know."

"It's not the thinking part I'm worried about," she countered.

"Then what *are* you worried about?" I demanded. "That Penny's going to steal me away from you?"

I knew the instant the words were out of my mouth that it was the absolutely wrong thing to say. But the words were already gone, and it was an eternity too late to call them back. Bayta's throat tightened, her eyes again those of someone who's just been slapped. Without a word, she spun around and stalked away from us across the room.

I started to follow her, paused; started to speak; paused again. Indecision and inertia won out and I didn't do anything. "That was helpful," Fayr murmured.

"*Thank* you," I growled back.

"You'll need to find another opportunity to talk," he said. Again, it was more order than suggestion. "In the meantime, the Nemuti sculptures as bombs cannot be the whole story."

"Why not?" I asked, my eyes and half my attention still on Bayta's stiff back.

"If he seeks to reproduce the effect, he needs only one sculpture to experiment with," Fayr said. "He certainly would not need to go to this much risk to obtain the last Lynx."

Resolutely, I shook Bayta and her anger at me out of my mind. Fayr was right. "Unless he doesn't think he can duplicate the technology," I said. "In that case, he'd want every one he can get hold of."

"No," Fayr said, shaking his head. "Something is still missing."

"Maybe we can figure it out once we have the Lynx," I said. "Earlier you said—"

I broke off as his left hand suddenly snapped up in a gesture for silence. He spun to face the archway leading out of our gallery into the rest of the museum, his Rontra popping into view from beneath the concealing poncho.

I resisted the urge to make extraneous noise by hauling out my own gun, opting instead to freeze in place and listen. The typical sounds of a large, mostly hollow, mostly deserted building whispered across my ears.

And then my ears and brain edited out the background noise, and I heard the slow, measured footsteps coming our way.

Bayta heard the footsteps, too. She turned back toward Fayr and me, her eyes wide with sudden urgency. I motioned for her to stay put, and got a grip on my gun. The footsteps came closer . . .

"Compton?" a familiar voice called softly from somewhere beyond the archway.

It was Gargantua.

Fayr threw me a sideways look. I threw him one back, making sure mine had a little curdle to it. So much for his sunburst grenade knocking Gargantua and the other Halkan walker out of the game for the rest of the night.

"Compton?" Gargantua called again, a little louder this time. "Please come out. I plan no action against you, but wish merely to talk."

Bayta was shaking her head, pointing insistently at the service door we'd used on our way in. I looked at Fayr again, saw my own ambivalence reflected there. Bayta's choice of a fast cut and run seemed the logical response. Certainly it would be the smart military move.

But if the Modhri wanted to take us, he would have cops surrounding the building by now. Actually, he would probably have had them lobbing in sleep gas already. Chances were good that, for once, he was telling the truth.

Fayr was still waiting for my call. Keeping hold of my gun, I gave Bayta a reassuring smile and made my way across the gallery. Carefully, I peeked around the corner.

I was looking into another gallery, this one every bit as elegant as the one I was standing in. More elegant, actually, since no one had set off a bomb in the middle of it.

Seated on one of the contemplation benches about twenty meters away was Gargantua.

He was, to put it bluntly, a mess. His eyes were heavily bandaged, the bandage riding over the top curve of his snout and half covering his ears. The facial skin the bandage didn't cover had gone a deep purple, the Halkan version of serious sunburn. Gripped in his hands was a sensor cane, its bottom end planted firmly in the soft-floor, its aperture swiveling back and forth across the width of my archway.

"Hello, Modhri," I greeted him as I came the rest of the way around the corner. "You're looking good."

"You lie," Gargantua said calmly. The hand resting on the top of the cane rotated a little, swiveling the sensor aperture to point directly at me. "A very effective weapon, that."

"Especially against someone like you who shares pain and all the other unpleasantries of life," I agreed. "How are you doing with the Tra'ho'seej vertigo? I notice you decided to sit down."

His lips curled back to reveal his teeth. "I'm not in a position to force you to my will, if that's what you mean," he said. "Still, never forget that I can eliminate that particular effect whenever I choose."

Translation: at any point the Modhri colonies inside the Tra'ho'seej could simply kill themselves and their hosts, eliminating the vertigo flowing through the local Modhri mind segment by eliminating the central nervous systems that were generating it. Rather like curing dandruff by cutting off your head, except that in this case it would actually work. "I don't think that would be a good idea," I pointed out. "By my count, you're down to two functioning walkers at the moment."

"That, too, is easily changed," he said. "But I didn't come here to talk about me. I came to talk about your Human friends."

I felt a lump rise into my throat. Penny . . . "How are they doing?"

"They are in pain," the Modhri said. "Also frightened. Also very angry."

I grimaced before I could catch myself. "I imagine so," I agreed, wondering fleetingly what kind of visual resolution he was getting from his cane. With Humans, it took a month or more of practice before the brain learned to read the input stream well enough to decipher faces and read expressions. I didn't know how long that adaptation took with Halkas, and had even less of an idea how long it took with the Modhri.

Apparently not as long as I would have liked. "You seem distressed," he said.

"I've seen you in action," I reminded him. "I dislike the thought of any civilized being falling into your hands."

"As well you should," he said coldly. "But at the moment there is no need for concern. The only damage perpetrated on either of them was that inflicted by the Human McMicking."

"Who?" I asked innocently.

And this time I *did* manage to keep my face from giving anything away. So the Modhri thought it was Larry Hardin's troubleshooter Bruce McMicking who had thrown the sunburst grenade, and not the rogue Belldic commando *Korak* Fayr. A reasonable mistake for him to have made, and one that might prove to be useful.

"Do not play innocent," Gargantua admonished me. "I saw him throw that grenade."

"Actually, all you saw was a street drifter fumbling with something," I corrected him. "You never saw the actual grenade."

Gargantua snorted. "This is a foolish lie," he said. "I know you had no such device with you."

"Do you?" I countered, raising my eyebrows.

For a long minute he remained silent, his face turned to me as if he was trying to stare straight through his bandages into my mind.

Because I was right. All he actually knew was that he'd had me under surveillance since before we'd left the Quadrail, and that I hadn't had a chance to pick up any military hardware along the way.

And of course, he knew that no one was permitted to carry such things aboard a Quadrail.

But he also knew that I was in league with the Spiders . . . and allies of the Spiders might operate under entirely different rules.

"I know what I saw," he said at last. "But even with the Human McMicking's aid, it will not be possible for you to locate the other Humans." His face hardened. "I would presume you won't wish the Ghonsilya authorities to call you in to identify the Human Auslander's body."

He was bluffing, of course. We both knew that. He couldn't afford to damage the only levers he had to use against me.

But even so I still felt a tingle of dread ripple through me at the thought of what he might do to Penny.

And we also both knew that I couldn't and wouldn't

let anything happen to her. "There won't be any need for that," I said between dry lips. "There's an art auction scheduled here for tomorrow evening. Bring Morse and Ms. Auslander with you."

He leaned the cane a little toward me, as if trying to read my face. "You have the Lynx?"

"I will by then," I promised. "A straight trade: the Humans for the Lynx."

"I accept," he said. "But be warned. If you don't have the Lynx, things will not go well for your friends."

"I'll keep that in mind," I said. "There's just one more thing, then. Since I can't have you following me—"

He never even had time to react as I pulled out my gun and shot him.

He slumped limply over the back of the bench, his cane thudding to the softfloor, as the snoozer's drug hit his bloodstream and knocked him cold. Mindful of what Fayr had once told me about a Modhran colony's resistance to such drugs, I fired again, then put a third snoozer into him just to be on the safe side. Slipping the gun back beneath my poncho, keeping an eye on the archways leading off into other sections of the museum, I gave his clothing a quick search.

I'd had some faint hope that the Modhri might have been careless enough to let Gargantua head off to our meeting with a hotel key or other significant clue on his person. But no such luck. Nothing in his pockets gave any indication of where he might have Penny and Morse hidden.

Keeping an eye on him over my shoulder, I returned to the other gallery. Fayr and Bayta had moved to the edge of the archway in my absence, no doubt the better to eavesdrop on the conversation. I gave them a thumbs-up, a finger across the lips for continued silence, and gestured toward the exit.

Five minutes later, we were back out in the rain, making our way across the museum grounds. I'd half expected the Modhri to have stationed his other Halkan soldier out here as backup, just in case I pulled something on Gargantua. But there was no sign of anyone hanging around, and neither Fayr's sensors or the ones in my gimmicked reader indicated any evidence of electronic surveillance focused on us.

It retrospect, I decided I wasn't really surprised the other Halka wasn't here. Locking up a trained ESS agent like Morse somewhere was tricky enough without having to trust him to stay that way on his own. The Modhri had apparently decided keeping tabs on me was less important than making sure he held on to his bargaining chips.

Especially since the only way out of the Ghonsilya system was through the Quadrail station. If I double-crossed him and ran, he knew where I'd eventually have to turn up.

We were out of sight of the museum building itself before Fayr spoke again. "*Do* you know where the Lynx is?"

"Not yet," I said. "But now that we're here, I don't think we'll have any trouble laying our hands on it."

"And you genuinely intend to trade it to the Modhri for your friends?"

"We'll see what we can do," I hedged. "But before we can cross that bridge we need to find Daniel Stafford. You said you know a place where these artist types hang out?"

Fayr was silent for a few more steps. Maybe he wasn't sure anymore whether to trust me or not. "There's a place a short distance away on the other side of the museum grounds," he said at last. "It's called Artists' Paradise."

I turned to glance down a side street as we passed, the movement tilting my hood just enough to send a rivulet of rain into my eyes. "Sounds interesting," I said, brushing away the water with the back of my hand. "Lead the way."

SEVENTEEN

We continued walking directly away from the museum for a couple more blocks, then changed direction and made a wide circle around the whole museum area.

I also discovered I'd been wrong earlier about the neighborhood buttoning up for the night. Now that the dinner hour was over, the streets and sidewalks were starting to fill up again as the locals ventured out into the rain and their evening activities. The increasing number of pedestrians made it harder to be sure we weren't being followed, but at the same time it offered more cover if we needed to make a break for it.

The neighborhoods themselves also began to change again, this time definitely not for the better. Whereas on the other side of the museum the homes had ranged from lower-middle-class pleasant to full-blown high-class snooty, the real estate on this side seemed to be sliding rapidly toward the opposite end of the scale.

"Not what I'd consider your typical paradise-type area," I commented as we walked past a row of houses that were little more than closely packed shacks. "Who named this place, the same real estate fogger who tagged a frozen wasteland as Greenland?"

"This is not the Paradise," Fayr said. He pointed two

blocks ahead, to a large structure looming over the smaller homes around it. "*That* is the Paradise."

I eyed it. Even from this distance, I could see that the building included a few hints of the same architectural style as the art museum.

But where that place had been carefully and lovingly maintained, this one had been allowed to go straight to the dogs. "I don't see a lot of improvement," I told Fayr.

"It looks like a theater," Bayta said.

"It's an amphitheater, actually, with a central, open-air performance area," Fayr said. "The reference listing states that after it fell into disuse and disrepair poor street artists moved in. They turned the dressing rooms and equipment shops into their homes and studios."

I nodded. It was the same move-in-and-squat technique the down-and-out had been doing for centuries, probably everywhere in the galaxy. "The authorities couldn't get rid of them?"

"On the contrary," Fayr said. "Over the past decades the authorities have created an aura of local attraction around the Paradise and its residents. Many artists, particularly offworlders, have journeyed to Ghonsilya specifically to spend time here."

"They want to *live* there?" Bayta asked.

"I'm certain they're surprised at what they find," Fayr said grimly. "But by the time they learn the truth, many aren't able to leave."

"I don't understand," Bayta said.

"It's a matter of economics," I said. The Chahwyn who'd raised her, I suspected, had passed over many of the more sordid facts of modern life. "Artists come to Ghonsilya, lured by the Tra'ho reputation as art lovers and maybe stories and out-of-date photos of the Artists' Paradise."

"The first part is true, certainly," Fayr murmured.

"Absolutely," I agreed. "The Tra'ho'seej are certainly eager to buy up their art—that hotel lobby was loaded to the gills with the stuff."

"Then I don't understand the problem," Bayta said.

"The problem is that the Tra'ho'seej probably don't pay very much," I told her. "If they keep the prices low—and there are any number of ways to do that—then the artists end up stuck. They have to keep cranking out artwork to survive, but are never quite able to scrape together enough money to pull up stakes and go somewhere else."

"I've heard that some of the poorest trade their art directly for food at the local restaurants and markets," Fayr said.

"Where again the buyer gets to set the exchange rate," I said. "When love turns to obsession."

Bayta gave me an odd look. "What?"

"Art-loving becoming art-obsession," I clarified.

"Oh," Bayta said, the odd look not going away. "I thought you were talking about . . . never mind. But surely not all their work is traded by barter."

"The more expensive pieces are sold directly to customers," Fayr said. "In fact, many of the transactions take place right here in the Paradise." He looked around at the lower-class Tra'ho'seej milling around. "Though only during the daylight hours."

"We can't afford to wait," I told him. "With all those Tra'ho walkers lying in bed watching their ceilings spin around, the local Modhri mind segment is as weak and inattentive as it's likely to get. We need to find Stafford tonight."

"You believe he's in the Paradise?" Fayr asked.

"If he's not, he should be," I told him. "If you want to find art, go where the artists are. If you *really* want to find art, live where the artists live."

Fayr lifted his head to look at the top of the dilapidated building. "There's a great deal of area here for three people to search," he commented. "We'd best get started."

"Right," I said. "He's my species. Let me do the talking."

The Paradise main entrance was a large archway of the

same style as the ones we'd seen in the art museum. Leading inward from the archway was an entrance tunnel lined by closed doors and a number of shabbily dressed Tra'ho'seej. Most of the loiterers were sitting around talking, inhaling aromatic censer smoke, or moodily watching everyone else. The tunnel also had a double row of light fixtures set about head height, but only one light in six or seven was actually lit. "I can see why the buyers only come during the day," I murmured.

I'd barely finished the comment when a group of five Tra'ho youths leaning against the tunnel fifteen meters ahead detached themselves from their section of wall and sauntered their way into a loose line across our path.

"Compton?" Fayr asked.

"It's okay," I told him as I studied the youths. All had long knives displayed prominently at their sides, but I didn't see any of the telltale clothing bulges or strains that would indicate heavier weaponry. Focusing on the tallest of the five, I nodded a greeting. "Evening, young honoreds," I called. "Is this the Artists' Paradise we've heard so much about?"

[The Paradise is closed to business,] the Tra'ho said brusquely in Seejlis.

"All the artists have gone to sleep, have they?" I asked. "Nestled all snug in their beds, with visions of sugarplums and all that?"

[The Paradise is closed,] he repeated, dropping his hand warningly to his knife hilt. [Come back with the sunlight.]

"Sorry, but we can't do that," I said, watching his friends out of the corner of my eye as I continued forward. The whole group seemed a little confused by my strange inability to take the hint.

Which implied this was probably not just some random group of toughs looking for someone to rob. If they were, they'd be moving in for the kill instead of trying to wave us off. Guards, then, hired by the artists to protect them after dark?

If so, we might be able to work that to our advantage. "I'm afraid we're running a tight schedule and have to be gone by morning," I continued. I was about three steps away from the leader now, and his hand had wrapped around his knife hilt in preparation for a quick draw. "I'm told there's a Human here who's looking for the sort of thing we're selling."

His ears twitched with surprise. Apparently dealers didn't come around at night, either. [What is it you sell?]

"An item one of the artists very much wants," I said. "*And* is willing to pay a great deal of money for."

That one got an ear twitch from all five of them. A Paradise artist with spare cash was probably something of a rarity.

For a gang of lower-class toughs, it would be an extremely intriguing rarity. [What Human could that possibly be?] the leader asked. He was clearly trying to be casual about it, but there was enough body language going on to light up a small city. [There are no such Humans here.]

"There's at least one," I said.

[Perhaps if you gave us a name?] he suggested.

"His name's Stafford," I said, trying to watch all five of them at once. No reaction. "He may be going under the name Daniel, or Dan, or Danny. Or possibly Künstler."

Still no reaction. [There is no one with any of these names,] the leader said, sounding a bit disappointed.

"Or maybe he simply calls himself Artist," I suggested.

The leader still didn't react. But out of the corner of my eye I saw a distinct ripple of recognition run through one of his buddies.

Bingo.

Maybe the leader didn't think I'd caught the mark. [All here call themselves Artists,] he scoffed.

"We still want to look for him," I said. "We can pass peaceably, or otherwise."

The leader snorted. [Search all you like,] he invited, stepping aside and motioning the rest of the group to do likewise. [You won't find the Human you describe.]

"We'll see," I said. "By the way, I don't suppose any of the food vendors in here are still open?"

[Some sellers of sculpted foods will be preparing their wares for tomorrow,] the Tra'ho who'd reacted to the name Artist spoke up. [One of them may be willing to sell to you.]

"Thank you," I said, watching for a last-minute sneak attack as I stepped past them. But they were apparently genuinely willing to let us pass.

Small wonder. They knew this place; we didn't. They figured they would be able to get to Stafford and his cash sticks long before we did. Especially if we stopped for supper first.

Fayr and Bayta passed through the line, too, and we continued down the tunnel. " 'Artist'?" Fayr asked.

"The English translation of the German word Künstler," I told him. "Could be that's what got the late Mr. Künstler interested in art collecting in the first place."

A few meters ahead, the tunnel opened up into a curved corridor, probably a ring paralleling the amphitheater's central performance area. As we turned to the right into the curve, I glanced casually over my shoulder, just in time to see the last of the five toughs disappear through one of the tunnel's left-hand doors.

"They're hoping they can reach Stafford before we do," Fayr warned.

"That's the idea," I said. "They're going to play native guides for us."

"There will be an entire roundrun of rooms and corridors in a place like this," Fayr countered. "If we let them out of our sight, we'll almost certainly lose them."

"Stafford won't be in any of the rooms," I assured him. "The nicer quarters will have been grabbed up by the older residents years ago. Newcomers like Stafford will be stuck in the central area out in the elements."

"Unless he's visiting someone," Bayta said quietly. "Or has persuaded a new friend to let him move in."

I stared at her, my stomach knotting. Somehow, neither of those possibilities had even occurred to me.

For a moment my tongue was frozen. Fortunately, Fayr interpreted my silence correctly. "No fears," he said, and headed back down the tunnel at a brisk trot.

Bayta was still staring at me, and I didn't much like the expression on her face. "Don't look at me like that," I reproved her. "I know what I'm doing."

"Do you?" she countered. "You don't seem to be thinking clearly lately."

"Let me guess," I growled. "Penny. Right?"

The last time I'd brought up Penny's name it had sparked an instant and decidedly unpleasant reaction. This time, Bayta didn't even twitch. "Not necessarily," she said, her voice tight but under control. "But since you bring her up, yes, I'm concerned at how you've been behaving. How both of you have been behaving, actually."

"You don't think a woman like her could possibly want anything to do with someone like me?" I demanded.

"She's not in your class, Frank," Bayta said. "If there's really something there . . ." Her throat worked. "Danger and tension can bring people together. I know that. People who otherwise might not ever even look at each other—"

"Is there a reason we're having this conversation right now?" I cut her off. "Because if not, we need to get out there and find Stafford."

"That *is* the reason," Bayta said. "I'm wondering if you really want to find Mr. Stafford. Or at least, whether you want to find him alive."

Once, years ago, a criminal kingpin I'd just nailed had offered me a bribe to let him go. This felt exactly the same way. "If you really believe that, you don't know me at all," I said stiffly. "Come on. We have a job to do."

Turning my back on her, I continued down the curved corridor, walking as fast as I could without breaking into a jog. I didn't know if Bayta was having any trouble keeping up with me. For the moment, I didn't care.

The area we'd come to was somewhat better lit than the tunnel had been, and certainly better populated. Small booths lined the walls, most with the appearance of art dealerships, most of them deserted and closed. As the toughs had suggested, a few of the booths with food and drink products still had people working them. The less artsy types, the ones selling flatcake, soups, and Tra'hok vegetable twists, were doing a fairly brisk business.

The general atmosphere of the place was more or less as expected. Most of the beings wandering through the gloom had a generally disheveled appearance, with ratty hair, feathers, or fur and old or at least rumpled clothing. Many had cobbled together outfits and adornments that were bizarre blends of their particular culture's class indicators. There were Juriani with the unpolished scales of commoners, yet wearing the tiered—though badly faded—clothing of midlevel royalty; Cimmaheem with their yarnlike hair braided, upper-class style, but only on one side; and Pirks who had preen-glossed feathers but wore no status headdresses. Either they were trying to hang on to the status they'd once had, or else were hoping an odd look would make them stand out of the crowd when the paying customers came around.

One of the artsy booths still had a lone Nemut on duty. He was polishing some jewelry, his gaze drifting across the collection of colorful characters as he worked, his truncated-cone mouth orifice making little silent motions as if he was humming to himself. His rainbow-slashed eyes passed across us, paused, and came back again.

Someone who could distinguish between Human faces well enough to recognize we didn't belong there. That would be a good place to start. Changing direction, I headed toward his booth.

"Fine evening to you, Humans," he said in better than passable English as we reached him. His angled shoulder muscles flexed briefly in traditional Nemuti greeting. "Have you come to shop for fine artistry?"

"Perhaps later," I said, glancing over the necklaces, rings, and ear cuffs in his display case, most of them composed of nested strips of copper, gold, and silver. It wasn't a style I'd seen before, but I found it rather attractive. "First, we have to locate a friend."

The Nemut gave a long, sibilant sniffle. "Few here have friends," he said. "Has your friend a name?"

"He's a Human," I said. "I understand he goes by the name Artist."

The other tossed his head, his tight middle-class curls glinting in the faint light. "Ah," he said, his tone changing subtly. "Artist. Yes, I know the one."

"I take it you don't like him?" I asked.

"We are all artists," the Nemut said scornfully. "But this Human almost doesn't deserve such a title. All he does is play with his claywork and pester those of us who are Nemuti with questions about ancient sculptures."

"Yes, that sounds like our friend," I agreed. "Do you know where we might find him?"

He nodded his head back over his shoulder. "His dwelling is in the courtyard," he said. "A small gray tent with green edges."

"Thank you," I said, eyeing the jewelry again. "How late will you be open?"

"Another hour at least," he said, his eyes reflecting cautious hope. "Longer for anyone truly interested in my work."

"We'll be back," I promised. Glancing around, I located Bayta, standing a couple of steps behind me with smoldering fire in her eyes, then headed toward the nearest corridor angling inward. Two corridors later we stepped out again into the cold night rain onto a landing about five meters above the old amphitheater's performance ground.

It was like a scene from an apocalyptic dit rec drama. The yard stretched out in front of us, dark and wet and gloomy, a combination tent city and tenement with a bit of macabre street fair thrown in. The open ground was crowded with tents and small pavilions of random sizes and shapes, their surfaces glistening in the rain. Wedged into some of the unoccupied areas were small furnaces, probably pottery kilns, with tendrils of steam rising wherever the rain hit. Hooded figures hunched around them, their faces red in the glow of the small fires.

In the center of the courtyard was a much bigger fire pit, maybe thirty meters across, with a fading bonfire in the center. The pit was surrounded by a shin-high wall built of stone, with numerous long indented pathways leading to within three, four, or five meters of the blaze. All the indentations were occupied, some by glass blowers, others by blacksmiths working bits of metal. There was a painter halfway down one of the indentations as well, working briskly at an easel hooded against the rain. Either the smoke of the burning wood was an integral part of his painting, or else he was just looking for free heat.

There were figures moving all through the area, some of them hooded, many of them not. Their conversation formed a low rumble punctuated by the rhythmic clinking from the metalworkers and an occasional shout or barked laugh that rose above the general background.

"Here we are," I said, waving a hand over the scene.

"Wonderful," Bayta said with an edge of sarcasm. "Now all we have to do is find a single Human in all of this."

A movement a quarter of the way around the courtyard caught my eye. It was the five toughs from the entry tunnel, spread out in a search line and working their way through the mass of tents and artists. "No problem," I said, nodding toward them, feeling a surge of wounded vindication. I'd been right about this one, anyway. "Our bird dogs have arrived."

"And?" Bayta prompted, gesturing toward the stairs leading down from our landing to the main yard.

"Patience," I said. "Once we head down into the courtyard we'll lose sight of them. I want at least a general idea of where they're going first."

We didn't have long to wait. Midway through the grounds they converged on a small tent. "Is that the tent the jeweler described?" Bayta asked.

"Hard to tell in this light," I said, forcing myself not to charge immediately to the rescue. If Stafford wasn't home and the toughs headed somewhere else, we wouldn't have a hope of finding them again in that maze.

Sure enough, the leader pulled open the flap, glanced inside, and let it drop again. He held a brief consultation with his friends, and then the whole group continued their inward path.

"The bonfire," Bayta said suddenly. "The jeweler said he did claywork."

"And he needs a fire to bake it with," I agreed. Automatically, I started to take her arm, remembered at the last second she was mad at me, and let my hand fall back to my side. "Let's go."

The main ground was every bit as densely packed as it had looked from the higher vantage point. Most of the residents were milling around slowly, not in any hurry to get wherever they were going. I was, and I must have winged at least half a dozen of them on my way through.

The toughs had reached the low wall and were working their way around it in our direction when we came within sight of them again. I caught Bayta's arm as she started around the last tent between us and the fire pit, pulling her back into partial concealment. "Easy," I murmured. "Don't want to spook them until they've finished doing the legwork for us."

They had made it past three of the indentations when the one who had reacted to the Artist name suddenly pointed into the next pathway ahead.

I squinted through the blaze of the fire. A lone figure

was crouched at the far end of the indentation, wearing a metalworker's protective face shield, full-torso apron, and gauntlets. He was fiddling with something on the stone barrier in front of him.

What with the glare and the garb, I couldn't imagine how the Tra'ho could recognize anyone. But the leader apparently had no doubts. He glanced furtively around, tapped one of his gang on the shoulder, and headed in. Three of the toughs followed, the one he'd touched staying behind and planting himself in the center of the indentation's entrance, his hand resting casually on his knife hilt.

"That's our cue," I told Bayta, and headed around the tent.

The Tra'ho spotted us as we came around the last curve of the wall. Like an idiot, he decided to try a bluff first. [We are seeking your friend,] he said as we came up to him. [We think he might be—]

He broke off in midsentence as I kept coming, finally drawing his knife from its sheath. Too late. I swung my left arm down, catching his wrist with mine and deflecting his thrust to the side. As I did so, I jabbed downward with my right fist, catching the nerve center at the top of his hip.

He went down in a flailing tangle of limbs as his leg collapsed beneath him. I caught him with a cross-punch to the top of his right shoulder as he fell, paralyzing that arm as well and sending the knife clattering against the fire pit wall. Scooping up the weapon, I pitched it over the wall into the ashes and took his place in the center of the pathway.

By now the other four Tra'ho'seej had collected their victim and were heading back toward me. One of the toughs was on either side of the man, gripping his apron straps, his knife hand pressed against the victim's sides. The other two strode along in front of them, their own knives pressed into partial concealment against their sides. I couldn't see any of their expressions with the glare of the fire behind them, but I could imagine they weren't looking very pleased to see me standing in their way.

Six paces away, the leader motioned for the rear group to stop. He and the other front man took another pace forward and also stopped. [Out of the way,] he ordered me, tapping his knife against his leg for emphasis.

I folded my arms across my chest. "Make me," I invited.

EIGHTEEN

For a moment he just stood there, probably wondering what kind of suicidal moron faced down two knives without any weapon of his own.

Then I saw his eyes flick down to their friend, moaning quietly on the ground where I'd left him. That was apparently all the answer he needed. He and his buddy started toward me again, leaving their companions and their prisoner still hanging back out of danger.

I let them get two more steps, then held out a hand like a cop directing traffic. "Let's all calm down," I advised. "You really don't want to do this."

The pair took one more step before coming to a somewhat leisurely halt, putting them almost within knife-thrust range of my stomach. [You think not?] the leader asked.

"I'm sure not," I assured him. "All that blood and pain. Yuck."

[Then move from our path and live,] he said.

"You misunderstand," I said. "I wasn't talking about *my* blood." I inclined my head to my left.

For a moment he just stared at me. Then, cautiously, he turned his head.

And froze. Fayr was standing in the next indentation over, halfway in toward the fire where he had a perfect view of all four toughs' backs. His poncho was draped up and over his Rontra 772 as he held it shoulder-slung at his side, only the tip of the muzzle coyly peeking out.

"Trust me, he can take out both of your friends before either has a chance to do anything," I said. "The knives go away now, right?"

All four Tra'ho'seej were staring at Fayr now. They were still staring when their prisoner abruptly twisted his arms out of his captors' grips and dropped flat on his stomach onto the ground.

I tensed, as I'm sure the toughs did, waiting for Fayr to take advantage of the newly cleared field of fire to mow them down. But Fayr was cooler than that. More to the point, he also knew we needed to keep a low profile. "The knives go away now, right?" I repeated.

The leader muttered something under his breath, and the knives disappeared back into their sheaths. I gestured, and the two toughs in back moved up to join their friends. "Have a seat," I invited, waving at the low fire pit wall, and headed in to get their newly freed prisoner.

He had gotten back to his feet by the time I reached him. "Good evening," I greeted him. "Mr. Da—?"

"What the hell was *that*?" he cut me off tartly, his voice muffled by his face shield. "I gave you a perfect opening against those killers, and you just stood there."

"It's called restraint," I said, frowning. People rescued from kidnapping and robbery were usually a little more civil toward their rescuers. "You have something personal against those kids?"

"You mean aside from the fact one of them could have stuck his knife in me while I was lying on the ground?" he retorted.

"But they didn't, did they?" I reminded him patiently. "It's also called not drawing extra attention to yourself. I assumed you were as interested in that as we are."

"Well, yes," he said, less truculently. "Sorry. I guess I should be more grateful for the rescue, shouldn't I? Thank you."

"You're welcome," I said. "And I think you may be overreacting a little. All they were after were your cash sticks."

I couldn't see his expression with the face shield still in place, but I could nevertheless sense his surprise. "My cash sticks?" he echoed. "Why in the world would they think I even had any?"

"Because I told them," I said.

"You *what?*"

"We needed to find you quickly," I explained. "That seemed the easiest way to do it."

"I see," he said. The growing annoyance in his voice had vanished, replaced by a cautious anticipation. "Is this about the item?"

"Yes, but not in the way you're thinking," I said, looking over his shoulder. With the rain still falling the bonfire was starting to die down, but it was still quite warm where I was standing. "Is there a private place where we can go to talk?"

"That depends on what you have to say," he said, some of the wariness coming back. "Do you have the item I'm looking for?"

"I'm afraid the item you're looking for no longer exists," I said. "But the item you already have is still greatly in demand, Mr. Stafford." I raised my eyebrows. "Or should I say, Mr. Künstler?"

His shoulders went rigid. "Who are you?" he demanded.

"My name's Frank Compton." I hesitated, but there was no good way to say this. "I was with your father when he died."

For a long moment he stood rigid. Then, carefully, he pulled off his gauntlets and removed his mask.

It was Daniel Stafford, all right. But the face before me was a far cry from the neat, clean-cut professional college student in Morse's dossier photo. This version had wild and ragged hair, several weeks' worth of beard, and was sheened with sweat and grime. "My name is

Stafford," he said quietly but firmly. "Rafael Künstler was my uncle."

"Ah," I said. So even now his true parentage was to be kept secret. That was fine with me. "My mistake."

His eyes searched my face. "So you're Frank Compton," he went on. "Uncle Rafael sent me a couple of messages about you."

"Anything interesting?"

"Only that you came with a high recommendation as a man who could be trusted." His lip twitched. "I also heard the news report of his death. What happened?"

"We can go into that later, if you don't mind," I said, looking over my shoulder. The four toughs were still sitting on the fire pit wall, with Fayr facing them from a couple of meters away with his gun still mostly hidden. So far the milling populace didn't seem to have noticed or gotten curious about any of it, but that wouldn't last forever. "Right now, we've got more pressing matters to deal with. Specifically, we need to grab the Lynx and get out of here."

"And I'm just supposed to hand it over to you?" Stafford asked. "Just like that?"

"Unless you want to join the rest of the bodies littering the trail of these damn sculptures, yes," I said tartly. "The people who've been creating that trail are already on Ghonsilya looking for you."

His throat tightened. "How do I know you're not one of them? You said you were with Uncle Rafael when he died. Maybe you're his killer."

"You said he gave me a vote of confidence."

"He gave someone named Frank Compton a vote of confidence," he countered. "I only have your word that you're the same person. And don't bother showing me any ID," he added as I reached for my wallet. "I've got lots of ID, too."

"So I gather," I growled. We didn't have time for this. "Let me lay it out for you. You have three choices. Only three. Option one: you give the Lynx to the people who killed your uncle."

His eyes flashed. "No," he bit out.

"Good for you," I said. "Option two is you trust me and let me get you and the Lynx out of here."

"And option three?"

I looked him squarely in the eye. "You reject my help, they track you down and kill you, and they get the Lynx anyway."

His gaze unfocused over my shoulder at the crowd of impoverished artists. He was scared all right, right down to his socks. But unlike a lot of people I'd met over the years, he wasn't going to let fear or panic make his decisions for him. "You still haven't given me any reason to trust you," he said.

I chewed at the inside of my cheek. There weren't a lot of ways for one stranger to prove to another that he could be trusted.

But there was one that might work. "Fine. Come with me."

I headed back down the indentation toward Fayr and Bayta. Stafford, with only a moment's hesitation, followed. "How are they doing?" I asked Fayr as I stepped to his side.

"They're quiet, and very unhappy," he told me.

I looked at the toughs. "Taking the opportunity to make their peace with the Creator, I hope?"

The leader twitched at that. "If they're wise," Fayr said.

"I don't think wisdom has ever been much of a burden for any of them," I said. "But there's still a chance they'll get to live out the rest of the night. Maybe even longer than that." I pointed to the leader. "You know of a nice, quiet place where you won't be tempted to make trouble?"

[There are rooms behind the entryway,] he said, his eyes seemingly glued to the bulge in Fayr's poncho that concealed the Rontra's muzzle. [We live there.]

"Who else uses those rooms? Or any of that area?"

[No one,] he said. [The foundation and walls are damaged. No one else is willing to take the risk.]

Apparently, plain simple common sense wasn't any more of a burden for them than wisdom was. "Good enough," I said. "Fayr, take them back and get them settled in for the night. Keep them quiet, of course."

"No fears," he assured me, gesturing with his gun.

Silently, the four Tra'ho'seej got up, two of them assisting their still wobbly companion, and filed off through the crowd. Fayr was right behind them. "Why not just use snoozers and put them to sleep?" Bayta asked.

"Because we may still have some questions for them," I told her. "Don't worry, they're way beyond the point of making trouble. The sight of submachine guns will do that to a person."

"What now?" Stafford asked.

"First, we pretend this is a civilized universe," I said. "Bayta, this is Daniel Stafford. Stafford, my partner and assistant Bayta."

"Pleased," Stafford said shortly. "What now?"

"Now we prove ourselves to you," I told him. "Question: if we're involved with your uncle's murder, why haven't we already killed you?"

He snorted. "Obviously, you want the Lynx, and you know killing me won't get it for you."

"Right," I said. "Now, what if we *did* have the Lynx, and still didn't kill you? Would that prove we could be trusted?"

He studied my face. "Probably," he conceded. "But that assumes I'll just hand it over to you."

"Not at all," I said, letting my gaze drift slowly around the courtyard as I settled my mind back into Westali investigator mode. The Lynx had to be here somewhere, I knew. Stafford wouldn't risk stashing it someplace where he couldn't keep a close eye on it.

But he wouldn't be carrying it on him, either, especially not after what happened to Künstler. He also wouldn't leave it someplace where one of his fellow artists might stumble over it. That left out most of the maze of rooms and cubbies in the amphitheater, which were out of his sight as well as being out of his control.

Buried in the courtyard somewhere, then? But ground that had been recently turned over was pretty obvious even to a casual observer. Besides, unless Stafford was digging under his own tent—which was itself way too obvious—the operation would be bound to attract unwelcome attention.

Unless he'd buried it under someone else's tent? Someone he knew would be gone at a given hour, thereby giving him the necessary privacy, or someone he trusted enough to bring at least partially in on the secret?

I looked at Stafford, at the taut wariness in his eyes and cheeks and throat. No, he wouldn't have risked a stranger noticing something odd about his tent and investigating. And he *certainly* wouldn't have trusted anyone here that far.

So it wasn't hidden in the amphitheater complex or in the courtyard. What was left?

I looked past Stafford toward the end of the indentation where he'd been working. Silhouetted against the smoky firelight was the lump of claywork he'd been playing with when he'd been so rudely interrupted.

Clay.

I smiled. Rule number one in the investigators' handbook: if you can't hide something, disguise it.

I started into the indentation. Before I'd gone five steps Stafford was at my side. "Where are you going?" he demanded, an anxious edge to his voice. "Don't mess with my sculpture."

"I'm not going to touch it," I assured him. The fire was still pretty hot, but no longer unbearably so. I reached the inner edge of the indentation and looked down.

The logs feeding the fire had been stacked in the middle of the pit in a standard crisscross pattern. There were four layers of them, the ones in the top tier mostly burned to ash, those on the bottom blackened but still reasonably intact. Each of the logs was about sixty centimeters long and twenty in diameter, a convenient size for handling.

Stafford was hovering at my side now, trying very hard not to look nervous and not succeeding very well. "Clever," I complimented him. "Even if someone figured out where it was, he'd have to wait until the fire died down to get at it."

"I don't know what you're talking about," Stafford insisted.

"There's only one small problem," I said. "Remember I told you the Viper you came here to buy didn't exist anymore? That's because it exploded."

He seemed to shrink back a little as he looked down into the fire pit. "What do you mean, exploded? How?"

"I don't know, exactly," I said. "Best guess is that the sculpture's made of some kind of exotic explosive." I looked back at the logs, searching the lower tier for one that didn't show the same scorch pattern as the others on its level.

And there it was. The closest one, naturally, to our particular indentation. "So far you've been lucky," I said, pointing to it. "You put it there on the bottom, where it's coolest, and all that glazed ceramic clay wrapped around it probably protects it pretty well from the heat. But we'd still better get it out of there as soon as possible."

He looked at me, his eyes uncertain for the first time since I'd met him. "This isn't just a scam, is it?" he asked hesitantly. "I mean . . . to get me to . . . ?"

"To admit to what I already know?" I shook my head. "As to the Viper blowing up, I've seen the damage. In fact, they're holding an art auction at the museum tomorrow night to raise funds to fix the pit it made."

He exhaled carefully. "I'd heard stories," he murmured. "I thought they were just rumors."

"They weren't," I assured him. "So. You trust me yet?"

He gave me a tentative smile. "Well, you at least have to keep me alive until you can get the Lynx out of there, don't you?"

"Absolutely," I said. "While we're waiting, let's find a quiet place to talk."

THE BEST PLACE for a private chat turned out to be the damaged section of the amphitheater where Fayr had taken the five Tra'ho juvenile delinquents. We kicked the six of them back out into the tunnel—Stafford confirmed that the gang really *did* help keep out the riffraff at night—and Bayta and I settled down to hear Stafford's story.

"He'd been getting offers to buy the Lynx for probably three weeks before the robbery attempt," he told us. "Strange offers, from a mysterious unnamed buyer."

"How strange?" I asked.

"The man was naming a price way above what the Lynx could possibly be worth," he said. "That alone made Uncle Rafael suspicious. He started looking into the current status of the rest of the Nemuti sculptures, which was how he found out they'd been disappearing right and left. He doubled the guard on his estate and the gallery and started trying to backtrack the would-be buyer."

"Only they got in anyway," I said.

Stafford winced. "Yes," he said grimly. "I think that was what hit Uncle Rafael the hardest. There was no way they could have penetrated the security system without the help of one of the guards."

"Not necessarily," I said. "There are techniques people in my former line of work would know."

He looked sharply at me. "Oh?"

"And I was out of the solar system when it happened," I hastened to assure him.

"I'm sure you were," Stafford said. "Anyway, Uncle Rafael decided he'd better get the Lynx off the estate before whoever it was tried it again."

"So he gave you the sculpture, a handful of cash sticks, some fake ID, and told you to lose yourself?"

"Basically. I hopped the next flight out of Paris and headed for the Quadrail."

"Did Mr. Künstler also suggest you come to Ghonsilya to find the Viper?" Bayta asked.

"Actually, that was my idea," Stafford said. "I'd been off the estate a couple of weeks, just riding the Quadrail and staying away from anyplace where I might be recognized, when I got a message from him. His would-be buyer had surfaced again, this time offering to trade the Lynx for the Hawk that had been stolen from a collector on Bellis. He told me he was thinking about going to Bellis to contact the person and size up the situation."

"Secure in the knowledge that the Lynx was well out of the buyer's reach," I said grimly. "Unfortunately for him, the buyer didn't know that."

"And I gather arranged an ambush," Stafford said, a shiver running through him. "What the hell *are* these damn sculptures, anyway? And don't tell me they're just bombs. No one kills just for bombs."

"I don't know," I said. For the moment, at least, there was no need for him to know about the sensor chameleon aspect. "But for our current purposes it doesn't really matter. Just on general principles, if the bad guys want something, you want to keep it away from them."

"And hope you can stay alive in the process," Stafford murmured. "Do you at least know who killed my uncle?"

"We know who ordered the attack," I said, choosing my words carefully. "It's not quite clear yet which specific individuals carried it out."

"But you'll get them, won't you?"

"The plan is to ultimately nail the whole gang," I said. "But it might take a while."

"Doesn't it always?" he said. "So what's the plan? Grab the Lynx and get out of here?"

"We definitely grab the Lynx," I said. "The getting out

part is going to be a little trickier. It turns out that the gang is holding a couple of hostages for my good behavior. An ESS agent named Morse, who was sent to find you and bring you back to Earth." I braced myself. "And a young lady named Penny Auslander."

Stafford stared at me, and even in the dim light I could see some of the color drain from his face. "*Penny's* here? In God's name—?"

"Easy," I soothed him. "She was just following your instructions."

He swore under his breath. "She and the others were supposed to go to Ian-apof," he said. "They were just supposed to throw anyone looking for me off the scent." He glared at me accusingly, as if Penny's presence here was my fault.

Which, technically, it was. "So I gathered," I said. "Unfortunately, the gang saw through it. Anyway, the point is we have to get them free before we take off."

"Do you know where they are?"

"No, but I know where they'll be tomorrow night," I said. "Tell me, in your time here in Paradise have you found out who the best ceramic workers are?"

"I know a couple of good ones," he said. "But I can do ceramic work, too, you know."

"No offense, but what we need right now is a professional," I said. "You think you could go get one of them and bring him here?"

"Probably," Stafford said, not moving. "What's the plan?"

"The plan is for you to go get your sculptor friend," I said patiently. "That's all you need to know right now." I took another look at his face. "Don't worry, you're not going to just be sitting around twiddling your thumbs. Oh, and we might need a set of metalworking tools, too, including a small plasma torch."

For a long moment he gazed hard at my face. Then, abruptly, he got up and strode out of the room. "I don't think he trusts you," Bayta said.

"Nothing I can do about that," I said. "If Uncle Rafael's recommendation isn't good enough for him—"

"I meant I don't think he trusts you about Penny."

I broke off. "Oh."

For a moment we stared across the room at each other in silence . . . and as I gazed into her eyes something she'd said earlier suddenly penetrated my consciousness. *Danger and tension can bring people together. I know that.*

I know that . . .

I'd thought I'd been accepted into Bayta's inner circle. Apparently, I'd made it inside that circle a little farther than I'd realized.

"Bayta, this has nothing to do with you," I said quietly. "It's me."

"I know that," she said. "That's what has me worried. You've closed yourself off from people for so long that . . . well, it all just seems to be happening too fast. For anyone, but especially for you."

"And especially with someone like Penny?"

Her lip twitched. "I just don't want you to get hurt."

"Hurt is my middle name," I told her, trying to strike a little lighter note. "I can handle it." I stood up. "Come on."

"What are we going to do?" she asked, standing up, too.

"We start by getting the Lynx," I told her. "The fire should have burned down enough by now."

"What about Ms. Auslander and Mr. Morse?" she asked.

"Well, we can't just leave them here," I said reasonably. "Much as I'm tempted in Morse's case."

"So again, what are we going to do?"

"Whatever it takes," I said. "Come on. I want the Lynx in hand before Stafford gets back."

NINETEEN

Fayr had said earlier that Ghonsilya was a relatively poor world, as these things went, with only a few of the utterly obscenely wealthy that formed the upper crust on many other planets. Still, the place clearly boasted at least a fair representation of the only moderately obscenely wealthy.

And judging from the crowd still flowing into the Magaraa City Art Museum's auditorium, it looked like every one of them had turned out for the auction.

I was seated in one of the aisle seats about three-quarters of the way back from the stage when Bayta returned from her reconnoiter and sat down beside me. "Anything?" I asked.

She shook her head. "I saw three Halkas, but they weren't the Modhri's soldiers. At least, they weren't either of the two we've met. You?"

"I've collected a lot of dirty looks for hogging the aisle seats," I told her. "Other than that, nothing."

She peered up over the heads of the people, mostly Tra'ho'seej, seated around us. "What if he doesn't come?"

"He will," I assured her. "The big question is what kind of backup he'll have with him."

"He doesn't want the local police authorities in on this," she reminded me.

"Unless he's brought in walkers high enough in the pecking order to keep the cops under control."

Abruptly, Bayta craned her neck upward a little. "Frank—that Tra'ho in the back of the room in the rider chair," she said. "Is that one of the oathlings from last night?"

I studied the distant alien face. "Could be," I said. "Especially in that chair. He's probably still having trouble with his balance."

"But he *is* now able to see," a gruff Halkan voice said from above me.

I looked up. It was Gargantua, standing in the aisle beside me, glaring intimidatingly down his bulldog snout at me. There was no sign of his sensor cane, so apparently his eyes had recovered, too. "There you are," I said conversationally. "How's it going?"

"You have the item?" he asked, ignoring the attempt at small talk.

"You have our friends?" I countered.

His eyes flicked to my jacket, then to the empty area beneath my chair. "Where is it?"

"Nice and safe and easy to get to," I assured him. "*When* we see our friends."

He studied my face a moment. "They await in a car out front."

"Good," I said. "Bring them here."

"You have my word they're unharmed."

"Glad to hear it," I said. "Bring them here anyway. The trade's going to happen in this room."

Gargantua's gaze lifted almost furtively to the crowd around us . . . and with a sudden and unexpected flicker of empathy I had a glimpse of just how vulnerable the Modhri truly was. His main body was composed of lumps of coral, helpless against a determined attack, while his only allies were co-opted beings who had no loyalty to either him or his cause, but who had to be literally forced to do his bidding.

The Modhri had been designed by the Shonkla-raa as

a secret weapon, someone who would operate in the shadows. Now, with the truth of his existence out in the light, he was fighting not only for conquest, but for survival.

Ruthlessly, I crushed back the flicker of sympathy. Sympathy of any sort was a weakness the Modhri could turn to his advantage, exerting limited influence through telepathically planted thought viruses that traveled the lowered mental resistance lines that existed between friends and trusted associates.

Fortunately, unlike the irresistible control he had over his walkers, thought viruses could be successfully fought, provided you didn't let them get a foothold. "We're still waiting," I reminded him.

"They have arrived."

I turned around in my seat. Flanked by two more Tra'hok oathlings in rider chairs, Penny and Morse were standing in the back of the room. They were steady on their feet, looking around the room, and seemed to be all right.

Morse's scanning eyes found me. I raised my eyebrows in wordless question, got a subtle thumbs-up in wordless response.

"The Lynx," Gargantua said.

"Certainly." Turning back around, I nodded to the stage. "It's right there."

He looked that direction, the wrinkles in his snout deepening. "Where?"

"Right there," I said again, pointing. "Peeking out from behind that green and blue landscape painting. See it?"

He turned startled eyes on me. "You entered it in the *auction*?"

"You got it," I said. "Lot one hundred thirty-five, I believe. Afraid you're going to have to make an evening of it—late donation, you know. Anyway, the point is that all you need to do is wait for it to come up, buy it, and it's yours."

He looked back at the stage. "We agreed to a straight trade."

"I changed my mind," I said. "Mr. Stafford spent a lot of money coming here, and I thought he should at least get some of it back. Besides, it was your fault the museum was damaged. It's only right that you help pay to put it back together."

"I see," he said, sounding calmer. "Only half the monies collected go to the museum. How will the Human Stafford receive his share?"

"That's the best part," I said. "We'll have a couple of hours to get safely hidden away before you take possession, just in case you have something nasty up your sleeves—"

"I have given you my word."

"And as I said before, I've seen how well you keep it," I reminded him. "Meanwhile, the museum will hold our share until we're ready to come get it."

He cocked his head to the side. "*Our* share?"

"I'm charging a small commission for services rendered," I said. "Not that that's any of your concern. Do we have a deal?"

Gargantua looked at the Lynx again. "Take the other Humans and go," he said.

"Good," I said, standing up and motioning for Bayta to do the same. "See you around."

His eyes glittered. "Absolutely," he promised.

"What's going on?" Penny asked as Bayta and I reached her and Morse.

"We're getting out of here," I said, watching the two oathlings out of the corners of my eye as I took her arm. Neither was paying any attention to us. But then, I doubted either had the faintest idea that he was on guard duty. "Your luggage still back at the transport depot?"

Morse nodded. "The Halkas wouldn't let us go get it."

"Good enough," I said. "It can stay there until we're ready to leave the planet. Come on—your friend Daniel's waiting."

"Her *fiancé* Daniel," Morse corrected pointedly as the four of us headed for the nearest exit.

I grimaced as I glanced sideways at Penny's profile. Out of sight, out of mind, and over the past day I'd almost been able to bury my feelings for her. Now, with her right here beside me, they were flooding back with a vengeance.

Even knowing how it was hurting Bayta, they were still flooding back with a vengeance. It was like high school all over again. "Whatever," I said to Morse. "Regardless, we need to make tracks."

"Where are we going?" he asked.

"You'll see."

There was a line of autocabs pulled up beside the curb. We piled in and I gave the vehicle the address of the Artists' Paradise. "What about the Lynx?" Morse asked as we set off through the evening darkness.

"We're leaving it here," I told him.

"The hell we are," Morse bit out. "That's evidence in a grand theft case. Possibly also a homicide."

"Sorry, but I made a deal," I said.

"With whom?" Morse countered. "The gang, or Stafford?"

"Pick one," I said. I'd also nearly forgotten how annoying Morse could be.

The autocab let us out at the Paradise's main entrance, and I led us inside. Halfway down the tunnel, I found that the five Tra'ho'seej juvenile delinquents had taken up their old posts. They seemed considerably more subdued than they'd been the previous night. "Evening," I greeted them. "I trust we're not going to have any trouble from you?"

[No,] the leader said, his ears twitching nervously. [But he's gone.]

"What?" I asked, letting my voice drop half an octave.

[He's gone,] the Tra'ho repeated, holding out a data chip. [He said to give you this.]

Wordlessly, I pulled out my reader and plugged in the chip.

The message was very brief. *Compton: I can't wait this out. I thought I could, but I can't. You can have my share of the auction money—I just want out. See you when I see you.*

It was signed *Daniel S.*

"Terrific," I growled, handing the reader to Morse and Penny. "Just terrific."

"He can't do this," Morse growled. "He's still under suspicion for grand theft."

"Maybe he doesn't realize that," I said.

"Or maybe he *does*," Morse shot back. "Maybe that's why he ran."

"He didn't even mention me," Penny murmured.

I looked at her, my heart aching in sympathy with the quiet pain in her voice. I wanted to tell her the truth, but of course I couldn't. "He didn't know you were here," I lied instead. "I never told him."

"Time stamp's only three hours ago," Morse pointed out, handing back the reader. "If he's headed for the spaceport, we might still be able to catch him."

"Worth a try," I said. "Let's see if our autocab's still there."

Unfortunately, it had already driven off. "Doesn't matter," I said. "The subway's not far."

I set off at a brisk walk. "Wait a minute," Penny said as she worked to keep up with me. "Shouldn't we call the spaceport first?"

"And say what?" I countered, pulling up the torchliner schedule on my reader. "We have no authority to ask them to hold him."

"I could start extradition proceedings," Morse offered, sounding doubtful. "But that would take time."

"Way too much time," I agreed. "Besides, the police may still be mad at me over that hotel incident. We'd do better to keep our heads down."

"I could try to call him," Penny offered. "I know his comm number."

"Except that the Halkas never gave us back our

comms," Morse reminded her. "We'd have to find a public."

"No time for that now," I said, handing Morse my reader. "If I'm reading these schedules right, we're going to reach the spaceport with less than an hour to book passage on that torchliner and get ourselves aboard."

"We're *leaving*?" Penny asked. "We don't even know if Daniel's aboard."

"The next one doesn't leave until tomorrow," Morse told her as he flipped through the schedule. "Compton's right—he'll definitely be making for this one. But we should be able to book our staterooms on the way from one of the comms in the suborb."

"Good idea," I said. "Ms. Auslander can also try calling Mr. Stafford from there. The trick will be to catch the next suborb before it leaves. Otherwise, we won't make that liner."

"Then let's stop talking and hurry," Morse said.

LUCK, AND THE express subway schedule, were with us. We made the depot with fifteen minutes to spare, grabbed our luggage and got tickets for the suborbital transport to Portline, and were soon arcing our way through the darkened Ghonsilya sky.

Penny insisted on trying to call Stafford before we did anything else. But there was no answer. Either his comm was off or else he'd lost it sometime during his residence at the Paradise. She tried a dozen times before reluctantly agreeing to stop long enough to call the torchliner station about booking passage. There were, as I'd expected, several staterooms still available, and her credit tab was healthy enough to reserve four of them for us. Brushing off Morse's promise to try to get ESS to reimburse her for at least his part of the fare, she resumed her efforts to get through to Stafford.

The flight took three hours, during which time we

passed from the early evening of Magaraa City to the midafternoon of Portline. The torchliner was already in the middle of flight prep, but we had time to sign in and get settled before it lifted.

The staff was, of course, not at liberty to give out the names of other passengers. Morse suggested trying to tap into their computer, but since none of us knew what name Stafford was traveling under there wasn't much point in that. So instead, the four of us settled in to keep a close watch on the dining rooms and public areas. Sooner or later, he would have to come out of his state-room.

Only he didn't. We were two days out when even Morse was forced to accept the conclusion that Stafford wasn't aboard.

"This is all your fault," Penny bit out, glaring at me across the dining-room table. "*You're* the one who said he'd be on this torchliner."

"You saw the message," I reminded her, fighting to stay professional about this. It wasn't easy, what with her anger and sense of betrayal hitting me like high-radiation solar wind. "What other assumption could we have made?"

"Maybe he decided at the last minute he didn't want to leave without his share of the auction money," Bayta offered.

"Or else he knew we would read his note and go charging off like a pack of idiots," Morse growled. He was clearly with Penny on the plan to drop all the blame for this into my lap. "He probably went to ground in Portline to wait for the next torchliner."

"So that we could be waiting for him when he reached the Tube?" I scoffed. "That doesn't make any sense."

"Maybe he thought we'd turn around and go charging back to Ghonsilya as soon as we hit the transfer station," Morse said. "Thereby being conveniently out of position when his actual torchliner came in."

"Only we won't be doing that, I take it?" I said.

"Bloody right we won't," he said firmly. "There's only

one way out of this system, and that's through the transfer station. I'm prepared to set up camp there and wait all month if I have to."

"Well, best of luck to you," I said. "You want Bayta and me to escort Ms. Auslander back to Earth?"

"I'm not going back without Daniel," Penny said firmly. Her eyes softened a little as she looked at me. "You aren't going to leave us, are you?"

And with that, all three sets of eyes were on me: Penny's pleading, Morse's unfriendly, Bayta's merely watchful. "I guess we'll see," I said. It was a lame answer, but it was the best I could come up with.

Because I knew that by the time we reached the transfer station I very likely wouldn't have any choice as to whether I stayed or not.

TWENTY

We reached the transfer station four days later, tying up at our dock ten minutes ahead of schedule. The disembarkation listing called for our particular grouping to exit about an hour after docking, and at Morse's suggestion we spent the time in the aft observation lounge, where we'd at least have a view of something besides the station hull.

I studied Penny's face as we sat there, wondering if she was thinking about what had happened between us the last time we were in one of these aft lounges together. But it was clear that her thoughts were on Stafford, with me running a distant second.

If I was even in the running at all. Whatever that kiss had meant to me, I was starting to suspect it had meant a great deal less to her.

The transfer station was busy today. Docked a safe distance away from us was a small-capacity torchferry, presumably making its run from one of the asteroid mining regions scattered throughout this part of Ghonsilya's outer system. Farther down were a pair of the even smaller torchyachts, plus a third currently maneuvering away from the station at the low-power drive setting necessary to keep from frying everything within reach of its heavy-ion plasma exhaust. For a minor system, Ghonsilya seemed to have a lot of traffic.

Finally, the lounge's speaker called our disembarkation grouping. Gathering our luggage, we joined the line of passengers passing through the hatchways, walked down the entry corridor, and emerged in a large and crowded reception room. Fifty meters directly ahead I could see a row of customs tables with a line of passengers at each, with the doors into the main part of the transfer station just beyond them. A little ahead and to our right was a group of Tra'ho'seej I didn't recognize from our flight, possibly some of the passengers from the torchferry.

And eight people ahead of us and two lines to our left, freshly disembarked from their rented torchyacht, were Fayr and Stafford.

Stafford was in front, with five Tra'ho'seej and a Nemut between him and Fayr. He was wearing the same plain, nondescript clothing he'd had on at the Paradise, but at least he'd taken the time to get the outfit cleaned during the torchyacht trip. Fayr, in contrast, was resplendent in upper-class clothing, as befit a Bellido wearing four handguns in a matched set of double shoulder holsters.

Stafford had two carrybags rolling alongside him, plus a heavy-looking backpack. Fayr had a single carrybag—an expensive one, naturally—and a long, flat shoulder case for his Rontra 772.

I watched Penny and Morse as we settled into position in our own line, wondering if either of them would recognize Stafford. The odds were low, I knew. Only a little of the younger man's face was visible at our angle, even less with all that extra hair and beard obscuring it. Between the hair and the clothing, he looked more like a wilderness wanderer than a rich college student. Still, it was a concern, and I kept my eye on Morse and Penny in hopes of stifling any cry of recognition before it got started.

Which was probably why Stafford was nearly to his customs table before I spotted the Tra'ho oathling standing quietly among a group of armed guards in the far corner of the room.

An oathling I'd last seen in Magaraa City outside the Fraklog-Oryo Hotel.

I looked sideways at Bayta, found her looking tensely back at me. She'd obviously spotted him, too, probably before I had. Morse and Penny, in contrast, still seemed oblivious to this new threat.

But then, he wasn't a threat to either of them.

Stafford had moved up to the table and opened his backpack, revealing a strange half log, half sculpture hybrid that looked like that odd breed of rough-hewn folk art so dearly beloved by sentimental tourists. The customs agent was frowning as Stafford gestured and talked, most likely explaining it was kiln-fired clay and not real Ghonsilyan wood. The agent cut him off, peering at his sensor display, and gestured for the next bag to be put on the table. A minute later, with the procedure completed, Stafford packed up his last bag and strode off through the doors into the station. The customs agent beckoned, and the next Tra'ho in line moved up to the table.

I looked back at the oathling. His eyes were still searching the crowd, having missed Stafford completely. Now all the kid had to do was get aboard one of the shuttles and get to the Tube before the balloon went up. Fortunately, with this much traffic the shuttles were likely to be running pretty continuously.

And then, as I watched the oathling out of the corner of my eye, his drifting gaze abruptly locked on to my face.

I forced myself to stand still, waiting tensely for him to sic the guards on me. But no cry was given, no signal passed. Apparently, the Modhri had decided to play it cool.

And it suddenly occurred to me why. Back during our

private parley in the art museum, I'd hinted that I had concealed weapons that the Spiders permitted me to carry aboard the Quadrail.

I'd spun the story mainly to try to obscure Fayr's role in our rescue. But the Modhri had apparently taken the conversation seriously. He was therefore waiting to make his move until after I hit the customs tables, hoping their scanners would pick up any such weaponry and deprive me of it.

Ahead, the Nemut directly in front of Fayr moved up for his turn under the microscope. "Morse?" I murmured.

"What?" he said distractedly.

"Whatever happens, make sure to get Bayta and Ms. Auslander to the Tube," I said. "Got that?"

I had his full attention now. "What are you talking about?" he demanded quietly.

"Just get them to safety," I said. I started to drift to the side.

Morse caught my arm. "Don't even think about it," he warned. "Whatever *it* is."

"We don't have a choice," I said. "See that oathling over there, the one with all the mobile firepower? He's looking for me."

"What, over the hotel thing?" Morse scoffed.

"No, over the fact that the Lynx I gave the art museum to auction off was a fake."

Morse's grip tightened. "A *what*?"

"One of Stafford's friends in the artists' colony sculpted it for me," I told him. "It was late enough in the auction schedule that the gang wouldn't have gotten hold of it and learned the truth until we were already off planet. Obviously, they lasered a message ahead."

"So how did the oathling get here before we did?"

"They probably sent him off right after Bayta and I gave the rest of you the slip," I said. "They would have wanted one of their own here as backstop in case I managed to get off Ghonsilya with the Lynx."

"Are you saying you have it with you?"

In answer, I nudged my larger carrybag with my foot.

Morse hissed softly between his teeth. "This won't be easy."

"No kidding," I said. "Just stay clear, wave your badge around if necessary, and get the women to the Tube."

The Nemut sealed his last bag and strode off through the doors, and it was Fayr's turn. The customs agent was obviously familiar with Bellidos; even as Fayr stepped forward, he reached down and pulled a pair of Quadrail lockboxes from beneath the table, one for the handguns, the other for the Rontra in its case.

Stepping out of line, I started toward the row of tables, walking with a determined but casual gait that I knew from experience tended to slow people's reactions. For a half-dozen steps no one even seemed to notice me, and for another two they remained frozen out of sheer puzzlement as to what I was doing. By the time the oathling in the corner recovered from his own paralysis and snapped an order I was nearly there.

And as the customs agent frowned, and the Tra'ho guards started forward, I took a final step to Fayr's side and plucked one of his handguns and a clip from the open lockbox on the table in front of him.

The customs agent gave a startled screech and lunged toward me. But he was too late. Taking half a step back, I jammed the clip into the gun, chambered a round, and aimed the weapon at the oathling and his guards. "Hold it," I called.

The whole room froze, no one speaking, no one twitching, and for that first few seconds possibly no one even breathing. Out of the corner of my eye I saw Fayr shift his weight subtly—"You—Bellido," I growled, gesturing to him with my free hand. "Back away from the guns and you won't get hurt."

Fayr caught the cue. "You have my status gun," he said stiffly.

"Don't worry, it's not personal," I assured him. "Now,

back off. You—over there," I added to the guards standing like a set of overwound springs beside the oathling. "Hands on your heads. No need for anyone to be a dead hero."

Silently, they complied. I was just reaching over to shut the lockbox with the rest of Fayr's guns when I heard the faint sound of rapidly approaching footsteps. I turned my head, wondering what Morse had in mind.

But it wasn't Morse. "What are you *doing*?" Penny demanded as she ran toward me, her eyes wide with disbelief. A startled Morse, I saw peripherally, was in pursuit, but a crucial four steps too far back. "You mustn't—"

There was no time to think. No time to do anything but what her action had forced on me. As she came within reach, I grabbed her wrist and pulled her close, shifting my left arm to wrap around her throat. "Play along," I muttered into her ear as she gasped with surprise and perhaps a little pain. "You hear me?"

Whether she heard me or whether sheer disbelief finally succeeded in freezing her muscles, she went rigid. Lifting my gun hand over her shoulder, I peered around the side of her head.

If I hadn't burned my bridges before, I had definitely dynamited them now. The Tra'hok culture might have a strong undercurrent of specism to it, but they drew a strange but solid line at females. Especially their own, but also those of other species. By taking a female hostage, I had just taken a giant step over that line.

The entire crowd knew it. All around me, Tra'hok ears were twitching with anger and injured honor, and I had the feeling that we were one spark away from a full-fledged lynch mob.

I focused on the oathling. He was as outraged as the rest of them, his eyes burning like he was trying to set me on fire through sheer willpower.

But his Tra'hok sensibilities weren't alone behind those eyes. I waited, letting the Modhri mind segment think it through, hoping he would come to the same conclusion I'd already reached.

In the deathly silence, the oathling stepped forward. [What do you do, Human?] he demanded. [What purpose have you?]

"I want to get on the Quadrail and go my way," I told him. "That's all."

[You have committed criminal acts.]

"Only this one," I said. "And if I get to leave and don't hurt anyone, it won't count."

It was a strained and completely implausible line of reasoning, of course. But I wasn't counting on reason to get me out of this.

[Interesting logic you present,] the oathling said dryly, taking another step toward me. [Let us examine your claim. Have you murdered any Tra'ho'seej? Or committed Assault One?]

"No, to both," I said. Fortunately for my presumed part in the sunburst grenade incident, Tra'hok law defined Assault One as an attack causing actual injury. Dazzled eyes didn't count.

[Theft?]

Technically, I hadn't stolen anything that had ever belonged to a Tra'ho. "No."

[Arson?] he continued, still coming toward me. No doubt he believed he was being very brave, approaching an armed and obviously unhinged alien this way. Distantly, I wondered what he would think if he knew his current behavior was coming from an alien mind that would sacrifice him in a second if he thought it would gain him anything.

"No," I said.

[Fraud?] he asked, his eyes glittering a little brighter.

"Not against the Tra'hok people," I said.

His ears pricked up at that one. [I'm told you offered a piece of counterfeit art for sale.]

"Where it was bought by a Halka, not a Tra'ho," I

pointed out. "Besides, since I never received any money for that sale, it was technically not fraud."

He finished his walk in silence, stopping three meters in front of me. [Then you may leave this place in peace,] he said. [You will go aboard the Quadrail, and you will never again return to any world of the Tra'hok Unity.]

"Understood," I said, and meant it. If we got out of this in one piece, I would willingly and gladly write off this entire region of space.

The oathling drew himself up. [Then go,] he said. [I will serve as your shield and safe-conduct. You may release the female.]

Released to his guards so she could be returned to bargaining-chip status? "The female comes with me," I said firmly. "But you're welcome to tag along if you want."

For a long moment I thought he was going to cancel the deal right there. He looked at Penny, glanced sideways at the crowd, then looked back at me. [Very well,] he said. [A shuttle will be prepared to take you to the Tube.]

"Good," I said. "Lead on."

He started toward the doors behind the customs desks. "Just a second," I said. Keeping my eyes on him and the guards, I reached down and scooped up my larger carrybag, clutching it to my chest like a combination armored vest and medieval shield and leaving the other carrybag to continue rolling along at my side. "Wouldn't want this getting lost along the way," I explained. "Start walking."

The wide corridors were deserted as we headed toward the shuttle docking stations. I wondered uneasily where all the people had gone until we passed the first restaurant and I saw the wide-eyed crowd huddled inside staring out at me. A line of station security was standing as a barrier between them and our three-person parade, their hands on their heads away from their weapons. Someone had made sure to clue them in on the rules.

The same silent mob scene was repeated at every restaurant, bar, waiting room, and shop we passed. My own tension notched up a bit each time, wondering if and when the station personnel were going to make their move.

But to my mild surprise, none of them did. The oathling, under urgent Modhri prodding, had apparently managed to convince, persuade, or threaten the station manager into letting me go without a struggle.

"You take great risks," the oathling murmured as he walked stolidly beside Penny.

I looked at him in surprise. It was the first time he'd spoken English. I hadn't even realized he knew the language.

And then my brain caught up with me, and I belatedly recognized the subtle change in voice and face and body language. "It wasn't that big a risk," I told him. "You can't afford to have a fracas now."

"What means fracas?"

"A disturbance," I explained. "Like the kind of mob scene we left in there."

Penny half turned around, frowning at me. "Frank?" she asked tentatively.

"It's okay," I said. "Turns out he's part of the gang who's after the Lynx."

She twisted her head around toward the oathling, the one eye I could see widening. "He's—?"

"Relax," I soothed her. "For the moment, we all have the same goal. Namely, to get me out of here and onto the Quadrail."

"I do not control station security, you see," the Modhri explained to her. "If they were allowed to take him, they would impound his effects. A routine inquiry would show the Lynx had been stolen, and it would be returned to Earth."

"Putting him back at square one," I said. "Even worse, the guards could start shooting." I drummed my fingers on my carrybag. "That would pretty well end the hunt for good." I cocked an eyebrow at the oathling. "You really should have infiltrated the local law enforcement establishment better, you know."

The oathling gave a strange catlike hiss. "Indeed," he conceded. "But there are other needs, and more urgent priorities. And this is such a small, useless world."

"And playing the odds usually does work," I agreed. "Still, one never knows where the cards are going to be dealt, does one?"

"True," the Modhri said. "Yet at the end of each hand the cards are always gathered and dealt anew."

I grimaced. "True."

"So they're letting us go?" Penny asked, grabbing on to the part of this she could understand.

"Only temporarily," I said. "Like I said, he's playing the odds. In this case, he's hoping that on the Quadrail he'll have a better chance of stealing the Lynx from us."

I saw Penny's throat muscles tighten. "Maybe it would be better if we *did* turn ourselves in."

"Maybe better for *you*," I said. "Unfortunately, after that little drama it would hardly be better for me. Besides, the Quadrail has one big advantage over this place."

"What's that?"

I hefted Fayr's gun. "No weapons."

The oathling looked sideways at me, an odd expression on his face. I was still wondering what that meant when it abruptly changed again. [I'm sorry,] he said, his voice also returning to normal as he shifted back to Seejlis. [My thoughts wandered. Were you speaking to me?]

"Just rambling," I said. So a wandering mind was how the oathling had chosen to explain away this latest blank spot in his memory. A puppet on golden chains, and he didn't even know it.

Damn the Modhri, anyway.

The debarkation lounge the oathling led us to was as deserted as everywhere else we'd been since leaving the customs area. [There is your escape,] he said, pointing to the invitingly open hatchway.

Way too invitingly, to my mind. "You first," I said, gesturing with my gun. "Don't get too far ahead of me."

I'd expected the shuttle to be the standard Tra'hok passenger model, with ten rows of seats offering lots of cover to a determined assault team. To my surprise, it was instead a cargo version of the same ship, a single empty chamber lined with straps and anchor rings with literally nowhere for anyone to hide. "Nice," I commented as Penny and I stepped cautiously inside. "Okay, then. Let's get this show—"

Without warning, the oathling turned and lunged.

Reflexively, I twisted away, swinging the barrel of my gun toward the side of his head.

But he wasn't going for me. Ducking under my wild blow, he grabbed Penny's upper arms and shoved her hard back through the hatchway. Even as I dropped my carrybag and dived after her, her gasp of surprise and pain was swallowed up by the slam of metal on metal as the hatch slammed closed.

Cursing, I switched direction toward the hatch control. But again I was too late. With a multiple popping of released clamps, we were away from the station and into the vacuum of space.

I turned back to the oathling, leveling my gun squarely between his eyes. "Go ahead," the Modhri voice said. "Shoot, if it will appease your anger and shame." He gave me an almost human smile. "I can afford to lose this one."

With a supreme effort, I eased my forefinger back off the trigger. *A puppet who doesn't even know it.* "Clever," I bit out. "Passenger shuttle doors can't legally close that fast except in a decompression emergency. Hence, the cargo version."

"I thought it would also soothe any fears of a trap," he said, gesturing around the empty compartment. "But don't be concerned. The Human female is in no danger."

"Provided?"

His eyes flicked to my carrybag. "Provided you now deliver to me what you promised."

"You'd like that, wouldn't you?" I countered, thinking furiously. This whole scheme depended on the Modhri thinking he knew where the Lynx was. Briefly, my thoughts flicked to Stafford, wondering if he'd made it across to the Tube yet or whether he was still stuck in one of the waiting rooms. "Okay, you got me," I told the Modhri. "You can have the Lynx." I cocked my head as if considering my options. "But not here."

His ears twitched in a way I'd never seen a Tra'ho's ears move before. "Where, then?"

"The Terra Quadrail Station," I told him. "My friends in the transfer station will be allowed to leave, and then we'll all travel together back to Human space. You can message ahead and have a walker waiting."

For a long moment he gazed at me. "Very well," he said at last. "I can wait a little longer. But *only* a little longer," he added, his voice deepening. "And don't try anything clever. Remember, I'll be watching you the entire way."

"Yes," I murmured. "I'll bet you will."

A PAIR OF drone Spiders were waiting for me when the shuttle's upper hatch opened, one of them plucking the gun from my hand without comment and tucking it in close beneath his silvery sphere as he and his companion strode off toward the stationmaster's office. I wasn't sure what happened to confiscated items; hopefully, Bayta could persuade them to put the weapon in a lockbox to be returned to Fayr later.

His job of living shield completed, the oathling stayed aboard the shuttle for transport back to the transfer station. There was no need for him to stay; the Modhran colony inside him had already linked up with whatever mind segment of travelers happened to be in the Tube at the moment, transferring all the necessary information about me, the Lynx, and the exchange agreement.

Nor was there any need for any of them to change

their own travel plans in order to shadow me. When my train pulled in, the walkers aboard—be there one or twenty—would similarly be clued in on the situation. Someone would also probably send a message ahead on one of the Spiders' message cylinders, alerting Modhri mind segments down the line. Once the Modhri was alerted to something, you didn't have a hope of outflanking him.

Not unless you were clever.

Stafford had indeed made it across ahead of me. As per our arrangement, he was sitting in one of the clinger-plant–covered gazebos near the stationmaster's office, pretending to be engrossed in his reader. I took a seat fifty meters behind him, out of his line of sight, and settled in to wait for the others.

And to figure out what exactly I was going to say to them.

Fayr arrived on the eighth shuttle after mine, his plastic substitute status guns bouncing prominently beneath his arms. He was wearing a scowl of wounded dignity, probably for the benefit of any of his fellow passengers who might have witnessed my performance. He consulted the schedule, carefully avoiding looking in my direction, and marched off toward the platform where the next Terra-bound train was scheduled to depart.

Bayta and Morse arrived two shuttles later, with their own luggage plus Penny's abandoned carrybags in tow. They had moved out of the main traffic patterns and were looking around when I reached them.

"*There* you are," Morse growled. "What the bloody hell was *that* in aid of?"

"It's called a diversion," I explained. "Any problems back there after I left?"

"Only the expected ones," he said, frowning slightly at me. "What kind of diversion?"

"Where's Ms. Auslander?" Bayta asked.

"Not here," I admitted. "I'm afraid I got finessed at the last moment."

"Well, that's clever," Morse said heavily. "First you lose Stafford, and now you lose Ms. Auslander, too?"

"You're half right," I told him. "Come with me."

I led the way to the gazebo where Stafford was waiting. "Agent Morse: Mr. Daniel Stafford," I introduced them as Stafford stood up. "Mr. Stafford: EuroUnion Security Service Agent Ackerley Morse."

"Honored," Stafford said shortly, his eyes probing the milling crowd of Quadrail passengers behind us. "Where's Penny? You said she'd be with you."

"I'm afraid there's been a slight hitch on that front," I told him, bracing myself. "We'll be meeting Ms. Auslander back at Terra Station."

His roving eyes locked on to me. "You *lost* her? What in *blinking*—?"

"She'll be all right," I interrupted, holding out a soothing hand. "All they want is the Lynx."

"Well, then, let them have it," he said, starting to turn toward the backpack on the seat beside him.

"Easy," I said, catching his arm. The Modhri would undoubtedly be watching all of this.

Stafford shrugged off my hand. "Don't touch me," he snapped. "You promised that if I cooperated they'd let Penny go."

"And they will," I assured him. "It's just going to take a little longer, that's all. Don't worry, she'll be fine."

He looked down at Penny's luggage, clustered around Bayta's feet. "It's coming out of your hide, Compton," he said darkly. "From now on. Anything and everything that happens comes straight out of your hide."

"I'll get her back," I promised.

"Then let's get to it," Stafford said, squinting at the nearest schedule holodisplay. "Next express that direction is in an hour. Do we need tickets, or did you already get them?"

"No, we still need tickets." I cleared my throat. This was going to be awkward. "Speaking of which . . ."

He looked at me with disgust. "You still need me to cover your fare, I suppose."

"If you wouldn't mind," I said, feeling my face warming. Originally, he was supposed to be so grateful that I'd reunited him with Penny that he wouldn't even bat an eye over me stiffing him for a measly little Quadrail ticket back to Earth. Obviously, gratitude wasn't exactly at the top of his mind right now.

I could only guess what was at the top of Morse's.

"Fine," Stafford growled. "You really are a piece of work, Compton, aren't you?" Pushing past me, he headed toward the stationmaster's office.

I caught Bayta's eye and nodded. She nodded back and set off after him. "Well, *that* went well," Morse commented.

"It'll be all right," I said, watching Stafford's stiff back.

"Your record is so convincing so far." Morse paused. "There *is* another way to play this, of course."

"You mean just give them the Lynx?"

"I mean we wait for them to bring Ms. Auslander across to the Tube," he said tartly.

"And then what?" I asked.

"We grab her back, of course," he said. "At least here it's a level playing pitch. No guns for us; no guns for them."

I snorted. "Like that'll matter when they can bring ten thugs for each of us."

"Can't the Spiders help?"

"Can't and won't," I said. "No, the only way to get Ms. Auslander back is to play it straight."

His eyes narrowed slightly. "You have a plan, don't you?"

"Not yet," I admitted. "But it's a long way back to Terra. I'll think of something."

TWENTY-ONE

Stafford, as befit his status and the number of zeroes on his cash sticks, booked himself a first-class compartment. As befit his frustration at my inability to deliver his fiancée, he booked *me* a seat back in the second to the last of the third-class cars.

"It's bloody unfair," Morse grumbled as we made our way down the narrow aisle to our seats. "It's not *your* fault she isn't here. If she'd stayed with Bayta and me during your little performance, she'd have been fine."

"You don't hear me arguing," I said as I took my seat beside a pair of Shorshians. Honeymooners, from the look of them. At least I wouldn't need to sit next to Morse, whose seat was three rows ahead of mine. "You don't have to do this, you know," I added. "Your pass will be good the whole way to Terra, and there's a good chance there are still first-class seats available."

"Only if you let me take that with me," he said, his eyes following my every move as I heaved my carrybags up onto the rack above the seats. "Evidence in grand theft and homicide, remember?"

"Forget it," I said as I sat down.

"Then I stay here."

"Suit yourself," I said. I wasn't exactly happy about

leaving Stafford out of my sight in first class, either. But Bayta was there, and had even managed to get the compartment that connected to his. If the Modhri tried anything, she could whistle up the Spiders and get a message to me. Hopefully in time to do something.

Besides which, Fayr was also aboard, though I wasn't exactly sure where. With luck, the Modhri hadn't made the connection between him and us, which would leave him free to play the role of wild card if necessary.

I very much hoped it wouldn't be necessary.

We were about an hour out of Ghonsilya Station, and I'd just put my reader away in favor of a nap, when the vestibule at the front of the car opened and Bayta appeared, an expression on her face that I'd seen before. She looked around, spotted me, and headed back. I focused on the top of Morse's head, visible over the top of the seat back, and hoped hard that he was asleep.

No such luck. As Bayta passed he rose from his seat and stepped into the aisle behind her. "Let me guess," I said as Bayta reached me. "Now?"

"Right now," she confirmed, her voice tight. "They say it's urgent."

"Who says?" Morse asked from behind her.

She looked over her shoulder, startled at his unseen entry into the conversation. "It's nothing to do with you," she told him.

"Anything that affects Compton has to do with me," he countered as I stood up. "Where are we going?"

"*You're* staying here," I said firmly. "Don't worry, we won't be long." Without waiting for a reply, I ushered Bayta past me and we headed toward the rear of the train.

The Chahwyn, apparently, wanted to speak with us again.

We traveled through the rest of the Quadrail's third-class section and two of the three luggage cars. "Any idea what it's about?" I asked Bayta as we moved through the last baggage car toward the train's rear door.

"The Spiders didn't know," she said. "But I suppose—"

She broke off at the soft sound of the car's forward vestibule door opening behind us.

I spun around, peering forward through the car's dim lighting, my hands curling reflexively into fists. There was a vague figure approaching down the aisle between the stacks of crates . . .

"There you are," Morse puffed, my larger carrybag clutched across his chest. "What in bloody hell are you doing back here?"

"What in bloody hell are *you* doing back here?" I countered, sorely tempted to deck him anyway just for startling us that way.

"You forgot this," he said, thrusting the carrybag toward me.

"I didn't forget it," I said, making no move to take it. "I didn't want it."

"Thought so," Morse grunted, lowering the bag to the floor. "The Lynx isn't in here, is it?"

I grimaced. But then, I shouldn't have expected a trained investigator to be taken in that easily. "Of course not," I said. "Way too obvious."

"So where is—whoa!" he interrupted himself as the car abruptly began to slow down. "What's going on? Are we stopping?"

"Just this car," I told him.

He stared at me. "In the middle of bloody nowhere?"

"Trust me," I said, gesturing to one of the nearby stacks of crates. "Might as well have a seat and make yourself comfortable."

He eyed me another moment, then eased himself down onto the floor. He was shifting his back against the crates when the car began to pick up speed again. "So where *is* the Lynx?" he asked. "With Stafford?"

"Well, *I* certainly couldn't risk carrying it," I pointed out. "My face was way too well known. Stafford, on the other hand, currently looks like a refugee from a dit rec war drama. We thought there was a good chance he could slip by them."

He cocked his head to the side in sudden understanding. "I'll be damned," he said. "That sculpture thing he had in his backpack that looked like a half-carved log?"

I nodded. "He'd built a fake log around the Lynx and hidden it at the bottom of a fire pit at the Paradise," I explained. "Naturally, you can't just carry a big ceramic log through customs without someone wondering. So I had him redo it as a sort of folk art piece."

"Clever," Morse murmured. "Of course, that means he *and* the Lynx are sitting all alone on that train right now."

"This won't take long," I assured him. "Besides, he's in a locked compartment, and the bad guys don't know who he is."

Morse grunted. "Let's hope not."

Given the urgency of the summons, I wasn't expecting the trip to take very long. I was right. We'd been traveling our private way for no more than fifteen minutes when we again began to slow down. "So what happens now?" Morse said, standing up and brushing himself off.

"Bayta and I go outside for a chat," I said. "You stay here and cultivate your patience."

For a moment I thought he was going to argue about that. He glanced at the stony expression on Bayta's face and apparently thought better of it. "Whatever you say," he said.

The car door irised open, and Bayta and I stepped out into yet another of the Spiders' secret sidings. Unlike all the others I'd visited, though, this one was playing host to a second train, another of the short pushmi-pullyu tenders like the one the Spiders had provided for our trip from Homshil to Jurskala. There seemed to be more Spiders around than usual, too, including several of the unknown stationmaster-sized class.

One of the latter was waiting on the platform, and led us to a typical meeting building. Inside, waiting at his point of the three-chair triangle, was a Chahwyn, a pair of

Spiders standing watchdog behind him. "Sit down, Mr. Compton," he said, pointing to one of the other chairs.

"Thank you," I said as I did so. His voice sounded very much like that of the Chahwyn who'd pink-slipped me earlier this trip, but given the species' malleable bodies and voice boxes that might not mean anything. "To what do I owe the pleasure of your company?"

"You have obtained the third Nemuti Lynx," he said, extending his hand. "I will take it."

"Will you, now?" I said, leaning back in my chair and crossing my legs casually. "Sorry—did I miss the part where you thanked me for tracking it down?"

"Frank," Bayta murmured warningly.

I glanced at her, paused for a second look. Her face was tight and pinched, the look of someone walking through a graveyard in a midnight mist. "What?" I asked.

For a moment neither of them spoke, their eyes locked in another of those annoying little telepathic conferences. "Hello?" I called. "Remember me?"

The Chahwyn's eyes dipped briefly away from the contact, then rose again to face me. "You are not Chahwyn," he said flatly. "You cannot be told."

I felt my ears prick up. There was a deep, dark secret lurking behind that plastic face, just waiting for me to weasel it out of him. "No, I'm not Chahwyn," I agreed calmly. "That's precisely why I need to be told everything."

"You no longer work for the Chahwyn."

"Then you're in deep trouble," I said. Time to trot out the trump card I'd been saving for just such an occasion. "Because I'm the only guy in town who the Modhri's afraid of."

His face wrinkled like an old dishrag. "What do you say? You make no sense."

"Why not?" I countered. "Don't you think the Modhri can feel fear?"

"Not toward you," he said flatly. "Not toward a single Human."

I smiled tightly. "But I'm not just *a* single Human. I'm *the* single Human. I'm the Human who took on an entire trainload of his walkers and destroyed them."

The Chahwyn gave a short, two-toned whistle. "That's not how it happened."

"Isn't it?" I countered. "A few months ago Bayta and I boarded a Quadrail with a Modhri mind segment that was ready and willing to take over the entire train in order to nail us to the floor. There was surely another mind segment at the platform who knew of that intent. Only we came out alive, while the train's mind segment *and* the rest of the whole damn train vanished without a trace. If you were the Modhri, what conclusion would *you* come to?"

His face was rippling now like a lake in a stiff breeze. "No," he said firmly. "I know what happened aboard that train. It wasn't as easy as you imply."

"I never said it was," I said. "But what you and I know doesn't matter. As far as the Modhri's concerned it's a big fat unknown. Big fat unknowns always make people nervous."

"The Modhri does not panic so easily."

"I never said he was panicked, either," I said. "I said he was afraid of me. An entire mind segment was destroyed, aboard a Quadrail where we theoretically had no access to weapons. The Modhri has no idea how we pulled it off, and he's sure as hell not ready to risk us doing it again."

I gestured to Bayta. "But don't take *my* word for it. Ask Bayta whether or not the Modhri's been playing us with tweezers and cotton batting ever since we tripped over Künstler's body on the way to Bellis."

They locked eyes in another miniconference. This time I stayed quiet and let them finish at their own speed.

It took over a minute, but when the Chahwyn again turned to face me I was pretty sure Bayta had won. "What do you want?" he asked.

"Number one: I want to be reinstated," I said. "I didn't

ask to get into this war, but I'm in it now and I'll be damned if I'll quit before the final whistle. That includes reactivating my fancy unlimited first-class compartment pass, and all the bells and whistles that go with it."

"It will be done," the Chahwyn said.

"And I want a monthly stipend, as well," I added. "There are all sorts of out-of-pocket expenses in this job, plus I still have an apartment in New York I'm paying rent on. Say, ten thousand dollars a month?"

The Chahwyn's face contorted slightly, but he nodded. "It will be done."

"Number two: I want to know what this new big secret is about the Lynx," I said. "First point on that list being how to make sure it won't blow up on me."

"The Lynx will not explode." He looked at Bayta again, possibly trying one last time to argue for silence in front of this upstart alien.

He might as well have saved himself the effort. Bayta was wearing her set-in-concrete stubborn expression, another of the looks I knew all too well. "I'm listening," I prodded.

"Have you ever heard of—" He glanced at Bayta, as if searching for the right English word. "Of trinary weapons?"

"I'm familiar with binaries," I said. "Explosives built from two components that you have to mix together to get the desired boom."

"Trinaries are not explosives," the Chahwyn said. "They're shock or energy weapons composed of three separate sections."

"You mean like breaking a rifle down into component parts?" I asked, frowning.

"Not at all," he said. "A rifle component is instantly recognizable as part of a weapon. A true trinary is a weapon whose components are completely inert when they are alone. Only when they are joined is the weapon's true nature awakened."

Something with cold feet ran up my spine. Three components. Hawk, Viper, Lynx. "Are you saying *that's* what the Nemuti sculptures are? Some exotic alien weapon?"

"Not just an alien weapon," he said grimly. "A weapon created by the Shonkla-raa."

"Terrific," I murmured. The Modhri and the Nemuti sculptures. One weapon of the Shonkla-raa busily collecting the pieces of another. "How do they work?"

"As I say, the three components are joined together," the Chahwyn said. "Each component then activates the others and is activated in turn by them."

"And in the meantime, not only are they dormant, they're also effectively invisible to sensors," I said. This whole thing was sounding more unpleasant by the minute. "Do we know which sculpture is which component?"

He shrugged, a fluid rolling of the shoulders like a move in a scarecrow dance routine. "From their shapes, I would assume the Lynx is the emitter and the Hawk the handle."

"Yes, that makes sense," I agreed, pulling up my mental image of the pictures that had been on Morse's data chip. "And that would make—" I broke off, fumbling for my reader as something suddenly occurred to me.

"What is it?" Bayta asked.

"I just had a thought," I said, plugging in the dictionary chip. "I was about to say that would make the Viper the power supply."

"And?"

"Remember what the Spider report said about that Nemuti scholar doing an etymological study on the sculptures' names and coming up with alien equivalents?" I punched in the word *Lynx*. "Okay, let's see. *Lynx* comes from Middle English, from Latin, from Greek from—see *leuk*—" I hit the link. "Bingo. The Indo-European root *leuk* means *light* or *brightness*."

"Light?" Bayta asked, sounding confused.

"As in shock or energy," I said.

Her expression hardened. "Oh."

"Exactly," I agreed, keying for the other names. "Hawk . . . from *kap,* meaning to grasp. There's your grip, all right. And Viper . . . from *gwei* and *pere,* meaning to live and to produce."

"The power supply," Bayta murmured.

"Right," I said. "This scholar was smarter than I thought. With this kind of hint, I'm surprised no one's figured it out before now."

"This is all interesting, but of no immediate usage," the Chahwyn put in. "Now that you know the truth, you see that you must give me the Lynx."

"I do, and I'd love to comply," I said. "Unfortunately, we've picked up a couple of complications along the way. For one thing, I don't have it with me. For another, it looks like we're going to have to trade it to the Modhri for one of our friends."

The Chahwyn's back stiffened. "You cannot do that," he insisted. "You *will* not do that. I demand that you retrieve the Lynx at once and bring it to me."

"Easy," I calmed him, holding out a soothing hand. "You're missing the big picture."

He snorted. "Do you have any idea what the Modhri could do with such a weapon?"

"He could create havoc across the galaxy, including and maybe especially aboard the Quadrail trains," I said. "And I wholeheartedly agree that's something we very much want to avoid. But that's not the big picture I was referring to."

"Then what is?"

"I can get you the Lynx," I said. "But what you really want are all the rest of the sculptures."

"Except the one that exploded in the Ghonsilya art museum," Bayta murmured.

I stared at her, her words echoing through my brain. Suddenly, with that simple comment, the whole thing had taken a sideways tilt. A very, very dangerous sideways tilt. "Right," I said, keeping my voice steady. I needed time to think this through. "Of course not that one. So retrieving the rest of them is next on the agenda."

"How can you do that?" the Chahwyn asked suspiciously. "You don't even know where the sculptures are."

"No, but I know where they were going," I said. "That first group of Bellidos, the ones with the stolen Hawk, were on their way to Laarmiten in the Nemuti Far-Reach."

"You think to find the sculptures there?"

"If they're there, we'll get them back," I promised. "Which brings up my third request."

"Your third request?" the Chahwyn asked, sounding confused.

"After reinstatement and the truth," I said to him. "Request three is that I want a gun."

"Impossible," the Chahwyn said flatly. "No weapons are allowed inside the Tube."

"Of course they are," I said. "*You* have one."

The room went a dark gray shade of silence. The Chahwyn's eyes darted to Bayta's, turned back to me. "Explain," he said, his voice tight.

"You Chahwyn were designed by the Shonkla-raa to be incapable of aggression, which is why you bred the Spiders to run your Quadrail for you," I said. "It stands to reason that you wouldn't have ventured out into the big bad universe without some way of protecting yourself."

"That does not imply a weapon," he said stiffly. "I have Spiders to protect me."

"Who are as useless in a fight as you are," I said. "No, you've got some kind of weapon, all right. I want one, too."

He looked at Bayta, and once again the two of them lapsed into a brief telepathic conference. "Actually, I'd venture to say you almost don't have a choice anymore," I said into the silence. "The Modhri already suspects I'm being allowed to carry a weapon aboard the trains. If and when he gets desperate enough to jump me, I'd better be holding something heftier than a bluff. Otherwise, scratch me, scratch Bayta, and scratch any chance of using any other bluffs against him. Ever."

The Chahwyn's eyes came back to me. "It cannot be allowed," he said.

"Oh, I'll bet it can," I cajoled. "Come on, at least let me see what the thing looks like."

For a long minute he sat stewing in indecision. Then, reluctantly, he reached somewhere inside his toga and pulled out a device that looked remarkably like a set of brass knuckles made of antiqued pewter. "It's a neural shock weapon called a *kwi*," he said, holding it out for my scrutiny. "A relic of the war against the Shonkla-raa."

"What does it do?" I asked.

"It has two settings, each with three levels," he explained, indicating a pair of spots on the weapon. "It can either create incapacitating pain or bring about unconsciousness for up to six hours."

"Scope and range?"

"We believe it will work against any oxygen-breathing being, and up to a distance of perhaps forty or fifty meters."

Not much range, as such things went. Still, it was better than nothing. And the any oxygen-breather part was definitely promising. "Will the knock-out setting take out a walker's polyp colony?" I asked, just to make sure.

His face puckered. Not just the area around his mouth, but his whole face. "We are fairly certain that it will," he said. "But we haven't yet tried it against any living beings."

An untested weapon. Terrific. "Well, the things apparently worked back during the war," I pointed out. "Close enough. Wrap it up—I'll take it."

"Certainly you joke," he said, tucking the *kwi* out of sight again. "As you have already said, this is my single defense against danger."

"My apologies," I said. "In that case, I'll make do with your backup piece."

"My what?"

"Your backup weapon," I said. "The one you keep hidden in your tender in case the bad guys manage to take this one away from you."

The Chahwyn's face rippled again. "Would you care to tell me exactly where the other weapon is hidden?"

"I don't know the layout in there," I reminded him. "But it'll be somewhere within arm's reach of the most valuable thing you have." I paused, considering. "At a guess, it's near your map of the Quadrail system. The one that includes all these sidings, your new home system, and any other secret hideaways you have stashed around the galaxy."

He stared at me as if seeing me for the first time. "You're very sure of yourself and your conclusions, aren't you, Mr. Compton?"

"If you mean am I good at what I do, yes," I said. "That's why you hired me in the first place."

He looked at Bayta, and then stood up. As he did so, and in perfect unison, the two Spiders behind him also straightened a bit. "Come." He walked to the door, the two Spiders deftly inserting themselves between him and me, and we all headed outside.

We passed our truncated train, and I got a glimpse of Morse's face as he peered between the legs of a Spider who had taken up guard position directly outside the baggage car door. If Morse had been despondently clutching the nearest legs it would have been the spitting image of a dit rec prison drama scene, and it was all I could do to resist calling out something about the governor and a pardon.

The Chahwyn noticed Morse, too, and the door abruptly irised closed.

We continued forward to the tender. The door irised open at our approach, and the Chahwyn disappeared inside. Bayta didn't hesitate, but followed him in, so I did as well.

The interior layout was the same as that of the tender we'd ridden earlier, except that the forward set of bunks had been replaced by a workstation and a living area. The Chahwyn went to a wardrobe set against one of the side walls, opened it, and from a hidden compartment in the side withdrew another of the *kwi* weapons. He turned, and with only a little hesitation handed it to me. "Here," he said. "Do not lose it."

"Thank you," I said, trying it on. The thing was heavier than I'd expected, but not unreasonably so. The adjustment knobs were within convenient thumb range. "Which of these is which?"

"The left-side switch allows you to choose between pain and unconsciousness," he said. "Left is for pain. The right-side switch controls intensity, lowest at the left. Squeeze the grip to activate."

"Got it, I said, adjusting it for full-power unconsciousness. Might as well have it ready to go. "Don't worry, I promise not to misuse it."

"I'm certain you won't," he said gravely. "Because it is telepathically activated."

I froze with the *kwi* halfway to my pocket. "What?" I asked carefully.

"It must be activated before use by either Bayta or a Spider," he explained, and I could swear there was a hint of malicious amusement in his voice. I'd managed to talk him out of a forbidden weapon, but the last laugh was going to be his. "Once it is activated, you may use it at will."

"And how many shots will I get before it has to be reactivated?"

His face puckered again. "I don't know," he said. "We haven't yet—"

"Tried it on anyone," I interrupted. "Right—I forgot. I'll be sure to let you know how it works. Come on, Bayta. Time we were getting back."

THE SPIDER STANDING guard outside our car stepped aside as we approached, and the door irised open.

"About time," Morse said as we entered, the door closing again behind us. "Who in bloody hell was *that*?"

"Who was who?" I asked. Beneath us, the floor rocked slightly as we got under way.

"Don't be cute," he growled. "That alien. I've never seen one like that before."

"Who, Fred?" I asked. "He's just a Shorshic trying out a new Halloween costume. Don't worry about it."

"Compton—"

"The important thing is that we've now got a plan," I said. "You want to hear it, or not?"

"Please, don't keep me in suspense," he said sarcastically.

"For starters, we're not going to make the exchange at Terra Station," I said, pulling out my reader and keying for my Quadrail system map. "We're going to do it at the Nemuti world of Laarmiten."

"Why?" Morse asked.

"Because that's where the Lynx is going to end up anyway," I said. "We might as well make it easy for them." I paused, as if weighing how much I should tell him. "Besides, we already have a friend on the ground there," I added, remembering what I'd put on Fayr's altered message chip.

"You seem to have friends all over the galaxy," he said. "Just how big an organization are you part of, anyway?"

"I have no idea," I said. It was even the truth, for a change. "There's a train change coming up at Trivsdal a little over forty hours from now. Instead of continuing on down the main line toward Terra, we'll switch to the Claremiado Loop and go to Laarmiten instead."

"Fine," he said. "Incidentally, when we hit Bildim I'm going to see about upgrading back to first class. No sense in staying back here guarding your luggage if there's nothing in there worth guarding."

"Not really," I agreed. It was not, I decided, the right

time to tell him I was going to upgrade back to a first-class compartment, too. "Be sure to lift a fine Scotch whiskey to my health."

The corner of his lip twisted. "Of course," he said softly. "Maybe even two."

TWENTY-TWO

Forty minutes later we felt the slight bump that meant we'd been reconnected with our train.

"It occurs to me we may have trouble letting the other side know we want to alter the exchange point," Morse commented as we started down the aisle of the rearmost third-class car. "I don't suppose you have a forwarding address for them."

"No, but I don't think it'll be a problem," I assured him. "They have people all around."

"So I gather," he said. "I think it's about time you told me exactly who and what this group is."

"Later," I told him.

At the front of our car, one of the restroom doors opened and possibly the widest Cimma I'd ever seen pushed his way out into the aisle. With his eyes on the floor in front of him, completely oblivious to our presence, he started waddling in our direction. "This could be trouble," Morse murmured.

"No problem," I assured him, spotting an empty seat a few rows ahead. "We'll pull in there and wait for him to pass."

We were nearly there when the Cimma suddenly raised his eyes far enough to see us. "Ah—friends," he panted, his blubbery flanks wobbling their way around another pair of seats. Apparently even this much of a stroll was outside his usual endurance level. "Excuse pre please. I am bother of great height."

"That's all right," I said. Morse had already stepped into the gap, and I nudged Bayta to join him. There wasn't enough room for all three of us, so I slipped into the row just behind them, apologizing with a nod of my head as my feet brushed a little too close to the toes of the Juri seated there.

The Cimma worked his way to the row in front of Bayta, then suddenly turned an intense gaze on me. "But you not sit from this car," he said. "I would peer three Humans living here together."

"No, our seats are farther forward," I agreed. "We had to get something from our luggage."

"All three of you?" Abruptly his jaws cracked wide in a sly smile. "You on running, my friend?"

"What?" I asked. The casual Cimmaheem approach to grammar made them masters at mangling all languages except their own.

"You on running," he repeated, even more slyly. "You were cheating at cards, perhapsly, and went dark to hide?"

"No, of course not," I said stiffly, putting all the wounded pride into my voice that I could summon on short notice. The Cimmaheem might be terrible with languages, but they could read attitude and tonal nuance with the best of them.

And they were better than most at jumping to wrong conclusions. "Ah," he said knowingly as he got his bulk moving again, finally clearing Bayta's and Morse's row. "Never fear, friend. I will not orate upon you."

"Thank you," I said. "We appreciate it."

"Nothing littler can one do for a friend," he said, looking directly into my eyes as he cleared my row as well. "Be long-lived, friend, and do run safely to probable."

With that, he continued on back, bumping into every seat and most of the shoulders along his path. I stared at his back as he went, an odd tingling somewhere at the base of my brain. There was something wrong about him, but I couldn't put my finger on what it was.

"You coming?" Morse asked.

I snapped out of my reverie. "Of course," I said, nodding again to the Juri as I stepped back out into the aisle.

Bayta was looking oddly at me. "You all right?" she asked.

"I'm fine." I took a deep breath. "Come on, let's get back to our seats. I want a nap before we hit Bildim."

I WAS AWAKENED by a hand shaking my shoulder. "Compton?" Morse's voice called from somewhere in the distance. "Come on, snap out of it."

I blinked open my eyes. Everything around me was dim, which meant the car's lights had been lowered to their usual nighttime setting. That must mean we were about to come into Bildim Station. I lifted my wrist to check my watch.

It was only then I realized I wasn't sitting in my nice, comfy third-class seat amid the smells and sounds of dozens of Humans and aliens. I was, instead, standing amid the crates and trunks in one of the baggage cars, facing a stack of dark blue boxes safety-webbed to the side wall.

I snapped fully awake. "What the *hell*?"

"I was about to say that myself," Morse growled. "When did you start sleepwalking?"

"I don't sleepwalk," I told him, looking around. I was in a baggage car, all right. The front one, I tentatively identified it. "What happened?"

"As I said, you were sleepwalking," Morse said. "I heard you mumbling, and when I looked back to see what the problem was you were lumbering down the aisle like Frankenstein's latest science project."

A cold chill ran up my back. "Thought virus," I muttered.

"Come again?"

"Thought virus," I repeated. "It's a technique used by the enemy for planting suggestions in a person's mind."

"You mean like a hypnotic drug?" Morse asked, frowning.

"Similar, but a lot easier to deliver," I said. "Remember that Cimma who talked to us as we were heading back to our seats earlier? It didn't click at the time, but his hair didn't fit his supposedly lower-class status."

"Of course it did," Morse said, frowning with concentration. "I remember. It was hanging completely loose."

"Yes, but it had the kinking of having been recently braided," I said.

"You're right," Morse murmured. "Bloody hell. But what does that have to do with this?"

"You were there on Ghonsilya," I said. "You saw how most of the enemy's soldiers were from the upper and ruling classes."

Morse muttered something under his breath. "I was hoping they were just playing fancy-dress to throw the cops off the track."

"No, they were real," I assured him. "*And* the Cimma called me friend, four or five times at least. Friendship helps lower emotional barriers and gives the thought virus better access to the victim."

Morse hissed between his teeth. "You ready yet to tell me what the hell is going on?"

"Later," I said. "Right now, I need to figure out what I'm doing here. What happened after I came in?"

"You walked straight to this stack of crates and stopped," Morse said. "You were staring at the labels when I decided enough was enough."

I studied the stack of crates. All of them had destination labels for the same world, some place in the Cimmal Republic I'd never heard of. So did all the crates in the two stacks on either side of it. "Interesting," I said, pulling out my multitool. "Let's see what's in them."

"Easy," Morse warned, suddenly cautious. "This is illegal even by the Spiders' rules."

"Don't worry, I won't hurt anything," I said. Selecting the pry bar, I slid it beneath the lid of the top crate, digging into the plastic near one corner. With a twist of my wrist, I popped the lid half a centimeter up.

And as the train clattered around a curve and the car lurched, a spoonful of water rolled through the gap and trickled down the outside of the crate.

I touched a finger to it. It was cold water. *Very* cold water. The kind of water Modhran coral liked to live in.

I looked at the three stacks of crates. Suddenly this was feeling like a very unhealthy place to be. "Let's get out of here," I muttered, letting the lid back down and taking a careful step back.

"What is it?" Morse asked.

"Tell you later," I said, taking another step back and turning around. I half expected to see the Cimma and an entire group of walkers watching in silent anticipation of me pulling a Sleeping Beauty and jabbing my finger on the sharp coral. One scratch was all it would take to put me on the track to joining them.

But there was no one there. Having wound up his puppet—me—the Modhri had apparently just turned me loose.

I jerked as Morse suddenly gripped my upper arm. "Not later," he said flatly. "Later has become now. My life's on the line here. So are Mr. Stafford's and Ms. Auslander's."

"I suppose," I conceded. "All right. As soon as we hit Bildim and I can get a compartment and some privacy, we'll talk."

WE REACHED BILDIM, swapped out the usual assortment of passengers, and started up again. There were no compartments available, but Morse and I were able to get seats in the first-class car directly behind the compartment car.

And as we pulled out into the permanent twilight of the

Tube, he and Bayta and I settled into Bayta's compartment and I told him the whole story. Or at least as much of the story as it seemed advisable to tell him.

He was silent for a long minute after I'd finished. Apparently his standard *bloody hell* was inadequate to cover this one. "And you can prove all this?" he asked at last.

"*Prove* may be too strong a word," I conceded. "But Deputy Director Losutu can certainly vouch for the parts he was involved in. You can talk to him when we get back."

"I'll do that," he said, a hint of challenge in his tone. "In the meantime, we have Ms. Auslander as a hostage to these things—"

"*This* thing, singular," I corrected.

"Right," he growled. "Group mind. Even the bloody grammar is scrambled with this thing. As I was saying, our first priority has to be getting Ms. Auslander away from him."

"Agreed," I said. "We'll have a couple of hours at Trivsdal Station when we change Quadrails for Laarmiten. I'll just wander the platform muttering *message for Modhri* until someone takes notice."

"Sounds like the opening of that classic Hitchcock dit rec drama *North by Northwest,*" Morse commented. "A mistaken connection with the telegram boy launches the hero into danger and intrigue."

"Yes, I remember," I said. "Let's hope life doesn't end up imitating art. Anyway, once a walker comes forward I'll tell him about the change in plans."

"What if he can't get the message to the walkers holding Ms. Auslander in time?" Morse asked. "Or what if the Modhri doesn't go for it? He's bound to be suspicious about you resetting the rendezvous for the system where he's collecting the rest of the sculptures."

"That's his problem," I said. "Both are his problem, actually. If he wants the Lynx badly enough, he'll just have to play by our rules."

"Or else write up a set of his own," Morse warned. "The thing with you and the coral back there looks suspiciously like a recruitment effort."

"He's tried to get me to touch coral before," I said. "I'm not worried about it."

"Maybe you should be," Morse said, standing up. "Anyway, conspiracy stories make me thirsty. Join me?"

"Maybe later," I told him. "Bayta and I first need to discuss some of the details of the Laarmiten plan."

"And to talk about me, no doubt," Morse said, smiling slightly. "Fine. I'll be in the bar or my seat if you need me."

With a nod to each of us, he left the compartment. "He's right, you know," Bayta told me. "Maybe you *should* be concerned."

"What, about the Modhri sleepwalking me to the baggage car?" I shook my head. "That was never about me touching the coral."

"Mr. Morse seems to think it was."

"Mr. Morse is wrong," I said flatly. "He said himself that I was just standing there staring at the crates when he snapped me awake. I hadn't even gone for my multitool yet to try to open one of them. And when I did, I could barely get a corner of the lid open. I'd have had to cut the safety webbing and pull down a crate full of water and coral, and I *know* I wouldn't have stayed asleep through all that. No, I think all the Modhri wanted was for me to know what was in there."

"But why?" Bayta asked. "Was it a threat? A warning?"

"Neither," I said grimly. "I think he was offering me a trade."

"A *trade*?"

"You see, I now have two choices," I said. "I can go to Laarmiten and make the exchange for Ms. Auslander, with whatever scheme he suspects I've got lurking up my sleeve. Or I can leave that task to Stafford and Morse, played straight with no tricks, while I follow this colony to wherever he's sending it."

"Why would we want to follow the coral?"

"Because moving this much coral at once implies it's going somewhere important," I said. "It's possible he's started some new campaign and decided he needs a bigger baseline presence there."

Bayta was silent a moment. "We know where the crates are headed," she said slowly. "We could stay with Mr. Stafford and send word ahead to the Spiders to watch the crates. They could let us know whether they leave the Tube and go into the system or whether they're transferred onto a different Quadrail."

"Actually, we *don't* know where they're headed," I said. "That's the point. All we know is what their current labels say. Unfortunately, there's nothing to stop the Modhri from sending a team of walkers back there the minute we're off this train and changing the labels, maybe even moving the crates somewhere else in the car. No, if we want to see where the coral's heading, we'll have to sit on it the whole way."

"So what do we do?"

I shrugged. "I don't think we've got a choice," I said. "Finding out where they're moving this outpost would certainly be interesting. But if the Modhri's got a trick of his own up his sleeves I don't want to be the one to tell Stafford that his girlfriend has slipped through our fingers again."

"His fiancée."

"Whatever." I glanced at my watch. "I need to find Fayr and bounce this latest change of plans off him. Any idea where he's sitting?"

Bayta shook her head. "Second class somewhere," she said. "I didn't spot him when I was heading back to third to get you."

"He's probably changed his facial stripe pattern again," I said, standing up. "I'll find him."

"There is one other possibility," Bayta said from behind me as I turned toward the door. "Instead of starting a new campaign, it could be the Modhri has found a new prospective homeland and is starting to move his coral there."

"That's definitely a possibility," I agreed.

"I just wanted to make sure you understood the full implications here," she said.

I turned back to face her. "Are you suggesting we just throw Penny to the wolves?" I asked.

Her lip twitched. "I'm still wondering how your feelings for her might be affecting your judgment."

Somehow, I'd never noticed before how much quiet pain there was behind her eyes when she talked about Penny. It sent a ripple of guilt through me. "Any feelings I might or might not have for Ms. Auslander have nothing to do with my decision," I said. "Okay?"

"If you say so."

"I say so," I said. "I'll be back later."

I headed out into the corridor, some lingering guilt and shame heading out with me.

Because I'd lied to her. My feelings for Penny did indeed have a lot to do with the new plan.

In fact, in a way, they had everything to do with it.

THE NEXT TWO and a half days went by slowly. Stafford and Bayta stayed mostly in their compartments, while Morse and I suffered, mostly in silence, through the boisterous company of our first-class car. I could tell that Morse was now looking at our traveling companions with wary eyes, wondering which of them might be Modhri walkers.

If he believed my story, that is. The other possibility was that he was simply wondering which of his fellow passengers he might be able to call on for assistance if and when the time came for pinning me to the floor and fitting me with a straightjacket.

I didn't see Fayr at all after that single talk with him. Presumably he was having a fine time of his own back in second class. Though of course not quite as good a time as the first-class crowd was having.

I did have a couple of long conversations with Stafford in the privacy of his stateroom. He still blamed me for losing his fiancée at the Ghonsilya transfer station, and in general didn't seem to like me very much. Fortunately, he seemed able to put those feelings aside while we discussed possible strategies for getting her back. If Künstler *had* been grooming him to take over his business empire, I reflected, he'd chosen his successor well.

As for the Modhri, whatever mind segment he had aboard stayed quiet and kept to himself.

Trivsdal, like Homshil, was a node station where several Quadrail lines came together, and as Bayta, Morse, Stafford, and I trooped off the train we found ourselves amid a teeming crowd of interstellar travelers. "What now?" Stafford asked as we found a relatively safe corner off the main walkway beside a waist-high planter filled with aromatic flowers.

"Bayta will go and get our tickets," I said. "You and Agent Morse will stay here and watch the luggage."

"What about you?"

"I'm going to look around," I told him. "We've got three hours before the next Claremiado Loop train, and it's possible Ms. Auslander and her escort will arrive here before then."

"If she does, we'll do the trade here," Stafford said firmly, sliding his backpack off his shoulder and onto the ground. "Frankly, I think this new plan of yours stinks. There's no reason for all of us to go all the way to Laarmiten."

"Objection noted," I said. "And we do the trade where I say we do it. Watch the luggage closely."

"Don't worry, we will," Morse assured me.

I made my way into the crowd, watching for the fancy or official clothing that was most likely to mark

Modhran walkers. Two platforms away I spotted a pair of Halkas dressed in their Peerage's distinctive tricolor layered robes and headed over. "Message for the Modhri," I murmured as I walked past them. "Message for the Modhri."

Neither of them so much as looked at me. Shifting direction, I made my way toward a group of well-dressed Juriani a dozen meters away. "Message for the Modhri," I murmured again. "Message for the—"

I broke off as a sudden hoarse cheer came from behind me. I spun around just in time to see a group of Shorshians hoist a flailing and clearly protesting Morse and Stafford up onto their shoulders and march off in an impromptu parade across the station.

I hurried toward them, dodging between and around the other passengers, many of whom had paused to watch the spectacle. But the Shorshians were moving briskly, and by the time I reached the planter where I'd left them the whole crowd had traveled another twenty meters onward.

And all our luggage had disappeared.

"The Shorshians do so love a parade," a voice said from beside me.

I turned. It was one of the two Halkas I'd tried my telegram-boy routine with a few minutes earlier. Only now his eyes and expression were those of the Modhri. "Nicely done," I complimented him. "How'd you get that many walkers here so quickly?"

"Oh, only two are my Eyes," the Modhri said, nodding toward the procession. "The others are merely bystanders caught up in the excitement of the moment."

"Leaving the rest of your walkers to make off with our luggage," I said. The Shorshians had finished their tribute now and were lowering Morse and Stafford back to the floor. "What exactly was this moment of excitement, if I may ask?"

"You may," the Modhri said magnanimously. "An elderly Shorshian walking stiffly with a cane dropped his ticket. One of your fellow Humans reached down and picked it up for him."

"A simple thank-you would have been sufficient."

He shrugged. "As I say, Shorshians enjoy a parade."

"So I see," I said, watching Stafford and Morse trying to force their way through the still lingering crowd of onlookers. Clearly, both of them knew a setup when they'd been caught in the middle of it. "So much for you keeping your word."

"The Human female will be delivered to you here once my Eyes have left with the Lynx," he assured me. "I have no further need of her."

"Actually, you might as well have her delivered to Laarmiten," I said. "That's where we're going next."

I turned to find the Halka staring hard at me. "Laarmiten?" he asked almost casually.

"Regional capital of the Nemuti FarReach," I said helpfully. "Population eight hundred million, major exports foodstuffs, gemstones—"

"I know of it," he interrupted. "The Lynx is not in your carrybags."

It was a statement, not a question. Apparently, his walkers had finished their search of the stolen carrybags. "That's right," I confirmed anyway. "Never was, actually. I trust you'll be returning the luggage to us, by the way. It's four more days to Laarmiten and a couple of changes of clothing would be nice to have."

"We were to make the exchange at Terra Station," the Modhri reminded me.

"And I've changed my mind," I said. "Now we'll be doing it at the Laarmiten transfer station."

I could see the wheels turning behind those dark eyes. Once out of the Tube and in the transfer station, we would have access again to weapons and any other Spider-forbidden items I might want to bring to bear. "You plan something foolish," he said. Again, it wasn't a question.

"Maybe," I said. "But that's not your problem. Your problem is that you want the Lynx, and I still have it."

He hissed softly, an eerily chilling sound I'd never heard a Halka make before. "Very well," he said. "The Laarmiten transfer station." His eyes glittered. "Make very sure you have the Lynx."

He turned and strode away. I watched his back, and caught the moment of subtle change of stance as the Modhri relinquished his control. I wondered how the Halka would rationalize this particular blackout.

A moment later, Stafford and Morse made it through the last line of people. Stafford looked flushed and anxious, Morse looked just flat-out furious. "Bloody hell," he said as he looked at the spot where the luggage had been. "Bloody, *bloody* hell."

"Relax," I calmed him. "It'll all be returned."

"Except the Lynx, of course," he bit out. "I imagine they'll be keeping *that*."

I looked at Stafford. His face was still flushed, but I could also see a hint of grim satisfaction there. "Oh, I don't think so," I said.

"What are you talking about?" Morse asked, looking around as if the thieves would have been stupid enough to be still hanging around.

"He means he called it, straight down the line," Stafford told him. "Right down to them hitting us here in the station. I hate to admit it, Compton, but you're not bad at this."

"You mean, for a washed-up has-been?" I suggested.

"Something like that."

"Wait a minute," Morse said, frowning. "If the Lynx wasn't inside that log sculpture—" He broke off, a flash of sudden understanding on his face. "It *is* inside the sculpture, isn't it? It's that—what did you call it? That chameleon effect."

"Actually, the sculpture is what we call the diversion effect," I said. "We pulled the Lynx out of the log before I had Mr. Stafford recarve the surface."

"So where *is* it?" Morse asked, looking at Stafford.

Stafford shrugged. "No idea," he admitted. "For all I know it could still be somewhere on Ghonsilya."

"Don't worry, it'll be at Laarmiten in time for the exchange," I assured him. "Anyway, I hope you enjoyed your moment of adulation. Let's go find Bayta and see what kind of tickets she was able to get."

TWENTY-THREE

"Thank you, Mr. Compton," the Nemuti customs agent said, his truncated cone-shaped mouth orifice and extra-deep voice making the words echo like they were coming out of a deep cave. "Enjoy your visit. May your heart give joy to your soul."

"And may your soul rest peacefully in its joy," I said, giving the proper response. Setting my carrybags on the floor, I keyed my leash control and headed through the doorway into the main part of the Laarmiten transfer station.

"How long before they show up, do you think?" Morse asked as he came alongside me.

"No more than a few hours," I said. "The Modhri's as anxious to get this over with as we are."

Morse glanced back at the carrybags rolling along behind us. "I'll be very interested to see where you've hidden the Lynx."

"I hope it'll be worth the wait."

We passed through another doorway into a wide, mall-like area with the usual selection of restaurants, shops, waiting rooms, and entertainment centers. Stafford and Bayta were standing off to one side, waiting for us. "Any problems?" I asked as Morse and I came up to them. "That agent seemed awfully interested in your artwork."

"He was mostly wondering why I was still bothering to lug the pieces around," Stafford said sourly. The Modhri had been very thorough in his search for the sculpture back at Trivsdal, to the point of making five or six pieces out of Stafford's log. Stafford was clearly still annoyed about that. "I told him it had sentimental value."

"Why *are* you still lugging them around?" Morse asked.

"Sentimental value," he said. "What now?"

"We'll set up camp over there," I told him, pointing to the nearest waiting room. "If we stay near that archway we should be able to see all the entry doors. We don't want the Modhri to have to come looking for us."

My time estimate turned out to be a bit on the pessimistic side. We'd been in the waiting room less than two hours when Penny appeared through the door from customs, looking pale and stressed but otherwise unharmed. Accompanying her, to my complete lack of surprise, were Gargantua and his fellow Halkan soldier.

Stafford was out of his chair and over to Penny before she'd made it five steps past the doorway. "You all right?" he asked anxiously, taking her hands in his. Gargantua made as if to interfere; a brief warning look from Stafford and he changed his mind.

"I'm fine," she said, some of her old fire showing through the tension in her voice.

"They've been treating you all right?" he persisted as the rest of us came up.

"She is unharmed," Gargantua said.

Stafford sent him another look, this one managing to combine utter contempt and complete dismissal. I made a mental note to learn how to do that one. "They've been treating you all right?" he repeated.

"Yes," Penny said, turning a brief glare of her own on Gargantua. "But he's made a few veiled threats as to what will happen if he doesn't get the Lynx."

"Don't worry, he'll get it," I said. "Whenever you're ready, follow me."

We set off across the station, heading past the waiting areas toward the long wing where torchliners waited to carry our fellow Quadrail passengers into the inner system. Gargantua, I noted, kept a firm but casual-looking grip on Penny's upper arm as we walked.

Just outside the embarkation stations was a room containing the lockboxes that the Spiders had ferried over from the Tube. I stepped to one of the tables, presented my claim ticket, and was given a long, flat shoulder box. "I should have guessed," Morse commented as we went to a small conversation nook off the far side of the corridor. "Nice, safe, and inaccessible during the trip."

"Do you seek again to trick me?" Gargantua rumbled warningly as I set the case down on the nook's low table. "I saw all items leaving Ghonsilya."

"And probably scanned them, too," I agreed. "Observe, and learn." With a little flourish, I popped open the case.

Penny gave a little gasp of surprise. "That's a *gun*!"

"It is indeed," I confirmed, lifting it out and putting it on the table beside the case. "A Rontra 772 submachine gun, to be precise."

"Impossible," Gargantua said, prodding at the case's custom-molded interior with a thick finger. "There's no room in here for the Lynx."

"Not in the case, anyway," I agreed, producing my multitool.

And as they watched, I unfastened the Rontra's barrel and slid it off, revealing the Lynx tucked away inside the weapon's outer shell.

"Bloody hell," Morse muttered as I set to work taking apart the rest of the gun. "I wouldn't have believed the Lynx would fit into something even that size."

"It *is* a cozy fit," I conceded. "I had to pretty much gut the thing to get it in, and then add on this extra cooling sleeve to make it work."

"Where did you get it?" Penny asked, still sounding stunned. "I mean . . . I didn't think you worked for Westali anymore."

"That's the wonderful thing about the free enterprise system," I told her. "You can find anything you want on the galaxy's various black markets."

She shivered. "I suppose."

I finished the operation in silence. A moment later, with the pieces of what was left of the Rontra scattered around the table, I held up the Nemuti Lynx. "Okay," I said, turning to Gargantua. "Your turn."

"Take her," he said, letting go of Penny's arm and taking the sculpture. Without another word, he and the other Halka turned and joined the line of people heading for the torchliner boarding areas.

Morse heaved a sigh. "So that's it," he said. "No crime, no suspect; and now no evidence. Might as well not even have made the trip."

"No, we still have a crime," I said. "Mr. Künstler's murder, remember?"

"Like we're actually going to solve that now," he said with an edge of bitterness.

"We might," I said. The two Halkas had passed through a wide archway and angled out of our sight. "As for the evidence, don't count that out yet, either," I added. "I'll be right back."

I crossed to the edge of the archway and cautiously looked through. There were a fair number of passengers streaming down the corridors, but Gargantua's size made him easy to pick out of the crowd. As I watched, the two of them turned into the third of the five hatchways, paused briefly at the registration desk, and disappeared inside.

I looked at the schedule listing above my archway. The torchliner behind that door was heading for the city of Parrda, on the Central Continent, and was scheduled to leave in three hours. Smiling, I retraced my steps to the rest of our group.

"Well?" Morse asked as I came up.

"They're taking the Lynx to Parrda," I told him.

"Good," Stafford said. "Let's get us some tickets."

Penny and Morse both looked at him in astonishment.

Penny got the words out first. "What in the *world* are you talking about?" she demanded. "I just got away from those people."

"They killed Uncle Rafael," he reminded her.

"You can't do anything about that," Penny protested.

"Maybe not," Stafford said. "But they also have my sculpture, and I want it back."

"Relax," I put in as Penny visibly gathered herself together for another try. "We're not going to just charge aboard the torchliner and demand they return Mr. Stafford's property. I had something a little more circumspect in mind."

"Such as?" she asked.

"Such as renting a torchyacht and seeing if we can get to Parrda ahead of them."

"Following them from in front, in other words?" Morse suggested.

"Something like that," I said. "People with guilty consciences tend to focus their attention over their shoulders."

"I'm in," Stafford said firmly, digging a cash stick out of his pocket. "The rest of you can do whatever you want. Where do we go to hire this torchyacht?"

IN THE END, we all decided to go. Even Penny, who was equal parts aghast that we would pull such a bonehead stunt and adamant that she wasn't going to head back to Earth alone.

I'd never been inside a torchyacht before, and was rather surprised by both its roominess and the plainness of its decor and furnishings. But then, this one *was* a Nemuti craft, and the Nemuti as a species weren't especially noted for their love of ruffles and flourishes.

Stafford didn't have a pilot's license—probably one of the few university majors he hadn't gotten to yet—but Morse and I both had current military-grade certificates that covered civilian craft this size. We got ourselves checked out on the torchyacht's control systems, drained a hefty up-front fee and an even heftier deposit out of Stafford's cash sticks, and headed out.

The universe was an incredibly beautiful place. Beautiful and lonely both. It was something I tended to forget sometimes, traveling inside a cozy Quadrail Tube or flying cross-system wrapped up in a torchliner with a thousand other people, with only the occasional visit to an observation lounge to remind me of what things looked like outside.

But from the cockpit of a torchyacht, with the stars and nebulae spread out in front of me through a wraparound canopy, it was all very clear. And very humbling.

Morse, whose license was more up-to-date than mine, handled the job of maneuvering us away from the transfer station. After that I took over, feeding in the positioning data and keying in our course. Laarmiten was currently on the far side of its orbit from the Quadrail station, which translated to a twenty-day trip. Fortunately, torch vessels scooped their own fuel from the interplanetary medium around us, and even a ship as small as a torchyacht routinely packed enough food, drink, and air for trips three times that long.

Even more fortunately, I had no intention of taking us all the way to Laarmiten.

I gave it two hours, just to be on the safe side. Then I changed course, locked in the autopilot, and headed back to the dayroom.

Stafford and Penny were seated together on a small couch, holding hands and talking quietly but earnestly together. Bayta was reading in a chair a quarter of the way around the room from them, while Morse was at the center table, splitting his attention between a Scotch and something he was writing. "Your report to ESS?" I asked as I came over to him.

"The latest version, yes," he said, taking a sip from his drink. "I don't think I've ever been on a job that required such a massive rewrite every third day."

"I wouldn't worry about it," I said, sitting across the

table from him, resting my right hand in my lap out of his sight. "From this point on, I think the report's pretty well finished."

He frowned. "How do you figure? We still have to get to Laarmiten and find the Lynx—"

"Or rather," I said quietly, "*you're* pretty well finished."

Across the room, Penny and Stafford stopped talking. Bayta laid aside her reader. "So I was right, after all," Morse said into the silence. "That story was nothing but the truth turned inside-out, wasn't it?"

"What story?" Stafford asked.

"He spun me a tale about some villainous group mind called the Modhri," Morse said, his eyes locked on me. "They supposedly arose during a war—"

"Yes, I know the story," Stafford interrupted. "What do you mean he turned it inside-out?"

"He claimed that vanished Quadrail train a few months ago was him and UN Deputy Director Losutu foiling a plot by this Modhri group mind," Morse said. "Only I think it was the other way around. I think *he's* the one who's gone over the side, and it was Colonel Applegate who was trying to stop *him*."

A shiver of memory ran through me. Colonel Terrance Applegate had once been my superior in Westali. He'd subsequently become my ex-superior, and later my deadly enemy.

My reaction to his name must have shown on my face, because Morse gave me a faint smile. "Oh, yes, I knew the colonel," he said. "Quite well, in fact. I met him after he left Westali and started working for the UN Directorate. He recognized my potential and helped me start climbing the ESS ladder. I returned the favor by recommending he be offered a job with the Service." His face darkened. "And then he stepped aboard a Quadrail train with you and Losutu and disappeared."

"I guess that explains why you hate me," I said as the final piece of Morse's personal puzzle fell into place. "It also explains how you came to be a Modhri walker."

"A what?" Penny asked, sounding bewildered.

"An unsuspecting member of the Modhri group mind," Stafford told her, his eyes on Morse. "You sure about this, Compton?"

"I'm positive," I said, watching Morse closely. Somewhere along here the Modhri colony within him would realize the jig was up, take over his body, and make a fight of it. "Applegate was probably the one who got Morse infected."

"Ridiculous," Morse spat. "I've never touched Modhran coral in my life."

"I'm sure you don't remember," I said. "The Modhri's been working on keeping a very low profile, especially on Earth."

"So you therefore argue from silence?" Morse snorted. "What dazzling logic."

"No, I argue from my knowledge of the Modhri and how he works," I said. "Particularly how he uses thought viruses to carry subtle suggestions between friends and trusted colleagues. Which is how I know for certain you're carrying a Modhran colony beneath your brain." I gestured to Penny. "You really shouldn't have tried to make me fall in love with her."

Beside Penny, Stafford stiffened. "What?" he asked carefully.

"It started aboard our private train to Jurskala," I said. "Morse spent those couple of days filling Penny's mind with suspicions about Bayta and me. That naturally drew the two of them closer together emotionally, enabling the Modhri to slide in his thought viruses."

Stafford looked sideways at Penny. "What kind of suggestions was he making?" he asked.

"Don't worry, they're pretty short-lived." I focused on Penny. With her fiancé sitting there beside her, I knew, this was likely to be awkward. But it was important that she hear this. "You haven't had any sort of feelings of attraction toward me lately, have you?"

The tip of her tongue swiped quickly across her upper

lip. "It wasn't the way you make it sound," she said. "I was just grateful to you for your help in finding Daniel. That's all."

"Of course," I said, looking into her eyes. Backpedaling and spindrifting it for all she was worth.

And with that, the last faint lingering hope within me finally died a quiet death. The last lingering Modhri-counterfeited hope. One more reason, I reflected, for me to hate him. "The point is that you switched your opinion of me just a little too quickly," I told her. "Especially after all of Morse's horror stories."

I looked back at Morse. Still none of the telltale signs of a Modhri takeover. "At the same time, the Modhri inside him was also working on me."

"Only you claim thought viruses need a line of friendship between the two parties," Morse said acidly. "I don't think you and I exactly qualify."

"I said they work best that way," I reminded him. "But whether we personally liked each other or not, we were still colleagues who'd been thrown together on the same case. That relationship also lowers emotional resistance walls. Besides, the Modhri didn't need to make me do anything outlandish, at least not at the beginning. All he wanted was to tweak my emotions a little."

"Why?" Stafford asked, clearly not happy with this line of conversation.

"To distract me, of course," I said. "The Modhri wanted my mind on Ms. Auslander instead of focusing my full attention on the problem of finding you and the Lynx and getting you out of his reach."

Abruptly Penny stiffened. "Is *that* why I ran after you in the Ghonsilya transfer station when you grabbed that gun? Because he *told* me to?"

"I'm afraid so," I said. "The Modhri had only a few walkers under his control on the scene. He needed to move you into a position where the oathling would have easy access to you."

"And so I supposedly persuaded her to go running

toward a lunatic with a loaded gun?" Morse demanded. "Do you have any idea how ridiculous this whole thing sounds?"

"Do you have a better explanation for what's been happening?" I countered.

"As a matter of fact, I do," he said. "If I'm right about Colonel Applegate tumbling to this scheme and having to be eliminated, then this whole charade is just an attempt to do the same to me." He nodded toward Stafford and Penny. "If there even *is* a Modhri walker among us, who's to say it's not Mr. Stafford or Ms. Auslander?"

"Good question," I said. "Unfortunately for you, there's an equally good answer. For starters, Mr. Stafford is definitely out. If he was a walker, he wouldn't have run off with the Lynx in the first place."

"And Ms. Auslander?"

I shook my head. "Doesn't work. She wasn't anywhere near the Künstler estate the night the Modhri tried to steal the Lynx."

Morse's eyes narrowed. "What are you implying?"

"Don't act the innocent," I reproved him. "It doesn't fit well on you. There was a Modhri walker waiting outside the grounds of Künstler's estate the night of the botched robbery. I know that because one of the captured robbers tried to get Künstler to tell him where the Lynx was, which only makes sense if there was another part of the local mind segment within contact distance."

"That could have been anyone off the street."

"Except that the average person off the street isn't Intelligence trained," I said. "I read the police report, remember? The would-be burglars knew far more about penetration and stealth techniques than they should have. Someone with Intel training had to be running the show."

"Maybe it was someone else from ESS," Morse said, a hint of desperation starting to edge into his voice. He was too good an agent not to recognize how quickly this box was closing around him. "Applegate knew a lot of people. It could have been any one of them."

"It could have," I agreed, wincing with sympathetic pain for the man. This had to be a terrible shock to him, like having the diagnosis of an incurable disease thrown in your face without warning.

But I pushed the feelings away. Compassion formed the paving stones to the same hell Morse was now in. "But it wasn't someone else . . . because you were the only Intelligence agent with me when I was persuaded to visit the coral crates in the Quadrail baggage car."

Some of the last remaining color drained out of Morse's face. "You said that was the Cimma."

"Of course I said that," I agreed. "The last thing I wanted was for the Modhri mind segment aboard the train to know I was on to you."

"But why *couldn't* it have been the Cimma?" Morse persisted.

"What, a stranger who called me *friend* more times than a used-car salesman?" I shook my head. "There's not a chance in hell he could have planted a thought virus that quickly and effectively."

Morse's eyes darted to Bayta, then to Stafford and Penny, a cornered rat looking desperately for a way out. But there wasn't one. He knew the truth now, and there was nothing left to do but accept it. Deliberately, I settled my mind and body into combat mode as I waited for the Modhri mind within him to make its final, desperate move.

But to my surprise, it didn't. Morse turned back to me, his eyes haunted but with none of the telltale signs of a Modhri takeover. "So why tell me now?" he asked.

"So that you'll understand this," I said, lifting my right hand above the tabletop to reveal the Chahwyn *kwi*. The weapon gave a slight tingle against my palm as Bayta telepathically activated it. "I've been assured it'll just knock you out for a few hours. You *and* the Modhri inside you."

He swallowed visibly. "All right," he said. "If this is

the only way to persuade you I'm not your enemy . . . go ahead."

And still not a peep from the Modhri. For a moment I hesitated, wondering if I could possibly be wrong.

But I wasn't. And whether the Modhri was learning how to play it subtle or was simply floored by my logical brilliance, he was still the Modhri. Mentally crossing my fingers, I squeezed the *kwi*.

Quietly, without any sound, fury, or fuss, Morse's eyes rolled up and he fell forward, his torso sprawling on the tabletop.

Stafford muttered something startled-sounding in French. "Is he all right?"

I reached over and checked Morse's pulse. It was slow—too slow for him to be faking—but steady. "Near as I can tell," I said.

"Okay, that's it," Penny said, her voice shaking but determined. "Before we go any farther, I want to know what's going on."

"You will," I promised. "Starting with the fact that we're *not* going any farther. We are, in fact, on our way back to the Tube."

That one caught both of them by surprise. "We're *what*?" Stafford demanded.

"Laarmiten was a false front from square one," I told them. "The Modhri never intended to bring any of the Nemuti sculptures here. It was just a convenient destination to slap on the walkers' tickets back at Bellis."

"Then what are we doing out here in the middle of nowhere?" Penny asked.

"We're playing his game right back at him," I said. "First we had to convince the Modhri, via Morse, that we'd fallen for his Laarmiten scam. Hence, the rented torchyacht. Second, we had to get Morse out of range of all the other colonies while we executed our about-face." I waved a hand around me. "Hence, the middle of nowhere."

Penny was still looking at me like I was speaking ancient Greek. But the light of comprehension was starting to dawn on Stafford's face. "I see," he said. "And since we're not due into Laarmiten for three more weeks, none of the other mind segments will even suspect anything's happened until then."

"Exactly," I said. "Though if I'm right, our mission will be over a lot sooner than that."

Stafford looked at Morse's motionless form. "Of course, you're assuming the Modhri colony in there is also unconscious. So unconscious that other colonies won't detect it once we're back at the Tube."

"That *is* the assumption," I conceded. "And since we've never used this gadget on a walker, we don't know for sure that that's true. We'll just have to play our odds as short as we can and keep our fingers crossed."

Stafford grunted. "Doesn't exactly fill me with confidence."

"As I say, we'll do the best we can," I said. "When we reach the Tube we'll circle around and approach the station from the far side, out of view of the transfer station and any other ships that happen to be wandering around. We'll enter through one of the access hatches in the maintenance end—"

"How do we do *that*?" Penny interrupted.

"We ask the Spiders nicely," I said. "Then, if things are on schedule, we'll board a special train"—I glanced at Bayta, got a slight confirming nod—"and head out to our real destination. There, Mr. Stafford and I will go to the transfer station, rent us another torchyacht, and come around the back side of the Tube again to pick up Morse and the ladies."

"I don't know," Stafford said hesitantly, looking at Penny. "I don't like the idea of leaving the girls alone with Morse."

"They'll be fine," I assured him. "They'll have the *kwi,* and we'll want him to be unconscious the whole time anyway."

"I could stay here with them," he volunteered. "You could go get the torchyacht by yourself. I'm pretty sure I've got enough left on my last cash stick to cover it."

"Unfortunately, they'll also want to see the renter's ID," I reminded him. "If my name pops up on any official database from now on, it's going to set off alarms from here to Bellis and back again."

"I hadn't thought about that," Stafford said, making a face. "Okay, then. We'll get the torchyacht, and the girls will mind the store."

"They'll be fine," I assured him again. "Anyway, we should be back inside the Tube in a few hours. I hope you haven't unpacked yet."

"We haven't," Stafford said. "Do we get to know where we're going once we're aboard our Quadrail?"

"The place where the Modhri's taken the sculptures, of course," I said. "It turns out they're actually components of something called trinaries, with one of each type fitting together into some kind of exotic energy weapon."

Stafford gave a low whistle. "That sounds bad."

"It's worse than just bad," I said. "Which is why we have to get in there and stop it."

"And you know where they took them?" Penny asked.

"I know the exact spot," I said. "Remember the art auction at the Magaraa City Art Museum? It seems one of the Vipers blew up while the Modhri was trying to steal it a few weeks ago."

I paused, looking expectantly at them. But all I saw was blank stares. "Don't you get it?" I asked. "One of the Vipers blew up."

"Yes, you said that," Stafford said. "What does that have to do with anything?"

I suppressed a sigh. "Look. The sculptures form a trinary weapon, right? One Lynx, one Hawk, one Viper."

"You said that, too," Stafford said, starting to sound impatient.

"The third Viper is gone," I said. "So *why does the Modhri even want the third Lynx?*"

Penny caught her breath. "He knows where there's another Viper!"

"Exactly," I said. "And where are you most likely to find a tenth Nemuti sculpture?"

"The same place they found the first nine," Bayta said. "The Ten Mesas region of Veerstu."

"Which is just two Quadrail stops before Laarmiten," I said. "All the walkers bringing in the stolen Hawk from Bellis had to do was step outside their train and make a quick handoff to another group waiting on the platform. Then they could continue on to Laarmiten as if nothing had happened."

"So Veerstu it is," Stafford said. "I don't suppose there's time to whistle up any cavalry?"

"All the cavalry we could get would either be too late or too suspect," I said regretfully. "No, it's up to us. Well, it's up to Bayta and me, anyway. You two can stay with the torchyacht at Veerstu if you want. For that matter, once we have the torchyacht rented, you can just go home."

"Not a chance," Stafford said firmly. "They killed Uncle Rafael. This isn't just justice, not for me. It's also personal."

He considered. "Besides which, I still have to get my sculpture back."

TWENTY-FOUR

The return to the Quadrail went off without a hitch. I brought the torchyacht around in a big circle to make sure we avoided any curious eyes, then rendezvoused with the Tube a good thousand kilometers away from the station itself and the shuttle traffic associated with it. I eased us in along the back side, keeping it slow and unspectacular, finally bringing us to a floating halt half a kilometer away from the station. The torchyacht would be all right there until we finished up on Veerstu and sent word back to the rental company telling them where they could go to retrieve it. We all suited up and crossed the empty space to one of the service access airlocks near one end of the station, in a maintenance area a couple of kilometers from the passenger platforms. Bayta signaled the Spiders to open up, and a few minutes later we were inside.

The tender Bayta had requested was ready, fitted out pretty much like the one we'd used earlier on our trip to Jurskala. I'd wondered how it was the Spiders even had such rigged-out trains available, or I had until our last meeting with the Chahwyn. Apparently, these were the vehicles of choice for any of the Quadrail's masters who decided to venture out into the universe.

The Chahwyn had said the *kwi*'s highest sleep setting

would work for up to six hours. Just to be on the safe side, I gave Morse a new jolt every three. It would have been far more convenient to use one of the plethora of long-term sleep drugs specially developed for this sort of situation, but I had no access to anything like that and didn't have time to scare up a source.

It would have been equally convenient to simply kill him. But I was only ninety-eight percent sure that he had a Modhran colony lurking inside him, and without that other two percent I couldn't justify an execution. Even if I'd had the full hundred I knew I probably still couldn't do anything without an overt act against me or one of the others.

Maybe that was why the Modhri had kept quiet in the torchyacht instead of making a bid for freedom. Maybe, like me, he was learning how to play the short odds.

It was a five-hour trip back down the Claremiado Loop to Veerstu Station, and I spent most of that time bringing Penny and Stafford up to speed on the Modhri and his plans to take over the galaxy from the inside. I wasn't entirely happy about giving them the full picture this way, but they'd already stuck their necks way over the line for me and it seemed only fair that they know the truth.

Besides, if I was right about Stafford being Rafael Künstler's son, the kid stood to inherit a sizable financial empire. With Larry Hardin spreading hate mail about me throughout the Terran Confederation, it might be nice to have at least one trillionaire who was on my side.

I avoided any mention of the Chahwyn, of course, as well as the fact that the Quadrail system was fundamentally a fraud. *That* part of the picture *no* one else was going to get if I had anything to say about it. The galaxy's current struggle with the Modhri would pale in comparison to the chaos that would erupt if the Twelve Empires suddenly learned there was a way to go out conquering and pillaging among their neighbors.

Bayta spent most of the trip sleeping.

We reached Veerstu Station, again disembarking in the service areas far from the passenger platforms. The trick now was how to insert Stafford and me back into the general populace without the kind of unwelcome notice that would come if we simply strolled in from the far end of the station in plain sight.

Bayta solved that problem by diverting one of the Spider-run lockbox shuttles to our end of the station. Stafford and I got aboard and were transported directly to the transfer station, conveniently bypassing the Quadrail platforms, the passenger shuttles, and even the Veerstu customs setup. Stafford unloaded another stack of money at the torchyacht rental desk, and I flew us ostentatiously toward the inner system. As soon as we were off the local traffic control monitors, I circled back to the Quadrail station and picked up Bayta, Penny, and the dozing Morse. Three hours later, after another cautious skulk around the backside of the Tube, we were finally and truly on our way to Veerstu.

The Quadrail station was somewhat closer in toward the primary in this system, and in addition Veerstu was also about at its nearest orbital approach to the Tube. The result was that our flight took only four and a half days.

I let Morse wake up during most of the middle two days, making sure of course to wristcuff him securely to whatever conduit or large piece of furniture was handy. Bayta and the others weren't happy with the arrangement, but I felt it was only right to give the man the opportunity to eat, shower, and perform all those other necessary Human functions.

It also gave us a chance to test how long a single *kwi* jolt lasted. In Morse's case, it was just over five and a half hours.

In addition—and I didn't mention this one even to Bayta—I was also secretly hoping the Modhri would finally make some move that would clear away my last two percent of doubt. I'd seen the transition on two Human walkers and any number of alien ones, and I knew that when it happened he wouldn't be able to hide it from me.

But again, the Modhri refused to take the bait. Finally, a day out of Veerstu I gave up the effort and reinstated the three-hour zap regimen.

Veerstu was a much less developed world than Laarmiten, with only two spaceports capable of handling torchships. I landed us at the farther of the two from the Ten Mesas region and ran us through the entry procedure. It was largely a formality, given that our carrybags were properly marked with the customs stickers I'd managed to swipe from the transfer station while Stafford was renting the torchyacht. They were a little bemused by the coffin-sized box we'd put Morse into, but it had a sticker, too, and so they merely recorded its number along with the rest of them and let us pass.

Of course, when evening came and they lasered their updates to the central office the computer there would undoubtedly notice that stickers that had supposedly never left the transfer station had nevertheless managed to make it all the way to the planet's surface. Still, the first assumption would be computer or agent error, and we should have at least a couple of days before anyone began seriously looking for us.

Veerstu had only four suborbital transport routes, none of which took us close to our destination. Fortunately, there were aircars and trucks available for rent. Half an hour later, with Stafford's cash sticks depleted a little more, we were on our way.

It was as I was looking over the data chip I'd picked up from the travelers' desk at the spaceport that I discovered the Ten Mesas region had been closed to all visitors.

"That tears it," Stafford growled as he handed the reader to Penny. "He's on to us."

"Not necessarily," I said. "If he's got his walkers engaged in a major excavation, he wouldn't want *anyone* snooping around, not just established troublemakers like ourselves."

"Why not?" Stafford asked. "There are archaeological digs all over underdeveloped worlds like this."

"Only this isn't a standard archaeological dig," I reminded him. "Archaeologists sift through the landscape with a comb and a soft brush, looking for anything bigger than a good-sized piece of lint. The Modhri's looking for stuff the size of the Lynx, and he's not going to be shy about using rakes and shovels. Actually, I wouldn't be surprised if he's brought in gravel excavators to expedite the job."

"So what do we do?" Stafford asked.

"It only says the area's off-limits to visitors," I pointed out. "If we can find an official or quasi-official reason to go in, we might be able to bluff our way through the fence."

"What, a bunch of Humans on a Nemuti world?" Stafford scoffed. "Right."

"It's not as crazy as you might think," I told him. "The bureaucratic mind-set is pretty much universal among the Twelve Empires. All we have to do is find the right buttons to push."

"You know, it doesn't actually say that the whole region is closed," Penny spoke up, studying the reader. "If this boundary line is drawn correctly, the three biggest mesas are still accessible: the ones to the east, south, and southwest of the dig area."

Bayta craned her neck to look over her shoulder. "She's right," she confirmed. "Their outer edges are all outside the perimeter fence."

"If the Modhri's ignoring them, it's because you can't get up there," I said. "That, or you can't get down anywhere inside the fence once you are."

"Who says you can't get anywhere?" Penny countered.

"We *do* have an aircar," Stafford added.

"Which will be tagged, intercepted, and escorted out the minute we get within five klicks of the perimeter fence," I explained patiently.

"I wasn't talking about the aircar," Penny said, just as

patiently. "I was thinking we could hike up the outer slope of one of the mesas, cross to the inner side, then rappel down into the dig area."

"You must be joking," I said, my stomach suddenly tightening.

"Why?" she countered. "The mesas are only a couple of kilometers long. And the outer edges don't look all *that* steep."

"The leading edge isn't the part that concerns me," I said. "Or didn't you notice those things they call the Spikes?"

"What, you mean those little peaks on the inner edge of the bigger mesas?" Penny scoffed.

"Those 'little peaks' are a good ten meters higher than the rest of the surface," I countered. "*And* very steep, *and* just a little tricky to get over."

"It won't be a problem," Penny assured me. "You can't tell much from these pictures, but there's always a way over or around something like that. I've done some rock climbing, and this is hardly a master-class slope."

"I don't think it's the over or around part that's bothering him," Stafford said, an all-too-knowing look on his face. "I think our courageous ex-Intelligence agent is afraid of heights. Didn't Westali train you to rappel down buildings and such?"

"They trained me as best they could," I said stiffly. "And for the record, it's not the heights that bother me. It's the possibility of falling from them."

"You'll be fine," Penny assured me. "This whole region is perfect for climbing, which means there'll be shops all over that'll carry the equipment we'll need. We can stop off somewhere along the way and I'll get us outfitted."

She gave me a pseudo-innocent look. "If you want, I'll even partner with you for the descent."

"You should instead make sure Mr. Stafford is safe," Bayta put in before I could think up a suitable answer. "I can partner with Frank."

Penny's smile went just a bit brittle. Bayta's attitude toward her, I'd noticed, had thawed somewhat since my public revelation earlier that the Modhri had been manipulating my feelings. But their relationship was still nowhere near warm. "Of course," Penny said. "I was just offering."

"You have a choice of which mesa we take?" Stafford asked.

"Let me look over the pictures a little more before I decide," Penny said.

"We'll take the south one," I told them.

"Why, is that the shortest?" Stafford asked.

"I have no idea," I said. "But that's the one we're taking."

"Don't you think—?"

"That's the one we're taking, Mr. Stafford," I said. "If you don't like it, I can drop you off at the next town. Ms. Auslander, get busy and figure out our best route."

I kept my eyes on the view out the canopy, but I could feel the sudden tenseness of the silence. Apparently, Stafford and Penny had started to think of themselves as full partners in this enterprise. The reminder that this was a benign dictatorship must have been a little upsetting. "Okay," Stafford broke the silence after a moment. "You're the boss."

I glanced over my shoulder at Bayta. She was watching me closely, a slightly troubled look on her face. But if she was also wondering what I was up to, she kept it to herself.

Turning back to the canopy, I returned my full attention to my flying. This, I knew, was about to get interesting.

A LITTLE BEFORE sundown we landed in a town at the foot of some craggy mountains to get some food and fuel, collect the gear Penny wanted, and buy some comms to replace the ones Gargantua and his buddies had taken from us back on Ghonsilya. Before we lifted off again I also gave the sleeping Morse another jolt from the *kwi*.

I could tell that both Penny and Bayta were a little concerned about the possible effects of such continual zapping on the man, but I brushed such worries aside. My only concern was whether we could land, get to our target mesa, hike across it, and rappel down again before our five-and-a-half-hour clock ran down and the polyp colony inside Morse woke up and alerted the rest of the local Modhri mind segment to our presence.

We flew most of the rest of the night. I dozed in the pilot's seat, awakening every half hour or so to check on our progress and make sure the autopilot was keeping us on track. The others, as far as I could tell, slept a bit restlessly but more or less straight through. Morse, with the usual help from the *kwi,* didn't wake up at all. During the quiet and privacy of the night I also made a small but significant adjustment to my newly purchased comm.

A couple of hours before sunrise, we arrived.

I set us down three kilometers outside the perimeter fence, landing in a shallow pit where the aircar would be partially concealed from casual observation. The whole region was arid and rocky, dotted with mesas and buttes and tall granite rock spines. Trees and clumps of vegetation were few and far between, concentrated mostly along streambeds and around natural springs, but nearly every minor dip and depression where dew might collect had sprouted stands of feathery, waist-high brown grass. It was easily pulled out of the loose soil, and I set Bayta and Penny to work gathering a few bunches to scatter across the top of the aircar. While they did that, Stafford and I got the unconscious Morse out of his carrying crate and set him up in one of the rear seats, wristcuffing him to the armrest to make sure he stayed put. It seemed unlikely we would make it to the dig and back before he woke up, but with luck by the time he did the local Modhri mind segment wouldn't be in any shape to respond to his warning. I gave him one last jolt from the *kwi* and we set off.

The air was bitterly cold, typical of arid regions with little ground and atmospheric water to hold heat. The sky was clear and the stars shone brilliantly down on us.

I particularly noticed the stars, as much of my attention was focused on the sky and any telltale occultations that might indicate curious aircraft nosing around. But I didn't spot anything, and in retrospect I decided that was as it should be. The Modhri wouldn't want to attract unwelcome curiosity by putting up nighttime sentry aircraft over a supposedly innocent archaeological dig.

An hour's walk brought us to the Ten Mesas area and the base of the mesa I'd chosen for our climb. Penny had assured us that the upward slope wouldn't be difficult, but looking at it from below in the dark it certainly looked daunting enough. But I needed to get in, and this was probably the simplest way.

Besides that, Penny was already striding briskly up the black rock, Stafford and Bayta right behind her. Taking a deep breath, deciding I hated this, I headed up after them.

The slope was every bit as challenging as I'd guessed it would be, and if I'd had any knee trouble at all I probably wouldn't have made it. As it was, we were all puffing to one degree or another by the time the slope began to level off onto the top of the mesa. Here the required level of physical exertion was much lower, but on the minus side much of the upper mesa surface was covered by the same waist-high grass we'd already encountered below. It was easy enough to push through, but because we couldn't see the ground below us we now had to pick our way carefully lest we twist an ankle on a hidden dip or pit or rock.

Once again, I kept an eye out for sentries. Once again, I didn't spot any.

The sky to the east was starting to show a faint reddish glow when we reached the northern end of the mesa.

"Yes, that's exactly what I was talking about," I

commented in a low voice as we stood facing the Spike. It looked just the way the pictures had shown it: a sudden upward sweep of the mesa's surface into a steep-sloped, more or less pointed formation towering ten meters above us. At the same time, the sides of the mesa on either side of us also rose sharply, leaving us in a sort of natural cul-de-sac.

"No problem," Penny assured me, digging a coil of rope from her backpack. "We'll anchor the rope here and toss the coil over the lip around the side of the Spike. Its own weight, plus the friction of the rock up there, ought to give enough counterbalance for me to get to the lip. Once I'm there I'll anchor it, we'll all climb up, then we'll rappel down the other side."

To me it seemed more likely we would simply slice the rope in half on the edge of the lip. But Penny was already tying one end of the rope to a rock outcropping below the Spike. I checked my watch and peered across the wasteland at the easternmost of the mesas perhaps two kilometers away, its own Spike silhouetted against the increasing glow of the approaching sunrise like the prow of an ancient Viking dragon ship. Digging out the thick leather gloves Penny had bought with the rest of our climbing supplies, I pulled them on.

She finished securing the rope and heaved the coil up and over into the darkness. With one hand on the rope and the other searching out crevices and protrusions on the rock face itself, she started up.

I held my breath, but she made it without falling. "Okay," she called softly as she crouched down and got a grip on the rope. "Bayta?"

Bayta started forward, but I touched her shoulder and shook my head. "I'll go," I said. Getting a grip on the rope, I started up.

I made it to the top, to find that the razor-edged ridge I'd envisioned was instead a narrow but relatively flat shelf with plenty of room to stand or sit. Climbing up beside Penny, I eased a careful look over the other side.

That side, unfortunately, was every bit as dizzying as I'd expected it to be. It was nearly as sheer as a skyscraper wall, dropping sixty meters to the ground below. With an effort, I forced my mind and eyes away from the cliff and focused my attention instead on the archaeological dig spread out before me.

Even knowing what was at stake, I was surprised at the size of the operation. The glow in the east wasn't yet strong enough to shine any real light down there, but I could see the firefly glow of hundreds of small guide lights, some marking pathways across the area, others delineating the edges of pits or marking other hazards. In their faint reflected light I could see at least fifty tents of different sizes, plus the unmistakable shapes of a dozen portable sanitation facilities. There were vehicles, too: aircars and trucks, water and fuel tankers, and something that was probably a portable kitchen setup. Clearly, the Modhri was pulling out all the stops.

"I'll go first," Penny murmured beside me, starting to fasten the rope into her rappelling harness. "I'll tug the rope three times when I'm ready."

I took a careful breath. "That's okay," I told her. "I'll go first."

"It'll be easier for you if I'm down there belaying the other end."

"I'm the one in charge," I reminded her. "If there are any surprises waiting down there, I should be the one to find them."

I couldn't see her expression in the darkness, but I fancied I could perhaps sense a little new respect. "Okay," she said. "Let me help you with your harness."

A minute later I was ready. "Remember, three tugs," she said, giving the harness's rope channel one final check. "Then if you don't mind belaying it, it'll be easier for Bayta and Daniel."

"Got it," I said. "Don't panic if I don't tug right away—I'll want to check out the area a little first." Giving her an encouraging smile—a waste of effort since she couldn't see my expression any more than I could see hers—I got a grip on the rope, leaned backward, and fell off the edge of the cliff.

It was as bad as I'd expected. All my acrophobic feelings came rushing back as the wind swept past me and my feet bounced off the rock face like a vertical kangaroo in full emergency reverse. I could hear the faint and only marginally reassuring hiss of my harness feeding the rope through the channel exactly the way it was supposed to, and could feel the sliding of the rope on my palms even through the leather gloves.

And then, abruptly, it was over. The harness kicked into deceleration mode and slowed me to an almost gentle landing on the rocky ground. Helping myself to a few lungfuls of fresh air, I freed the rope from my harness and took a quick look around.

The terrain was basically the same as it had been on the other side of the mesa: rocks, stands of tall grass, no trees to speak of. More to the immediate point, the nearest of the tents was a good thirty meters away, and there was no one wandering around that I could see or hear.

Pulling out the comm I'd gimmicked during the flight, I plugged in its battery pack and I keyed in the code I'd set up. Making sure it was working properly, I slipped it back into my pocket. Then, removing my right glove, I snugged the *kwi* into position against my palm, adjusted it to its highest pain setting, and pulled the glove back over it. The weapon's bulk pushed rather blatantly against the leather, but if I kept my hand curved and at my side it shouldn't be too noticeable, especially not in this light. Given that the thing apparently worked just fine through the victim's clothing, I didn't expect the glove to impede it any. Then, wrapping the rope around my right forearm, I gave it three sharp tugs. Eyes turned cautiously upward so that I could move out of the way before I got landed on, I braced myself.

A few minutes later we were all down. None of the others, as near as I could tell, had had nearly as traumatic a time of the experience as I had. "What now?" Stafford whispered.

"We find the trophy room," I whispered back. The sky, I noted, had brightened considerably during this last stage of our trek. Most of the dimmer stars were already gone, and the predawn glow was hard at work engulfing the rest. "Should be one of the larger tents toward the middle of the camp. Keep it quiet—the walkers could start waking up anytime now."

We set off in single file, me in front, Stafford and Penny behind me, Bayta bringing up the rear. The rocky ground didn't lend itself to silent travel, but with me trying to pick out the best route and the others trying to stay in my footsteps it wasn't too bad. Fortunately, at this hour it shouldn't be unreasonable for an early riser or two to be up and about.

Of course, that misconception would only fool anyone if the site included nonwalkers who'd been pressed into digging duty. If the entire site was nothing but a single Modhran mind segment, the sound of extra footsteps in the camp would damn us instantly as intruders.

But we passed the outer lines of tents and equipment without incident. Directly ahead, nestled into the middle of the encampment as I'd predicted, were a pair of large tents that were obviously more than simple residences.

We were still fifty meters away when I heard a sharp intake of air from behind me. "Oh, no," Stafford murmured.

I turned sharply, opening my mouth to remind him to keep quiet.

The warning wasn't necessary. It was also too late. Standing at the doorways of each of the tents we'd already passed were three or four beings in rough work clothing, all of them standing stiff and silent.

The Modhri had us.

TWENTY-FIVE

I stopped, the other three following suit. "Good morning, Modhri," I called cheerfully. "You're an early riser."

For a moment nothing happened. Then, in typically perfect unison, the walkers in front of the tents started toward us. As they did so, more began to file out of the tents behind them.

It was like a reunion of first-class Quadrail passengers, except in grubbier clothing. Virtually every species in the Twelve Empires was represented, from Bellidos and Juriani to Pirks and Shorshians. The largest percentage were Nemuti, hardly surprising given we were in their territory. I didn't spot any Humans in the crowd, but decided not to feel insulted by our lack of inclusion.

"So you didn't take that torchyacht to Laarmiten after all."

I turned around again. Now that the trap was sprung, the sleeping tents on the far side of the camp were also disgorging their complement of walkers. Striding toward me at their head was a familiar figure: Gargantua. "You didn't stay on your torchliner, either," I reminded him. "I think that makes us even."

He continued on toward me in silence. So did the rest of the crowd. I could hear Penny's rapid, frightened breathing behind me, as well as some tense and venomous-sounding

French mutterings from Stafford. Bayta, in contrast, was as watchfully silent as the walkers.

The crowd formed themselves into a ring about ten meters away from us. Gargantua continued into the circle, stopping a few steps in front of me. The light was now strong enough for me to see his expression, which to my mild surprise looked more bemused than angry. "You're a remarkable being, Frank Compton," he said at last. "You're like no opponent I've ever faced."

"That's only because you usually absorb your enemies before they're really up to speed as to who and what they're up against," I said. "If you gave us a level playing field, I think you'd find a lot of us able to give you a good run for your money."

He hissed. "Enough of a reason in itself for me not to provide such a level field. Tell me, what did you hope to accomplish here?"

"Oh, come now," I chided. "I can put two and two together as well as the next man." I raised my eyebrows. "Or should I say, I can put three and three together?"

Up until that point I hadn't been a hundred percent sure that the Chahwyn's guess about the Nemuti sculptures had been correct. But the subtle darkening of Gargantua's expression more than filled in the uncertainty. The sculptures were indeed the Shonkla-raa weapons the Chahwyn had described.

"As I said," Gargantua murmured. "A remarkable being. Where is the fifth member of your group?"

I looked around as if I hadn't realized until then that Morse was missing. "Huh," I said, turning back to Gargantua. "He was just here a minute ago. Must have lost him somewhere along the way. Don't worry—I'm sure you'll find him again soon enough."

"You think to prepare an ambush against me?" Gargantua demanded.

"You can pass on the games," Stafford put in. "We know he's one of you."

A hint of a frown crossed Gargantua's face. "An

interesting thought," he said. "I must consider adding him to my Eyes when the rest of you have been dealt with."

"What do you mean, dealt with?" Penny asked tightly.

"The Human Compton has left me very few options," Gargantua said. "You cannot simply be added to my Eyes—you would hardly be unaware of my presence within your bodies. Nor can you be allowed to leave here untouched."

"Which I gather leaves just one option," I said. "You propose to turn us into your Arms." I pointed at Gargantua. "Like that one."

Gargantua nodded. "You are correct."

"What's he talking about?" Penny breathed. She was standing very close behind me now, close enough for me to hear her teeth chattering with fright.

"He's talking about a permanent takeover of your body," I told her, looking casually around the silent circle around us. There were probably two hundred walkers present. "Like he has with the rest of these fine citizens."

"Hardly," the Modhri said. "Most here are Eyes, not Arms. And I intend for them to remain so."

"That'll be a good trick," Stafford muttered.

"Not at all," the Modhri assured him. "Fortunately, your appearance is at an hour when they will be able to surmise afterward that they were still asleep."

"Interesting how important self-deception is when you're part of the Modhri's army," I said. "So how many Arms do you have here?"

"Why do you ask?" the Modhri countered.

"Simple curiosity," I said. "Part of what makes us Humans the remarkable beings that we are."

"I have twelve Arms present," Gargantua said, eyeing me closely.

"Which ones?"

Gargantua smiled faintly. "Begin trouble, and you will find out."

"Did Rafael Künstler create trouble?" I asked. "Is that why you beat him to death?"

"He promised to bring the Lynx," the Modhri said, his voice darkening with the memory. "But when I queried him aboard the Quadrail he admitted that he had lied, that he had come to Bellis hoping instead to buy it from me."

"And if you weren't willing to sell, he was hoping to blackmail you into it?" I suggested. "After all, you *were* in possession of stolen property."

"He did make some such threats," the Modhri said. "I wasn't concerned."

"Certainly not with all those armed soldiers between him and the transfer station," I said as that part finally clicked. "I presume that was why you had them there, anyway. You figured Künstler would arrive with a full security team of his own and wanted to be ready for any surprises."

"I thought he might choose to secure the Lynx in a Quadrail lockbox instead of carrying it aboard with him." Gargantua smiled thinly. "An idea you yourself later took advantage of. If he had done so, I wouldn't have been able to obtain it until he arrived at the transfer station, where his presumed guards would have access to their own weapons. I thought it prudent to be prepared with a superior show of force."

"You still shouldn't have killed him."

Gargantua's eyes flicked pointedly across me and the others. "In retrospect, I agree," he said. "But the error will be fixed soon enough."

"Not necessarily," I said. The Modhri had implied earlier that Morse wasn't one of his walkers. It might be interesting to see just how far he was willing to go with that game. "There's still Mr. Morse to consider."

Gargantua gave me another tight smile. "Do you really think he can elude me?" Abruptly his expression changed, and as it did so a pair of Nemuti detached themselves from the crowd and came toward me. "No—I see now," Gargantua continued. "Remain where you are."

"Don't worry, I'm not going anywhere," I assured

him, lifting my arms slightly away from my sides to make the search easier.

The Nemuti found the comm, of course, on the second pocket they tried. "A foolish trick, Human," Gargantua said as one of the Nemuti punched the off switch and put it away in his own pocket.

"Just a high-tech version of the same trick you used on Künstler's estate after the robbery attempt," I reminded him.

"Which also didn't work, did it?" the Modhri countered.

"No, I suppose not," I agreed. "But in the end, you got what you wanted." I lifted my left hand and pointed toward the two big tents behind him. "Speaking of which, I don't suppose we could have a look at your prize."

"Why not?" the Modhri said. There was a ripple from one of the big tents' flaps, and another Halka appeared, a white and vaguely rifle-shaped object cradled in his arms. As he stopped just beyond the circle of walkers, I got a close enough look at his face to see that he was the other soldier from Gargantua's original foursome, the one who had killed Penny's friend Pyotr. "I presume you'd also like to see how it operates?" the Modhri offered.

Behind me, Penny caught her breath. "Relax—he doesn't mean on us," I told her. "We're more valuable to him still breathing."

"I won't let them do it," she said, her voice trembling but defiant. "Not to me."

"You won't have a choice," Gargantua said. Behind him, the other Halka lifted the white weapon to his shoulder, aimed at a rock spine fifty meters away, and fired.

It was like nothing else I'd ever seen. The green flash that burst from the weapon's business end was definitely energy—the way it erupted silently and without a whisper of recoil showed that much. But at the same time, there was also a strange sense of flowing liquid to it, like the blazing fluid from a flamethrower, as well as the very unlaserlike way the beam or flow or whatever fanned out from the muzzle.

But if there was a question about its nature, there was no doubt whatsoever about its effect. The green flow sizzled into the spine, shattering it with a crackling thunder crack that sent bits of rock flying across the landscape.

"As you can see," Gargantua said as the echoes of the explosion faded away, "it was well worth the effort to obtain."

With an effort of my own, I got my tongue working again. "Indeed," I said. "So how many of them are there?"

"Just the three," he said. "I have found five more Vipers, but no more samples of the other two." He waved a hand around the area. "Still, if there are Vipers, surely the other components must also be here somewhere. We need only find them."

"Could be," I said. "And once you've dug them all up, what then? You plan to kill all the Spiders and take over the Quadrail?"

Gargantua's eyes flicked over my shoulder to Bayta. "I'm sure there will be no need for anything so violent," he said, his voice going all silky smooth. "Provided the Spiders are prepared to be reasonable."

"Well, I wish you luck," I said. "You may find a few unexpected obstacles in your path, though."

"Such as?"

I pointed at the Halka holding the weapon. He had it hefted in his arms again, the Lynx/muzzle end pointed toward the sky. "For starters, I don't think those weapons were really designed for your use."

"On the contrary," the Modhri said. "They're perfectly suited to me."

"I presume you're referring to the fact that there's no trigger, and that they're fired telepathically?" I suggested.

Gargantua cocked his head. "Interesting. Not one in a trillion would have noticed that."

"I have a little more experience than most people with how you and the Spiders do things," I said. "My point is that telepathic controls are a two-edged weapon. Tell me, what happened to the Viper on Ghonsilya?"

The stillness around us abruptly seemed to darken. "It exploded during my attempt to acquire it," Gargantua said, his eyes narrowing as he studied my face. "As you well know."

"I meant how did the explosion happen?" I asked.

"The second guard surprised my Eyes," he said, still watching me closely. The Modhri was very sensitive to atmosphere, and could clearly sense I was heading somewhere important. "He fired his weapon, striking the sculpture, and the power source inside exploded."

"I don't think so," I said. "A properly designed power source doesn't explode when it's damaged. My guess is that it simply went off, and without the Hawk section to moderate the energy and the Lynx section to funnel off and focus the flow it had no choice but to become a bomb."

"And how did it simply go off?"

"I have a theory," I said. "With your permission, I'd like to test it. Bayta?"

Gargantua's eyes flicked over my shoulder again; and as I felt the familiar activation tingle from the *kwi* concealed beneath my glove, I raised my fist to point at Gargantua's stomach and fired.

The great strength of a group mind is its near-omnipresence and instant communication. Its great weakness is the equally instant sharing of pain. Gargantua jerked as the *kwi*'s jolt lanced through him, the entire ring of walkers staggering back as the same pain echoed into their nervous systems through their own Modhri colonies. I fired again and again, hoping like hell my theory was right. I could tell Gargantua was starting to adjust to the pain, starting to fight it back to a level where he could function again, the look in his eyes proclaiming that his first action once he was back on balance would be to rip the *kwi* from my hand, taking my entire arm with it if necessary.

And then, behind him, the Shonkla-raa weapon exploded.

Distance, plus Gargantua's own sizable bulk standing in front of us, protected our group from the worst of the blast. The walkers immediately in front of the weapon weren't so lucky. The concussion ripped through them like a massive green fireball, shattering their bodies and throwing them in all directions. The Halka who'd been actually holding the weapon was vaporized where he stood.

The blast sent a second, even more violent wave of pain through the remaining walkers. Again they staggered, enough to give us a little breathing space. "Get out of here!" I snapped, grabbing Penny's arm and giving her a shove back toward the mesa we'd come from. I picked out one of the nearer walkers at random and gave him a jolt from the *kwi*. "You and Stafford. Head for the perimeter fence and keep going. We'll hold him here."

"How?" she gasped, waving a hand at the ring of beings still surrounding us. "They're there. They're all *there*."

"Don't worry about them," I told her. "They're walkers, remember? He isn't going to risk them getting hurt—he wants them alive and intact. Now, run—I want you out of here before he brings in the rest of his soldiers."

But it was too late. I turned back around to find Gargantua looming suddenly over me, his eyes blazing with rage and hatred and pain. Even as I tried to dodge to the side he grabbed my right wrist, twisting my arm over to point my fist and the *kwi* harmlessly toward the sky.

And behind him the large tents erupted with Modhran soldiers.

There was no doubt whatsoever as to who and what they were. While the walkers in the disintegrating circle were staggering away from me and my weapon as fast as their pain-spasming legs could carry them, the eight newcomers were staggering with equal determination directly toward us.

"And now you will die," Gargantua spat into my face.

I didn't doubt for a second that he meant it. With the *kwi* no longer adding to their pain, the soldiers' staggering and twitching was starting to fade as Modhran stamina reasserted itself with a vengeance. By the time they reached me, they would almost certainly be up to the task of tearing me into confetti-sized pieces.

And after they'd vented their rage, they would take Bayta, Penny, and Stafford to wherever the nearest coral outpost was and turn them into zombies like themselves.

Only it wasn't going to be that way. "No," I said, looking Gargantua—the Modhri—straight in the eye. "I think not." Turning my head toward the Nemut still carrying my supposedly silenced comm, the comm which I'd wired to be permanently active, I filled my lungs. "*Now!*" I shouted.

And as if he'd been hit by a thunderbolt from the rising sun, one of the approaching soldiers leaped a meter sideways in midstep. He hit the ground, skidded a few centimeters in the dust, and slid to a halt.

The Modhri was fast, all right. The dead soldier had barely stopped moving when the last soldier in line reversed direction and disappeared back into the tent. As he did so, another of the soldiers also jerked and fell.

The third and fourth soldiers had joined their comrades in death before the sound of the first shot crackled faintly through the air.

Gargantua twisted around, squinting into the sun, the Modhri trying desperately to find the source of the unexpected attack. The last three soldiers had dropped, and the distant gunfire from Fayr's hypersonic rifle had settled into a steady cadence, when the one who'd gone back inside reappeared, a glistening Shonkla-raa trinary weapon clutched in his arms. Dropping to one knee in the partial concealment of the tent door, he turned the weapon toward the east.

And suddenly the air was filled with a fury of green fire, stitching a pattern across the ground at the base of the mesa silhouetted against the rising sun.

With the Modhri's attention temporarily focused elsewhere, I got a grip on Gargantua's wrist where he still held my right arm, lifted both feet off the ground, and kicked with all my strength into his torso.

He folded backward and collapsed with an agonized grunt, his grip suddenly going limp and sending me sprawling onto the ground. I scrambled back to my feet, leveled my *kwi* at the last soldier, and fired. He jerked, the flashes from his weapon weaving briefly off target as a fresh jolt of pain lanced through him.

And I was thrown a meter backward and slammed flat onto my back as the weapon and its handler disintegrated in another massive green fireball.

Once again I climbed back to my feet, blinking against the dust and smoke and afterimage . . . and it was only then that my brain belatedly caught up to the fact that only *eight* soldiers had come charging out of the tent at the Modhri's urgent summons. Gargantua, lying gasping for breath on the ground, made nine, while his vaporized fellow Halka made ten.

Two soldiers were still unaccounted for.

I dropped into a crouch, bringing up my *kwi* as I started to look around. An instant later, I threw myself flat onto my stomach as, out of nowhere, an aircar roared past, nearly taking my head along with it. I twisted around, tracking his movement, tensing for the moment he would spin around and come back for another try.

But the Modhri knew his priorities, and at the moment I wasn't one of them. The aircar kept going, jinking back and forth like a hooked fish as it grabbed for altitude and blazed at top speed toward the eastern mesa. A second later, a motion to my left caught my eye, and I looked to see a second car lift from somewhere north of us and begin corkscrewing its own way toward the mesa.

Fayr saw them coming, of course, and the thunder of the distant rifle fire abruptly changed pitch as he switched from single fire to three-round bursts. But the Modhri was as good at this as Fayr was. The two aircars dodged madly as they drove toward Fayr's sniper post, neither of them creating a discernible pattern he could anticipate and capitalize on, the two craft angling in from widely different directions to keep from presenting an easy one-two target.

And unlike normal fighter pilots, they had no regard whatsoever for their own lives. When they reached the other end of the target range they wouldn't bother with strafing or shockwaving or any other fancy maneuvers. They would simply ram full speed into Fayr's position.

There was nothing I could do to help. Nothing, except to keep pouring pain into the Modhri mind segment, distracting him as much as possible. I stood over Gargantua's broken body, hitting him with jolt after jolt from my *kwi,* watching the aircars closing the gap, knowing that my feeble efforts weren't even delaying the inevitable.

And then, straight out of the glare of the rising sun, a third aircar appeared, driving close along the side of the mesa.

With his attention on the other attackers, I doubted Fayr even knew it was there, and I tensed helplessly as it neared his position. But to my surprise, it shot past the end of the mesa, shifting direction to head straight for the nearer of the approaching Modhri aircars.

The Modhri turned sharply to avoid him, dropping his nose and trying to half-ring beneath him. But the newcomer knew that one, too. Instead of shooting harmlessly past overhead, he did a half roll of his own and dropped down onto his target. Their sterns met, and both aircars wobbled furiously as their pilots fought to bring them back under control. The newcomer won the race, straightening out and curving hard back around toward the Modhri.

And then, both aircars lurched again as the second Modhri aircar caught a fatal burst from Fayr's gun and exploded in a blazing yellow fireball. The surviving Modhri, wobbling furiously in the shockwave, had barely regained his equilibrium when his vehicle was shattered by the stutter of sustained gunfire from the mesa.

The third aircar, his mission apparently completed, made a leisurely turn away from the mesa and headed in our direction. "Morse?" Gargantua breathed, his voice strangely gurgling with the unmistakable mark of massive internal bleeding.

"Morse is wristcuffed and asleep," I told him, wondering who the hell it was in the other vehicle. Had Fayr managed to get one of his other commandos to Veerstu in time for the party?

"You will die, Compton," Gargantua breathed again, his eyes glinting with hatred. "I will gut you like a food animal."

"Possibly," I said. "But whatever happens to me, in the end you *are* going to lose."

"We shall see," he said. "And we *will* meet again." With one final glare, he closed his eyes.

And one more Arm of the Modhri was gone. Hefting the *kwi,* I lifted my eyes again, wondering what the Modhri would throw at us next.

But the battle was over. The surviving walkers were in full flight now, most of them still staggering with residual pain as they hurried across the lightening landscape.

It was only then that I noticed that the ground was giving little shakes beneath my feet.

I frowned, looking around. The tremors were small and distant, like the feel of a heavy ground-pounder driving foundation pylons a block away. One of the distant walkers abruptly staggered a little harder, and a second later I felt another rumble. This one was accompanied by a small puff of dust a meter from the walker's feet, looking rather like the blow from a surfacing whale.

And suddenly I understood. The massive surge of pain through the Modhri mind segment was triggering explosions in the Viper power sources still buried beneath the dig site as the agonized walkers ran over them.

"I don't get it," Stafford said as he and the two women gathered beside me. "Is he just giving up?"

"Actually, he hasn't got much choice," I told him. "With his soldiers gone and Fayr holding the high ground, we hold the edge in firepower."

"But those walkers outnumber us twenty to one," Stafford objected. "He could arm them with nothing but rocks and still win."

"Not really," I said. "You see, he's in something of a no-win situation here. As long as he maintains control of the walkers' bodies, he's vulnerable to the full level of pain we're throwing at him."

"Ah," Stafford said, nodding as he finally understood. "But if he releases control back to the hosts to try to stop the pain from spreading, he can't make them fight us."

"Actually, it's even worse than that," I said. "If he releases control now, he won't be able to keep them ignorant that something violently strange has happened to them. You get a hundred rich and powerful people rushing to their doctors in a panic and *someone's* eventually going to find those polyp colonies. The last thing the Modhri wants right now is for hard evidence of his existence to leak out to the galaxy at large."

I nodded toward them. "Besides, if he continues to fight and loses, this mind segment will be wiped out, and the rest of the Modhri will never know what happened here."

"That happened to him once," Bayta said quietly. "He doesn't want it to happen again."

"So they just run away and wake up in the wilderness?" Stafford snorted. "Like *that's* not something strange?"

"He'll probably bring them back here once we're gone," I said. "That won't be nearly as hard to explain away."

"Except for all the bodies and destruction we're leaving behind," Stafford pointed out.

I shrugged. "I'm sure he'll be up to the challenge."

"Why do we have to leave at all?" Penny asked.

"Because if we don't, we'll probably be arrested for mass murder," I told her. "*You* want to try to explain all this?"

"Why not?" she countered. "We've got all the hard evidence we need, don't we?"

"We certainly have enough," I said. "Only *we* don't want to blow this into a full-court confrontation yet any more than the Modhri does. Don't forget, for all his vulnerabilities he still controls a lot of the power centers in the Twelve Empires. We go head-to-head and things will get very, very messy. For everyone."

"So that's it?" Stafford demanded. "We just walk away?"

"We just walk away," I confirmed. "*And* we keep our mouths shut."

"I don't think I like that," he said, an edge to his voice.

"Would you rather get a midnight visit from a couple of these?" I asked, nudging Gargantua's body with my foot. "You two just sit back, pretend this never happened, and let us deal with it."

"All right," Stafford said ominously. "For now."

I turned as the surviving aircar set down between us and the main tents. I lifted my *kwi* as the door opened, hoping against hope I would see a striped Belldic face peering out.

"Easy," Morse said as he climbed stiffly out of the pilot's seat. "It's just me."

For a moment I couldn't find my tongue. Neither, apparently, could anyone else. Stafford recovered first. "Well," he said, his tone studiously casual. "So much for him being a Modhri walker."

"As I believe I told you in the first place," Morse growled, walking over to us. "Maybe you'll trust me a little now. Incidentally, Compton, just for the record, that gadget of yours apparently builds up a resistance in the victim if you use it too much." He lifted his eyebrows. "Unless you *planned* for me to wake up while the party was still going on."

"Hardly," I managed. "How did you get out of the cuffs?"

He smiled. "Come now. I'm ESS. We aren't entirely without our resources, you know." He looked around. "So this was it?"

"Still is it, actually," I said. I looked around, too . . . and as I did so, I suddenly understood what this place really was.

God in heaven.

"Frank?"

I looked around. Bayta was frowning at me. "Are you all right?" she asked.

"Of course," I lied. "Back to business. By my count, there should still be one complete trinary weapon lying around somewhere. We need to find it and get it out of here, along with any spare Vipers that might have survived."

"Preferably before someone starts wondering what this strange glitch is on the weather satellite feed," Morse warned. "Let's get the loot, and get the hell out of here."

TWENTY-SIX

We said our final farewells on the platform as the next Terra-bound train worked its way down the Tube toward us. "Good luck," I said to Stafford as we shook hands. "And watch yourself. If and when the Modhri decides to step up his operations on Earth, you'll be an obvious target for him to go for."

"I'll be careful," Stafford said grimly. "If he tries it, he'll have a serious fight on his hands."

"And not just from Mr. Stafford," Morse added. "I'll be with them the whole way."

"I appreciate that," I said. "Don't forget your promise."

"To keep all of this secret." Morse hissed between his teeth. "I know. Still, galling though it is to let Earth stroll along in blissful ignorance, I can see your point. We'll keep quiet."

"But if the silent routine changes, you let us know," Stafford said. "I still want justice for Uncle Rafael's murder."

"We all do, and we're working on it," I promised. I nudged my carrybag with my foot. "This should definitely help."

"I still can't believe the Spiders let you into the Tube with that thing in your bag," Morse commented.

"We have a good working relationship with them," I said, passing over the fact that with the weapon separated into its components again the Spiders couldn't have spotted it even if they'd wanted to.

"And don't forget *your* promise," Stafford added. "Whenever your friends get done studying the thing, I'd appreciate it if they would let me have the Lynx back."

"If they'll allow it, I'll deliver it to you personally," I promised.

"Someday you'll have to tell me the whole story of how you ended up in this war," Morse said, glancing around the station. "You *and* your sniper friend. Be sure to thank him for me, by the way."

"I'm sure he thanks you, too," I said. "Your timing was perfect."

"Actually, I could probably have shown up two minutes earlier and no one would have objected," Morse said dryly. "How did you arrange for him to be up there, anyway?"

"I didn't actually arrange anything," I said. "I just told him where we were going and the day and approximate time I expected us to arrive. He worked out the rest of the details himself."

"Except that you *did* know he'd be on the easternmost mesa," Stafford said. "I assume that's why you wanted us to come in via the southern one."

"I didn't *know* that was where he'd be," I said. "But that was the most likely place for him to set up shop. He would want the sun at his back if he could manage it."

With a squeal of brakes, the Quadrail came to a stop on the track in front of us. The conductors took their places outside the doors, and the exodus of passengers began. "You be careful," Morse said. He hesitated, then held out his hand to me. "I'm sorry for—well, you know."

"I understand," I assured him, feeling an unpleasant tingle as I shook his hand. "Good-bye, Mr. Stafford; Ms. Auslander."

"Good-bye," Penny said, offering me her hand. "And

thank you. You and Bayta both. I don't know how we'll ever repay you."

I took her hand and gazed into her eyes, trying to rekindle the attraction I remembered once having felt for her.

But there was nothing. The Modhri-induced feelings were gone, and I found myself wondering that I'd ever taken them seriously at all. "No problem," I told her. "Send me an invitation to the wedding."

Her eyes flicked sideways toward Stafford. "We'll do that," she promised.

The stream of disembarking passengers ended, and the conductors called the all aboard. "Say good-bye to Bayta for us," Morse called to me as the three of them climbed aboard. I waited, and after a minute Penny appeared at the window of her compartment. She smiled and waved, I waved back, and she disappeared out of my view, probably to start unpacking. The conductors went back aboard, the doors closed, and the Quadrail was once again on its way.

"Any trouble?"

I turned as Bayta came up beside me, her eyes following the train as it picked up speed along the tracks. "No, everything went fine," I said. "What kept you?"

"I was making our arrangements." Resolutely, she pulled her eyes away from the departing train. "The stationmaster says we'll be contacted somewhere between Trivsdal and Ian-apof for the transfer."

"Good." The sooner the Chahwyn pulled their little detached-car routine and took the remaining Shonkla-raa weapon components off our hands, the sooner I would be able to relax. A little. "The others said to say good-bye. And to thank you."

Bayta didn't answer, but turned and started walking. "We'll be leaving from Platform Eight," she said over her shoulder.

I caught up and fell into step beside her. "Come on, now," I cajoled. "It worked out all right, didn't it?"

"Did it?" she countered.

I sighed. "Look. I know I behaved like an adolescent idiot. I also know that I hurt you, and I'm really and truly sorry. But you know now that the whole thing was straight Modhran manipulation."

"How?" she countered. "What happened on Veerstu rather disproved your theory that Agent Morse is a walker. Are you going to suggest next that all that manipulation came from one of the Halkan soldiers?"

"No, of course not," I said, taking her arm.

She twitched it away from me. "It's none of my business," she said, trying to hide the trembling in her voice. "Whatever you feel for her—"

"*Felt* for her, past tense," I said. "And whatever I felt wasn't real."

"It's none of my business," she repeated in a low voice.

"It's every bit your business," I corrected, glancing around. None of the other passengers wandering the station was in earshot. "Because Veerstu didn't prove anything. Morse *is,* in fact, a walker."

She spun, her eyes angry and hurt and shimmering with tears. "Don't *lie* to me, Frank," she said fiercely. "You hear? Don't ever lie to me."

"I'm not lying," I said, catching her hands in mine and forcing her to a stop. She tried to pull away again, but this time I didn't let her. "It's the only way this makes sense."

"Unless you really did fall in love with her."

"Would you get off Ms. Auslander for a minute?" I growled. "I'm talking about the thought virus that got planted in me on the Bildim train."

"Which must have come from the Cimma."

"Which couldn't possibly have come from the Cimma," I shot back. "We've been through this, remember? Morse had probably already set up the thought virus for me to go to the baggage car, only there was no time to embed another one strongly enough to cancel it. All the Modhri could do was throw in the Cimma and hope I'd think it was him."

"Then why did Agent Morse help us on Veerstu?" she

countered. "The Modhri was on the edge of winning it all when he showed up. If he's a walker, why didn't he help defeat us?"

"Because we made a mistake, Bayta," I said quietly. "All of us. A *huge* mistake." I braced myself. "We let Morse see a Chahwyn."

She stared at me, her face suddenly rigid. "Oh, no," she breathed.

"I'm afraid so," I said heavily. "The Modhri doesn't know who they are yet, of course, or where they're based, or even what their relationship is with us and the Spiders. But he knows now that there's another player in this game. And he's desperate to know more."

"Desperate enough to play Agent Morse against himself?" Bayta asked, clearly still having trouble believing it.

"No, it's much more subtle than that," I told her. "Don't forget, Fayr and I both have military training, and the Modhri knows it. Trying to choreograph a battle without one of us picking up on it would have been way too risky."

I looked back along the Tube, just in time to see the last car of Morse's Quadrail disappear through the atmosphere barrier into the depths of interstellar space. "No, the Modhri colony in Morse is now in what's called deep cover. That means no manipulation, no suggestions, no nothing. Morse is free to do exactly whatever he would if he'd never touched the damn coral at all."

"With the Modhri hoping we'll eventually start trusting him," Bayta said with a shiver. "And maybe show or tell him more."

"With pretty good odds that we would, actually," I conceded. "We don't have a lot of allies in this war. He probably figures that somewhere along the line we'll have to call on Morse for more help."

For a moment neither of us spoke. "The Chahwyn will have to be told," Bayta said at last, turning away from me and starting to walk again. "They won't be happy."

"It's partly their own fault," I reminded her. "The one we met with should have had the Spiders close the door before he came out onto the platform."

"Not that dividing up the blame makes any difference."

"No, it doesn't," I agreed, looking around again. "If it helps any, it could have been worse. A lot worse. The Modhri might have gone bird-in-the-hand and decided that the weapons dump on Veerstu was worth more than possible future information on the Chahwyn. We might still have gotten out, but we'd have left him in possession of the area."

"In which case we'd have invisible weapons to deal with," she agreed soberly. "Maybe other things, too. All those Viper power supplies must mean the place was a supply dump for other equipment besides just the trinaries."

"And nothing he might have dug up would have mattered in the slightest," I said grimly. "If the Modhri had held on to the region, invisible hand weapons would have been the least of our worries."

She flashed me a puzzled look. "What do you mean?"

I closed my eyes briefly, visualizing again the horrible revelation I'd had on that horrible morning. "Remember the Ten Mesas, Bayta? Specifically, remember the three big ones with those odd spikes jutting up from one end? Have you ever heard of something that geologically odd that nevertheless repeats itself so similarly on three separate rock formations?"

"No, I don't think so," she said slowly. "Some kind of Shonkla-raa cannon or rocket launcher, maybe?"

I shook my head. "Think about the Quadrail tender we rode on," I said. "Think about the way the loop gantries stick up at one end so as to bring the car's closest bit of matter a little closer to the Coreline."

She frowned in concentration, her eyes gazing unblinkingly into mine. And then, abruptly, she caught her breath. "Are you saying the mesas are—?" She looked furtively around us. "They're *spaceships*?"

"Why not?" I asked. "Where better to hide Shonkla-raa battleships than at a Shonkla-raa equipment dump? Besides, we've already seen the Modhran tendency to put all his eggs in one basket. Ten to one that's a weakness that came straight from their creators."

"Oh, Frank," she said, her voice shaking openly now. "If you're right . . . Frank, we have to destroy them. We have to get in there with explosives and destroy them."

"I wish to God we could," I said heavily. "But that's the very last thing we can afford to do."

"We can do it," she insisted. "Even something that big. We can find a way."

"You don't understand," I said. "We could certainly destroy this bunch. But what if there are more hidden somewhere else? We can't afford for the Modhri to even suspect such a prize might exist out there."

"But—" Bayta took a deep breath, exhaled in a strained huff. "No, you're right," she said reluctantly. "This just gets worse and worse, doesn't it?"

"Life is like that sometimes," I conceded. "A lot of the time, actually. All you can do is deal with the problems as they pop up, and hope the ones you can't solve don't pop up until you *can* solve them."

I dug into my pocket. "And speaking of solving problems . . ." I pulled out a small box and handed it to her. "Maybe this will help."

Frowning, she took the box and opened it. "Oh," she said, sounding surprised and puzzled and pleased all at the same time. "Frank, they're—they're beautiful."

I looked over her shoulder at the matching set of necklace and ear cuffs, their intertwined strips of copper, gold, and silver glinting in the light from the Coreline. "I'm glad you like them," I said. "I got them from that Nemut in the Artists' Paradise. They're sort of a peace offering."

"You don't need a peace offering," she said, pulling out one of the ear cuffs for a closer look. "But thank you."

"You're welcome," I said. "Are we . . . ?"

"Yes, we're friends again," she assured me, slipping the cuff onto her ear.

Friends. Earlier, I'd wondered if perhaps I might have drifted a little closer to her than just friendship. But if I had, I had apparently been moved back out again.

But that was okay. Bayta was a good companion, and a good ally, and very definitely a good friend.

We could leave it at that. For now.

"Meanwhile, we can start solving one of our other problems by getting these sculptures to the Chahwyn," she said as she slipped on the other ear cuff.

So it was back to business. Typical Bayta. "Right," I said. "After that, maybe we should look into those crates of coral the Modhri tried to bribe me with."

"Definitely," Bayta agreed. "We can check with the Chahwyn and see if they've learned anything from the Spiders."

"Good idea," I said. "And that, I think, should be enough for our plate for the moment." I cocked an eye at her. "That is, assuming you still *want* to share the same plate with me?"

"Of course." She gave me a tentative smile. "If you still want *me* as a partner."

"Well, it's either you or a Spider," I reminded her, patting the pocket where I had my *kwi*. "And you're definitely better company than any of them are."

She winced. "At least when I'm not being jealous."

"Even when you are." I took her arm. This time, she didn't fight me. "Come on—we've got an hour yet before our train," I said. "If Nemuti bars stock lemonade, I'll buy you a drink."

Turn the page for a preview of

Odd Girl Out

TIMOTHY
ZAHN

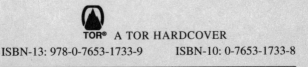

TOR® A TOR HARDCOVER

ISBN-13: 978-0-7653-1733-9   ISBN-10: 0-7653-1733-8

They took me to West Seventy-fifth Street and the familiar blazing lights and yellow tape of a crime scene. A dozen more cops were already on the scene, the uniformed ones guarding the perimeter and directing traffic, the plainclothes contingent milling around in the cold November air, collecting evidence or scanning for clues.

In the center of the stage were the guests of honor: one male, one female. Their torsos were covered by preservation cloths, but I had no trouble recognizing the dark gray clothing the woman was wearing.

Lorelei had said she was in danger. I'd been too tired to care.

A middle-aged man with receding hair and a serious seven-o'clock shadow stepped in front of me. "Compton?" he asked.

I pulled my eyes away from Lorelei's body. "Yes," I said.

"Detective Kylowski," he identified himself, holding out an ID badge. "Sorry to drag you down here at this time of night."

Sure he was. "What happened?"

"I was hoping you could tell me," he said. "Neither vic has any ID, and we haven't been able to track them down."

"The woman came to my apartment tonight," I told him, deciding to skip over the fact that she'd already been there when I'd arrived. "She said she was in trouble and asked for help."

"And you said . . . ?"

"I told her to call the cops or try the women's shelter and sent her on her way."

"After giving her one of your guns?"

"I didn't *give* her anything," I said. "Obviously, she helped herself."

"Without you noticing?"

"I was very tired," I said. "I still am."

"Uh-huh," he said, looking closely at me. "And you're sure this is the same woman?"

"I recognize her clothing," I told him. "I doubt there are two women dressed that way who've had access to my apartment lately."

"Don't you think you should at least take a look at her face?" he persisted, gesturing me toward the bodies. "It'll only take a minute."

"If you insist," I said, frowning as I walked over with him. Usually homicide cops weren't so eager to foist the details of their gory little world on people.

"This might shock you a little," he warned as he crouched down, his fingers getting a grip on the edge of the preservation cloth, his eyes locked unblinkingly on my face.

"Thanks for the warning," I growled. Did he think the sight of a couple of dead bodies was going to shock an ex-Westali agent? "Go ahead."

He flipped over the cloth.

And I nearly lost my dinner.

Lorelei's face above and in front of her ear was blood-spattered but mostly intact. Her head and neck below the ear, in contrast, were effectively gone, shattered into a mess of blood and shattered bone and pulp.

I twisted my face away from the sight, keeping my stomach under control by sheer force of will. I was still standing there, staring at a storm-sewer grating, when Kylowski took my arm and steered me away. "You all right?" he asked.

"How do you *think* I am?" I managed between clenched teeth. Turning my face away from him, I smiled hard, an old trick I'd learned for suppressing the gag reflex.

"I understand," he said. "Come on—have a seat over here."

I let him sit me down on the curb. "I don't suppose you have any idea why anyone would want to do something like that," he went on, sitting down beside me.

I shook my head. My stomach was starting to recover, but my brain was still reeling with the shock of the mutilation. "Looks like a ritual murder."

"Yeah, that was my first thought, too," Kylowski said. "Trouble is, we don't have any of the other usual trappings. No robes, no weird jewelry or tattoos, no strangled chickens. Not to mention that they were killed and mutilated here on the street and not in some abandoned warehouse or tenement."

"Maybe it's a new—" I broke off as a key word abruptly penetrated the haze of nausea. "*They* were mutilated?"

"That's right," he confirmed. He was back to scrutinizing my face. "Both of them were done the same way."

I hauled myself to my feet, my stomach suddenly forgotten. One mutilation was a sick perversion. Two mutilations was a potentially intriguing pattern. "Let me see," I said.

We retraced our steps to the bodies. Kylowski crouched down beside the man and twitched aside the cloth.

His head behind the ear was a copy of the mess that was now Lorelei's, with the lower part of the skull torn to shreds. But there was one vital difference between his upper face and Lorelei's: right in the middle of his forehead was another thudwumper hole. "Which of them was shot with my gun?" I asked Kylowski.

"Funny you should ask," Kylowski said. "Both of them."

I frowned at him. "*Both* of them?"

"Near as we can tell," he confirmed. "Kind of a puzzle, isn't it?"

I stepped back over to Lorelei's body and lifted the cloth, searching her torso. This time I spotted what I'd missed on the first go-around: two small wet spots where blood had oozed rather than flowed.

The marks of snoozer rounds. "So much for your big puzzle," I said, pointing to them. "This guy and at least one friend got the drop on Lorelei and got in the first shot. Once she was out, they took her gun and did all this."

"The vic's *friend* did this to him?" Kylowski asked, gesturing to the dead man. "That's one hell of a friend."

"Yes," I murmured, staring at the man's mutilated head as it suddenly made sense. The plane of destruction torn by the thudwumper rounds had sliced right across the lower part of his brain.

Right where the collection of polyps that formed a Modhran colony would have been located.

The men who had assaulted and killed Lorelei were walkers.

I looked at the man's closed eyes, a shiver running through me. One of the creepiest aspects of the Modhri group mind was the way it could infiltrate other living beings, Humans and Halkas and Bellidos, setting up small, sentient colonies within their bodies that could telepathically link with other nearby colonies to form a larger and smarter mind segment.

The puppetmaster scenario was bad enough. What made it worse was the fact that the walkers themselves were completely unaware that they'd been drafted into the Modhri's little war of conquest. Most of the time a polyp colony lay quietly, controlling its host with subtle mental suggestions that the host would usually obey, coming up with the most bizarrely convoluted rationalizations afterward for his or her behavior. Under more extreme conditions, though, the colony could push the host's own mind and consciousness aside and take direct control of the body.

The Modhri hadn't infiltrated the Terran Confederation nearly as extensively as he had most of the other governments and cultures around us, but I knew he had a few walkers down here keeping an eye on things. It was a good bet that Lorelei had somehow wandered into his sights and been eliminated.

But why? The Modhri didn't kill just for the sick fun of it. Had Lorelei known something the Modhri didn't want getting out? Had she been another Spider agent like me, someone the Spiders had neglected to tell me about?

Or was it something to do with her sister? The sister on New Tigris, the girl Lorelei had said bad people were trying to find?

"Well?" Kylowski prompted.

"Well what?" I countered, stalling for time while I tried to think. To me, what had happened here was now obvious. Lorelei had shot and killed the first walker, but had been nailed with snoozers before she could take out his companion. The Modhri, rightly guessing that her gunshot wouldn't go unnoticed or uninvestigated, had had the second walker obliterate the dead man's polyp colony, lest an autopsy discover it. He'd then created the same damage to Lorelei's head to make it look like ritual murder or a psycho killer.

But knowing the truth was one thing. Talking about it was something else. The galaxy at large was unaware of the Modhri's existence, let alone his plans and ambitions and techniques, and for the moment those of us in the know wanted to keep it that way. "Okay, so maybe *friend* was too strong a word," I added. "Either way, there was a third person on the scene."

"Obviously," Kylowski said. "That still leaves us with

the question of why he took the time to do all this. Especially since multiple thudwumper shots draw a lot more attention than just one or two."

"I can't answer that," I said, which was perfectly true if slightly misleading.

"Yeah," he said. "You always load your guns with thudwumpers?"

"I load them with snoozers, like my permit specifies," I said. "It doesn't take a criminal mastermind to change clips."

"Assuming he or she can find a supply of thudwumpers for that new clip."

"Finding thudwumper rounds doesn't take a criminal mastermind, either," I said. "I presume some other gun fired the snoozers into Ms. Beach?"

"Small-caliber Colt," Kylowski confirmed. "So her name was Lorelei Beach?"

"That's the name she gave me, anyway," I said. "By the way, did any of your people remove anything from either body?"

"No," Kylowski said. "Why, is something missing?"

"She had a silver necklace when she was at my apartment," I said. "It's not there now."

He made a note on his reader. "Why was she at your apartment?"

I shrugged, running a quick edit on the brief conversation Lorelei and I had had. The fact that her attackers had been walkers changed everything. "Like I said, she told me she was in danger and wanted my help," I said. "That's all."

"And instead of helping you sent her out." He nodded back toward her body. "Into this."

"If I'd known this would happen, I wouldn't have done that," I said stiffly.

"Obviously," he said. "Any idea what she might have been doing this far from your place?"

I shook my head. "None."

"Heading for Central Park, maybe?" he persisted. "Or to see some friend who lived uptown?"

"I said I don't know."

He pursed his lips. "Okay. What did you do after she left?"

"I double-locked the door and went to bed."

"Any way to prove that?"

I grimaced. Here was where it was going to hit the fan. "Not unless we had a cat burglar working the neighborhood who looked in my window."

"Yeah," Kylowski rumbled. "See, here's my problem. Four problems, actually. First, by your own admission you met with one of the vics a few hours before her death. Second, you have no alibi for the time of the murder."

"You must be joking," I said. "Cops and vampires aside, precious few people have alibis for this hour of the morning."

"True enough." Kylowski raised his eyebrows. "Problem number three is that the murder weapon hasn't been recovered."

I frowned. "I thought you said it was my gun."

"Oh, it was," he assured me. "We were able to do a micro-groove analysis on a couple of the slugs. Most people don't even know we can do that."

"*I* know it," I said. "So what would be my reason for taking the gun away?"

"Because you also know that the chances of recovering a slug in good enough shape for a positive groove ID are pretty small," he said. "The point is that in my experience there's only one reason why a murderer risks getting caught with the murder weapon on him. Namely, if he knows it can be traced to him."

"I already told you Ms. Beach stole it."

"Did you report the theft?"

"I didn't know it was gone until your buddies came knocking on my door an hour ago."

"Uh-huh," he said. "And that brings us to problem number four. The witness who called it in also reported a man of your general height and build running from the scene."

I sighed. "Is there any point mentioning how many people in Manhattan match my general height and build?"

"Not really," Kylowski said. Half turning, he gestured to a pair of nearby uniforms. "Frank Compton, you're under arrest. For murder."

ABOUT THE AUTHOR

Timothy Zahn is the author of more than thirty original science fiction novels, including the very popular Cobra and Blackcollar series. His recent novels include *Odd Girl Out*, *The Third Lynx*, *Night Train to Rigel*, *Angel-mass*, *Manta's Gift*, and *The Green and the Gray*. He has had many short works published in major SF magazines, including "Cascade Point," which won the Hugo Award for best novella of 1983. Among other works, he is the author of the bestselling Star Wars novel *Heir to the Empire*, *The Hand of Thrawn* duology, and other Star Wars novels. He currently resides in Oregon, where he is working on *The Domino Murders*, the next volume in the Quadrail series.